HMS TROUBADOUR   2001.   7th.

Eugene Earnshaw.

With the compliments and good wishes of the author.

Yours.

Walter Bazley.

By the same author

Bunyoro, Tropical Paradox

HMS TROUBADOUR

Walter Bazley

JANUS PUBLISHING COMPANY
London, England

First published in Great Britain 1996
by Janus Publishing Company,
Edinburgh House, 19 Nassau Street,
London W1N 7RE

Copyright © Walter Bazley 1996

British Library Cataloguing-in-Publication Data.
A catalogue record for this book is available from the British Library.

ISBN 1 85756 226 7

All rights reserved. No part of this publication may be reproduced, stored in a retrieval system or transmitted in any form or by any means, electronic, mechanical, photocopying, recording or otherwise, without the prior permission of the publisher.

The right of Walter Bazley to be identified as the author of this work has been asserted by him in accordance with the Copyright, Designs and Patents Act 1988.

Cover design Harold King

Phototypeset by Intype London Ltd

Printed and bound in England by
Antony Rowe Ltd,
Chippenham, Wiltshire

The characters and situations in this book are entirely imaginary and bear no relation to any real person or actual happening.

Chapter 1

BRAITHWAITE LOOKED AT Edmund and his eye was glazed.

'What are you doing here?'

Edmund put down his binoculars and turned toward his captain.

'You know what I'm doing here. I'm the officer of the watch.'

'Well, I want this place to myself. Get off the fairway. Take these men with you. Go and get in the whaleboat, all of you. Signalman, lookouts, quartermaster; go and get in the whaleboat and I'll lower it . . . and turn off that asdic. The noise is driving me . . .'

'I won't do anything of the sort. You're not well. This is wartime and we need the asdic every moment of the day and night. Why don't you go to your cabin and rest? When you're feeling better you can . . .'

'Get off the bridge,' Braithwaite roared.

'No, sir.' Edmund said it quietly.

'Very well, I'm going down to get my revolver and I'm going to shoot you, Casswell. If you're still here when I get back you'll be dead. Is that clear?'

'Yessir, quite clear. I'm the officer of the watch and if I'm here when you come back you'll shoot me.'

Braithwaite looked perplexed, went to the bridge chart table and snatched the chart. It was the one currently in use, the North Atlantic; the other charts representing the coasts of England, the United States and Canada were kept in drawers in the chart room below. Braithwaite tore it to shreds and threw the pieces upwards where the breeze caught them and carried them like cavorting seagulls in the air currents which surrounded the ship . . .

Edmund entered the bishop's palace behind his mother, helping her by carrying an armful of flowers. Passing through to the pantry he put down his burden, at which moment Jim, head servant in the household, appeared from the direction of the kitchen.

'It's 'ere, mister Edmund. Couple of minutes ago. I gave the boy sixpence.'

If the telegram had been for Edmund's father or Mrs Casswell it would have been offered on a tray, but for Edmund it was enough to pass it by hand.

'Thanks, Jim. Thanks very much. Sixpence? I don't have it with me.'

'It'll be your notice, mister Edmund. They're calling up the reserves. And may I say now, sir, 'case I don't get another chance, that Amy and me and the others wishes you very well. Very well indeed.'

'Thank you, Jim.'

Edmund tore open the flimsy envelope.

'Yes, you're right. Sub-lieutenant Casswell is ordered to put down the flowers and repair to Chatham dockyard.'

He looked at the clock.

'I'll pack before supper. Can you get my ticket, Jim? Tomorrow's train.'

'Right sir. And a taxi for seven in the morning and Amy's going to do a nice sandwich lunch.'

'Thanks. I'll get some cash to pay for all this. They'll reimburse me at the other end.'

Edmund bounded upstairs to his bedroom. His steel uniform case was set across two hard chairs, open and ready to receive the clothes that lay in piles. He took his wallet, went down again and handed Jim the money.

Now, he thought; the difficult part. He'd have to face his mother first and then his father. He returned to the hallway, and as he read the telegram again a sinking out-of-body feeling came over him. His mother was calling from another room, her voice sounding plaintive and far away.

'You're being careful with the flowers, aren't you? I want to do something nice for this room; sort of . . . oriental. It always pleases your father.' She went on about the flowers but he wasn't listening.

His mother was a handsome woman in her early forties; gentle, artistic, but a step removed from the practicalities of life. Her world was one of trivia, baroque without foundations; flowers, but not the earth from which they sprang. She lived comfortably on an income derived from her own side of the family.

'Mother, will you please listen to me?'

She turned toward him and he noticed that she still wore the shapeless garden coat which she used to protect her dress. Seeing the telegram she flung out a hand as though to restrain him.

'Oh, Edmund, you're not leaving again, are you?'

'Yes, mother, I am to repair with all despatch to Chatham dockyard, there to join HMS *Troubadour*. I wonder why they say *repair*. I'll get there just as fast if I simply *go*. It sounds like the King James version.'

'But you'll get it over quickly, won't you? Can't it be put off in some way?'

'No, not really. This country has been putting it off too long already.'

'Then you must insist on a nice cabin on the top deck.'

'Mother, I expect that *Troubadour* will be an escort vessel. It can't be very large or I'd have heard of it. As you know, I've taken a course in anti-submarine warfare so it's going to be an anti-submarine ship of some sort. There aren't any cabins on the top deck.'

'What will become of you?' She grasped her son's arm and laid her head on his shoulder.

'Come, mother; be brave. I see a good omen here. In the Middle Ages the troubadours came from southern France, where your family originated. The glorious sunlit hillsides of Provence; the reek of wine; wild boars in the forest; truffles under the oak trees. And the troubadours sang of valiant deeds and courtly love.'

Edmund suddenly became serious. 'In those days the word *King* was not a shameful word in France; one of them was made a saint.' He paused. 'They were ruled by God, and there was a chicken in every pot.'

'You won't forget all you've learned, will you?' she said in a whisper. 'Your father has such high hopes for you. If anything went wrong it would break his heart.'

'No, I won't forget, and perhaps I shall learn more. Now mother, your flowers await you in the pantry, and for me I must repair to my room and pack my kit.'

Edmund was a methodical person and he had drawn up a list of clothes and other articles which would be needed aboard ship. He stood and contemplated the steel trunk, his name and rank painted on the lid. It was of standard size, long enough to hold an officer's sword which, as a reservist, he didn't possess, so he began to pack, the white tropical uniforms going in first. After that came his best blue uniform and then two older ones. His second best he hung behind the door for the journey to London.

On each cuff of his uniform was sewn the single gold stripe of a sub-lieutenant of the 'wavy navy', appearing awkward, almost absurd as it zig-zagged round the sleeve. He had been a sub-lieutenant for nearly two years and had suffered a variety of indignities as the wearer of those wobbly gold stripes. He had been asked whether he was a wireless officer, had overheard a seaman describe him as 'not a proper officer.' He couldn't imagine any other navy labelling its reserve officers with badges of rank that were distinguishable and, by implication, inferior to those of the permanent officers. The army didn't expect their reservists to wear insignia on their shoulders that were different from the crowns and pips worn by the regulars. It was English class consciousness in full bloom, the official way by which regulars could imply, 'you are not as good as us and it shows on your sleeve.' One of the complaints, fully justified, which the regular officers levelled at the reservists was that their training had been haphazard. Exactly, and who was supposed to train them if not the regulars?

Edmund had joined the Royal Naval Volunteer Reserve during his first year at Cambridge. It was a gesture of subdued rebellion, a small act of defiance against his father. No one could recall a previous instance of a Divinity student joining the naval reserve, but he was able to claim that his situation was unusual. His uncle on his mother's side, uncle Philippe, had business interests in

France and had himself been a naval reservist in the 1914–18 war. His twenty-ton yacht, *La Belle Poule*, served as his business headquarters during his summer forays up the rivers which led to the heart of the wine-growing country. Edmund had spent his holidays aboard *La Belle Poule* and his inquisitive mind had recommended him to Captain Watts, the professional skipper, in consequence of which his instruction in seamanship and navigation had been remarkably thorough.

During his first university year he began, slowly at first, to lose the sharp edge of enthusiasm for his theological studies. He knew parts of it already, had a good grounding in Old Testament Hebrew and New Testament Greek; had read many of the standard texts and was, in consequence, ahead of his classmates. The subjects of study had often been topics of discussion by the clergy who regularly gathered in the precincts of a great cathedral. The syllabus, therefore, carried the ring of familiarity so that he was not overwhelmed by his work and found time to probe around the edges, read texts that were not on the required reading list, even pick up books that were critical.

Edmund was fascinated by the history of the first century AD as disclosed by sources other than biblical. He attempted to form a solid framework in his mind in which to set the dramatic events of Christianity, a stage that would complement and enhance the central drama. He discovered, however, that these were dangerous waters. Every fact established by the historians seemed to contradict the gospels, every discovery of archaeology ran contrary to some cherished belief.

His training in the naval reserve had been a relief from these perplexities, a change from the esoteric to the mundane. He loved the simple practicality of ropes and flags, of compass bearings, charts and tides. He enjoyed the sea itself in all its moods, its glory and its agony; he rejoiced inwardly as he took morning and evening star sights and learned the names of the first-magnitude stars and tried to visualise the flotillas of planets that might encircle each. He made friends easily, so the monotony of shipboard life posed little threat, the fellowship delighted him and the discipline worried him little. Happily he never had a problem with seasickness.

Edmund spent the summer of 1937 as a midshipman in a battleship of the home fleet, his first summer away from *La Belle Poule*. As a reservist he was regarded as an intruder, but he enjoyed the experience and found that in seamanship and navigation he was at the same level as the regulars who had been trained at Dartmouth. Torpedo, gunnery and signals were his weak subjects and he resolved to concentrate on them during his second year at Cambridge.

Whether it was the effect of the gunroom mess of a great battleship, sleeping in a hammock, handling the ship's boats, keeping watches or perhaps a combination of many influences, he returned to the world of carved stone, books and ideas with a different outlook. He continued to get good marks, indeed he was in the top two or three of his class, but a change had taken place. Instead of searching and questioning as he had done during his first year, he became more conservative and conformist. The doubts were there, but the navy had taught him to suppress them, to accept that unanswerable questions were best left unasked. The professors, he realized, avoided opinions that jolted the fragile structure of myth and artifice on which their world was built.

If Edmund's first act of insubordination had been to join the naval reserve and devote time to it, his second was almost as reprehensible in his father's estimation. He was an athlete of considerable promise and was persuaded by the captain of athletics to join the university track and field team. He practised regularly, developed as a middle distance runner and was soon running for Cambridge.

The best part of this diversion was the people he met and the places he visited. His brother students in Divinity were much addicted to each others' company and were, on the whole, self-centred with few outside interests. His college had not even resolved in its corporate mind whether Divinity students ought to live monastic or near-monastic lives and shun the society of those who were not like-minded. Edmund became known as the student who consorted with discus throwers and runners who, on a Saturday morning, would set aside the spiritual life and drive off with a busload of noisy undergraduates to take part in a track meet. His companions might be engineering or medical students, mathematicians or linguists, scientists or historians, and he asked himself how it was possible to have lived so close to these young men in colleges clustered up and down the street and not hitherto to have acknowledged their existence. These people, he said to himself, worldly, profane and not faintly interested in religion, would one day be his parishioners, assuming he ever became ordained and acquired a parish.

So it was that Edmund Casswell, in the summer of 1939, wrote his end-of-year tests and with only a brief visit home to see his parents accepted the navy's offer of a month's course in anti-submarine warfare. This was undertaken at Portland and when it was finished he learned that he had done well enough to merit the attention of his superiors. In truth he found anti-submarine work simple and rather to his liking. The years he had spent in the cathedral choir had given him an advantage when it came to identifying the subtle changes in tone between the outgoing broadcast of the asdic, or sonar, and the return echo which bounced off the hull of the submarine. Some of the others had difficulty distinguishing between one tone and another, and one or two were so tone deaf they dropped from the course.

'We want to send you on another brief course of instruction.' he was told by a red-faced, white-haired veteran of many wars, and Edmund and a group of others were sent to Whale Island to be trained in gunnery. July slid into August and he next went to Greenwich for navigation. It had become obvious that England was on the brink of war. On 21st August he was given a leave pass and told to hold himself in readiness for appointment to one of His Majesty's ships.

Edmund had discovered, almost to his surprise, that for an officer or man aboard ship, be he of high rank or low, there was only one thing that he could call his own and that was his kit. The table at which he sat, the food he ate, the charts and sextant, even the binoculars round his neck were not his but belonged to the navy. His personal possessions, his kit, might have to last him month after month, from Arctic to tropic latitudes, from ceremonial occasions to the dirtiest of tasks. Even the official Seamanship Manual, a copy of which was passed to every seaman in the navy, gave tacit acknowledgement to this fact by devoting a full page to a photograph of a seaman's kit laid out on the deck.

Edmund now packed his trunk, also a kitbag and a small piece of hand luggage containing overnight necessities. He ticked off each item as he put it in, not only clothes but such things as shoe-cleaning equipment, books, coat hangers and safety pins, the latter because the motion of the ship would dislodge clothes from the hangers if they were not secured. In went his Cambridge track suit, a soft pair of shoes for wearing in his cabin, thick woollen trousers for bad weather, sweaters and gloves. Before closing his trunk he added a coloured cloth which he used as a bedspread. It brightened up his bunk and somehow improved his morale.

The kitbag was next; seaboots, duffel coat, woollens and much else, and soon it was full and ready for its padlock. Lastly it was the overnight bag; pyjamas, razor and hairbrush, until only his keys and wallet lay on the dresser and his uniform for to-morrow on the chair. Helped by Tom he carried the trunk downstairs and placed it in the hall with the kitbag on top. He then returned to his room to wash and change.

Edmund's father, bishop Casswell, was a tall man, stooped, sharp of feature and with thin hands which people always noticed when they met him. His language was delicate and so well enunciated that he appeared almost to be an actor playing the part of a bishop on the London stage. His eye glittered and held lesser mortals in awe and fascination. His opinions were inflexible on every subject and delivered with a precision that put an end to all discussion. Even his handwriting was thin, precise and unadorned. In his youth he had modelled himself on Saint Bernard of Clairvaux, believing him to the greatest of western saints after Thomas Aquinas. If he had lived in an earlier age he too might have influenced popes and emperors to believe that he was worthy of the Church's highest accolade. He had many times been pronounced a saintly man and it was widely speculated that the archiepiscopal see of Canterbury was not beyond his reach.

The bishop elected to wear the habit of a Victorian prelate, which was not unusual in the 1930s. His black frock coat, black gaiters and top hat were subordinate to the splash of purple silk beneath his white collar. He carried a black walking-stick and wore glasses for reading suspended round his neck and tucked into an upper pocket when not in use. He drew attention to his hands by probing endlessly to find his glasses or return them. His pectoral cross, of primitive metal and wood, was said to have been fashioned by the very hand of Saint Anselm of Canterbury.

As he entered the house he stiffened perceptibly as his eye fell upon Edmund's luggage. He handed his top hat, cane and gloves to his servant and inclined his head to his wife who was at the far end of the hall, still fussing with the flowers.

'Do I assume from this that Edmund is going to the defence of Poland?' he asked.

Anne-Marie Casswell, his wife of twenty-five years, had heeded her brother's advice when confronted by the bishop's more outrageous statements. 'Never miss the easy shots,' he had counselled, 'and don't waste a cartridge on the impossible ones.'

'You're late,' she said amiably, 'what kept you? One of those tiresome committees?'

Without waiting for a reply she altered course.

'Let's go in to dinner where we can talk.'

At the sound of the gong Edmund came down the stairs at a controlled gallop and entered the dining room behind his parents.

'Evening father,' he said as he went to his chair, 'I have to be off in the morning.'

'And where are you going, may I ask?'

'I'm not just going, I'm *repairing* to Chatham with all despatch. A ship called HMS *Troubadour*.'

His father seated himself and took the linen napkin from its ring with his delicate fingers, then inclined his head and pronounced the grace in sonorous tones. Jim had held the chair for Mrs Casswell and now proceeded to the sideboard where two dishes, under their covers, were set on a hot plate.

'What do we have this evening?' she asked.

'Sliced beef, ma'am, in gravy with potatoes, and broad beans here, which is mister Edmund's favourite.'

It occurred to Edmund that most ladies who employed a cook would have known what had been prepared for a family meal, but his mother distanced herself from the running of the house. She could rely on Jim and Amy and left it at that.

'*Miroton* of beef,' his mother announced when hers was placed in front of her.

'How delectable,' his father added from his end of the table.

Last Sunday's roast jazzed up a bit, Edmund thought to himself. That's the trouble with this house, we always have three different ways of saying the same thing.

'*Troubadour*,' his father said finally. 'Would that be a warship?'

'I've never heard of *Troubadour*,' Edmund replied. 'I think it's certain to be a warship. I'll know by this time to-morrow.'

'Edmund will write a long letter and tell us about it; won't you, Edmund?'

'Yes mother, of course. I'll tell you what sort of ship it is, and I'll write about my brother officers.'

The conversation remained in a minor key until the end of the meal when his father called Jim to serve the port.

'Not for me,' his mother said. 'I'll leave you to drink by yourselves.'

Edmund rose and opened the door for her, then resumed his seat. He knew what was coming next, not a cheerful or encouraging word, nor yet a toast to his good health and to the navy; no, it would be in the nature of a sermon.

'In my heart,' his father was saying, 'I deplore this,' he gestured vaguely toward the hall where the steel trunk and kitbag were guiltily exposed. 'These warlike preparations, the courses of instruction which have doubtless taught you to kill more efficiently; but they fill me with foreboding. I see no good coming of it. Another war? To what purpose? Poland? I hardly know where Poland is to be found on the map. I can only pray that the folly of our politicians will be averted.'

Edmund reached for his wineglass but said nothing.

'You are well into your sacred studies and by all accounts acquitting yourself with credit, although the Dean informed me that some of your written work tends toward a distressing want of orthodoxy. But you have seen fit to taint your life with diversions, none of which are relevant to a person of your aspiration. Come now, Edmund, see it from my point of view, the Church's.

Though you run with the swiftness of angels it will avail you nothing in the performance of your priestly duties.

'As for this navy madness,' he went on, 'I am at a loss for words except to admit my own fault in the matter. I should not have permitted you to take your holidays abroad. Your mother claimed that Philippe was well-intentioned and with no children of his own would be as a father to you. Now I realise that he and captain . . .'

'Watts, father. Captain Watts.'

'. . . planted false seed; led you toward a life that God does not intend.'

Edmund took a sip of wine and looked at his father. Finally he spoke.

'I don't want to say anything much on my own behalf or plead my case, because I know that you'll demolish my statements to your absolute satisfaction.'

The bishop glared at his son.

'But let me put it like this. I've had a wonderful upbringing for the first twenty-three years of my life. A good education, a scholarship, the choir, a strong physique, happy home life and summer holidays with uncle Philippe which always contained an element of adventure. Yes, I have had the best of everything and now, in this uncertain hour, the time has come to put something back. That's what I'll do, roll up my sleeves . . .' he hesitated, 'I do sound so conceited . . .'

There was silence in the room. His father fingered his pectoral cross and looked at the walls as though searching for lost inspiration.

Edmund was thinking to himself how like his father he had become. He spoke like him, put himself in the right, exaggerated. Shouldn't this moment be spent on simple thoughts and plain speech, the uncomplicated recollections of past happiness? Are there not moments in life when cleverness is merely burdensome?

His father had begun again.

'For you, Edmund, the curtain of Heaven parted momentarily and allowed you to see what others are denied. Your life is sanctified and must be so lived. I pray sometimes for those against whom the curtain is tightly drawn. Yours was the gift which compels your footsteps along a prescribed path. You owe a service to your church, not to your country.' He wagged his finger at Edmund. 'I want you to admit your error and leave the navy. I could use my influence . . .'

Anger boiled up inside Edmund, but before he could reply the door opened and Jim appeared.

'May I pour another glass, my lord?'

Jim didn't normally address the bishop as 'my lord' unless he was trying to impress visitors. It was usually 'sir'. The bishop gave him a sour look, a snarl almost.

'No, no more.'

'And how about you, mister Edmund?'

'I think not, thank you, Jim. I still have a few things to do. I must write a note to the bank manager.'

'Bank manager? Why the bank manager?' his father asked, suddenly alert.

'Because I'm making arrangements for most of my pay to go into my bank account. The manager will pay the naval tailors on a quarterly basis so I can shop in any of their branches and order what I need. A lot of officers do it.'

Edmund was grateful to have something different to talk about. It was better than the discussion which had preceded it.

'Some of them,' he went on, 'get into debt, but as long as they go on paying on a regular basis Gieves, the naval tailors, carries it until the officer is promoted. They remain loyal customers for the rest of their time in the navy.'

'I see. How interesting.'

The bishop did not hide the sarcasm in his voice. 'But you also receive an allowance from your uncle; is that not so?'

'Yes, I do.'

'And may I ask how much he gives you?'

'At university it's enough to keep me in books, pocket money and sporting equipment.'

What Edmund did not tell his father was that uncle Philippe had promised to double his allowance for as long as he was in the navy.

Jim put down the decanter and left the room and the bishop rose wearily to his feet.

'And now I suppose you want me to give you my blessing?'

Edmund had been expecting this and hated the thought of kneeling in front of his father on the dining room carpet.

'No sir. You have expressed your disapproval and asked me to resign from the navy. I haven't earned your blessing; just your good wishes.' Edmund remained obstinately standing.

They shook hands and the bishop forced a very feeble smile.

The train was crowded with August holidaymakers returning to London. Edmund, conspicuous in uniform, found a seat in a first-class compartment and put his hand luggage and cap on the rack. As the train pulled away he glanced at his travelling companions who seemed to know each other and were talking about their holiday. He unfolded the morning paper and read it through, then to signify that he did not want to be included in their conversation he leaned back and closed his eyes. He had made this journey many times and could visualize the scenery that flowed past the windows. In his mind he saw the countryside in full flower, rich and replete under the late summer sun. The harvest was coming in, apples hung heavy on the trees, even the gray towns and villages of the northland basked in an austere beauty.

He had not revealed the full truth to his father the night before. If this was an hour of crisis in his country's history then he felt he owed a debt and wanted to repay it, but there was much he had not mentioned, his desire for change, a respite from the confined existence of a divinity student. He had asked himself whether he really wanted to be committed for the whole of his life to the Church, the highest of all callings his father said constantly, when he didn't really believe the doctrine that he would be preaching. He wanted more time to think about it; a change of scene and different companionship. He wanted to be where his father's ice-cold grip would not be felt; where he could think uncensored thoughts. Besides that, there were things about the Church itself that left him perplexed and angered. Only the week before he had overheard a group of talkative clergy, well out of his father's earshot, discussing how to prevent other travellers from entering their railway compartment.

'An infectious disease,' one of them suggested. 'Just say you're suffering from severe alcoholitis, which is highly contagious...'

'That's amateur stuff,' another said, 'the best way is to go down on your knees and pray. Do it ostentatiously in Latin with much wringing of hands, and mind you take up all the floor space. There's nothing that repels the laity more thoroughly than the sight of the clergy at prayer. It's guaranteed to keep them out of your compartment.'

They all laughed and one said that he would have expected someone to say: 'Come on, get up! You're not in church now.'

'The answer to that's easy,' another retorted. '*This is my church.*'

And why, Edmund asked himself, are the clergy attempting to bar people from entering their church, even in jest?

Edmund had only one hero in the Church, John Donne, the dean of St Paul's under the first Stewarts. His has been a raucous youth followed by conversion and then the glorious sermons which captivated London society and were still quoted. 'I am involved in mankind,' he had said. 'I weep for them, I don't try to bar them from entering my railway compartment.' Well, no; he didn't say exactly that. 'The death of any man diminishes me. Don't send someone to find out who the church bell is tolling for,' then he shocked his listeners, 'because really it's tolling for you.'

John Donne, a white lily sprung from the red earth; but did one have to serve a wildly disreputable apprenticeship in the taverns and brothels of London to find such words and the courage to use them?

What of his mother, Edmund asked himself. A former beauty with money in her own right, a lady of accomplishment but little substance. She could speak three or four languages but couldn't converse seriously in any of them; she was the kind of hostess who flitted from one topic to another and never put her visitors at ease. She was not serious by nature, had few friends and allowed the servants to run her house. Neither she nor her husband had learned to drive a car, so they proposed that the Church provide them with a Rolls Royce and chauffeur, but nothing came of it. Edmund had once heard his mother say that when she had been a child she had prayed that she would never grow up. Her tragedy was that her prayer had come so perilously close to being answered.

The question that perplexed Edmund and which left even the knowledgeable uncle Philippe at a loss was why his parents had married in the first place. Uncle Philippe recalled that they had met in Aix-en-Provence when Jonathan Casswell was returning from a tour of the Holy Land. Beyond this, the circumstances of their courtship left him baffled. It all seemed out of character; the dull English clergyman, the fun-loving, well connected young woman whose father was one of the great wine merchants of Europe. Uncle Philippe hinted darkly that he had somehow got her pregnant or, more likely, someone else had. The first child, a daughter, had died at birth. Edmund often thought of the little girl who would have been his sister and he wondered if his father might have been a different person if she had lived. Then again Edmund knew that there was a tradition in the Church; secretive, rarely mentioned, but a tradition nonetheless, by which a priest might take a fallen or discarded woman to be his wife. His mother, fallen, discarded?

During the early years of their marriage his mother's influence had been of assistance in his father's career. She knew the right people and pleaded tirelessly on his behalf. Her efforts bore fruit and his elevation to bishop at a young age and subsequent appointment to a great and historic northern see had come in swift succession. A price, however, had to be paid, and they found themselves in an ancient and uncomfortable palace that had only one bathroom. The stone walls were a yard thick so that plumbing and electrical work were impossible. It was there that Edmund had lived since the age of six and his education had begun in the cathedral choir school. His teachers, many of them young curates seeking to curry favour with his father, had taught him well because at the age of twelve, when his voice broke, he went to Winchester on a scholarship.

In Edmund's affections it had been Jim and Amy who held pride of place during those years. A child truly loves those who care for him, cook his food, answer the questions and comfort him through the misadventures of childhood. Jim taught him to swim and skate, to fish in the pond as the monks had done for many centuries and do simple carpentry. Amy sewed on his buttons, bandaged his knees and cooked with a sure hand and a kind heart.

As he reached his teens Edmund spent little time at home. He was at boarding school for almost three quarters of the year and with uncle Philippe for the summer holidays. Only at Christmas and Easter was he at the palace and he began to realise, slowly at first, that his mother was diminishing, that she had more to hide than she had to tell. She had grown weary of a husband who was more pompous than God, who never laughed and treated her like an imbecile. She grew tired of the façade, the pretence of domestic tranquillity and took to eating her meals in silence; spending her holidays in Provence. When Edmund was at home he attempted to draw her out and make her talk; talk about anything.

'What was he like, mother, Enrico Caruso? You heard him sing. What was there about his voice that the recordings missed?'

'I don't know,' she replied. 'I don't know what it was.'

'Mother, the newspapers of those days said that women broke down and wept, men appeared shaken and silenced, that his voice was seamless and velvet. Tell me, please, the sound of his voice, the dark quality. What was it that people still talk about?'

But it was always the same, there was no reply. Even with all her languages, words failed her.

How strange, Edmund thought, that when he put his head back against the upholstered headrest the voices within the compartment faded and train sounds took over. They entered his consciousness, dulling the sharp edge of spoken words and lulling him to sleep. Predominant was the sensation of distant earthquakes, the subdued conflict of wood and steel measured by the click of the wheels as they passed over the joints between lengths of rail.

He slept for a full hour and woke gradually, realising that the train was well into the Midlands. A wash and brushup seemed in order so he took down his hand luggage and went to the washroom. As he dug down for soap, towel and hairbrush he found Amy's sandwiches and decided that he would eat them standing in the corridor. He had no wish to challenge the convention that had been established by the travelling public to the effect that sandwiches would not be consumed in a first class compartment.

Chapter 2

EDMUND TOOK A taxi from the train station to Chatham dockyard although the journey was more than twenty miles. He didn't begrudge the expense because to go by train would have meant crossing London to another station, a porter for his luggage and a second taxi when he reached Chatham. Besides that, he was *repairing* to Chatham with all despatch as the telegram had instructed. The taxi was bright yellow and the driver, an older man, climbed down from the cab and secured Edmund's luggage with a leather strap. Edmund noticed the man's limp.

'The war?' he asked.

'Yessir, Mesopotamia; and a real mess it was, but by all accounts not so bad as the western front.'

'I've been on the train all day. Anything new?'

'What I 'eard at the teashop was that Poland were invaded yesterday and Mr Churchill's back at the Admiralty.'

'How are people reacting?' Edmund asked.

'Quiet, yer know. Most of me mates is saying that it's gotta come, no avoiding it, but I hope it ain't like the last time.'

Edmund nodded and climbed into the back seat which was cool and smelled of leather. London taxis had been designed early in the century with two features that had survived the years. First, they were required to have enough headroom for a gentleman passenger to wear his top hat, and secondly it was presumed that little or no communication would take place between the driver and passenger, so a glass partition separated them. It was this second feature that irked Edmund. He wanted to talk to the driver and test his belief that a quiet determination had overtaken the majority of ordinary people in face of the certainty of war.

They passed through the dockyard gates and found *Troubadour* lying alongside the jetty. Edmund jumped out and for a full minute while the taxi meter continued to run he stood staring at the ship and taking in the details. What a handsome ship, he thought, not overburdened by top hamper, a single funnel and sturdy bridge structure. A gun was mounted on the forward deck and machine guns on the deckhouse aft. Her quarterdeck was a mass of depth charge chutes and mortars, although the weapons themselves, the depth charges, were not in place. She looked defiant, a little cocky, with her high bow and forward gun. She was painted dark grey which enhanced her air of purpose.

Edmund knew that trawlers had been taken over by the Admiralty while the reserves were being mobilised. Many had been equipped as minesweepers so that Britain's fishing fleet was depleted of sixty or more of its best vessels in the course of a few days, predominantly the larger Iceland trawlers which plied their trade in northern waters. *Troubadour*, however, did not fit the description. Her curving bow, rounded at deck level, the absence of any facilities for storing fish and, most of all, the fact that her gun was not set on a makeshift platform but was mounted at deck level and protected by a breakwater, all suggested she had been built for a purpose other than fishing.

Someone wearing overalls and an officer's cap emerged from the deckhouse and stood wiping his hands.

'Hello,' Edmund said, 'is this *Troubadour*?'

'Sure is. I'm chief engineer Dobreiner.'

He saw Edmund's kit in the taxi.

'You won't be sleeping aboard to-night. Probably to-morrow night. Can I have a ride with you? We're all at Chatham barracks.'

Edmund nodded and Dobreiner threw away his rag and stepped ashore with hand outstretched. 'Excuse my dirty hands,' he said.

'I'm Edmund Casswell. I got my orders yesterday.'

They shook hands and both climbed into the taxi.

'The captain and first lieutenant have arrived. Are you anti-submarine?'

'Yes. I took the course.'

'By the way, I've often wondered what *asdic* stands for. Anti-submarine. . . .'

'No, its *Allied Submarine Detection Investigation Committee*. It was set up with the French after the last war. Strange to say the French had more to do with it than we did. As you know, the idea is to use sound waves to locate objects underwater. They think that whales use it, and of course bats do in the air.' He paused. 'Now let me ask you a question, where did *Troubadour* come from?'

'Well may you ask! All four of these ships were built in our shipyards for a South American government. They wanted a high performance vessel for the far south among those thousands of islands; you know, fisheries protection, research work, chasing god-knows-who. *Troubadour* is about a thousand tons and has speed and endurance. And the best thing is she's well built and powered by steam turbines. Wait till you see some of the details, you're going to be impressed.'

'And the navy took her over?' Edmund asked.

'Yes. The Admiralty can't let good ships slip away, not now. The situation for escort vessels is frightful. Chile can get its ships from somewhere else.'

'And the range?' Edmund asked.

'Four thousand miles or more, which is remarkable for a ship of this size. It's better than a lot of destroyers, but then the armament isn't up to much, just depth charges and a four-inch gun. A destroyer would have four guns like that plus depth charges, torpedoes and a speed of 30 knots. Mind you, it takes a bigger crew to man a destroyer. We'll have to manage with about eighty or ninety men.'

'Well, she's a fine-looking ship,' Edmund agreed.

'By the way, they call me *chief*, because I'm chief engineer. In fact I'm a commissioned warrant engineer; I used to be in destroyers.'

They alighted at the officers' mess of Chatham barracks which was busier than it had been for many years. Edmund reported his arrival and a bed was found for him in a corridor among many other reserve officers who, like himself, had just been recalled. He pushed his kit under the bed and went to the wardroom for a meal but found the dining room and ante-room crowded. As he stood and contemplated the scene a lieutenant approached him.

'Are you Casswell?'

Edmund nodded.

'Good. I'm Pemberton, first lieutenant of *Troubadour*. We're expecting you. Come and meet the captain. Got a place to sleep?'

'Yes, thanks.'

Pemberton, Edmund thought to himself as he followed him through the press of officers, Pemberton. Yes, of course; yachtsman, the skipper who had been in a close race against some shipping bigwig. His opponent had lost a man overboard and they had thrown a lifebelt. Pemberton, however, put about although he was in the lead, lowered sail and went to the man's rescue. The other yacht had taken first prize and actually accepted it, which outraged British sensibilities, particularly when the camera caught a shot of Pemberton and his crew members helping the rescued man into an ambulance. From then on nothing could dislodge the impression of sheer decency which the unassuming Pemberton had created in people's minds, the sort of person whom the British describe as a real sportsman.

Funny, Edmund thought, how a single impression can govern your whole judgement. With the prime minister it was Munich, the scrawny figure, the umbrella and the pathetic bleat of 'peace in our time.' With Churchill, the first lord, it was the combative look, the cigar and the Dardanelles fiasco. For his mother the picture was a mass of flowers, as though she had been born among them and would die among them. For King George the Fifth, of happy memory, it was the unblinking stare from postage stamps, silently commanding all Britons to do their duty.

'Captain, sir,' Pemberton was saying. 'I've found Casswell.'

He turned to Edmund.

'Lieutenant-commander Braithwaite, Royal Naval Reserve.'

'Good show, Casswell. Glad to meet you,' Braithwaite said. 'That only leaves one more, what's his name? Marko Cyr.'

Edmund spoke up.

'Oh, I know him, sir. I met him at Portsmouth.'

'Where does he come from with a name like that?' Braithwaite asked.

'It's a French name, but he's from Canada. I think his father owns fishing boats in the Gulf of St Lawrence.'

'You'd expect him to join the Canadian navy,' Pemberton suggested.

'He was in England as a graduate student and with his experience the RNVR accepted him without argument. If I may say so, he's quite a character.'

'Well, character or not, he only had to come from Portsmouth and he ought to be here by now,' Braithwaite said flatly. He turned to Edmund. 'Chief was saying you've done the anti-submarine course at Portland.'

'Yessir.'

'Well, we're not going to wait for Cyr. Is that how you pronounce it? I say we go to a pub and get some supper and a drink. It'll be an hour before our names are called for the dining room. Besides, I want to sit down and explain about to-morrow.'

The four of them retrieved their caps and were about to follow the captain outside when he gestured them round.

'I just heard that a chauffeur-driven car drove up to the main gate and an able seaman got out. He saluted the officer of the watch and handed him a newspaper clipping; the one about the King's pardon being extended to deserters. The able seaman turned to his driver and told him he might as well keep the car because he wouldn't need it any more.' They all laughed and at that moment a taxi drew up and an R.N.V.R. sub-lieutenant got out.

'It's Marko Cyr,' Edmund exclaimed.

Sub-lieutenant Cyr was out of the taxi even before it stopped. He saw Edmund.

'Ed, you old bastard, what are you doing here?'

'Same as you, Marko, we're shipmates. Now pay attention, this is the captain, lieutenant-commander Braithwaite.'

'Brait-waite' was Marko's first try.

'Braithwaite,' the captain said, extending his hand.

'And lieutenant Pemberton, the first lieutenant; and commissioned warrant engineer Dobreiner.'

'Pemberton. Do-breiner.' Marko tried them cautiously.

'And what sort of a capital ship is it; or is she just a destroyer?' Marko asked.

'Get your kit unloaded and stowed away. We're in a hurry to

get something to eat and make plans for to-morrow.' A note of impatience was in Braithwaite's voice. 'She's a sloop.'

'Aye aye, sir,' someone said, and the four of them crowded round the taxi and pulled out Marko's kit. This was the first time Braithwaite had seen his four officers together. At least, he thought to himself, they're not stupid and they're not lazy. It took a few minutes for Marko to report to the desk and be allocated a bed for the night. This done, he joined the others at the main entrance.

'We were expecting you earlier than this.' Braithwaite's voice still had a harsh edge. 'They told me you were at Portsmouth and would be released the moment you received your telegram.'

'Yessir, but I had to pick up the rest of my kit in London; I did my damndest to get here.'

'Very well,' Braithwaite said, 'you're here now. I hope you learned something at gunnery school.'

'Well, mostly, they marched us up and down the parade ground. God knows what it had to do with gunnery. No one yet told me what guns there are aboard *Troubadour*.'

'Single four-inch; no director,' the captain answered. Marko's face fell.

'Gosh, that ain't much. You want the gunnery officer on the gun platform or on the bridge?'

Braithwaite seemed not to have thought about it and hesitated.

'I'll consider it.'

Dobreiner, who knew Chatham, led the way to a tavern. They found a table and a game of darts was held up while the five officers made their way across the room with their drinks.

'Excuse me.'

'Not at all.'

'Sorry to cross your line of fire.'

It was good natured, but it had its small sense of drama which was not lost on Edmund as he sat down for the first time at the table with his captain and brother officers. This group, so arbitrarily chosen, so hastily assembled, were now comrades in arms whether they wished it or not. They were bound together with ties stronger even than those of marriage; after all, men didn't face death because they loved a girl. Now they would obey their captain's command to the very end. A couple of days previously the captain had known none of them and only because of Edmund and Marko's accidental encounter had the two met previously. As of this moment they were committed together in a hundred unspoken ways.

'We've all chosen different sandwiches,' Pemberton said. 'I'm going to put half of mine in the middle of the table and if someone else does the same I'll take his half and hope he takes mine.'

'*Très bon*,' from Marko; 'families always share their food.' A pause. 'I'm going for more to eat. I missed breakfast and lunch and I want to try something they call a Scotch egg. Was it laid in Scotland?'

When hunger and thirst had been satisfied Braithwaite looked at each of them and pushed away his glass.

'We have to start somewhere so let's begin with the ship. It was built for the government of Chile and taken over by the navy. She's about a thousand tons with twin screws and standard turbine propulsion machinery which should give 24 knots. The main armament consists of two depth charge racks which drop the charges directly over the stern, and four throwers, two each side. The number of charges carried will be 120, so we'll have twelve patterns of ten charges. The asdic set and depth charge armament was not part of the original specifications but has been added in recent weeks.'

'Now let's think about flotilla organization. *Minstrel* is the leader and she's a few days ahead of us. She's done her sea trials and there don't seem to have been any difficulties. These ships weren't built on the cheap; the specifications were demanding. Admiralty policy, on the other hand, has always been to get the largest number of ships for the smallest outlay. The workmanship and detail in a fishing boat is a cut above most navy ships, and of course the habitability factor in fishing boats is far superior.'

At this point Pemberton asked about the flotilla commander.

'His name is de Bongard Sykes; yes, you heard me correctly, he's a commander RNR, and a master mariner with a lot of navy experience. He told me that in eighteen years he never missed his annual navy training. I want to keep in close touch with him during the next few days because if *Minstrel* has trouble we can be on the lookout for the same thing.'

Dobreiner nodded.

'It's been impressed on me that we must prepare for sea immediately. Once we're commissioned and take over the ship we'll have a week to get our various trials completed including full power, swinging the ship and firing the gun; not to mention provisioning. In normal times we'd have a month. I repeat, we get a week.'

'What about the rest of the flotilla?' someone asked.

Harp and *Chorister* are a few days behind us. I don't know if the commanding officers have been named so I can't say which ship will be senior to which. By the way, the names of the ships were chosen by the Naming Committee of the Admiralty. I have no idea why they hit on the names they did. And there's something else, commander Sykes couldn't discover whether they were going to build more of this class. A full flotilla would be eight ships.'

'Now let's talk about officers' duties. Our full complement of officers is supposed to be seven, but god only knows when we'll get two more including someone to act as navigator. In the meantime we'll share navigation duties. At action stations I'll be on the bridge,' he went on, 'and the first lieutenant will be aft by the depth charges. The rule is that captain and first lieutenant are separated when the ship's in action so we don't both get killed by the same bomb, shell or mine.'

He paused.

'So far so good?'

They nodded.

'Casswell gets a variety of duties. Anti-submarine officer and action officer of the watch. He'll also be in charge of correspondence and pay. Cyr, you have the gun, the forecastle when going in and out of harbour, also sports and recreation which won't keep you busy, because there won't be any sports and recreation'.

'Very well, let's leave that and talk about the ship's company. We'll get a list of names to-morrow and I want the first lieutenant and Casswell to make out the Watch and Quarter Bill. When the men come on board in the afternoon we have to be ready for them.

'Sir,' Edmund said. 'There's a custom that when men come aboard a new ship they get a few hours to sling their hammocks.'

'You don't need to remind me of naval customs,' Braithwaite broke in. 'Within an hour of stepping on board there'll be a quartermaster on the gangway, the cooks will be cooking the evening meal, the stokers firing up the boilers and the rest of the ship's company will be cleaning up the mess left by the dockyard. Do I make myself clear?'

Edmund nodded.

'One last thing,' Braithwaite went on. 'In this ship the officers' cabins and wardroom are aft as they were in the days of sail. It's not the best arrangement, because when the alarm is sounded we have a distance to go between our cabins and the bridge. However, there are two bunks in the chartroom and I'll use the lower one as a sea cabin when we're in dangerous waters. Casswell or Cyr can use the upper bunk. By the way, I'll take my meals in the wardroom, not my cabin. My cabin has no proper facilities.

'Well now, I've left out a lot, but we should at least know what we're doing to-morrow. It's getting late, last drink anyone?'

'One more question, sir.' It was Cyr. 'What sort of men are we getting? Will they be regulars or reserves?'

Braithwaite had stood up, glass in hand.

'The senior ratings, the petty officers, are regular. The rest will be reservists. That's the best way for small ships.'

He sat down again.

'In my experience the regular petty officers are excellent; they've survived a difficult system and they know their business. The enlisted ratings are another thing; they get their training in big ships; you know, before anything happens there must be an officer standing there, a petty officer and a dozen men. They are not taught to think for themselves but rather to wait for orders. They get accustomed to a repressive routine to the point where it's an accomplishment merely to survive the disciplinary system. The reserve ratings aren't like that. They're volunteers, often well educated and looking for adventure. Keeping out of trouble isn't the problem. In small ships they're the best men you can have.'

He stood up again.

'A captain doesn't have much say as to who he gets, but they did tell me they'd find a good crew with no troublemakers. Does that answer it?'

Edmund's first impression of his new commanding officer was that he was clear about what he wanted and single-minded in getting it. The severity and waspish tone was perhaps understandable in the circumstances, but at the same time Edmund wished he had been addressed with more courtesy, more acknowledgement that he and his brother officers were loyal and didn't have to be put down. Braithwaite's tone, if not his words, seemed more appropriate to conscripts than volunteers.

On the way back to barracks Braithwaite turned and asked for their attention, so Edmund and Marko, who had fallen a few paces behind, closed within earshot.

'I haven't spoken about your conduct, and hope I don't have to. Two of you have come from university and I want it clearly understood that your university days are behind you. A small ship is no place to act the fool.'

'I was a serious student,' Edmund said. He was about to add more but Braithwaite broke in.

'What were you doing there? I always assumed that university was a place where you went to learn the things you should have learned in school.'

'Theology, sir. They don't teach it in school.'

'Good God!'

'Yes, sir.'

'So you were steering a course for the church steeple?' He tried to sound humorous. 'Sermons, tea with old ladies, marrying young idiots. May we anticipate your career and call you Reverend?'

'No sir. That would be a mockery of those who have been called to Holy Orders. It would be . . . *acting the fool*, and you just spoke about that.'

Silence fell on the little group and they walked on for several steps before Braithwaite spoke again.

'What were you doing at university, Cyr?'

'Law, sir. I was also a serious student.'

'Very well,' Braithwaite said, 'I would like one thing to be clear.

In the wardroom mess we'll follow the old custom of not discussing religion, women or politics.'

'What does that leave that we can discuss?' Marko whispered.

Chapter 3

3RD SEPTEMBER 1939 dawned clear over Chatham's ancient dockyard. A light westerly wind stirred the night-time odours of London and carried them, in all their reeking profusion, down the narrow streets and across the little river Medway. Edmund had awoken while it was still dark, sat up and looked down the corridor at the sleeping figures. He roused Marko who greeted the intrusion with dismay but got up immediately. The officers' bathroom was empty so they took their time, shaved and showered and were ready with their baggage at the main entrance an hour later. The events of the evening before were in the minds of both, but the excitement of going aboard *Troubadour* and the feeling that this day would be a milestone in their lives kept them subdued.

Marko went in search of a navy motor vehicle and found a fifteen-hundredweight lorry parked nearby. It had no key in the ignition, but after a few minutes' work under the hood he had it running. Braithwaite had told him to get a vehicle for the officers and their luggage and he assumed that the captain was not a man to quibble over the details. The five of them, less talkative than the evening before, breakfasted in the mess at seven and informed the duty officer they were leaving. With Marko at the wheel they drove to HMS *Troubadour*.

Edmund savoured the moment when he would enter his cabin. In more normal circumstances he would have shared with Marko, but because there were only five officers, not seven, each sub-lieutenant would have his own. It was an unexpected luxury for such junior officers and one that would end if the staffing situation were to change. A cabin to himself, Edmund thought, in which to read, write letters, sleep and, in time, resolve the complexities and doubts that occupied his mind. He would take care of it himself, keep it clean and make it his private sanctuary. He pushed open the door to find, even at that early hour, two dockyard workers squatting on the floor playing cards. They were surrounded by litter and cigarette butts. One of them looked up at Edmund as he stood in the doorway.

'Fuck off,' the man said.

'But this is my cabin,' Edmund announced. 'The first lieutenant said so.'

He put down the kitbag he was carrying.

Marko was behind him.

'What's yours like?'

'There are two dockyard employees sitting on the floor.'

'Tell them to bog off.'

'That's what they just told me.'

'Theology,' Marko muttered, and pushed past Edmund.

'Now get out of here you little rats,' he shouted, kicking the nearest in the ribs, 'or I'll go and find six very big sailors who'll rearrange your ugly faces. You're no more use than two soft ones in a whorehouse.'

Grumbling, the men got up and slunk out.

'You know,' Marko said, 'I learn my English in the street and aboard the fishing boats, but it gets understood well enough.'

'Thanks, Marko. I'm going to leave my kit on the floor and come back later. I'm supposed to go and help the first lieutenant.'

'What do you know about the Watch and Quarter Bill?' Pemberton asked him as they sat down at the wardroom table. 'I've never done one and I wasn't going to admit my ignorance when we were in the pub last evening.'

Edmund was rather taken aback. This was something the first lieutenant was always meant to do because it embodied the internal organization of the ship. Edmund had never actually done one either but had learned the principle when he had been a midshipman.

'Well, it shows each man where he must be in every situation; action stations, messdeck . . .' He paused. 'What you have there is the ship's complement. That's been decided by the Admiralty and shows the number of men and the qualifications they must have.'

Pemberton continued to look perplexed.

'They are saying, in other words, that to serve the weapons and fight the ship we're going to need these men. We don't know their names yet, but that will come later from the barracks. Let's start at the top. "One petty officer coxswain." He's the senior rating of the ship and your right-hand man. When the ship is in action he's on the wheel. It goes without saying that he's in the petty officers' mess.

'Second, one leading seaman gunlayer. He aims and fires the four-inch gun. We'll put him as leading seaman in charge of the forward mess deck where he's close to the gun. For entering and leaving harbour he'll be on the forecastle under sub-lieutenant Cyr dealing with anchors and cables and all the other stuff that goes on forward.

'Now it says, "Two able seamen AA3." They fire the anti-aircraft guns. After that we get able seamen and ordinary seamen with no special qualifications. The distinction to be made is between an AA3 who has a gold badge on his arm and must be placed on an anti-aircraft gun, because that's what he's been trained for, and an able seaman with no badges who can be given any one of a dozen jobs.'

'Like what?' Pemberton asked.

'Lookout on the bridge, loading the gun, ammunition supply.'

'Now let's look at the asdic operators, three of them, which means that one will be on duty every moment the ship is at sea. In harbour they only have to keep the equipment clean, which is nothing much, so one of them can help me in the ship's office and a second one can act as ship's postman.

'Torpedomen,' Edmund went on. 'You may ask why we need torpedomen when we don't have torpedoes. It's because torpedomen fire the depth charges and do all the ship's electrical work. And remember that we're going to need six or eight men to get the depth charges up from the magazine. It's a rotten job in bad weather because they weigh three hundred pounds each. The off-watch stokers are probably going to be needed.'

'Hold on,' Pemberton said, 'how do you think the chief engineer will react if I use his stokers when they'll be needed in the boiler room?'

'No,' Edmund replied. 'The stokers are in three watches. When the alarm bells go for action stations the watch on duty might as well stay on duty, because it doesn't take three times as many stokers to keep the boilers going when the ship is in action. Oh, and by the way, here we are shown as having a Sick Berth Attendant. He can't be given any duties other than the sick bay.'

At Edmund's suggestion the two of them went on a tour of the mess decks to discover how many men each mess would accommodate. They counted the numbers of lockers and hammock spaces and checked that the lockers themselves carried a number stencilled on the door. All were brand new and could be padlocked. The experienced men would keep padlocks on their kitbags and transfer them to their locker doors when their kit was stowed inside.

'What's this *G or T* column for?' Pemberton asked when they were back at the wardroom table. He pointed to a column on the Watch and Quarter Bill.

'G means grog,' Edmund replied, 'in other words he takes his rum ration. T stands for temperance in which case he gets threepence a day for not taking it. If he's under the age of twenty we write "U" for underage. I tried navy rum and I think they should be paid for drinking it, not for not drinking it.'

A moment later the captain came in.

'Names,' he said. 'Now you can go to work, but before you do I'll tell you the different states of readiness I want. *Action stations*; every man at his battle station. *Relaxed action stations*; cooks, stewards and men not concerned with the fighting readiness of the ship can prepare and carry round the food. Third, *Cruising stations* in three watches, red, white and blue, with enough men at the guns and depth charges to fire in an emergency. At sea in wartime the ship will normally be at cruising stations.

Pemberton and Edmund sat down again and within an hour they had the names pencilled in and the duties assigned.

A few minutes before eleven Braithwaite came in again. 'Turn on the wireless; it's the prime minister.'

For years afterwards Edmund remembered that voice; not, he

thought, the voice of a statesman but of a schoolmaster or civil servant. Nor, from what he said, did he leave the impression that he was in control, but rather than there was nothing further he could do, his options were exhausted. 'A state of war exists,' he said, which meant that the war had begun, it was upon them. The words were unmemorable until, as he concluded, London's barrage balloons, fat silver absurdities, were floated upwards into the clear air on the theory that they would inhibit low-flying aircraft. Some good anti-aircraft guns, Edmund thought, would inhibit them even more. At that moment the sirens wailed in a rising-falling cadence with the object of testing the country's preparedness against air attack.

'Anything we should be doing?' Pemberton asked the captain.

'Yes, man the anti-aircraft guns. And don't tell me there's no ammunition, because I know perfectly well.'

They all moved up to the roof of the deckhouse and unlaced the canvas covers which protected the twenty-millimetre guns.

'It seems that we're lucky to have them,' Braithwaite said. 'Trawlers are getting leftover Lewis guns from the last war; useless.'

They stood talking until the air-raid sirens wailed on a steady, continuous note to signal the end of the exercise. To Edmund's ear they were about the key of D in the soprano range. They secured the guns, but since, according to the prime minister, the war had started, they were not re-covered.

The ship's company arrived in the early afternoon in four navy vehicles with a regulating petty officer in charge. He ordered the men onto the jetty, each one standing with his kitbag and hammock.

'All present and correct, sir,' he reported to Pemberton. 'Will you inspect them, sir?'

'No,' Pemberton said. 'Have them stand easy and remain where they are.'

He went aft to the captain's cabin and a moment later Braithwaite stepped out on the upper deck. Edmund, Marko and the chief engineer were standing together and came to attention as Braithwaite approached the rail.

'Pay attention,' he said to his new ship's company and his eyes travelled across their slightly upturned faces. 'I am your captain and this is your ship. I welcome you. You have the distinction of coming aboard on the very day and the very hour that war has been declared. If you haven't heard, the prime minister spoke to the nation and said we are at war against Germany.'

He paused.

'This is my first order to you. Get settled in and then get the ship cleaned up, provisioned and ready for sea. Go to it with a will and good luck to all of you.'

He turned to Pemberton.

'First lieutenant, carry on.'

The officers saluted and the captain turned to go.

It was Pemberton's turn.

'You are now going to your mess decks,' he said.

'Number one mess. Leading seaman Harding and the following seamen . . .'

He read out the names.

'Come aboard and follow the sub-lieutenant.' He pointed to Cyr.

A group of men came over the gangway with their kitbags and hammocks.

'Now the stokers. Stokers, follow the chief engineer. All of you are in the same mess.'

'The second seaman's mess,' he went on. 'Leading seaman Fenway and the remaining seamen, follow sub-lieutenant Casswell,' and Edmund found himself leading the way with Fenway and a group of seaman behind him. Finally Pemberton took the miscellaneous ratings to their messdeck; the wireless operators, signalmen, asdic operators, two cooks and the sick-berth attendant. That only left the officers' cook and steward who had a small mess deck of their own next to the officers' quarters.

There was no one left on the jetty except the drivers and the regulating petty officer from barracks.

'That looks right to me,' Pemberton said when he was back on deck. 'Thanks for your help and I'll sign for them.'

'They're a good lot, sir. They won't give you trouble. Oh, and by the way, all these men have had their dinner and their grog.'

Meanwhile, in the second seaman's mess Edmund was allocating clothes lockers and hammock spaces to the seamen.

'My name is Casswell,' he began. 'I'm going to start by allocating a locker to each of you. If your locker isn't clean here are buckets, soap and cloths. You are to stow your blue kit in your lockers and your white tropical kit can go under the seats, here. When you've done that, get changed into working clothes and scrub out the mess, top to bottom. After that we'll be taking stores aboard.'

He turned to leading seaman Fenway.

'Very well, leading seaman. You carry on from here.'

They can do it perfectly well without me standing there, Edmund thought, and he went up on deck and found Marko.

'So far, so good,' Marko said. 'No delay, no standing around, no silly inspection. The Watch and Quarter Bill was ready.'

'Only just,' Edmund added. 'I liked what the captain said. He actually welcomed them.'

It took only half an hour for *Troubadour* to take on life. The quartermaster and boatswain's mate were on duty by the gangway, a brand-new log book was opened and the ship's bell began to sound the half-hours. Since he was the officer of the day Marko noted in the log the times that officers, petty officers and men came aboard, and the arrival, during the afternoon, of stores and provisions.

Edmund opened the ship's office which was at main deck level below the flag deck. He dragged in the box of stores that had been deposited outside the door and arranged them in the drawers and on the shelves. There were plenty of pens and steel nibs, even blotting paper, but no typewriter. The key of the safe had not been included, but a petty officer brought it during the afternoon and at the same time turned over the secret code-books and other confidential material.

The navy prided itself on its ability to keep paper work to a minimum, so the bareness of the office did not surprise Edmund. He made a copy of the Watch and Quarter Bill for himself, then arranged King's Regulations and Admiralty Instructions on the shelf. Ink bottles were wrapped in newspaper and stowed where they couldn't move. When finished, he went on deck and watched as victualling stores were being brought on board. A thin wisp of smoke was rising into the afternoon air from the funnel. Below, in the engine room, a diesel was humming so that lights, refrigerators and fans had come to life. He went to seamen's mess No 2 and found it clean but deserted except for an able seaman who was washing the crockery and storing it in racks.

'You're able seaman Kirk, aren't you?' Edmund asked. 'And you're one of the three quartermasters.'

'Yessir, I'll be on for the first dog watch, meantime the leading seaman told me to wash all the mess traps and count them as I put 'em away. Twelve of everything.'

'What do you think of the mess deck, Kirk? It wasn't built on the cheap.'

'The lads was saying, sir, this is above navy standards; mahogany table, upholstered seats and a sink for washing up. Here we have an oven for keeping food warm, and a safe for butter, sugar, tea and the rest. And here's an electric kettle so we can have tea when we want it. What it means is that when men come off watch at midnight they can get a hot drink and some bread and cheese before they turn in. You don't even get that in battleships.'

'I hope the navy takes note of this,' Edmund agreed. 'This ought to be standard.'

A wireless operator approached Edmund with a pair of binoculars which he was to keep in his cabin.

'And the captain wants you in the wardroom,' he said.

'Thanks. Are you Jones or Carmichael?' Edmund asked. 'You have to be one or other.'

'Jones, sir.'

'Thank you, Jones, I'll be off to the wardroom.'

He turned to able seaman Kirk.

'Well done, Kirk. I think we're going to be all right.'

'I'll only take a minute of your time,' Braithwaite said as the officers assembled.

'First, there's to be no smoking on the mess decks. Smoking on the upper deck only. And no man may possess matches, other than safety matches, and no lighters or lighter fluid. I'll speak to the ship's company to-morrow, but I want you to pass that on now.'

'Second, cameras and diaries are not permitted in wartime. If anyone has a camera or keeps a diary it must be handed in and a receipt given.'

'Thirdly, the victualling stores are being loaded and we'll have some sort of a meal on board this evening. Fresh water is not a problem because we're hooked up to the water main. Oh, and speaking of liquids, I called the wine merchants Saccone and Speed and told them to send a van with a supply of wines and spirits for the wardroom. I said we had five officers and left the details to them.'

'Finally we must start thinking about security; censoring letters, all that. At the moment I have only one order for the ship's company, the speed and armament of the ship is not to be disclosed.'

A chorus of 'aye aye sir,' and he waved them away.

By late evening the stores were on board and the men sat down to their first meal. Some were talkative, others silent after the afternoon's exertions. A total blackout had been ordered and the ships was darkened with scuttles closed and black material draped across hatchways and doors. Foreign ships in the river had not complied, but carried their lights as usual, yet in a matter of days this country, Edmund said to himself, so often lauded as a beacon for other nations, would become darker than it had been since the Middle Ages. What was it in the Old Testament about a darkness that would cover the earth, and gross darkness the people? There would be groping and stumbling as there had not been for a thousand years; there would be injuries and even death as people tried to find their way in an unaccustomed blackness.

The officers gathered in the wardroom for dinner and the steward served drinks. Things were coming together, the day had gone well and Braithwaite was in good form.

'We've done naval stores and victualling stores,' he said. 'Tomorrow we'll get our ammunition.'

Conversation bounced from one subject to another.

'How are things in the engine room, chief?'

'Good, sir. No problems.'

'And the leading cook managed alright?'

'Yessir,' from Pemberton. 'We issued the food which is kept by each mess; bread, butter, jam, tea, sugar. There wasn't time for an elaborate supper this evening but we settled on corned beef, cabbage, potatoes and stewed fruit.'

'Did you get the office sorted out, Casswell?'

'Yessir, everything in place, but no typewriter.'

'We can scrounge one from somewhere,' Braithwaite said. 'Come to think of it I've got one at home that never gets used.'

'I see we have some Welsh names in the engine room department,' Edmund was saying. 'The Welsh have a tradition of music so perhaps we could form a small band.'

'Welsh boys make good stokers, specially if they come from coal-mining families. God knows why that should be,' Dobreiner commented.

'Easy,' Braithwaite replied. 'A few years ago when the navy ran on coal their fathers and brothers were mining the coal and our stokers threw it in the furnaces. Boys from mining communities are strong and they know about hard work.'

Braithwaite turned to another subject. 'The navy's lucky in one respect,' he said. 'We were at war twenty-one years ago against the same enemy and we know what to expect. At the Admiralty I was amazed by the number of people who could remember how mobilization was done last time. It wasn't something new, just a matter of reintroducing old rules and orders. They said that the arming of merchant ships and the organization of the convoy system was going like clockwork; and don't forget we have three thousand merchant ships worldwide.'

'And from our point of view,' Pemberton added, 'we got our stores in the right sequence at the right time.'

The steward announced that supper was ready and Braithwaite took his place at the head of the table, motioning Pemberton to his right and Dobreiner to his left. Edmund and Marko sat facing, leaving two empty seats at the end. The steward poured water in the glasses, put bread on the table and served a simple meal.

'We must think about a mess and wine caterer,' Braithwaite said. 'I don't know how familiar you are with these things, but it's usual for each officer to contribute a small sum on a weekly or monthly basis. Some ships charge officers according to rank, which is stupid because a commander doesn't eat more than a midshipman. I think we should all pay the same amount and then the steward can go ashore and buy a few extras; fresh fruit, vegetables, that sort of thing.'

They discussed it for a few minutes and Marko found himself saddled with the task. He admitted that he was interested in food having done his own cooking as an undergraduate.

'That's how I got decent French-Canadian food,' he said.

'Do the petty officers and the other messes do the same?' Edmund asked.

'Yes, the petty officers do. You'll often see a crate of oranges or other fruit in their mess. With the seamen and stokers it's a question of money. If a man's married he's not going to spend it on himself when it should go to his wife. One of the things we'll do, and you can take this as an order, is to collect everything that can be sold and not throw anything away.' He was speaking to Pemberton.

'Those large cans which the men call "fannys" can all be washed and stored; also bottles, old clothes, worn-out rope and canvas, pickle jars, even gallon paint pots can be cleaned up. In foreign ports they can be bartered for fruit, eggs, coconuts. Rope, in particular, which is too far gone for us will suit a fisherman perfectly well. With a bit of bargaining you can get fresh fish for the whole ship for a length of rope which would otherwise get thrown away. And by the way, the coxswain will hand out hooks and lines to anyone who wants to fish over the side when we're at anchor.'

Dobreiner was nodding his head. 'Yes, I remember in the destroyer *Wishart* when we were on detached duty the captain would go alongside a fishing boat at sea. Once we got a whole tuna fish and had a wonderful meal. Small ships can do that sort of thing, large ones can't. It makes a difference if one meal a week can be taken out of the sea and not out of the store.'

This was a side of navy life that Edmund didn't know about. His experience as a midshipman in *Nelson* hadn't included stopping the ship in mid-ocean and bargaining for fish.

That evening Edmund scrubbed his cabin, cleaned out the clothes cupboard and unpacked. He hung up his uniforms, arranged his other clothes on the shelves and put his whites in the drawers under the bunk. Lastly he made up his bed with clean sheets and arranged his coloured bedspread over it. He didn't finish till midnight and was standing admiring his handiwork when Marko came in.

'A ship called *Athenia* has been sunk,' Marko said. 'South coast of Ireland. Loss of life very heavy. Captain's upset because he was once aboard *Athenia* and knew the officers. What can you expect from those lousy Germans? She was a passenger liner, dammit; women and children.'

Edmund went to bed thinking of *Athenia* lying on the sea bottom and a German U-boat crew gloating over what they had done.

For Edmund the third day of September, 1939, had come and gone.

Chapter 4

THE WEEK THAT followed was passed in a blur of hard work and preparation. Ammunition for the four-inch gun was brought alongside where it was examined by Pemberton and the coxswain, then passed below decks by the gun's crew. The depth charges, ugly gray barrels of destruction, were lowered into the magazine. The throwers were loaded, two each side of the quarterdeck, and the racks which dropped them directly over the stern of the ship received their quota. The pistols, or hydrostatically controlled firing devices, were stored separately and were not installed in the depth charges until the ship went to sea. This was because depth charges were heavy and awkward, and in bad weather had been known to slide overboard by accident. Without its pistol a depth charge was no more than a cylinder filled with explosive that would deteriorate in water, but with the pistol in place it would explode by the pressure of water, or if the water was shallow it would lie on the bottom, a menace to passing ships. Perhaps it had been set for a hundred feet and had fallen in ninety feet. The high tide could alter the depth sufficiently to set it off, or the water pressure be increased by a ship passing over.

Troubadour's sea trials were carried out in a sheltered area off Foulness Island. The full power trials produced only one slight hitch; as she gathered speed the bridge shook at twenty-one knots, then became steady again as she went up to twenty-two. With a stop-watch over the measured mile Edmund calculated her top speed at 24.9 knots, almost 25. *Minstrel* had only done 24.4.

'She doesn't like 21 knots; we'll have to avoid it. Make a note in the log.'

Edmund did so and Braithwaite continued, 'some vessels shake at certain speeds. I was in a destroyer that went crazy at 27.5 knots. There's nothing you can do beyond informing the flotilla leader and asking him never to order that speed.'

The anti-submarine drill had been satisfactory as far as it went. To test the asdic equipment properly would have required a real submarine and the nearest place where such exercises could take place was Scapa Flow in the Orkney Islands. However, the 'ping' had gone out into the water, probing the depths ahead like the beating of a giant creature's heart. Amplified for all on the bridge to hear it would be their constant accompaniment, the sound by which they lived day and night as long as the ship was at sea. As an anti-submarine sloop *Troubadour*'s asdic was their only means of detecting a submerged enemy. If it surfaced they would expect to see it and the four lookouts, two each side of the bridge, relied on nothing more than their eyesight. Below the surface it was asdic alone that revealed an enemy. In that event the 'ping' would go out, strike the steel hull of the submarine and return the sound. It was a *ping* – pause – *ping* sound that would make the heart miss a beat, turn the voice dry and tell the hearers that the enemy was below.

The gun drills had gone according to the book under Marko Cyr's direction. However *Troubadour*, like the other ships of her class, was lively in the water, which made it difficult to aim the gun. At one moment leading seaman Harding's crosswires would be on the sea a scant thousand yards distant, at the next they would be pointing far over the horizon. To hold the target and pull the trigger was going to be a matter of luck as well as judgement. In capital ships and cruisers the slow roll of the ship made it easier for the gunlayer, but the smaller the ship the more difficult it became.

A full afternoon had been spent swinging the ship to determine the error of the compass. This was an age-old requirement for the magnetic compass which was attracted not only by the magnetic north pole but also by the residual magnetism of the ship itself. If this deviation had been consistent it would have been a simple matter to add or subtract it from a compass reading. But it varied as the ship changed from one course to another and the only way to compute it was to swing the ship in a slow circle, making continuous observations of a distant object. Edmund watched the compass and called out to Marko the slightly differing values while a tug pulled *Troubadour* in a circle round her own anchor. *Troubadour* had a gyroscopic compass which did not suffer the ills of deviation and gave true readings that needed no correction. The old-fashioned magnetic compass, however, was the backup system which had to be ready in case the gyro should fail.

There had been other drills and practices; fire and damage control, lowering a boat at sea to simulate the rescue of survivors, preparing to board a suspicious vessel, taking another ship in tow. Nothing had gone wrong and there had been no word of complaint against the long days and the fact that no shore leave had been granted. HMS *Troubadour* was duly commissioned in a brief ceremony and Braithwaite felt confident as he reported to commander Sykes that he was ready for sea duty. *Minstrel* had returned to Chatham from a task which had taken her into the North Sea and was by then lying alongside *Troubadour*.

'Very well,' commander Sykes had said, 'you seem to be doing well. Perhaps you and your officers will come across to *Minstrel* for dinner. I'd like to meet them and I think they should get to know their opposite numbers. You can grant shore leave until midnight. At 0800 to-morrow we sail.'

The meal in *Minstrel*'s wardroom was a revelation to *Troubadour*'s officers. It was a five-course affair, cooked to perfection, with different wines and port afterwards. It seemed that *Minstrel*'s six officers could afford extra luxuries which were beyond normal rations, but that didn't explain how it was cooked so professionally. The answer was forthcoming from *Minstrel*'s first lieutenant. The officers' cook had been trained at the Trocadero in London and was a man of decided views and artistic temperament. When he volunteered for the navy he was interviewed by an officer to determine at what level he should be inducted, but the interview had not gone smoothly, in fact it would not have been clear to a casual observer who was interviewing who. Instead of making him an officers' cook with the rank of petty officer or chief petty officer and sending him to a battleship he was sent to *Minstrel* as a put-down.

'He has to be treated properly,' *Minstrel*'s first lieutenant was saying. 'When we're in harbour he cooks our dinner but won't make the effort if he doesn't have the best ingredients. He tells us what food and wines to order and if he doesn't get them he sulks and deliberately makes a mess of things. He'll end up by being court-martialled, but until then we might as well make the best of it. Instead of giving him a challenging and suitable posting, why did some small-minded person send him to us?'

Later in the evening commander Sykes told Edmund to come to his cabin and bring his coffee cup with him.

'Your captain has told me about you, Casswell,' he said when they were seated. 'You were at Cambridge. May I know a little of your background?'

'Yessir. During my growing-up years I spent my summer holidays with an uncle who owned a yacht. He employed a skipper who taught me seamanship and tried to persuade me to apply for Dartmouth and a career in the navy. However, to please my father I chose differently; a scholarship to public school, the classics and Cambridge. When I got to Cambridge I joined the RNVR and for three years I've taken it quite seriously. I spent a full summer aboard *Nelson* as a midshipman and I was also in the destroyer *Brilliant*.'

'Haven't your other studies suffered? Braithwaite told me that you were preparing for the Church.'

'I can't answer that without sounding conceited. I'm a scholarship student and I can keep up with my studies fairly easily. After all, my father's a bishop, the books are on every shelf in the house and I've been listening to it all my life.'

He took a sip of coffee while commander Sykes regarded him attentively.

'During my first year at Cambridge I was nineteen and I rebelled in small ways, although I'm not completely sure what I was rebelling about. Perhaps it was the fact that I had been so insulated against what they call the world, the flesh and the devil. I joined Track and Field and ran for Cambridge in two events, then I wrote an essay proposing that Saint Paul had been a Roman spy. It found its way back to my father and in the argument which followed I refused to give up athletics but did agree to tone down my essays. It was then that the RNVR took over and I loved it because it countered the other-worldliness of my studies and brought me in touch with real people and their problems. To answer your question, therefore, the time I spent with the RNVR made me a better student because it filled a gap which, up to that time, I didn't know existed.'

'But isn't it true,' Sykes went on, 'that everything which can be said about theology has already been said; you can only follow in the steps of others.'

'Yes, I've set out on a well-trodden path, but whether I shall return to it I'm not sure. This is the best thing that could have happened because it's giving me time...'

'So you are considering...?'

'Yes, but the other side of it is that it might strengthen me in my commitment. This is...' he paused, 'a sort of forty days in the wilderness.'

'Thank you, Casswell. Let's go back to the wardroom. I think your ship will benefit from your rather unusual experience.'

How kind of him to have said it, Edmund thought, and he compared it in his mind with the rebuff that Braithwaite had uttered on learning of Edmund's course of study.

'Obey engine room telegraphs,' were Braithwaite's first words as he stepped on the bridge, and Edmund relayed the order to the engine room.

'Single up to a forespring.'

Minstrel slipped and got under way at the stroke of eight bells and *Troubadour* followed moments later.

Flag hoists appeared at *Minstrel*'s halyards.

'Answering pennant,' called the leading signalman. '*Order One. Ships in line ahead in sequence of fleet numbers. G-8. Speed eight knots.*'

Braithwaite turned the ship astern of *Minstrel* and with half ahead on the engines he ordered 120 revolutions. Their course took them past Sheerness, then to the north-east with Foulness Island away to port.

'Can you see the ship ahead, coxswain?'

'Yessir, see her well,' came Clancey's voice.

'Follow in her wake.'

Edmund had the hand-held rangefinder to his eye.

'We're at a cable-and-a-half and closing.'

'One hundred revolutions,' Braithwaite called down the voice-pipe. 'Did you get a copy of *Minstrel*'s speed and revolution table?'

'Yessir; on the chart table,' Edmund replied.

'Good; that makes life simple. When *Minstrel* orders a certain speed we'll know what revolutions are on her shafts. No two ships are exactly alike, but it's a good point to start from. Take the ship,' Braithwaite went on, 'I want to look at the chart.'

Edmund stepped up to the gyro compass and turned his binoculars on *Minstrel*.

'Their seamen on the upper deck have been stood down.'

'Very well,' from Braithwaite, 'prepare the upper deck for sea. Tell Cyr to secure anchors and cables. I want to see the first lieutenant.'

'*G-14*. Speed fourteen knots,' the leading signalman called out.

'Very good. Wait for the order to execute and go up to...' Braithwaite hesitated.

'One-six-two revolutions,' Edmund prompted him.

'Right you are. We'll find the convoy between Foulness Point and Clacton-on-Sea. About 20 miles to go.'

'Execute 14 knots,' from the leading signalman.

Edmund ordered the increased revolutions, then took the range again. The low-lying coast of Essex lay to the west while on the other side, eastwards, the North Sea was calm and empty of ships.

Pemberton came up and saluted the captain.

'First lieutenant. I want you to pipe the cruising watch to their stations, but let them go down and change into seagoing rig. They don't need to stand their watches in blue uniforms. Any clothes can be worn at sea.'

'Aye aye, sir.'

'And turn out the seaboat on its davits.'

Cyr came up on the bridge.

'Forecastle secured for sea, sir.'

'Very good, but you took too long,' Braithwaite replied. 'You must learn to get the anchors close up and the cables secured in quick time. In weather like this and with a river estuary before we reach the sea you're in no danger, but there are ports in the world where you go out the breakwater and into a gale. The first wave can wash down the forecastle while the men are still working. You know the reason we secure the cables that way?'

'Yessir; in bad weather the cables would thrash down on the steel deck. It could crack the deck or crack a link of the cable, besides what it does for the men below who are listening to it.'

'Absolutely right, Cyr. Thank you.'

'Ships ahead on the horizon. Looks like the convoy,' Edmund reported.

'Very good. Switch on asdic and let it warm up.'

The duty watch were coming up and leading seaman Fenway detailed each seaman to his duty.

'Port lookouts, there's land in sight and the officer of the watch doesn't need to be told. You, Rogers, search sea and sky from right ahead to 90 degrees on the beam.'

He turned to the other man. 'Porrit, search from 90 degrees on the beam to right astern. And you should keep a bit of cloth in your pocket to dry off your binoculars.'

'It looks fuzzy to me,' Porrit said, 'something wrong with this lot.'

'Fenway, show him how to focus them,' Edmund called out.

On the deck below, the coxswain was still at the wheel, but now he stood back and a seaman took over.

'Following ship ahead,' the coxswain said, 'there you are, lad.'

The seaman spoke into the voicepipe over his head.

'Able seaman Knatchbull on the wheel, sir. Following ship ahead.'

'Very good.'

'Leading signalman,' the captain called out, 'until further notice you and one other signalman are to stay on the bridge. We'll be joining the convoy and there may be a lot of signalling.'

The convoy consisted of 22 merchant ships, mainly small coasters and general cargo vessels. They were bound for the Forth, four hundred miles distant on Scotland's east coast. The speed of the convoy was the speed of the slowest, so it would take almost two days for them to reach their destination. The navy's job, Braithwaite explained, was to guard against air and surface attack. It was not likely that they would encounter an enemy submarine in the shallow waters of the North Sea, but the asdic was kept running and the operators gained experience in its use. Two armed trawlers from Harwich had joined them and were under commander Sykes' command. They were stationed on each beam, east and west, while *Minstrel* and *Troubadour* led the procession a thousand yards apart.

This was the first convoy in which most of the merchantmen had sailed and the captains had difficulty maintaining a uniform speed. Some had no proper revolution counter and were reduced to shouting down the engine room voicepipe, 'Can't ye go a bit faster?' In others the engineers had little idea of what was expected of them and varied their revolutions at will. By the end of the forenoon watch, however, some semblance of order had been achieved.

'Lots of merchant skippers,' Braithwaite was saying, 'oppose the convoy system because they think it attracts the enemy whereas a single ship would be left unmolested. This is mistaken, because there's nothing an enemy likes better than to attack a single unguarded ship. The navy can't be there to protect it and the fire from one ship, if she has a gun, is obviously more effective when combined with that of other ships. Some skippers argue that a bomb dropped into the area occupied by a convoy is almost certain to do damage, but that's complete nonsense; a random bomb has only one chance in a thousand of hitting a ship. The convoy, in other words, offers a target more than 99.9 percent sea.'

Edmund knew that each merchant ship had been provided with a navy signalman whose job was to explain the orders of the commodore of the convoy. But signal discipline didn't come easily to many of the skippers so that the commodore received signals that were unnecessary of merely foolish. 'Tell him I think he's daft,' might get passed by a navy signalman as 'request clarification of your last order.' Better still, it wouldn't be passed at all.

When eight bells were struck at midday Edmund wrote up the log book and handed over the watch to Marko. He went down to his cabin, left his cap and binoculars on the bunk and stepped over the sill into the wardroom. 'My first watch on *Troubadour*'s bridge,' he said to himself, 'I've earned my lunch.' That afternoon he lay down and slept so that when he went back on the bridge at sixteen hundred hours he was ready for another watch.

Braithwaite was not on the bridge when Edmund took over again. They were up to nine knots and the English coast was over the horizon to the west although the lingering odours of land were still discernible on the evening breeze. It was said that hard-bitten east coast captains could estimate their position with remarkable accuracy based on the smells that reached them from the land. To the east the sea had become hazy as Edmund's binoculars swept the horizon. It was good to know that destroyers were patrolling between the convoy and the coast of Germany.

A light blinked from *Minstrel* and the signalman switched on his Aldis lamp and gave a 'T', a long flash, and waited for the message. Edmund picked up the signal pad and wrote it as the signalman read the letters. '*Expect to maintain this course during darkness. No signalling by light permitted and all ships to maintain total blackout.*'

'Captain,' Edmund called down the captain's voicepipe, 'From *Minstrel*...' He read it out and Braithwaite grunted. Edmund knew that the voicepipe in the chartroom branched so that there was one by the captain's bunk and another by the chart table. The captain had given orders that he was to be called if anything unusual, hazardous or of interest should occur. 'Be on the safe side and let me know,' he said. 'I don't mind being wakened and called on the bridge for something that turns out to be a false alarm. Look at it this way. You get me up to the bridge because you're uneasy; I'm doubtful and put the ship to action stations. It turns out to be nothing serious, but it wasn't necessarily a poor decision.'

Edmund looked back at the lines of awkward but determined merchant ships, each seemingly pushing a wall of white water above which could be seen the bows, bridge structure and masts. Those ships and their cargoes were his reason for his being there; it was the duty of the navy to see them safely to their destinations.

The watch was quiet and Edmund looked round and imagined what it would be like at night. He had to be able to put his hand on any telephone or voicepipe in darkness or storm and he had to know where handholds were located so that he could keep his feet in the roughest seas. The bridge was open with no shelter from rain or spray except in the lee of the screen which ran across the fore part. There were two steps down so that he could stand and look through the glass with a ledge overhead that gave some protection. From above he had an uninterrupted view over the ledge. On the port side the steps led down to a chart table where the chart was spread out in a recessed *cabouche*, as the navy called it. Canvas curtains covered the entrance so that the chart and log book were protected from the elements. There was a dim red light for use at night, red being chosen so that the night vision of the officer of the watch was not impaired.

He resumed his place by the compass and swept the horizon again. Leading seaman Harding's watch was on duty, the Blue watch, and Harding moved from one position to another to check that each man was at his assigned station and attentive to his duties. At the four-inch gun there were three men, gunlayer, gun trainer and loader, one of them wearing earphones so that Edmund had only to alert him and a sudden enemy attack would be met by a sudden response. In thirty or forty seconds the whole gun's crew would be in place, but it was those few seconds that might win or lose an encounter. Likewise two of the depth charge crew were in readiness by the depth-charge racks, one of them also wearing headphones so that Edmund could reach him at a moment's notice. If a German U-boat somehow managed to approach and was seen by the lookouts Edmund could turn the ship towards it, run over its last observed position and release depth charges.

There were also two men on the anti-aircraft gun deck, the oerlikon machine guns being the ship's truly rapid response weapons. The gunner had only to swing the gun toward the enemy, aim with the cartwheel sight and pull the trigger. A stream of explosive bullets, each the size of the handle of a carving knife, would stream toward the target. If an enemy aircraft were to appear suddenly out of the mist this would be its welcome.

Leading seaman Harding moved from one lookout to another, making sure that each man's binoculars were clean and well focused and that he was sweeping sky and sea in a systematic way. As he spoke he put a hand on the man's shoulder and held the bridge bulwark with the other. Finally he stopped to chat for a moment with the signalman who was at the after end of the bridge. He glanced up at the white ensign and, seemingly reassured, reported to Edmund that able seaman McVane was on the wheel and the Blue watch closed up at their stations.

The ship's bell sounded the half-hour as it had done in the navy for hundreds of years. Ding-ding, ding. Five thirty p.m. or 1730 hours on the 24–hour clock. The practicality of a ship's bell assured its survival throughout those years when timepieces had been a luxury. An hourglass which, in reality, measured half an hour, would be used by the quartermaster or boatswain's mate and each half hour would be sounded on the bell. A single 'ding' would mark thirty minutes after midday in, say, the afternoon watch. 'Ding-ding' would be struck at one o'clock or 1300 hours. It would continue building up until the end of the watch, 4 p.m., when eight bells were struck. Each watch began the count over again and the routine was only varied at midnight on New Year's Eve when sixteen bells were struck, eight for the old year and eight for the new. For sailors who had no access to a clock or watch it was like the church clock of an English town. Whether or not they could see the clock or even read the time mattered little because it was the chimes which kept the townsfolk informed, and the principle was the same at sea.

Another tradition which had survived from the days of sail was the boatswain's call, a curved silver whistle about six inches in length. The boatswain's mate wore it about his neck on a chain, usually tucked into his jersey when not in use. It was used to call attention to an order from the first lieutenant such as 'up spirits' or 'red watch muster at your stations.' The boatswain's mate would sound his whistle, with its high-pitched, attention-getting cadence, and then call out the order as he ran through the mess decks. It was also used when welcoming the captain on board, lowering the flag at sunset and for other ceremonies.

Edmund and Marko were each keeping ten hours of watches out of twenty-four while Pemberton kept only four, the morning watch from 0400 to 0800. This imbalance was because the first lieutenant was responsible for the internal organization of the ship while Edmund and Marko had few duties, besides watchkeeping, when the ship was at sea.

It was on this first patrol northwards that Edmund began to realize that at sea he lived a disjointed life. Day and night meant little, the unit of measurement was the four-hour watch, punctuated by the ship's bell and the boatswain's call. Days of the week and the month became insignificant and human existence was lived in short episodes of sleep and work.

When Edmund came up again at midnight the sky was clear and the moon lay low on the horizon leaving a path of light on the surface of the sea. He studied its face for many minutes, the face of a dead and lifeless planet that swung through space but did not nourish the tragedy and beauty of living things.

Chapter 5

MINSTREL AND *TROUBABOUR* led the convoy into the Forth and were instructed to refuel and hold themselves in readiness for a return to sea. Like the rest of the ship's company Braithwaite would have welcomed a slap-up dinner ashore, a drink or two and a full night of sleep. The misty hills of southern Scotland were displayed at their best and the public houses appeared inviting at no great distance from the ships. The pleasures of the land, however, were not to be sampled and by nightfall they were at sea again steaming northwards with St Andrews and the Bell Rock away to the west.

As the night progressed the weather deteriorated until by dawn the ships were labouring through a short, steep sea. This was *Troubadour*'s first trial in weather which, although not severe, was uncomfortable and made all shipboard activity difficult. Pemberton had attempted to take morning stars but gave up when he found the horizon impossible to define. Braithwaite found him talking to Edmund who had come up for the forenoon watch. Both were gripping handholds against the roll of the ship.

'Morning sir,' Pemberton said. 'Blowing up a bit from the nor-nor-west.'

Braithwaite steadied himself and watched the ship for a full five minutes. The bows, rounded at deck level, held the sea down and controlled most of the spray, but other spray was thrown upwards as she slapped into crossing waves. The navy had always shunned high, rounded bows because they would theoretically reduce a ship's speed and be less effective as a ram. As *Troubadour*'s bow dipped deeper into the sea the cutting edge was replaced by the more rounded and buoyant prow that pushed away the water rather than slicing through it. It was also disliked for another reason, being more difficult to paint when the ship was in harbour. This was because the stages from which the men worked were suspended from the upper deck which overhung the inside of the curve, so they found themselves several feet from the surface they were attempting to paint.

'Who's on the wheel?' he called down the voicepipe.

'Able seaman Rogers, sir.'

'How's she handling?'

'Carrying a slight amount of port wheel, but she's steady. Not giving me no trouble.'

'Thank you, Rogers.'

He turned to Edmund.

'Are we in station?'

Edmund took a rapid look at the compass and checked the rangefinder.

'Yessir. In station.'

'Speed?'

'One-five-eight revolutions, sir.'

'What would you say is the sea and swell?'

'Four and three, sir; perhaps four and four.'

'And the barometer?'

'Steady, sir.'

'Any ships fall astern during the night?'

'No, sir. There's an admiralty trawler astern to encourage the slow and the faint-hearted.'

'Slow and faint-bloody-hearted;' Braithwaite spat out the words. 'There must be a better way of saying it. Asdic working well?'

'Yessir.'

'I'll be in the wardroom having breakfast.'

Braithwaite made his way to the after end of the bridge, took his first step down the steel ladder, then turned; 'Tell the leading seaman to see there's no water in the seaboat and drain it if there is.'

'I'll tell him, sir.'

Edmund looked at the chart and realized that the convoy was bound for Scapa Flow or through the Pentland Firth and round the north coast of Scotland. Braithwaite probably knew where they were going, because commander Sykes must have told him when they were alongside the oil jetty. They were obviously not bound for Norway or the Shetland Islands, so they would be turning to the north-west at about midday and would steam through the Pentland Firth during the night, the worst time.

The Pentland Firth; he had read about it, heard stories from others and looked forward with some apprehension to his first encounter. It was there that the waters of the Gulf Stream flowed through from the west and, as they travelled over the uneven sea floor made the surface waters race and eddy, rather like a river in flood. An instructor had said that in a small ship an upsurge of water was uncomfortable, but when you fall into a hole it was far worse.

In the event the Pentland Firth was not at its most dangerous. The tide race which had been measured at seventeen knots on one historic occasion was no more than five that evening and the surface water was not alarming. Edmund had slept for three hours during the afternoon and had kept the first dog watch. He handed over to Marko at 1800, had some dinner in the wardroom and returned to the bridge at 2000. By this time the convoy was in the narrows searching for Cape Wrath, and by midnight they had turned into the Minches. Their destination was to be the port of Liverpool and their route took them between the Cumbrian mountains and the Isle of Man. It was a cool forenoon as they passed the little port of Whitehaven and Edmund's binoculars kept going back to the gray hills which rose, dream-like, beyond the shore. Late that evening they were in Liverpool and again it was a case of in and out and no leave granted. Would the whole war be like this, he wondered.

Their next task was a convoy of twenty ships which were to be escorted southwards through the Irish sea. Three of them, plus *Troubadour*, would detach themselves in St George's Channel and enter Milford Haven. Within sight of St Ann's Head *Troubadour* would leave her three charges, turn back to sea and rejoin the main convoy. *Troubadour* would find herself thirty miles astern of the convoy, but her speed would enable her to overtake in a few hours. The return would be made southwards to Land's End then into the English Channel, through the Straits of Dover and back to the Thames. *Troubadour* would then have completed the circumnavigation of the British Isles in the first two weeks of the war. It was a good shakedown cruise and they would return with more confidence than when they had set out.

'*Order One, G-8,*' the leading signalman called out as they turned in the Mersey river. 'Ships in line ahead, speed eight knots.'

Braithwaite ordered half ahead on the starboard engine and half astern port and fell astern of *Minstrel* as she moved downriver. The ship's bell sounded the hour and the Liver building with its atrocious birds atop the roof fell astern. This was the port from which slave ships had sailed, returning with their holds brimming with cotton and sugar from the southern United States and Cuba. Liverpool had doubtless redeemed its reputation since those years, but it had been an evil beginning.

Edmund was on the bridge, noting the time, writing the log and watching for signals when unexpectedly Braithwaite said, 'take the ship, Casswell.'

'Aye aye, sir.' Edmund replied. 'Up ten revolutions.'

'Hands to man the ship's side,' was being piped by the boatswain's mate and the seamen stopped what they were doing and formed lines down the rails facing outward. Marko was forward in the eyes of the ship, his men spread down either side. They passed a huge merchantman alongside the wharf and dipped their ensign in salute. Half an hour later they were into the waters of the estuary and soon had overtaken the convoy and were leading it westwards. *Minstrel* and *Troubadour* were ahead as usual, an admiralty trawler astern. Either the merchant captains had been well briefed or it was not their first attempt at convoy work because they formed their lines without confusion. Night fell with the Isle of Anglesey still over the horizon and visibility down to a few miles.

There had been a government order that all lighthouses were to be extinguished because it was thought that they helped the U-boats to fix their positions. Some had not complied but the Anglesey coast was in darkness and they could make out no distinguishing feature as they turned southwards with Holyhead, as they hoped, ten miles to the east. Dawn found them with the coast of South Wales hidden in cloud.

Braithwaite was responsible for leading the three merchantmen into Milford Haven, but he did not get star sights at dawn and was doubtful as to his exact position. In fact he was too far south and they had to turn north toward Saint Ann's Head instead of entering from the west. This wasted time and when he had brought them to within a mile of shore, too close for U-boats to be operating, the main convoy was well into the Celtic Sea. *Troubadour* delivered her charges to the embrace of the estuary and turned back toward the south-west. The weather was cool and the sea moderate, but a speed of eighteen knots gave her some pitch and roll. Her course was south-south-west towards Land's End; she was alone for the first time, not in company with other ships and Edmund was on watch.

Suddenly from the lookout, 'Fine on the port bow. Looks like . . .' but he didn't finish.

'How far?' Edmund asked.

''bout two mile, sir.'

'Can you see it now?'

'No sir, gone out of sight.'

'What did it look like?'

'Kind of square black . . .'

'Keep your binoculars up.'

Edmund lifted the cover from the captain's voicepipe. 'Come up, sir.'

Next he spoke into the wheelhouse voicepipe. 'Get the senior asdic operator here at the double,' then to the asdic operator on watch in the compartment, 'the lookout saw something fine on the port bow. About 4000 yards.'

By this time Edmund had decided that the ship should be at action stations and pressed the alarm button in a series of long bursts. Bells clanged throughout the ship. He looked at his watch, then swept the sea ahead with his binoculars.

'Port ten,' he called down the voicepipe. 'Steer 195 degrees.'

'I don't see nothing more sir,' from the port lookout.

'Keep searching.'

The captain appeared behind him.

'What's going on?'

'Right ahead, sir. I'm steering towards. Could have been the upperworks of a U-boat.'

'Who saw it?'

'Port lookout. I'd like to reduce speed. Give the asdic operators a better echo.'

'Do so.'

'One-five-four revolutions.'

The senior asdic operator ran across the bridge and into the asdic cubicle.

'Normal search,' Edmund said.

For agonising minutes the 'ping' of the asdic went unanswered and then suddenly a shout came from the starboard lookout.

'Periscope, sir. Green three-oh.'

'Starboard ten,' Braithwaite ordered. 'Take its bearing.'

The periscope had been a thousand yards away, moving north. Braithwaite made a quick calculation and set a course to intercept, and at that moment the asdic found the U-boat. The outgoing 'ping' was followed by a return 'ding'.

'Hold that echo,' Edmund told the operator. Then he picked up the telephone which connected him with the leading torpedoman on the quarter deck.

'We have contact with a U-Boat. We'll be firing a full pattern. Set depth charges for fifty feet. Stand by to obey the firing buzzer.'

There were confused noises at the other end. A voice asked, 'this a practice, sir?'

'No, it's the real thing. We've found a German U-boat. We're attacking it.'

'Oh, all right. We're going to fire, are we?'

'Yes, we are going to fire.'

'I have control of the ship,' Braithwaite said; 'I am attacking.'

'Echo high; no, let's say echo slight high,' Edmund reported as he listened to the return echo which differed in tone from the outgoing.

'She's on a course of about 260 degrees.'

Marko had given up his telephone and was shouting his orders to the gun over the fore port of the bridge. 'Load with armour piercing. Range point blank. Lookout bearing right ahead.'

Suddenly he turned to Braithwaite. 'At this close range I'll do better on the gun platform.'

Braithwaite nodded and Marko ran off the bridge.

'Fire on sight,' Braithwaite shouted after him.

The interval between outgoing and incoming sound was decreasing as the range decreased.

'Enemy range 500,' Edmund said. 'Echo slight high. She now bears 215 degrees so your throw-off is to starboard.' He had lost his nervousness and become very cool and detached.

'Enemy range 300. Echo same. She is turning to starboard. Enemy speed six knots. Start your throw-off.'

'Starboard twenty,' Braithwaite said. 'Steer 275 degrees.'

The lookouts could hear the asdic 'ping' going out followed by the return 'ding' a fraction of a second later and knew that the enemy was underneath the ship, perhaps no more than a few yards away. They peered downwards into the sea.

With earphones on his head, a stopwatch in one hand and the firing button in the other, Edmund waited for the moment to begin the firing routine. From the bridge they couldn't see the charges slipping out of the stern rails, but they saw two charges from the throwers arch gracefully into the sea on each side followed a few seconds later by two more.

'Take off headsets,' Edmund ordered and the operators removed them while the charges exploded.

The ten explosions fifty feet below the surface were not particularly loud because they were muffled by the water, but they seemed to shake the ship, to stun it. Huge piles of dirty water were thrown upward like vast bowls of whipped cream, tons of water from each depth charge, and Edmund wondered how any submarine made by the hand of man could survive such unspeakable punishment.

'Ten depth charges fired,' reported the leading torpedoman.

'I'm turning the ship to port which will put the enemy on the port side,' from Braithwaite.

When the last charge had exploded Edmund told the operators to put on their headsets and resume the search. The water was chaotic from the explosions, which confused the operators, but after two or three minutes they heard a reassuring 'ding' in reply.

'Echo bearing 342 degrees. Echo slight low,' Edmund reported. 'I recommend we stand off about six hundred yards and allow time to reload the depth charges.'

A thought occurred to him. 'Have we signalled Admiralty, sir? We're supposed to say we are over a U-boat.'

'No, for Christ's sake, we haven't because there isn't any navigator aboard this ship. I can't go and work out our position; nor can you; nor can Cyr.'

'Wouldn't it be best, sir, if we . . .' but Edmund trailed off when he realised he was questioning the captain. It was not his job to say what signals ought to be sent although he wanted to suggest something along the lines, 'Am over U-boat in approximate position 40 miles north of Land's End.' Better they know about the contact than know nothing.

The U-boat meanwhile was turning gradually to the west, the seaward side, and the operator was holding it with his echo.

'Range 650 yards. Echo high,' Edmund reported. 'No apparent damage from the last attack.'

A pause as the 'ping' went out and returned with its information.

'Depth charges reloaded, sir.'

'I'm going to attack again,' Braithwaite said.

'I don't advise it, sir,' Edmund replied. 'I recommend you send a wireless signal and find out if there are other ships nearby. Two or three working together have the best chance.'

'No, dammit, I'm going to attack. We'll get this one ourselves.'

'Aye aye, sir,' Edmund said. Next he spoke into the telephone, 'set all depth charges 300 feet,' and to the captain, 'Echo high, enemy speed seven knots; enemy course 290 degrees. I'd like the echo-sounder to be running when we go over.'

'One-five-four revolutions; attacking,' Braithwaite ordered.

'Stand by the depth charges, we are attacking,' Edmund told the leading torpedoman.

Troubadour gathered speed and ran over the U-boat a second time, releasing another full pattern of ten depth charges. Again Braithwaite turned the ship away after the attack and stopped engines leaving *Troubadour* at a presumed distance of about 600 yards from the U-boat. Again the explosions in the water created a huge disturbance and this time it prevented the asdic operators from regaining contact. The asdic sounds were mushy and confused with echoes returning from all points where the charges had exploded.

'Lost contact, sir.'

'Oil on the surface,' from a lookout.

Braithwaite turned his binoculars to the area where the explosions had been. 'We've got her! Oil everywhere.' Then to Edmund, 'of course you can't find her, she's sunk.'

Edmund's expression didn't change, so the captain went on. 'If you don't believe me, see for yourself!'

He took the ship through the area where oil was spreading.

'No doubt about it; that's oil.'

'Sir,' Edmund began, 'there doesn't seem to be wreckage or bodies and we didn't hear breaking-up noises. I recommend a standard search in case it slipped away.'

'Don't be ridiculous. We're not wasting more time.' Braithwaite was jubilant. 'Stand down from action stations. Put the ship back on her original course.'

Minutes later Braithwaite composed a signal to Admiralty: '*U-boat sunk in position . . .*' and gave the co-ordinates of latitude and longitude.

Within seconds the telegraphist was on the bridge with a reply from Admiralty, '*Well done.*'

Marko came up to relieve him and Edmund turned over the watch and went down to his cabin. He sat at his desk, pulled out a pad of paper and wrote the date at the top of the page. How he liked that small cabin of his; clean, efficient, everything to hand. In the lower desk drawer were the personal files of the men in his division; the drawer above contained paper, envelopes, pencils. In front of him was a small calendar.

Had he been forceful enough with the captain, he asked himself. How would Marko have handled it? Marko had an inbred toughness about him, the persistence of the trained lawyer; an ability to argue, bargain and negotiate. Edmund felt that if he differed with his captain he was being insubordinate, running the risk of disciplinary action. Or was it simply weakness? Had he taken the line of least resistance and allowed Braithwaite to do everything wrong? Someone, sooner or later, was going to tell him to prepare a report about it, so he might as well do it now while the events were fresh in his mind. Braithwaite had claimed to have sunk it, but at best it was a 'possible' success, not even close to a 'probable'.

He sat and contemplated his small cabin. The steel deadlight over the scuttle was secured by three butterfly nuts and would not be opened until they returned to harbour. The small curtain covering it moved back and forward with the motion of the ship, its colours, through half closed eyes, appearing like the wind on a valley of Alpine flowers. His bedspread was of the same pattern, all bright colours in contrast against the gray metal surrounding it.

Edmund did his own washing and took care of his cabin. Pemberton, on the other hand, employed a seaman and paid him for the extra work. A seaman's pay was so wretched that it was not difficult to find a man who would do a bit of washing, ironing, shoe cleaning and the like and send the money to his wife and children. In fact it was Nancy Pemberton who sent the sailor's wife a monthly cheque, so Pemberton and the able seaman didn't handle any money at all. Edmund, on the other hand, wanted his own touch on everything. He was meticulous where his room and clothes were concerned and he had a passion for order. When he bought his blue duffel coat at Gieves he found the buttons sewn on so badly that he cut them off and re-sewed them with fishing line.

There was a small picture frame on the shelf above his bunk. It was leather-covered and could be folded so that two photos were set in it, one at each side. On the left were his parents in a formal pose, his father stern and uncompromising with his hand on his pectoral cross. His mother looked past the camera, a little unfocussed, her expression hinted that she wanted to be rid of the present and return to an earlier and happier time. The picture as a whole spoke of respectability and the privilege of learning, of people who had been born in the previous century and who had been little affected, bypassed almost, by the convulsions that had beset the world after the death of Queen Victoria and her lust-dieted son.

On the other side was a photo that Edmund had taken with his own camera. Marguerite was mounted on her magnificent horse Bellerophon and behind her was the *château de Tilly*. She looked directly at the camera and smiled lightly, her hair stuffed under a hard riding hat. She was eighteen and he had taken it a few weeks earlier while on leave between the end of the asdic course at Portland and the start of the gunnery course at Whale Island. He had crossed to France and rushed to her side.

The asdic course had not taught them what to do if the captain goes plunging ahead and ignores advice. If a ship obtains a contact when not in company with other ships they had recommended that you take your time, signal Admiralty and try to get other ships to help you. Two asdic sets are better than one; three the ideal number. A single ship can lose contact, as *Troubadour* had done, but three ships directing their asdic from three different angles had a far better chance in the confusion of exploding depth charges. Surely other anti-submarine vessels could have been summoned from Bristol, Cardiff, Milford Haven or as far away as Plymouth. The Admiralty or the commander-in-chief; someone at a very senior level, would have signalled back with help and encouragement.

Even worse was to have abandoned the battle on such flimsy evidence. During the 1914–1918 war dozens of U-boats had been claimed by ships' captains which, when German records were examined after the war, turned out never to have been sunk at all. A bit of oil on the water meant nothing; it had probably been released intentionally by the U-boat. *Troubadour* should have conducted a systematic search in ever larger squares and continued to do so for at least two hours. Here was a gift, Edmund thought, a golden opportunity for *Troubadour* to have made a name for herself within three weeks of the outbreak of war. They had twice sighted the U-boat on the surface and had gained asdic contact, all within a few miles of the coast of England.

Edmund picked up his pen and began writing his report and he did so with a heavy heart.

Chapter 6

LIEUTENANT-COMMANDER HERBERT BRAITHWAITE, Royal Naval Reserve, was thirty-six years of age when he was appointed commanding officer of HMS *Troubadour*. He was born in Bremen in 1903 to an English father and German mother, his father having occupied a minor diplomatic position in the German seaport. Until the age of ten he lived in Bremen and from six onwards had attended a school for expatriate children. The fact that both English and German were spoken at home meant that he was able to adjust to his English surroundings when his father was ordered to return to England at the outbreak of war. His father died in the influenza epidemic which followed the war, and his mother, by then British by marriage, found a position as music and German teacher in a girl's school in Southampton. When he was old enough, Herbert was sent to training college for the merchant navy.

He began his career at sea as a quartermaster in the Peninsular and Oriental Steam Navigation Company, always known as the P & O, which was regarded as one of the best steamship lines in the world. When the Great Depression struck in 1929 he had been a second officer but, as world trade declined, was reduced to accepting any berth available. To keep up his spirits during those difficult times he joined the naval reserve which restored the gold to his sleeve and the spring to his step, if only for a month each year when he took his training. In 1931 his luck changed and he found a berth as second officer in a passenger and cargo vessel, the *Rio Claro*; he also passed the examinations for his master's certificate and married a wife, all within the space of a few weeks.

His marriage began as a disaster. His wife, Lucinda Trevellyan, was from a moneyed middle-class family and had been a music student under his mother's tutelage. His mother did not oppose the match and while it was beyond dispute that Lucinda would never be a competent home-maker, she seemed well behaved and willing to accept her husband's absences. She didn't work for a living because she didn't need to, but frittered away her time on the edges of the musical and artistic communities.

The problem began on their honeymoon. Herbert was an ardent man in the prime of his late twenties. He knew what he was doing and was not a clumsy lover, but he could make no progress with his artistic wife who wept copiously and shrank from his embrace. For a week he tried to reason with her, explained the simple facts of marriage but finally lost his temper and walked out. He was physically a strong man, but did not use his strength to overcome her reluctance, he simply packed his suitcase and went home, leaving her in the honeymoon suite of a comfortable hotel overlooking the sea.

Herbert had never thought it worthwhile to rent a house or even a room and then leave for months at a time, but enjoyed the use of an apartment in his mother's house which was necessarily close, indeed almost attached to the school where she worked. Conscious of the futility of the situation, he went home and within hours had secured a berth aboard a cargo-passenger liner bound for the Far East. Humiliated, he did not write and consequently received no letters, and when he returned nearly four months later he discovered to his surprise that Lucinda had moved in. This was not all, because a young German girl of his mother's choosing had also been employed as a domestic servant and Herbert lost little time in sizing up the situation and invading her bed. Indeed, his first evening at home found them engaged on the bathroom floor and then twice more in the bedroom.

This German girl was everything that Lucinda was not. She flaunted her sexuality, desported herself with abandon and encouraged him to try every artifice in the book. His mother viewed the situation with the tolerance of a woman who believes that her son could do no wrong, but the real surprise was Lucinda's reaction. It would have been impossible in that house to hide what was taking place, but Lucinda seemed more interested than jealous and asked to be allowed to come in and watch. From there it was only a short step to her becoming a participant. Her artistic sensibilities took over and she choreographed poses for the three of them in front of a large wall mirror. Her favourite pose involved German military ammunition belts, rifles and steel helmets but nothing else. So, from having no wife at all, Herbert found himself with two; from being the enforced celibate of long sea voyages he became the buffoon of bedroom orgies with a pair of women competing for his attention.

Sharing a house with three women meant that Herbert enjoyed the benefits of close attention in other ways. Lisa, the German, prepared most of the meals and was the kind of cook that men like, the food being on time, hot and sufficient. She only had to be told once to serve plates quickly and without fuss and that his jar of red Mexican chillies was always to be within reach. She didn't try to prepare complicated things like quiche when scrambled eggs were just as acceptable, or a boeuf à la something-or-other when stew with vegetables was equally appreciated. With her simple mind Lisa appealed to his simple instincts. She was consistent, kind and provided him with what he wanted.

Lucinda did little besides pay the bills and talk about art. If called upon to cook something she mustered cookbooks and newspaper cuttings and then went shopping for exotic ingredients. She could turn the kitchen into a madhouse within minutes, use every pot and pan in the house and produce appallingly mediocre results. Her ability to take the flavour out of food and serve it unappetizingly was a source of constant amazement.

Life in this eccentric household was not invariably placid, but when flareups occurred he turned his back and allowed his mother to deal with them. Lucinda, he realised, was a voyeur, but what he did not understand was that she craved physical ill-treatment, the brutality of a violent partner. The one thing she wanted was the one thing that Herbert did not provide so she settled for a different, more subtle form of humiliation, not only watching this German slut having sex with her husband but actually contributing to the process. It was her catharsis, her means of self-punishment and redemption.

That all this could have happened on the fringes of a school where nice English children were taught to be well scrubbed in body and mind, where the inheritors of Victorian prudishness were in full flower and where the teaching staff generally would not have said 'shit' if their mouths had been full of it was a tribute to the waywardness of human nature. Herbert's mother, epitome of the schoolmistress, stern of aspect but eternally devoted to her students, stepped with apparent ease from one stage to the other. She would give piano lessons or help a child with her German translation whilst on the floor above the mirror reflected a libertine threesome that most English people would have relegated to the decadence of an oriental harem.

Herbert himself saw no reason to change any of this and was as happy as a relatively unambitious man could be. When he saw an advertisement for a seamanship and navigation instructor at the marine college which he himself had attended some years earlier he applied for it, was interviewed and accepted. He was not a gifted teacher, but was painstaking and his mother showed him how to prepare his lessons. Celestial navigation, coastal pilotage and most branches of seamanship are technical and not unduly difficult. Teaching them calls for care and patience, not brilliance, but like so many others before him he discovered that he had not really understood it himself until he taught it to others. In his ten years at sea he had acquired mental shortcuts, ways of thinking and doing things that worked well enough in practice but which lacked the full explanation that a student requires. He found himself probing more deeply and in doing so he benefited from that year.

Finally he discovered to his surprise that the words 'Instructor, Navigation and Seamanship' carried weight with the shipping companies, and the fact that he was in the Royal Naval Reserve was no disadvantage. His next seagoing berth was that of first officer aboard a cruise liner, RMS *Homeric*, a berth he filled until the summer of 1939.

It was his mother's idea that Lucinda should accompany him on his first Mediterranean cruise. She paid for her own cabin, sat next to him at table and when she had overcome her seasickness began to make friends and enjoy herself. They went ashore at

Marseilles, Algiers and Naples, he visited her cabin and she his. He was an excellent dancer, which she had not previously known, and although not a tall man he was bronzed and handsome. She soon noticed that he was the focus of attention of other female passengers, some of whom regarded the ship's officers as part of the ongoing service provided by the shipping company to female holders of first class tickets. She began to be proud of his appearance, happy to be seen in his company and jealous of his attractions.

Their lives together grew in both an intellectual and physical sense, although there were occasions when she would lapse unaccountably into her old ways. When they returned to Southampton they found that Lisa was no longer there, as though her business in England was over and her duty done. When he and Lucinda visited Bremen the following year they learned that she had married and moved to another city.

Herbert and Lucinda Braithwaite were custodians of an even darker secret, because both had conceived an admiration for Hitler and the Nazi party. Since Hitler had come to power the casual observer might have been impressed by signs of change and improvement. The streets were clean, trains and buses kept to their schedules and there was an appearance of industry. Germany had always been an easy country to govern, Germans being hardworking and respectful of authority; they were the best soldiers in the world and discipline was not an objectionable word.

In the years preceding the war the German propaganda machine had presented the Nazis, not for what they were, but for what the German people wanted them to be. In subtle and unconscious ways they created the image of what was already deeply embedded in people's minds, an echo-Christianity. Hitler was presented as Christ himself, and it was trumpeted that Germans had no need of any Jewish saviour. The symbol of this new faith was the broken and distorted cross, the swastika, which adorned every public building and was worn on the arms of millions. The Hitler salute was their gesture of piety, the counterpart of a Christian crossing himself. The Nazi rallies were the high masses, while Hitler's voice on German radio was heard with reverence; the saviour himself on the air. Nazism, therefore, drew from the inexhaustible reservoir of Christianity, presenting itself as a system that was familiar and deeply embedded in the German mind.

Casual and unthinking visitors like Herbert and Lucinda Braithwaite saw little of what they were not meant to see and heard only what they were pleased to hear. Hitler's genius had provided something for everyone. For almost the first time in history women were courted, honoured and had compliments heaped on them. Their lives changed little but there was a new leadership and sense of direction. Children were recruited into the Hitler youth, a parody of the boy scout movement, where they sang the praises of Hitler and engaged in long route marches and uncomfortable bivouacs. From the outside it all seemed clean and wholesome; fresh air and pine forests; the embrace of nature and the pursuit of health. How it looked from the inside or what ends it was designed to serve were not emphasized.

When Herbert and Lucinda returned to England they spoke of the efficiency, full employment and sense of purpose which they thought they had witnessed. Neither of them possessed enough education to let them see what lay beneath the surface, and Herbert's German roots held in check the suspicions which might otherwise have tempered his enthusiasm. Herbert was a man of simplicities, so he allowed Lucinda to prattle on to her friends about the glory she had observed and the brilliant future she predicted for Germany and Europe as a whole.

It was with mixed feelings, therefore, that Herbert Braithwaite received the news of his appointment to command HMS *Troubadour*. His four years' seniority as a reserve lieutenant-commander, his master's certificate and experience as an instructor certainly qualified him for a command, but he would have preferred a troopship in which he would not have been actively engaged against the Germans. At the same time he was gratified that he had not been sent to minesweepers which he considered the most boring, dangerous and thankless service. He admired those who manned them as the unsung heroes of the navy, but he had no wish to follow their example.

Troubadour was a well-found ship, carefully built and as comfortable as could be expected for a ship of its size. His cabin was admirable, although it had no pantry nor facilities for cooking or heating food. He was obliged, therefore, to eat in the wardroom with the officers, despite the fact that this was not normal practice in the navy. For generations captains had remained aloof from their officers and taken their meals in their own quarters, which was possible if a pantry was attached. In this ship, however, he didn't even have a steward to attend to his needs. It seemed absurd that a ship's captain in wartime should have to concern himself with the trivia of daily existence which was so much more difficult at sea than ashore.

Troubadour's officers were an unusual group, but he was by no means displeased. Pemberton, as first lieutenant, was a good seaman, but his knowledge of the navy was slight. He had not known how to set up the Watch and Quarter Bill, how to administer the daily rum ration or account for the ship's stores. He had not even known that a seaboat's falls were to be of Manilla hemp, never the unreliable sisal rope, and that it was mandatory to change them end-for-end after six months and discard them altogether after a year. However, Pemberton was a quick learner and an intrinsically fair and decent person. He did not court popularity, but was the kind of officer who is respected for his good humour and even-handed approach. Time would tell whether he possessed the stamina needed in wartime and the persistence to turn the ship's company into an unbeatable team.

Gus Dobreiner was the least of his worries. He was a professional who had come up the hard way and would go higher still. He would never let the ship down and could be trusted completely.

The two sub-lieutenants were as unlike as could be imagined. He had expected them to be spoiled, undisciplined juveniles who would need months of instruction and supervision, but they turned out to be serious young men who had, in different ways, good backgrounds in seamanship and a fair amount of common sense. Casswell was the younger of the two, athletic of build but bookish and, as he thought, a bit pansy. He had helped the first lieutenant with the Watch and Quarter Bill; in fact done most of it himself. He had been well trained as a midshipman and had taken over the ship's office without a hitch. With his seniority of nearly two years as a sub-lieutenant he would get the second stripe of a full lieutenant fairly soon. Cyr, on the other hand, was tough, outgoing and looked as though he had stepped out of another century. His English was garbled, but he was an excellent seaman having handled fishing vessels since childhood. He was also resourceful and possessed enough brains to fill out the gaps. His presence in the wardroom mess was an asset because of his good humour and easygoing manner.

He wondered if the Admiralty were playing some sort of game by appointing Casswell, whose mother had been French before her marriage, to the same ship as himself whose mother had been born in Germany. But this was to impute more brains to the Admiralty than they had ever shown signs of possessing. A ship in which he had once served had two Pages, a Paget and a Paisley in the wardroom which suggested that the staffing of officers had been done on the basis of nothing more complicated than an alphabetical list.

Being two officers under strength was one of many reasons for Braithwaite's annoyance with the Admiralty. He shouldn't have to do the navigating himself and there should have been another watchkeeping officer which would make it easier on Casswell and Cyr. Six executive officers and an engineer wasn't asking much for a thousand ton sloop with asdic, depth charges and guns, not to mention the routine work of keeping the ship at sea for month after month. As always, the Admiralty had failed to plan ahead and train the officers who would be needed in wartime. The Germans, Braithwaite thought to himself, wouldn't have made such careless mistakes.

Chapter 7

WHEN *TROUBADOUR*'S LOOKOUTS sighted the Penwith peninsula Braithwaite was in familiar water and he cast caution aside as he brought the ship within a mile of Cape Cornwall and Land's End. The Wolf Rock slid past the starboard side as they turned into the English Channel and set course for the Lizard. When the convoy was overtaken off Portland he ran *Troubadour* between the merchant ships and into open water ahead of them. It was not a daring manoeuvre but a bit showy since he could have resumed his place on the screen by steaming round the northern side, toward the English coast. Some of the merchant seamen had lined the rails and cheered, having already received the news of *Troubadour*'s success.

'*Good show,*' *Minstrel* signalled. '*We are proud of you.*'

On this note the convoy and its two escorts skirted the Kent coast and entered the Nore which *Minstrel* and *Troubadour* had left only eleven days earlier. Once alongside, the men cleaned the guns and secured the depth charges while Marko put away the charts and Edmund opened the office and prepared to pay the ship's company. Edmund was so tired he scarcely took part in the conversation at dinner that evening which was to the effect that *Chorister* and *Harp* were to be commissioned within a few days and would join them before the end of the month. That night Edmund slept for ten hours.

He was awakened in the morning by Marko.

'Ed,' he said, 'are you listening? *Courageous* has been sunk. The telegraphist heard it.'

'*Courageous*? Aircraft carrier; quite old wasn't she? Converted battleship or something of the sort?'

'Yes, but I haven't told you the whole of it. She was sunk last night in the Bristol Channel with heavy loss of life. There were four destroyers escorting her; four!'

Edmund sat up.

'Are you thinking what I'm thinking?'

'Obviously. It was the same U-boat we contacted. We didn't sink the bloody thing and somewhere in the neighbourhood *Courageous* was on exercises with destroyers. A couple of them could have been detached and come to help us.'

'But how could *Courageous* be sunk with four destroyers in company?'

'My guess is she turned into the wind to land aircraft because they were running short of petrol and got away from her destroyer screen. The U-boat happens to be there and launches torpedoes.'

Edmund nodded.

'God, that's awful, and it's our fault; my fault. I should have tried harder; I mean, kept on at the old man. I knew we hadn't sunk it, I just didn't have the nerve to tell him he was wrong. At the same time,' he added, 'I can't see that *Courageous* was being handled intelligently. It's elementary that you keep your destroyers ahead of you, 'specially if there's evidence that U-boats are in the vicinity. They must have picked up our signal.'

Both were silent for a moment, then Edmund asked, 'do you think they'll order a court martial?'

'They can't court-martial the captain of *Courageous* because he's dead. Captain *something*-Jones; one of those hyphenated names. Our skipper could only be court-martialled on one charge; failing to make an immediate enemy report. His claim to have sunk it was an error of judgement, but failing to send a timely signal would be charged as negligence. The fact that he didn't have a navigator to write out the signal correctly with the ship's position might be taken into account, but it wouldn't get him off altogether.'

'Where did you learn your law, Marko?'

'Oh hell, I come from a family of lawyers. I used to go into court and listen to the messy cases. Better than going to school, and I learned more. My dad's side of the family owned fishing boats, my mum's side were the lawyers. Grandpa's the local judge.'

'So you divided your time between the fishing boats and the law court and for the moment...', Edmund waved his hand around the cabin, 'the fishing boats win.'

'Yes, but I studied law for five years...' he trailed off.

'Hell, look at the time, we have to get going and face the captain. He's going to be in a stinking bad mood.'

Braithwaite, however, did not come to breakfast in the wardroom. The steward took a tray to his cabin and at eight bells, in his best uniform, he went ashore. As he did so he looked over the mooring lines and called to the quartermaster to take up slack in the backspring, then he marched purposefully down the jetty toward *Minstrel*.

Commander Sykes was at his desk and motioned Braithwaite to be seated.

'You claim to have sunk a U-boat,' he began, 'do you persist in your claim?'

'No sir. Not now.'

'Why did you make the claim in the first place?'

'There was oil on the surface.'

'My leading telegraphist has told me that the only signal you made was to the effect that you had sunk the U-boat. You didn't signal when you first made contact. Why not?'

'As you know, sir, I haven't got a navigator. I didn't want to send a vague signal about being somewhere in the Bristol Channel. I had to include an accurate position.'

'That's a poor excuse, Braithwaite. Why not send a preliminary signal to say you had a U-boat contact? You could have followed it up later with details. We know now there were destroyers over the horizon.'

'I'm sorry, sir.'

'Sorry? Sorry *Courageous* was sunk? I expect you are, and I want your written report by midday to-day. I'll have to take it to the admiral's office and answer some very difficult questions. I'll say in your defence that you didn't have enough time to work up and exercise your ship, that you should have had three full weeks and practised anti-submarine warfare with a live submarine. I'll mention the shortage of officers, but I'm in treacherous water there because it seems you ignored the recommendations of the one officer you did have.'

How the hell did he find that out, Braithwaite wondered.

'In other words I'll do my best, but I don't guarantee the outcome.'

'I understand, sir.'

'I shall also recommend that *Minstrel, Troubadour, Chorister* and *Harp* be given two more weeks' training at some point in the future when things have settled.'

'*Chorister*, sir? *Harp*?'

'Yes. They're commissioning in a few days.'

'When are we going to sea again?'

'To-morrow afternoon.'

'But that hardly . . .'

'No, it doesn't, does it? These days, Braithwaite, our lives are measured by days and hours. The convoys have to be escorted and the Admiralty is short of escort vessels. It's as simple as that. Now, I'd be obliged if you'll go and prepare your report.'

For Braithwaite, the return to *Troubadour* was unnerving. His ship lay in the morning sunshine of late September, a beautiful vessel only a month out of the builder's hands. He had failed his ship and failed the white ensign, not by an act of cowardice but by sheer unmitigated folly. He wondered, deep in his mind, whether the German blood in his veins had contributed to his inability to fight the U-boat relentlessly. Had he, without fully realising what he was doing, allowed it to escape; given it a second chance? That he had been born in Bremen must be somewhere on file, although his father's status as a diplomat would presumably make everything all right. Or would it? Britain's ambassador in Berlin had made no secret of his Nazi sympathies and perhaps Braithwaite's background would not so much allay suspicion as arouse it.

Most potentially damaging was his flirtation with Nazism. He hadn't spoken to anyone in particular, but Lucinda had prattled to friends and relatives in a way that might turn out to be damaging at a court martial. Court martial? Yes, he said to himself, he had to face the possibility. As he stepped over the gangway and the boatswain's mate piped the side he made a decision. I'm a lousy writer, he said to himself, but I'll call Cyr and get him to do it. If anyone can state the case to my advantage, he can.

Braithwaite's misery was short lived because the following day found them at sea again. The ship shook itself to life, the upper deck became a bustle of activity as wet ropes were hauled inboard and the upper deck prepared for sea. Charts were carried from the chart room to the cramped and enclosed *cabouche* on the bridge. The land slipped away and the convoy of merchant ships appeared ahead of them. They passed *Chorister* and *Harp* which were on their sea trials and *Minstrel* signalled, 'Hurry, we need you.'

Braithwaite felt better as the bows rose and fell and the water of the North Sea parted as they plunged through. His wounded pride was a little healed by that most common spectacle for those who go to sea, the waves which are cast off by the ship in a V formation from the bows. Why do some waves break at the top and produce a white lather which seems stretched between one wavetop and the next? The sea that is pushed away forms small waves of its own and must have been an object of curiosity to millions of travellers, some too seasick to care, others, like himself, habituated to the sea's rough handling yet still fascinated by the phenomena of wave and wind. Watch followed watch and a routine settled over the ship and governed his life.

On the second night out the convoy was well into the North Sea and shaping course for the Forth. There was enough light in the sky to see the ships astern, at least to see their bow waves, and Edmund took the watch from Marko at midnight. It was a cool night but not cold, and for the first hour it was quiet. Edmund could hear voices in the wheelhouse below; the quartermaster, boatswain's mate and leading seaman Fenway, the tall man who, under Pemberton, was in charge of the upper deck and was known throughout the ship as Lofty Fenway. The smell of navy cocoa floated up the voicepipe. He wondered why no one had offered him any, when suddenly *Mistrel* opened fire, red flashes against the dark eastern horizon. 'Convoy's being attacked,' shouted a lookout.

Edmund had rehearsed what he would do in these circumstances and he didn't hesitate.

'Starboard twenty, quartermaster.'

'Full ahead both engines.'

'Captain come up, sir.'

'Action stations.

The wheel went over and *Troubadour* listed to port as the rudder gripped and she gathered speed from ten knots to twenty-four.

The leading signalman bounded up the ladder, followed by Braithwaite.

'What's going on?'

Another burst of fire from *Minstrel*'s guns and Edmund stated the obvious.

'*Minstrel* firing to seaward, sir. I've gone up to full speed and I'm taking her astern of *Minstrel*.'

A light flashed from *Minstrel*'s bridge and the leading signalman called out, '*Order one*. That's line ahead, sir.'

'Very good, I'll take the ship.'

'We're at full ahead, sir, steering due east.'

'Coxswain on the wheel.'

Next it was Marko's turn. 'Gun's crew closed up and ready. I'm loaded with semi-armour piercing.'

'Very good,' from Edmund. 'I'll pass it on.'

'Did you hear that, sir? Gun is loaded with semi-armour piercing.'

Edmund turned to the forward lookouts.

'Try and look past the gun flashes and see what they're shooting at.'

At that moment Edmund saw the enemy. They were E-boats, which he knew were fast and diesel-powered. They carried torpedoes and an 88–millimeter gun.

'E-boats, sir. I think I see three of them. Very fine to starboard. Moving toward the convoy.'

'I have them,' Braithwaite called back.

Suddenly there was a light detonation in the air a thousand feet above them and an enemy starshell burst and began its slow descent to the sea. It was pale green in colour and bright enough to light the convoy. Ships appeared where before there had been only darkness; figures on the bridge took on a ghostly glow and the E-boats became more difficult to see.

'Shall I order Cyr to fire starshell and light *them* up?' Edmund asked.

'No, leave it to one of the armed merchant ships,' Braithwaite said. 'We'll do more good firing high explosive.'

Minstrel had turned through 180 degrees and was now steaming southward at full speed to keep herself between the convoy and the enemy. She was firing over her port side and some of the ships in the convoy were also firing. *Troubadour* followed her round and came in two cables astern.

The E-boats were being engaged by the trawler astern of the convoy and they turned away to the east, which gave *Minstrel* time to execute yet another turn to the northward thus placing herself and *Troubadour* squarely in defence of the convoy.

'E-boats,' the captain called out to Marko. 'Lookout bearing green nine-o. Open fire at will.'

A moment later *Troubadour*'s four-inch gun began firing at the enemy which were in line ahead about two thousand yards distant. Splashes dotted the sea round them and the orange flashes from their guns indicated that they were returning fire. Edmund was amazed at *Troubadour*'s rate of fire, twelve to the minute, perhaps more, yet the E-boats maintained their formation and turned together at the convoy with the clear intention of launching torpedoes. They roared in to a thousand yards and both *Minstrel* and *Troubadour* turned towards them to reduce the target offered to an approaching torpedo.

A few moments later the asdic operator reported 'torpedo noises in the water', and Edmund grabbed his earphones from the hook and listened to the sound.

'Yes, he's right, sir. Torpedo noises.'

A shout from the leading signalman. 'One of the E-boats is hit, sir,' and then a dull explosion from inside the convoy as a merchantman was torpedoed.

'Bloody hell,' someone said.

As the E-boats turned away the oerlikon guns on the after deck were within range and poured a long burst in the direction of the nearest. It reminded Edmund of a stream of red cherries, shrieking across the dark sea; red because of the fiery tracers in the tail of each explosive bullet.

'What a gratifying sight. I hope they hit something,' Edmund said to no one in particular.

Pemberton knew that the E-boats offered the best target as they turned broadside and he had held fire until the chances were at their best. At that moment an 88–millimeter shell struck the seaboat's davit aboard *Troubadour* and exploded with a shower of metal. A signalman at the after end of the bridge fell with his hands to his face. Next, a second torpedo struck a merchant ship and exploded with a sheet of flame. Edmund turned his binoculars on the convoy briefly and then returned to the E-boats. Both *Minstrel* and *Troubadour* were still firing their four-inch guns at one that lay stopped in the water. Two others were in retreat. The battle was over for the time being and *Minstrel* was signalling the trawler to go to the assistance of the stricken merchant ships.

'Forty-two rounds expended,' Marko reported. 'One hit and several near misses.'

'Get Jennings up on the bridge,' Edmund ordered. 'He'll need bandages and a stretcher.'

Troubadour's men were kept at action stations for the remainder of the night. There was little danger from the same E-boats, because they must have expended their torpedoes, but once the convoy had been located there could always be other attacks, and at daylight twin-engine bombers came over and continued where the E-boats had left off. There were five of them, Junkers by the look of them, which flew over the convoy in formation not seeming to realise that the ships were armed.

A trawler was the first to open fire. Individual aircraft seemed to be picking individual targets and a large vessel in the centre of the convoy came in for more than its share of bombs. But it was well defended and its guns kept firing. Bombs dropped from the aircraft and landed with tall white splashes in the sea. The aircraft, however, had been hit and was trailing smoke and with a slow turn to port it flew on, losing height gradually over *Troubadour*. Pemberton on the after deck was ready and the oerlikon guns poured tracer into its fuselage. A wing crumpled and tore off and it went into the sea. The men on the upper deck let out a shout of delight.

Another aircraft had taken a hit and turned back to the east with a thin trail of smoke behind it. None of its bombs had scored hits but one had shaken a small coastal freighter by falling within a few yards of its bows. An hour later two Hurricane fighters appeared overhead but having circled the convoy they flew back toward the west.

Troubadour was still at action stations when they entered the broad estuary and the familiar outline of the Forth Bridge appeared in the distance. The depth charge, fire and damage control crews had been stood down but the lookouts and gun crews had been at instant readiness for thirty hours. They had only one casualty, the signalman who was struck by splinters from a bursting 88–millimeter shell. The steel davit which it hit had been bent and the boat itself shredded by the blast. The man was in the sick bay with splinters in the side of his face and neck. His messmates packed his kitbag and he was carried ashore on a stretcher and placed in an ambulance.

Minstrel had an astonishing story to tell. As they had turned toward the E-boat's torpedoes they had actually been hit by one which glanced off the keel without exploding. Everyone on the bridge had felt the thump and the lookouts saw the track in the water. It must have struck a glancing blow at an angle which did not detonate the firing device.

Edmund tried to analyse his own reactions to the events of the previous hours. Was it possible that he had felt exhilarated; had actually enjoyed it? He had not been particularly afraid; had watched the splashes from the German guns and listened to the torpedo sounds on the asdic almost with indifference. It seemed strange to be bathed in the pale green light of a German starshell, but he had felt no more apprehension than he would have felt while waiting for the starter's gun at a track meet. Is this the way you are supposed to feel in a brisk little action that had involved gunfire, torpedoes and bombs? His father, he thought to himself, would deplore the fact that he, Edmund, destined for the Church, had been more stimulated than sorry at the prospect of taking German lives.

Both *Minstrel* and *Troubadour* spent a few hours in the Forth and then returned south with another convoy. They were attacked again, but this time it was half-hearted and the sea too rough for the E-boats to use their speed. The convoy reached the Thames without loss.

Back in Chatham the mood was optimistic. Commander Sykes called Braithwaite aboard and spoke not about the U-boat incident, which Braithwaite had been expecting, but about the recent operations in the North Sea. 'Did you know,' he asked Braithwaite at one point, 'that up to a few months ago the Germans had E-boats for sale? They advertised them in our technical publications. They were inexpensive and contained details of diesel propulsion which is an area where we are behind. So what does the Admiralty do? Just what you'd expect; nothing.'

Chatham dockyard was not long in finding a new davit to replace the one that had received a direct hit. They lifted out the damaged one with a crane and dropped in the new one. A new boat was also supplied and Fenway set two men to painting it, reeving the falls and setting up the boatrope. He kept for himself the task of backsplicing the painter with a pointed end. This, he explained to the young seamen, was in case the boat was dropped with the drain plug not in place in which case the rope-end would serve as a temporary plug.

Chorister and *Harp* joined the flotilla during the first week of October. The commissioning took place on the upper decks in mid-morning, followed by a reception in *Harp*'s wardroom for all the flotilla officers. *Chorister* was commanded by an RNVR lieutenant-commander who had been a stockbroker and weekend yachtsman until only a few days before. Edmund took an immediate liking to him, but one of the junior officers in *Harp* produced the opposite effect. He was a loud-mouthed individual who thought himself qualified to entertain the visiting officers to a monologue that would have been considered unpleasant in any mess in the ship. In that crowded wardroom he told the kind of jokes and used the sort of language which, Edmund thought, was best ignored. Why do those fools laugh at him, he wondered; what can be funny about that sort of filth? He turned to face the man without smiling.

'Cheer up, old cock,' he was told. 'No need to look bloody miserable.'

He turned his back without replying and on the way along the jetty toward *Troubadour* fell in step with Pemberton who said that the man had been in the merchant service but somehow transferred to the navy. He was acting as *Harp*'s navigator which made him hope that *Troubadour*, when they got a navigator, wouldn't get one like that.

'You know,' Edmund said, as they approached *Troubadour*, 'I worry about that sort of person. What effect does he have on those round him and on the ship? What would you say if you had a sister and he came to take her out? He's the kind of person who creates an overwhelmingly nasty impression.'

Back on board, a youthful-looking officer was standing on the upper deck talking to Marko who had remained behind as duty officer.

'Terrific news,' Marko announced, 'we've got our navigator. Midshipman Reece, this is lieutenant Pemberton, the first lieutenant, and sub-lieutenant Casswell.'

'Good to see you,' Pemberton said, 'we really do need you. Where's your kit?'

'It went down to my cabin,' Marko broke in. 'He'll be sharing the cabin with me and immediately after lunch I'll help him unpack. And of course I'll show him the ship and introduce him to everyone. By supper time he'll be one of us.'

'How long have you been a midshipman?' were Braithwaite's first words on being introduced to Reece.

'Three weeks, sir. Before that I was at Pangbourne, training for . . .'

'Yes, I know about Pangbourne. And you say you're seventeen. You don't look it.'

'I'm always teased for looking younger than I am, sir.'

'Well, I have work for you. You'll be the navigator, and if you haven't been to sea before you'll probably be sick as a dog for the first few days.'

What a wonderful person Marko is, Edmund thought as he turned to go to the wardroom; 'help you unpack; be one of us,' were the words he used. Nine out of ten officers in Marko's position would have said 'get yourself unpacked and be quick about it.'

'Casswell.' It was the captain's voice.

'Sir?' Edmund turned and faced him.

'Signal for you. I'm not sure what you've done to deserve it.'

The look on Edmund's face reflected his perplexity. He took the signal from the captain's hand, read it and returned it to the telegraphist. *Troubadour from Admiralty*, it read, *Casswell promoted lieutenant RNVR with immediate effect*.'

'Get your uniforms changed. Who's your tailor? Gieves?'

'Yessir. Thank you, sir.'

'Well done, Edmund, that's terrific,' Marko said. 'Everything happens at once. Reece comes on board and the telegraphist appears with an order for your promotion.'

'You deserve it thoroughly,' Pemberton said.

Edmund went to his cabin and threw his cap on the bunk, then into the bathroom. Lieutenant Casswell, he said to his reflection in the mirror. The war's a month old, you've seen the enemy; U-boat, E-boats and aircraft. You're twenty-three and strange as it may seem you're rather enjoying yourself. But this wasn't the captain's doing; he looked even more bleak than usual. Could commander Sykes have intervened in some way?

During the first two weeks of October *Minstrel, Troubadour, Chorister* and *Harp* were continuously at sea guarding convoys between the Nore and the Forth, up and down the length of England's east coast. A rumour surfaced that they would be escorting an aircraft carrier to Scapa Flow, but they never did, and another, equally insubstantial, spoke of a *flak* ship armed with dozens of anti-aircraft guns which would join the flotilla under commander Sykes.

Opinion aboard *Troubadour* was that the German bombers would learn to recognise and avoid *flak* ships; they certainly weren't going to fly conveniently close and expose themselves to heavy anti-aircraft fire. For a twenty-ship convoy it would take at least three such vessels to create a deterrent.

On 14th October there occurred an event which shook the navy from the panelled halls of the Admiralty to the crowded mess decks. It demoralised the service and made it the laughing stock of its detractors. A German U-boat had threaded its way on the surface into the sanctuary of Scapa Flow and torpedoed HMS *Royal Oak*. Over 750 men had lost their lives including a rear-admiral.

In *Troubadour*'s wardroom anger and amazement gripped the officers, not so much against the U-boat commander but against the sheer incompetence of those responsible for Scapa's defence. It was the navy's great northern sanctuary, her safe haven while she waited for the opportunity to engage the German surface fleet. Scapa had been used in the first war and was being used again in this one, there had been twenty years of peace in which to secure its defences beyond all question of doubt, but now a U-boat passes through the narrows of Kirk Sound and when it had fired its torpedoes at a stationary target, retires from the scene without a scratch. Luckily there was only one battleship in the flow and an old one at that.

Unspoken thoughts in everyone's minds swirled round the politicians who presumed to direct the navy's affairs, admirals who paced their quarterdecks but couldn't see the obvious dangers and more junior officers who had been taught never to speak up and be heard. This want of comment and criticism had plagued the navy; it was enshrined in tradition and even in verse: 'thou shalt not criticise'. The few officers who had ever dared to say what they believed ought to be said were independently wealthy and didn't greatly care if they were dismissed.

It was the Admiralty, however, over the years, that appeared the most despicable, like a prima donna who flew into a rage at the slightest hint of disrespect. One could be sure that signals had been made and letters placed on file under the heading 'Improved Defences for Scapa Flow', but because reviewing the Fleet at Spithead was considered more important some 785 men had found their graves in the steel carcass of *Royal Oak*. As Pemberton pointed out there was not even an airfield at Scapa Flow which would allow the adjoining seas to be patrolled by air. 'Damn you, incompetent bastards,' people whispered through clenched teeth, and their hatred was not directed at the enemy but at those who directed the navy's affairs.

It was Marko, however, with his legal mind, who saw what the others had not seen. As he turned over the watch to Edmund he said very quietly, 'that gets Braithwaite out of the shit; they'll never court-martial him now.'

'What do you mean?' Edmund asked.

'Let's say he's being court-martialled,' Marko went on, 'a charge of negligence in connection with the U-boat in the Bristol Channel. He has a good lawyer who makes the case appear trivial when compared with Scapa Flow and *Royal Oak*. A bad decision made in the heat of battle by a reserve lieutenant-commander? Come on. It would be laughed out of court when counsel started to talk about the criminal negligence of senior people over a twenty-year period. See what I mean? They'd never dare order a court martial for fear of having it rebound on themselves.'

Chapter 8

'Come in, Crouch,' Edmund called out. 'Sit here; I want a word with you.'

Ordinary seaman Couch slunk in nervously. He was thin almost to being emaciated, his paint-stained overalls hanging on him as though there was little more than bones to hold them up. From his sallow face to his unlaced boots he looked more like a castaway than a seaman aboard one of His Majesty's ships.

'Leading seaman Fenway says you're not eating your food. He says you throw it in the gash. Why, Crouch? What's the matter?'

'I dunno, sir. I can't eat that 'orrid food.'

'What's wrong with the food? We get the same in the officers' mess. Same as yours.'

'It's disgraceful, sir. I wouldn't give it to a dog. At 'ome I'm accustomed to something better than that.'

'Oh, come on, Crouch; you know that isn't true. I've got your service record here; you don't live in a hotel.'

Crouch didn't reply; he looked round the small cabin and then back to Edmund, who picked up his file.

'According to the record you're twenty years old, you used to be a boy seaman, now you're an ordinary seaman. Your father died long ago and your mother remarried. You spend your leave with your elder sister in Pimlico. You don't take your grog; you last had uniforms issued about a month ago. You've never been in any serious trouble; just a couple of small things. Most important, you said you wanted to go on course for asdic operator and earn your badges. You know, Crouch, it's a difficult course and you'll never do it if you're not fit. I wish you'd tell me what the problem is.'

'Well, sir, I never 'ad no schooling. I can't write nor read. I mean, it's all very well for you.'

'Crouch; I'm your divisional officer and I want to help you. For a start I told the midshipman to write letters for you whenever you asked him. He's been doing it, hasn't he?'

'Yessir, but they all knows it ain't me that's writing it.'

'And they also know that while you're at sea serving your country you're thinking about them and wishing them well, even though someone else writes the words. And they know that when you leave the navy you'll take a literacy course and learn to read and write for yourself. Listen, Crouch, when the midshipman sits down and writes another letter I want you to have him say that it won't always be someone else who writes for you, that you're determined one day to do it with your own hand.'

'It's not only that, sir. There's a lot of things.'

Edmund tried to get to the bottom of Crouch's problems but finally put the file down in despair.

'How would it be,' he said, 'if you saw the Sick Berth Attendant? He's not a real doctor, but he might be able to help you. As you know, everyone calls him Doc Jennings.'

'All right, sir. It won't do no good, but I'll do what you say, sir.'

As Edmund expected, Jennings found nothing wrong with ordinary seaman Crouch. However, Edmund was not content to let the matter rest and mentioned it to the coxswain, petty officer Clancey.

'It's not uncommon this, when a man refuses to eat his food,' the coxswain said. 'He throws it away conspicuous like; he wants his messmates to see him throwing it away.'

'Yes, but why?' Edmund asked.

'Well sir, it's a form of disrespect toward authority. It's his way of saying, "this is what I think of the service." There's not many things a man can do to show disrespect and get away with it, but this he can.'

'But coxswain, he was in my cabin talking to me and he didn't seem disrespectful.'

'That's true, sir. He's got no quarrel with people he knows; yourself sir, leading seaman Fenway and me, but still he wants to have his protest and this is his way of going about it.'

Pemberton had been standing nearby and at this point he broke in.

'I've heard of this happening in a family. A teenage daughter refuses her food and it gets served back to her at the next meal. She's having her little mutiny against her parents and of course the food has symbolic value. Her father paid for it and her mother cooked it, so she's striking at them where they are vulnerable. It's probably the same with this man; it's his way of protesting; I don't think it has anything to do with the quality of the food.'

'That's right, sir,' the coxswain said, 'you find complaints about food come from boys from the poorest homes. Good homes and they don't complain; just the ones that's never had it as right as they're getting it here in the service. It's a way of showing off, pretending he's accustomed to something fancy. It's not the first time I seen it.'

Pemberton nodded. 'You notice that a man like that doesn't speak up and say he's not hungry when the food is being put on the plates. No, that isn't dramatic enough. He takes his plate and when everyone is looking he throws it in the gash bucket.'

'That's the way it is, sir. He's determined to draw attention to himself.'

'But as his divisional officer it's my responsibility,' Edmund said; 'I don't see what I can do. It's pointless mentioning it to the captain and trying to get him posted ashore. *If*, just *if* we did that, it would send a signal to the ship's company that a hunger strike lands them a soft job ashore.'

Pemberton had an easy smile which flashed over his face at unexpected moments. 'You know,' he said, 'the food served in the navy in wartime is far better than we got in an English boarding school.'

As the ship prepared for sea on that cold winter day during the last week of 1939, Edmund thought about his duties as a divisional officer. In civilian life it would have been considered a branch of the personnel function; in the navy it was simply shared among the officers. The hard-core personnel work such as pay, allowances and leave entitlement was done in the pay office ashore under the direction of a paymaster. Lieutenant 'Soapy' Hudson had begun as an executive officer who had been trained at Dartmouth, but his eyesight had been impaired following an attack of whooping cough and he had to wear corrective glasses and transfer to the paymaster branch. As a paymaster lieutenant he had an office and a team of clerks under his direction; clerks in the navy being rather curiously known as 'writers'.

In the ship's office, for which Edmund was responsible in *Troubadour*, most of the correspondence was with Soapy's office. Edmund paid the men the amounts shown on Soapy's lists and passed the duplicate personnel files to the officers designated as divisional officers. The divisional officer's task was to get to know his men, encourage ambition and write annual reports. Braithwaite was one of the many commanding officers who also required the divisional officer to be present at the defaulter's table when one of their men was charged with an offence. He would act as the defendant's friend and, if the man wanted it, would speak on his behalf. With a divisional system in place a man could never say that no one in authority gave a damn about him.

Meanwhile, in the engine room, Dobreiner was having problems of his own. As the boilers were being flashed up on that December afternoon the engine room artificer on duty, a petty officer, approached him and spoke in a low voice.

'Someone's trying to sabotage the ship, sir. I found sand and steel filings in the bearings.'

Dobreiner said absolutely nothing. He followed the petty officer down the ladder and into the engine room.

'My God,' he said when he saw it, 'get it cleaned up. Do it yourself. Any idea who?'

The petty officer took his thick leather glove off his left hand and scratched his head. 'Yes, I got my suspicions. It's a stoker.'

A stoker, Dobreiner thought; of course, a stoker would know enough to foul the bearings and wouldn't be noticed in the engine room the way a seaman would. A stoker had come to him a few days earlier saying he wanted leave to be married, and he had refused him point blank because no replacement could have been found at short notice. Yes, it was stoker Rostron, a cocky, handsome fellow of twenty-five; a bit too clever for his own good.

'Keep a very close watch,' he told the petty officer. 'Don't speak to anyone, and get that mess cleaned up immediately.' A few minutes later he reported to Braithwaite that steam was raised and the engine room ready to deliver power.

Troubadour and her sister ships had sailed from Chatham to Liverpool the week before and were now to escort their first Atlantic convoy. The fact that they had an exceptional range of over four thousand miles without refuelling meant that they were not restricted to brief sorties into Britain's Western Approaches as were many of the older escort vessels. They would sail from Liverpool with full tanks and remain wedded to their convoy until their charges were safely in North American harbours. Depending on the speed of the convoy they could be as much as three weeks at sea.

'Obey engine room telegraphs,' Braithwaite ordered. 'Let go forward, let go aft. Slow ahead together. Port twenty.'

Troubadour slid away from the jetty and turned westward in the stream. Flag signals went up *Minstrel*'s halyards and the signalman called out, as he always did, 'ships in line ahead; speed eight knots. Execute.'

'Very good,' from Braithwaite, then almost to himself, 'Where's the first lieutenant?'

Edmund leaned toward the voicepipe. 'Boatswain's mate. Captain's compliments to the first lieutenant and ask him to come on the bridge.'

'Aye aye, sir,' came a voice.

The sky was darkening and a fierce wind blew from the west. It raced across the brown waters of the Mersey in gusts that followed each other in rapid succession. A gust the size of a football field would seem to descend on the water, stir up a million small waves that were immediately toppled in dirty white foam by the sheer power of the wind. The clouds were low and menacing, trailing grey streamers of rain that lashed the ship. In more normal times such a storm would have kept all but the largest ships from venturing to sea.

From the lookout; 'there's a channel buoy half a mile on the port bow, sir.'

'What you mean,' Braithwaite snapped back, 'is port lookout to bridge. Buoy red two zero. Looks like a channel marker.'

'Yessir.'

Edmund crossed the bridge to where the port lookout was huddled against the bulwark.

'Knatchbull, the captain's quite right. Smarten up a bit, eh? No sloppy reporting.'

Pemberton ran up the steel ladder and saluted. 'Sir.'

'Secure the upper deck, Pemberton, we're in for some foul weather. Rig life-lines and set up a harness in the wheelhouse so the quartermaster doesn't get thrown around.'

'Aye aye, sir.'

A sense of foreboding took hold as the upper deck was secured for sea, the whaler turned out on its davits and the boatrope run forward. Lines were brought in and coiled in the storage space, fenders stacked on top. Leading seaman Harding looked over the four-inch gun, then climbed down to the ammunition store in the bottom of the ship to check that all was in place. Fenway went forward to the naval store and lashed the paint pots in their racks, then went round shaking everything in sight to make sure it couldn't move.

In the wheelhouse below the bridge the coxswain rigged a thick leather belt which the quartermaster, the man steering the ship, would secure round his waist. Lines held the belt so that it acted as a harness which left his arms free but made it impossible to be thrown in any direction.

Even within the estuary of the Mersey there was a short, pestering wave action, but when they were outside in the Irish Sea they were hit broadside by the waves which slapped at the port side as though trying to throw the ship off balance. The convoy was huge, over a hundred vessels, and it took much of the night for them to labour through the storm and find their places in the phalanx. The route chosen had been round the stormy north coast of Ireland. Their speed was only seven knots so that even the slowest could overtake and assume his right position if he lagged behind.

Minstrel was a mile ahead of the leading ship of the convoy, *Troubadour* on her port side, towards Ireland, and *Chorister* on her starboard side, toward the English coast. *Harp* was astern. As dawn broke next day the Isle of Man had been passed and Ireland was in sight ahead. They had a few hours of daylight to feel their way through the treacherous North Channel and out into the Atlantic.

Theoretically, at least, the three ships ahead of the convoy swept for U-boats that lay in their path while *Harp* would be in position to counter an attack from astern. But to feel secure two more escorts should have been stationed on the wings. Two more ships had not even been started but *Troubadour*'s officers had created them as a flight of fancy and named them *Dancer* and *Drum*. They would have brought the strength of the flotilla up to six and given it more of a fighting chance.

Edmund stumbled down to his cabin at four in the morning when Pemberton came up to relieve him. He took off his cap and binoculars, lay down on his bunk and listened to the creaking of the ship. He was tired and it was a joy to close his eyes. In what seemed a far-off time and place he remembered a tea-time conversation with two ladies who had taken passage from New York in the *Aquitania*. They had imagined themselves very bold and enterprising to venture across the Atlantic, albeit in a floating palace that was fifty times larger than *Troubadour*. With genteel sips of tea and a dainty nibble at the cucumber sandwiches they related how they had survived the miseries of the damned and the captain had said it was the roughest crossing. . . . Why does every amateur adventurer come home from a calm passage with that one about *what the captain said*? In a ship the size of *Aquitania* a passenger could travel across the Atlantic and hardly even see the sea. So the *captain said*, did he? Well, perhaps he did say something because he knew in the depths of his salty heart that it was what foolish old ladies wanted to hear. And Edmund's own captain, Braithwaite, was under a lot of strain. Edmund's thoughts grew misty and he drifted into sleep.

The three-week period that followed, at the end of 1939 and the start of 1940, was one of unmitigated storm, but the U-boats, happily, could not operate in such appalling weather. Once the convoy was clear of the coast of Ireland great waves like rows of houses came rolling in from the west having generated their ferocity across three thousand miles of ocean. Their crests broke off as though they were venturing into shallow water; their troughs were deep and cavernous. Ten-thousand-ton merchantmen laboured like angry giants lifting tons of water at every plunge and spewing it away from the foredeck as the bows rose and hesitated before plunging again. For *Troubadour* and her sisters it was many times worse. Being only a thousand tons they were like the playthings of the gods, able to say afloat and survive only because of their excellent construction and the seamanship of captains and crews. A strong able seaman, thrown about in his harness, would be exhausted after steering for a mere twenty minutes and another man would have to take his place.

Life on board was a fight for survival every minute of every day. As the ship fell downward into the trough of a wave a man's weight would be reduced to what felt like fifty pounds. It was a giddy, nauseating fall that made them lower their heads, fearing to be thrown upward at the steel deckhead. As the ship rose, his weight seemed to be increased to three or four hundred pounds, as though he were carrying an immense burden. To move from one part of the ship to another required an effort of will and body, aggravated as the days passed because the men were tired and hungry in the absence of proper cooked food. Pemberton had ruled that the danger of burning themselves was an unacceptable risk for the cooks, so the only food they ate was corned beef, hard bread and pickles.

Edmund found the best way to eat was while sitting on the wardroom floor with his legs and arms wrapped round the steel stanchion in the centre of the room. From there he couldn't fall or slide, even though the roll of the ship was thirty degrees each way. A metal bowl would be passed to him from the steward who grasped the sideboard. The food was cut in chunks and he ate it with his fingers. When he finished it was someone else's turn.

The only moments of comfort were when he was lying on his bunk, but even then he had to secure himself with a leather strap or the roll of the ship could have thrown him to the floor with bruises or broken bones. He made no attempt to shave or wash throughout the crossing; all he did was to sleep, eat a little and keep ten hours' watch out of twenty-four. He never changed out of the clothes he was wearing, never removed his boots and finally even lay down with his binoculars round his neck.

The ship's company were better off in one small respect because they slept in hammocks and a man can scarcely fall out of his hammock. The scenes on the mess decks, however, were indescribable, like something from the Middle Ages; a primitive confusion of wet clothes, moaning sleepers and distraught men; the smell of vomit pervading the whole. This was not the navy of the cigarette advertisements, nor yet of music-hall conception, although the daily rum ration was distributed and went some way toward restoring morale.

On the upper deck the whaleboat had been smashed by a huge wave, so Pemberton and Fenway turned in the davits and secured the falls. The potato locker had gone overboard and the armament was washing down so severely that Braithwaite ordered all the men on watch into the wheelhouse. If an emergency should occur they would have to reach the guns and depth charges as best they could.

Only the asdic compartment on the bridge was manned throughout, but the asdic dome, on the underside near the bows, came clear of the water as the ship rose and was not operating reliably. It was designed to send out its sound signal in water, not air, and the operators were hard pressed to make sense of the confused echoes that came back to their ears.

The four lookouts on the bridge, the signalman and the officer of the watch dressed themselves as best they could against the sheets of spray and blinding cold. The navy had never taken the trouble to issue special cold-weather clothing so the men wore standard duffel coats which soon became soaked.

The convoy was bound for St John's, Newfoundland, and after fifteen days at sea, having survived not one storm but three, Edmund climbed wearily to the bridge at midnight for the middle watch. He took over from Marko, glanced back at the convoy and then across a mile of sea to *Minstrel*. 'I have the ship,' he said. 'St John's to-morrow.'

Leading seaman Harding was on the bridge a minute later asking permission to place one lookout on each side of the bridge instead of two.

'Yes, all right, Harding.'

If there's nothing to be seen, Edmund thought, in this black, foul night, one might as well have only one person not see it.

'Give me a call when you've had enough,' Harding said to the man on the starboard side, 'I'll be in the wheelhouse.'

Edmund pushed his shoulders through the canvas curtains of the chart table and switched on the low, red light. A hundred miles or thereabouts and there would be a warm welcome, rest and the comforts of normal existence. He backed away from the table, the ship plunged and he fell on the wet steel plates. The signalman came to help him up and collapsed on top of him.

'Thanks,' he said. 'You all right?'

'Yessir. What we need is crash 'elmets; Jonesy took an awful bump on the 'ead. He's still half unconscious.'

'I heard. We need helmets like they wear on building sites.'

Edmund struggled to his feet and grasped the top of the bridge screen. The storm had reached its climax. A sheet of green water came up from the bows and flew over the bridge and its saltiness flowed into his eyes and mouth. He felt exhausted and for a moment the night overpowered him.

'Sir, please sir, God,' he said. 'Just listen, dammit.'

The bows rose again and the wind sounded like the high-pitched religiosity of boy sopranos in the cathedral choir. What, he suddenly asked himself, would those boys in white raiment and ruffs say to all this?

As the ship fell into the next trough he gripped the compass and held on while more sea water ran down his face.

'God,' he said again, 'your ship *Troubadour* doesn't deserve this. I mean, Sir, be reasonable.'

His mind went back to a quiet summer day three or four years before when God had been in his heaven and all had seemed right with the world. He had sat on a tombstone with a mind emptied of worldly things and his gaze rested on a distant stand of oak trees and he marvelled at their perfection. He was filled with a sudden joy and reverence as though he had stepped out of his earthly body and joined the stars, had stumbled into the hallways and galleries of God Himself. He lost all thought and feeling of himself, he was beside himself, a creature released momentarily from the gravity of earth, cleansed of the inheritance of flesh and blood. When the mood passed he knew that he would never be the same again, that his moment of otherworldliness would not forsake him for the remainder of his life.

With these memories he grew more calm as *Troubadour* plunged drunkenly into the night. An hour passed and then another. He wondered what the experience had done to him and whether it had changed him for the better. He had acquired serenity perhaps, but it had not prevented him from questioning his vocation. He had not become more innocent or trusting, his faith in the religious precepts of his youth continued to decline, although his sense of worldly participation had strengthened. Now he did not feel separate and élite; he rejoiced in the everyday, its beauty, unashamed carnality, misguided enthusiasm. He was no longer the exalted being who lived behind stone walls, who served God in His holy temple; no, he had become an addict, not of worldliness but of life itself. And to Edmund, the strangest thing of all was that when his father next saw him he perceived with certainty what had taken place.

'Starboard lookout,' Edmund called out. 'Did you see a flash from *Minstrel*?'

There was no answer.

'Starboard lookout.'

He waited till the ship was steady, then pushed away from the compass binnacle and grabbed at the bulwark on the starboard side. The lookouts kept watch in what Braithwaite called the 'wings' of the bridge, a narrow balcony two steps down from the main bridge where they were protected and could rest their binoculars or elbows on the outer bulwark.

The starboard lookout was slumped in the darkness but still held his binoculars.

'Harding,' Edmund called down the voicepipe. 'Come up and bring some men with you. The starboard lookout's in difficulties.'

There were some mumbled noises and Harding came up the ladder with three or four men.

'You'll have to get him in his hammock,' Edmund said.

Harding bent over the man for a full minute as the ship rose and fell in the dark. 'From now on he'll spend a lot of time in his hammock. He's dead, sir.'

'Who is it, Harding? I didn't see.'

'Ordinary seaman Crouch, sir.'

Edmund took a long, deep breath.

'Call Jennings. If Jennings says he's dead he can be sewn in his hammock.'

Edmund went to the chart table and wrote in the log, '0300 ordinary seaman Crouch found dead on lookout duty;' then to the captain's voicepipe, 'A man has died of exposure, sir. I'm having him taken below.'

There was a groan from the other end.

'Sure he's dead?'

'Jennings is looking at him.'

'Very well, we'll put the body ashore to-morrow. We won't bury at sea. It's too dangerous for the men at the ship's rail.'

Harding and the others lifted Crouch's body and passed it down the ladder. His place was taken by another seaman and Edmund returned to the binnacle and checked that the ship was in station.

'The Lord giveth,' he said to himself, 'but this time He taketh away. Child of heaven, child of God, child of earth; that's what they say when they make a saint, not when some poor sailor dies of exposure. Ordinary seaman Crouch, to-morrow I shall prepare a letter to your sister for the captain's signature. I won't say that you refused your food, but rather that you wanted to qualify as an asdic operator, that your burial was a simple but impressive ceremony with naval honours, grieving comrades . . . and I shall say that one of my officers had a discussion with you before the ship sailed and planned a bright . . . What did we plan that was bright? I'll think of something.'

The bleak and rock-studded coast of Newfoundland rose from the sea during the forenoon watch and it was appropriate that Marko, whose country they were approaching, should have been the officer of the watch. It was a good landfall, Cape Spear lighthouse appeared on the port bow, the sea moderated and *Troubadour* was ordered to act independently and enter ahead of the others. Braithwaite increased speed and made for the rocky entrance. The valley of the shadow was behind them for a few golden hours.

Of all the world's harbours, St John's is the one with the

shortest approach. A ship is at sea one minute and in harbour the next; there is no ante-room, no divide between ocean and harbour. Suddenly they were in quiet water. With her upper deck a shambles and the boats smashed the weary crew looked at the snow-covered landscape and were thankful to be in a safe haven of rest. Fuel was exhausted and *Troubadour* rode higher in the water than she had done when she sailed from Liverpool. Houses on shore grew larger and more distinct, the wharves and jetties took shape as they stopped engines to pick up the harbour pilot. The others would follow her in.

'Tower signalling, sir,' reported a lookout, and a signalman went to the Aldis lamp while another picked up pad and pencil.

'Signal from the tower, sir. *Your upper deck is a disgrace and your men are not in proper uniform for entering harbour. You will return to sea and when you have rectified these defects you may re-enter St John's.*'

The signalman handed it to Braithwaite while the pilot and Edmund stared in disbelief, first at the signal tower, then at Braithwaite.

For a few seconds Braithwaite stood looking at the paper in his hand, contemplating its enormity, then at the tower with its white ensign, signalling platform and glassed-in observation deck for whatever senior officer inhabited the place. Braithwaite was dirty, bearded and hungry, and at that moment something inside him disintegrated. He stumbled to the edge of the bridge, waved the signal in the air and shouted obscenities.

'You ignorant, stupid bugger,' he yelled across a mile of harbour. 'You're a fucking disgrace. The ship's cat shits something better than you . . .' There were tears running down his cheeks.

'Signalman,' he ordered, 'Reply to that arse-hole that I have not the slightest intention of going to sea with my ship in this condition. Tell the silly bastard he can go to hell. And tell him to send us an ambulance.'

Edmund took the signal from Braithwaite's hand and the pad from the signalman.

'I'll write it down, sir. Not exactly in those words but close.'

Edmund wrote, '*Unable comply with your order because fuel and fresh water reserves stand at zero. Send ambulance to carry away our dead and injured.'*

Edmund read it and Braithwaite nodded. He looked stunned, as though he had discovered his wife of many years *in flagrante delicto*. Then he brushed the tears from his eyes and told Edmund to take the ship alongside.

'Very well sir; starboard side to,' Edmund called out. 'Tell the first lieutenant. Port thirty and half astern together.'

Heaving lines curved through the air from fore and aft. There was a gentle bump as *Troubadour* nudged against the jetty.

Chapter 9

THE NORTH ATLANTIC had regained its composure by the time the flotilla sailed southwards to New York. It was Edmund's first visit to the great port and it turned out to be memorable for reasons that could hardly have been forseen. Shortly after their arrival he entered the wardroom for lunch and found, to his surprise, a full naval captain, four gold rings on each sleeve, talking to the other officers. Captain McCormick, he was told, stationed in New York, was paying an unofficial visit. He stood to attention for a moment after stepping over the sill and was rewarded by a smile and a nod of the visitor's head.

McCormick was a tall, elegant man who wore the blue and pink ribbon of the Distinguished Service Order, the French Legion of Honour, campaign ribbons from the last war and the Naval General Service Medal, dark red vertical lines on a white ground. He had evidently seen much active service. He was about fifty years of age with grey hair, a refined face and commanding figure.

'Part of my job,' he was saying, 'is to get out of my office and find out what you fellows are talking about. How can the convoy system be improved? Can we reduce our losses? The admiral on this side has been asking questions and he wants to know your ideas.'

He spoke about the organization of convoys, the administrative work that was needed to put a hundred ships, fully laden and ready for sea, into a few square miles of ocean so that an escort of navy ships could shepherd them to the Mersey. It was the crucial supply line of Britain's war effort, New York to Liverpool, the cord which, if it were cut, would encompass England's defeat. 'Remember,' he said, 'there may be twenty convoys at sea at any one time.' He looked round the tiny wardroom at their attentive expressions, which gave Edmund a chance to speak.

'Well, sir, we need some improvement to our asdic equipment. Even with good operating conditions we don't really know the depth of the U-boat and our chances of sinking it are remote. A depth charge has to explode within six feet of the hull to do real damage. The experts at home are saying that our success rate is in the order of two percent. If we knew the U-boat's depth it would make a big difference.'

'They are working on that.' captain McCormick replied. 'I can't say too much, but we expect the depth problem to be solved fairly soon. Another thing is that they're trying to provide a visual display of the enemy; to transform the sound waves into a representation on a screen. That means you could see the U-boat, measure his depth and watch your depth charges exploding. If the charges went off a hundred feet above him you'd know what to do with the next pattern. Up to now the problem has been that you had no way of telling where your charges explode in relation to the U-boat, so you can't be sure that a correction would be closer and not farther away.'

This was heady stuff, a visual display of a submerged U-boat a hundred yards or more below the surface. The depth charges would be seen falling and then the explosions which would appear on the screen. If the explosions were above and a bit behind, the next pattern would be given a deeper setting with more 'lead' in the direction that the U-boat was taking. What a wonderful prospect; it would make all the difference and was bound to tip the scales of battle in our favour.

At Pemberton's suggestion they adjourned to the lunch table where Captain McCormick was offered the head chair normally occupied by Braithwaite. He declined graciously, however, and seated himself between Pemberton and Edmund. It was a simple meal but they remained at table for an hour afterwards and continued to talk. Captain McCormick had raised a new and even more immediate topic.

'There's an expression being used to the effect that the enemy is moving as fast as we are. If we can make improvements he can do the same. The Germans are also sitting round their tables, discussing how the war is going, how they can build better U-boats, operate them more safely, avoid our depth charges and sink more ships. I'm sure you know that Hitler has boasted that he will build a thousand U-boats. It would be helpful if you people, with your young minds and first-hand experience, could give some thought as to what they might come up with in future. Obviously they're working on a faster, deeper-running U-boat. And what about torpedoes that "seek" their target by the sound of a ship's propulsion machinery?'

He turned to Edmund who had already identified himself as the anti-submarine officer. 'How would you react if they invented something that could be released from the outside of the U-boat and held itself stationary in the water? It would be electrified in some way and would distort your asdic echo. It's a nasty thought, but I'll bet they have it on the drawing boards.'

He paused and then went on. 'Usually there's an antidote. We think the torpedo which is designed to run toward the sound of a ship's propulsion machinery would run toward any noise. What we need is a steel box with a spring-loaded hammer beating on the inside. It would be electrically operated and towed astern of a merchant ship, creating a frightful din in the water. We have something like that already because the same principle is used in sweeping for acoustic mines. The torpedo isn't going to know the difference between one sound and another.'

The steward had been serving brandy and coffee and captain McCormick suddenly changed the conversation.

'What a civilised custom, brandy and coffee after a meal. With all due respect to my American friends, I think they have some catching up to do where the art of living is concerned. They suffer from eternal indigestion because they eat in a tearing hurry and half the time they don't even sit down.'

He smiled and spread his hands across the table.

'We think of sandwiches as a picnic food but in this country they even eat them for breakfast. If you think about it, a sandwich has to be consumed in haste. You get a grip of the thing with one or both hands and take a bite. If it's a hamburger with meat, lettuce and tomato you're reluctant to put it down because it's going to fall apart, so you keep hold of it until you've finished.

In consequence you eat too fast and get indigestion. American meals, much of the time, are not designed for conversation, pleasure or good fellowship; no, Americans eat as though they were cars filling up with petrol at the pump.'

They all smiled but then conversation returned to the war. Captain McCormick said that he had proposed, years before, an escort vessel specifically for North Atlantic duty. 'It was to have been 1,200 tons, very seaworthy and of long range, with its principal armament a forward-throwing depth charge. It was to be flush-deck with no torpedoes and with only a twin four-inch gun mounted on the forecastle and anti-aircraft guns aft. The engines would be those of a Hunt Class destroyer and give it a top speed of twenty-five knots. For ten million pounds they could have built between sixty and eighty. The crew would number about a hundred and ten, as opposed to two hundred or more for fleet destroyers. It would have been the perfect weapon for doing the job you're doing now.'

He paused. 'At the present time we're losing ten million pounds in merchant ships and their cargoes every week; sometimes every day. If only the politicians and admirals had listened and spent ten million at the right time on the right ships.'

He rose to leave and the officers accompanied him to the gangway. He thanked Pemberton for his hospitality, then turned to Braithwaite.

'You're so lucky,' he said, 'to have this command and such excellent officers. I envy you and I know that men like you will win the battle. I hope to see you again when you're back in New York.'

He returned their salute, smiled and shook hands all round.

When he was out of earshot Pemberton turned to Braithwaite. 'You know, sir, apart from commander Sykes he's the first senior officer I've ever really liked. What an extraordinary fellow and how decent of him to come and talk to us.'

'I imagine,' Braithwaite mused, 'that he was retired as a captain a year or two before the war and then recalled. He knows the navy all right, but he's picked up some characteristics of civilian life. He doesn't lose my respect, but he's at home with officers half his age and what he said made a lot of sense.' Then, as an afterthought, 'there's a Navy List in my cabin. I'll bring it to the wardroom.'

A few moments later he was thumbing through the pages. 'Captains,' he said. 'Lots of Mc and Mac. Here we are; McCormack, McCormick. Four in all, two with the initial J and both have the D.S.O. He must be one or the other.'

'When he came aboard,' Marko began, 'I asked him to sign his name in the log, which he did, and feeling rather foolish I asked to see his identification. There was a Port Authority identity card, among other things, which had a number on it, so I copied it down. I wasn't sure, from his signature, whether it was McCormick or McCormack.'

'It doesn't really matter,' Braithwaite said, 'we have an idea who he is. And now there are other things to think about.' He sighed. 'We sail at midnight. No shore leave. Postman to collect the mail at 2000. Full head of steam by 2300. Stations for leaving harbour at 2330.'

A chorus of 'aye aye, sir' erupted.

'And if you have any sense you'll all get some sleep.'

It was still winter and that night under clear skies *Troubadour* followed *Minstrel* out of New York harbour. Astern were *Chorister* and *Harp* always seeming breathless and over-anxious as they took station. The ships were blacked out except for their mandatory navigation lights, but these too would be switched off when the order came from *Minstrel* to darken ship. They passed through the Narrows with the massive, awe-inspiring brilliance of Brooklyn falling away on the port side and Staten Island to starboard. Over the calm water came the subdued roar of a city that was never at rest and never at ease.

'Feast your eyes on those lights,' Braithwaite said, 'we have some dark nights ahead of us; and tell me what all those people are doing at this hour?'

'Love-making, drinking and the occasional murder,' Edmund replied.

'You should know.' Braithwaite tried to make it derogatory.

In truth, Braithwaite didn't like having his frivolous questions answered; he thought his word should be the last, that it was intellectual insubordination for anyone to say more than 'yes sir; aye-aye sir; very good, sir.' He tried another tack.

'How many of our barnacles have we dropped to the bottom of the Hudson river, and how will it affect our speed?'

Edmund knew what the captain was driving at. When a ship had been at sea for any length of time it collected marine growth below the waterline which could reduce its speed. The Mediterranean had the worst reputation for producing a thick encrustation that had regularly to be scraped off or sandblasted. When a ship entered fresh water, however, some of it fell away and the ship was marginally better for it.

'Hard to say, sir. Perhaps two tons. May give us an extra half knot of speed.'

Before Braithwaite could pursue it further Edmund reported, 'Coney Island abeam to port, sir. Rockaway Point six miles on the port bow. Ship ahead signalling; probably an increase in speed and darken ship.'

'Very well,' Braithwaite mumbled. 'Where's the bloody convoy?'

'East of Sandy Hook, sir. Eighty ships.'

'Tell the first lieutenant to go to cruising stations. Start the asdic. Is the upper deck secure?'

And so it went, a routine that was becoming familiar. Speed was increased to fourteen knots, the ship was darkened and the cruising watch went to their stations. The convoy had assembled to the east of Sable Island and there they were, great groaning vessels, spread out over the sea, loaded to capacity with the cargoes of war. *Minstrel* led the way through them and took station a mile ahead of the commodore who was captain of a cargo-passenger liner, the *Star of Africa*. *Troubadour* took up her position a mile to the south of *Minstrel*, *Harp* a mile to the north. *Chorister* had remained astern and covered the rear. No orders were passed, no signals made and none were needed, at least until something went wrong. The captains of the merchant ships had met the day before and the commodore had laid out his plans. Each ship was assigned a place and it was impressed on captains that they would be disciplined if they failed to keep their ships dark and in proper station.

When Pemberton came up for his watch at 0400 Braithwaite

and Edmund were still on the bridge and the outlines of the merchant ships could be seen astern. After a few minutes to accustom his eyes to the dark he said, 'all right, I have the ship. You can go down, Casswell.'

Braithwaite added, 'don't bother with morning stars as long as we can see the glow from New York.'

Four hours later, after a fitful sleep, Edmund was in the wardroom having breakfast, a brilliant sun shining down on the convoy as it laboured eastwards. Marko had the forenoon watch, the captain was in his cabin. Pemberton breakfasted and then went on a tour of the ship while Dobreiner supervised the dismantling of a leaky pump. Edmund looked in the ship's office, found nothing to do, checked the asdic which was working perfectly and returned to his cabin. He would go up at midday for his next watch; meanwhile he might as well sleep. He had long ago learned the art of sleeping for an hour or two at a time.

Watch followed watch, daylight followed darkness; twice there were U-boat scares with *Minstrel* and *Harp* believing they had firm echoes but with no results to show after six patterns of depth charges. They sailed on to the east and on the fifth day two ships were torpedoed in rapid succession at the rear of the convoy. It was after midnight, the moon gave some light and commander Sykes decided to leave the task of rescuing survivors and hunting the U-boat to *Chorister*. If there was one U-boat there could be others and it was of prime importance for at least three escorts to maintain their position at the head of the convoy.

If only we had a full flotilla of eight ships, Edmund mused. Four more would cost a few thousand pounds, but some fool was going to say that the country couldn't afford it. Yet a single merchant ship torpedoed and lost with its cargo might be worth ten times the price of all the escorts put together. Indeed, the two ships that had just been torpedoed could easily have been worth a million pounds apiece. It took his mind back to captain McCormick and he realised that he had been pondering what he had said. He had seemed so knowledgeable, so reasonable, yet there were things about him which didn't ring true. He was sure, for instance, that the French Legion of Honour, although it was a high decoration, should be worn last.

Edmund knew that the sequence in which medal ribbons were sewn on a uniform was not haphazard but followed a prescribed order, a kind of seniority. A Victoria Cross would come first, that is to say top row, closest to the centre of the body. A Distinguished Service Order would be next and the more junior decorations, Distinguished Service Cross, for instance, after that. Campaign ribbons followed and foreign decorations came last.

It was easy to say that a New York tailor might not know this and make the kind of mistake that was always being made in films and theatrical productions. The costume designers, or whoever was responsible for actors' uniforms, often awarded medal ribbons in a manner which any military or naval man could see was bogus to the point of being absurd. Either they weren't the right ribbons for the war in question or were in the wrong sequence and were sometimes sewn on the pocket of the uniform instead of above it. The theatrical profession was just plain sloppy when it came to medals.

It was natural enough that *Troubadour*'s officers had noted the medals worn by captain McCormick because they revealed so much about him. The Distinguished Service Order had almost certainly been won during the First World War, the best guess would be as a destroyer commander. The Legion of Honour was more of a problem, but it suggested a successful operation in co-operation with the French. The Naval General Service Medal could have been for almost anything; anti-slavery in the Red Sea, Mediterranean service during the Spanish Civil War or post-war minesweeping. It added up to an officer of distinction with a varied career, whose conversation seemed to bear it out. He had a good fund of knowledge and some advanced ideas, and one pictured him in a specialised position like Naval Planning or Weapons Development. Why, then should a knowledgeable and fastidious officer overlook such an obvious mistake as a medal ribbon out of sequence? Technically it made him incorrectly dressed.

This wasn't Edmund's only thought. McCormick seemed to have put on a performance that was flawless. His words were on target and well chosen, his thoughts clearly expressed. At Cambridge even the most competent lecturers were no better than that; others didn't come close. Yet this man was a naval officer, a seaman; he might be studious and well read, but ideas and words were not his life in the way they would be for a university professor. Was he an exception to all the rules, the one in a hundred who stood out from his fellows?

Edmund decided to discuss his thoughts with Marko.

'I've been thinking about captain McCormick,' he began. 'I think he's a spy.'

Marko looked up from his book.

'You English, you all crazy,' he announced.

'A spy? He's the only half decent captain I ever bump into and you say he's a spy. Come on.' Then, on a different note, 'why the hell you think he's a spy?'

Before Edmund could answer Braithwaite stepped over the sill and taking his cap off threw it on the rack. He stood for a moment supporting himself against the roll of the ship before going to a chair.

'Spy,' he said, 'who's a spy?'

'Well, sir, I don't think that captain McCormick is all he claims to be,' Edmund replied. 'There's something there which looks fishy to me.'

'Funny you should say that. I thought him a bit of a fruit, but his conversation was impressive.' Braithwaite looked perplexed.

'And if he's a spy what the shit do we do about it?'

'I think we should make enquiries when we get to Liverpool. Soapy Hudson in the pay office has a foot in every door.'

'Well, all right.' Braithwaite was fussing with his pipe and tobacco. 'Don't make a fool of yourself in the process. Just say that while we were in New York a senior officer came aboard and we'd like to know more about him. Which of the captains McCormick is he; what's his official position and is it proper we should discuss service matters with him? Something like that.'

A few days later with the convoy safely in port, Edmund entered Soapy Hudson's office.

'I'll phone the Admiralty,' Soapy said when he heard the story. 'A post captain, you say; the Distinguished Service Order and French Legion of Honour which you thought were in the wrong sequence on his uniform. About fifty, tall and thin. Knowledgeable about the navy; well spoken.'

He phoned, evidently on a direct line, and asked to be put through to an officer whom he named. Soapy explained the position and was told he'd be called back. Edmund and Soapy chatted for a few moments and when the phone rang again it was the Admiralty. Soapy listened, thanked him and put the phone down.

'You're perfectly right. The first captain McCormick is dead, the second has command of a cruiser, number three is something to do with the Suez Canal and number four is on leave in Scotland. Had you thought this fellow might be a spy?'

Without waiting for an answer Soapy got to his feet and went on talking.

'I don't have much idea who deals with this, but I'll call a meeting for this afternoon. Captain Hibberd should be here, also your captain, the marine security officer, you and me.' He paused. 'Come back with Braithwaite after lunch,' then in an undertone, 'and make sure he's sober.'

Braithwaite's expression, on being told that McCormick was not all he seemed, was a study of injured innocence.

'That's what I said, a fruit. You can't trust those homo bastards; they're all spies. He didn't fool me for a moment.'

'They want to see us at 1400 and I thought it might be as well to take the log book so that captain Hibberd can actually see McCormick's signature.'

'But if he isn't McCormick . . .' he trailed off. 'Let's get some lunch.'

The meeting in captain Hibberd's office produced no particular surprises beyond a pretty WRNS secretary who was there to take notes. Soapy called her 'Audrey, darling' and she must have been an understanding girl because Edmund noticed that when the conversation became trivial or irrelevant, which it often did, her pencil stopped and she leaned forward to adjust her stockings. All that her notes need have recorded was that the matter should go forward from captain Hibberd to the Admiralty.

The marine security officer put a different slant on it. 'We must remember that the Americans are not at war. Their security is notoriously lax and I don't believe the federal authorities or the

New York police are going to take this seriously unless they think their own interests are at stake. I could be wrong, but this fellow doesn't sound like a spy to me. Spies don't work like that.'

Troubadour sailed a week later, but the McCormick affair was not forgotten and snatches of information about him continued to feed the mystery. It turned out that he had been a reserve naval officer during the First World War and had risen to the rank of lieutenant-commander. He was an avid reader, a thinker and a dreamer and, worst of all, he wrote letters. Nobody wanted to hear his ideas, his superiors thought him a pest and were happy to turn him out at war's end. He took up the theatre and did quite well in a succession of 'character' parts. He played an English butler, a scientist, a retired general. The outbreak of war in 1939 found him living in New York with a part in a Broadway comedy.

McCormick lived in a world of dreams and make-believe and he hit on the idea of becoming a war hero so that he could act out his fantasies in the very uniform that might have been his if he had been kept on as a permanent naval officer. He went to his tailor and got himself fitted out as a full captain with all the accoutrements, including medal ribbons. It was child's play for a trained actor and once in uniform he easily obtained a dockyard pass. He chose the name McCormick because there were two in the Navy List, both with the Distinguished Service Order and both with the initial J. If someone had previously met captain J. McCormick, DSO, he could say that he was the other one.

The question was what he gained by it. He went aboard the smaller ships, destroyers and escort vessels, which came into New York, always at lunch time when the officers were in the wardroom. He told his story, accepted a drink or two followed by lunch and he worked his charm on the young minds round the table. He was a teacher, as actors sometimes tend to be, and it was probably his desire to reach out and influence others that gave him satisfaction.

Braithwaite had cancelled him off as a homosexual, but Braithwaite would say that of anyone who seemed out of the ordinary. In fact the man lived in a comfortable apartment with a woman. He could be summed up as a harmless dreamer with an active mind that was not fully under control. His real name was Christopher Hussey.

The marine security officer in Liverpool had been right on all points. Neither the federal authorities nor the New York police were interested. He was not a spy and to masquerade as a British officer was not an offence in the United States. He hadn't given his correct name to get a dockyard pass, but that wasn't very serious so they investigated briefly, frightened him a bit and left him alone.

Braithwaite was determined to have the last word.

'What shits me off is the fact that the bloody Admiralty couldn't make use of him. His ideas were right on target and if someone had listened we wouldn't be in the mess we're in now.'

Yes, thought Edmund, the man of ideas rejected, the prophet despised. We've all heard that before. But why did we think so highly of him? Why were we so impressed? The only senior naval officer, as Marko said, whom he really liked was not a naval officer but an actor playing a part. Why was our admiration given so unstintingly to a dreamer and visionary, a man who had been cancelled off long ago as a letter-writer and a nuisance? Was it because he listened to us and took us seriously?

Chapter 10

IN THE EARLY spring of 1940 *Troubadour* and her sister ships sailed from Liverpool on what they expected would be another New York or Halifax convoy. They had no great love for the North Atlantic with its long and dark nights, rough seas and winds which tore through their clothes. The U-boats were a nuisance, although they had not developed into the mortal menace that they would later become. At the end of it all, however, there was New York, the city of instant gratification, easy shopping, even easier women, a million lights and almost as many delights.

The four ships, built for another country and for other seagoing purposes, had proved, during the months they had been at war, that they possessed the power and endurance needed by convoy escorts. They were dry ships, reasonably steady at sea and as comfortable as a thousand-ton ship could ever be in a winter gale. The sea had to be at its worst for the cook to be unable to produce hot meals, while sleep was usually possible in a swinging hammock. With food, sleep and New York over the horizon, life was just bearable.

It was with some surprise, therefore, that they picked up a small but fast convoy in the Irish Sea, were joined by two cruisers and shaped their course southwards and then south-west. This was not the route to New York and, come to think of it, the ships in convoy didn't look right for the North Atlantic run. There were two troopships, a passenger-cargo vessel and a dozen modern merchantmen. And why would cruisers be going to New York?

These were the old County class cruisers of ten thousand tons, armed with eight-inch guns. They had a First-World-War look about them and their appearance seemed to retain a touch of the passenger liner from which their class had evolved. It was said they were popular for their high deckheads and relatively spacious living quarters. It was also said that their machinery was complicated and no two exactly alike since all had been built in different shipyards. It was their tall funnels, however, that commanded attention when they were at sea. The centre funnel was broader than the others which gave the ships an odd but not unpleasing appearance.

Midshipman Reece had set a chart of the eastern Atlantic on the bridge chart table. After three or four days on a south-westerly course the weather became warmer and the pencilled chain of morning and evening star sights pointed southwards past Cape Finisterre.

'Gibraltar,' Marko said as he looked at the chart, 'but where after that?'

Petty Officer Clancey approached it from a different angle. 'Perhaps I should be warning the lads to look to their white uniforms,' he said to Pemberton. 'Make sure they're clean and don't have no buttons missing.'

Pemberton, however, was necessarily non-committal about their destination since he didn't know himself.

'Yes, coxswain. Good idea.'

Cape Spartel on the African coast rose up from the sea after six uneventful days. *Minstrel* led the way and turned northwards into Gibraltar's small harbour under the shadow of the rock. It was crowded with ships and all four escorts found themselves alongside each other so that the men thronged the upper decks in the warm winter sunshine to share humour and rumour with their friends. The old hands who knew Gibraltar cancelled it off as a rotten place with nothing to do or see.

'No restaurants or bars worth a damn,' Braithwaite sniffed; 'the governor lives in a shack called *The Convent* and beyond taking a walk you might as well stay aboard. The shopping is terrible, although I've heard you can get Spanish sherry at a reasonable price. If anyone in the wardroom drinks the stuff Cyr can go ashore and scrounge around. It always tastes to me like cough mixture.'

While Braithwaite was disposing of Gibraltar, damning the

Barbary apes that lived high on the rock and wondering where they would be going next, Pemberton walked down the jetty to speak to the first lieutenant of a minesweeper. It was secured up alongside, but the four escort vessels had crowded it to the point where it would be difficult to manoeuvre away from the jetty and out to sea.

'Sorry about this,' Pemberton began when he met the minesweeper's first lieutenant. 'I don't know when we're sailing, but we've made it tricky for you if you have to go first.'

'We'll find a way out,' came the reply. 'If I can't get a tug I'll lay out an anchor and warp myself away. We're single-screw and coal-burning.'

'*Single screw; coal-burning,*' Pemberton repeated in astonishment. 'I didn't know that navy ships . . .' he trailed off.

'Yes, this flotilla, what's left of it, was built around 1910 and saw service in the North Sea during the last war.'

'And you have to load coal in sacks?' Pemberton asked incredulously, 'and your stokers throw it in the furnaces with shovels?'

''Fraid so, and the fact that we're single-screw makes it devilish to control the ship when we're minesweeping. As you know, bad station-keeping or turning in unswept water is instant death.'

Pemberton surveyed the upper deck. It was clean and well kept and the minesweeping gear on the quarterdeck was freshly painted. What couldn't be hidden was the thirty-year-old appearance of the ship; dented, scraped, a mass of bruises gained over the years when it had plied its dangerous trade, added to the neglect of those times when it had been laid up and plied no trade at all.

'Would your officers care to come across and have dinner in our wardroom this evening?' Pemberton asked. 'We'd be honoured to have you and, for myself, I'd like to know more about your work. How many officers are you?'

'Four at present. We're supposed to have five. Yes, we'd be happy to get away from our cook for an evening. He's a seaman whose eyesight got so bad they made him a cook.'

'Then we'll be expecting you. *Troubadour,* second ship out from the jetty. How about seven o'clock?'

Marko was not put out by the prospect of four visitors for

dinner, and with the aid of a few tins plus his Gallic imagination he arranged a creditable meal. More memorable than the food, however, was the conversation, which lasted until late. Like most serving officers who are not actively engaged in minesweeping *Troubadour*'s wardroom knew next to nothing of this aspect of the navy's work which had always been the responsibility of the reserves, and a small percentage of them at that. The earliest minesweepers had been fishing vessels which took their crews with them when they were converted. A permanent naval officer from Dartmouth with straight stripes on his sleeve was almost unknown in the minesweeping service; he wouldn't even know the language of LL reels and oropesa floats.

Lieutenant Bell, RNR was their commanding officer and sat at Braithwaite's right. He had been a midshipman during the Dardanelles campaign in 1915 and spoke about the losses of minesweepers not only from mines but from the Turkish guns on shore.

'Rear admiral de Robeck was in command of the operation and his battleships came to grief on a line of moored mines across the narrows,' he began. 'Three battleships were lost and a fourth damaged. Minesweeping was hazardous because of the hostile guns on shore. The battleships could probably have silenced them, but the minesweepers with their fishermen crews had to be out ahead. They failed to get into the Black Sea where de Robeck's heavies could have pounded Constantinople into submission, sunk the Turkish fleet and joined forces with the Russians.'

Pemberton picked up the story at that point. 'If we had knocked Turkey out of the war and joined the Russians, then Germany would have been defeated earlier and there might not have been any Russian revolution.'

Bell nodded. 'The whole plan fell apart on a few moored mines which could have been swept if we'd had better minesweepers manned by navy crews. And the story doesn't end there, because de Robeck became an admiral of the fleet between the wars and you'd expect that after his experience in the Dardanelles he'd make sure that the navy had modern, fast minesweepers at the start of this war. In peacetime they can be used as patrol vessels, for fisheries protection, air-sea rescue and for training reserves, yet here am I in command of a vessel that was out-of-date not just at the beginning of this war but at the beginning of the last one as well.'

There was silence round the table which was broken by the minesweeper's first lieutenant. 'A few years ago these ships were offered for sale by the Admiralty at a hundred and fifty pounds each, but no one was interested. *One hundred and fifty quid*; the sort of sum that a wealthy man loses at a game of cards. And now they're back in commission, floating coffins, with fifty men on board.'

'All of them loading coal by hand,' someone said.

'It's worse than that,' Bell went on. 'Minesweeping isn't an exact science. Magnetic mines are temperamental and things often go wrong. If the degaussing gear doesn't work perfectly and a mine explodes under your ship the stokers and engine room crew stand no chance of escape. Minesweepers shouldn't be built of iron but of wood or perhaps a sort of concrete material so they don't set off magnetic mines. And they should have the kind of propulsion that doesn't need anyone to be in the engine room when sweeping. You see what I mean; engines controlled from the bridge and all the men up on deck where their prospects of survival are best. All this should have been thought out between the wars; after all, magnetic mines go back many years.'

'What was this guy de Robeck doing all that time?' Marko asked. 'He loses four battleships and he still doesn't get the point of the thing. Any one battleship would have paid for a hundred minesweepers.'

It was Edmund's turn to speak.

'I never knew that the course of western history had been altered by a few mines. They held up an admiral and his battle-ships and the Turks remained in control of the Dardanelles and Black Sea. Instead of a tight ring round Germany, and instead of Russia getting help and encouragement from us, we had to wait for the Americans.'

'Golly,' Reece announced, 'makes you think, doesn't it?'

Pemberton turned to him with a smile.

'Look, little brother, if ever you want to become an Admiral of the Fleet, *don't think!* It won't help at all.'

They laughed and the port was passed, but Reece was not to be deterred.

'When my mum married my dad she got a legacy of a hundred and fifty pounds. She could have had a minesweeper but no, she bought curtains instead.'

Early the following day Braithwaite was summoned to *Minstrel* and informed by commander Sykes that the flotilla would be sailing for Alexandria at the eastern end of the Mediterranean. This didn't mean they were joining the Mediterranean fleet but rather were on loan, because the Mediterranean fleet had been depleted of nearly all its ships in face of demands elsewhere. There were only three or four light cruisers, some destroyers dating from the last war and not a single capital ship. The commander-in-chief had been reduced to hauling down his flag and taking up residence ashore.

Both of the county class cruisers which they had escorted were to remain in Gibraltar for service in the Atlantic while the merchantmen and troop carriers would pass through the Suez Canal, sail down the Red Sea and into the Indian Ocean. There had been rumours of German U-boats penetrating the Mediterranean and it had been decided that merchant ships would have escorts. The Mediterranean fleet, however, having insufficient ships for such a task, was reduced to borrowing them when there was an important convoy, as in this instance.

Steam was being raised and Edmund sat in the ship's office with a pile of unsealed letter forms in front of him. He had learned to censor the men's letters without reading them consciously and he made a point of not looking at the name on the back. He skimmed each one, only half comprehending the sense of what was being said, then passed it to Reece who sealed it and dropped it in the mailbag. Suddenly he stopped reading, looked at Reece and then out the open door at the rock of Gibraltar towering above them. There were some words that seemed to jump off the page at him: 'have you paid the Prudential Insurance policy?'

'What do you make of this one?' he asked.

Reece studied it for a full minute and then laughed. 'Of course, the rock of Gilbraltar is the symbol of the Prudential Insurance Company.'

'Send for him,' Edmund said, and went on reading.

A moment later a stoker petty officer came in and took his cap off as he stepped over the sill.

'Oh it's you, Carslake. This is your letter and I'm not passing it. You know why. You're not allowed to say where we are.'

He handed it to Carslake and pointed out the door.

'*Prudential Insurance.* Either cross it out so it can't be read or else you can take it to the first lieutenant. I want one thing understood. I'm not saying that you don't have a policy with the Prudential Insurance Company and I'm not saying that it's not due for payment. What I am saying is that someone reading this letter might think we were in Gibraltar, which happens to be true. They might talk about it at work or in the pub and that might be the information the Germans were waiting for.'

'If the first lieutenant sees it,' Edmund went on, 'and thinks it was deliberate, you'll be put in the captain's report.'

'I'll cross it out, sir.'

'I wonder why he did that?' Reece asked when he was gone. 'Nothing to gain and everything to lose. The old man wouldn't have taken it kindly. He can't stand cleverness.'

Carslake returned with his letter and Edmund glanced at it and passed it to Reece.

'That's all right.'

'Would you have been so lenient,' Reece asked a moment later, 'if it had been someone else? A repeat offender, a thorough nuisance?'

'I don't know. What I do know is that we have a good crew and the occasional clemency won't hurt. Stoker petty officer Carslake has learned something from this.'

There are not many men in the navy, Edmund found himself thinking, on whom I wish harm, but the ones who allowed honest men to serve in thirty-year-old minesweepers come painfully close. Coal-fired, single-screw, battered beyond belief, with fifty men risking their lives unnecessarily. And no buyers at a hundred and fifty pounds. He looked up at the rock of Gibraltar. Does that embarrass the lords commissioners of the Admiralty? Is anyone up there ashamed? You can't feel much anger over the folly of petty officer Carslake when politicians and admirals are responsible for such outrages.

The passage eastwards down the length of the Mediterranean was a pleasure cruise for the four escort vessels. The convoy speed was twelve knots and the weather fine. The Mediterranean fleet had not been ordered into white uniforms and the temperature, something like that of an English summer, called for light clothes by day and a coat at night.

'Two thousand miles, as near as dammit,' Braithwaite recalled from memory. 'Two hundred and eighty-eight sea miles every twenty-four hours and Alexandria in seven days and a bit.' This was a sea he knew well and he didn't bother to look at the chart. 'We'll have the African coast in sight for the first three days.'

Watch followed watch and with Pemberton keeping the morning and Reece the forenoon, Edmund and Marko had only eight hours each out of twenty four. Edmund found time to plunge into Gibbon's *Decline and Fall of the Roman Empire*; Marko read Marcel Proust.

As they reached the eastern Mediterranean and the brown hills of Malta dropped astern, Braithwaite announced that the threat of enemy action was so remote that the depth charge and gun's crews would be stood down and only the asdic watch maintained. During the afternoons the men slept or sunbathed, the forenoon providing enough time for the ship to be maintained in perfect condition. It was like a sudden outbreak of peace and only the high superstructures of the merchant ships and the sour note of the asdic reminded them of serious business.

Marko was intrigued by the number of fishing boats that the Mediterranean seemed to contain. Whole fleets were encountered, many under sail, and in the early mornings and evenings they gave the scene a picture-postcard appearance.

'I'd like a decent meal of fresh fish,' Braithwaite grumbled, 'but when we're in company like this we can't just abandon our place on the screen to go and barter with some wog.' Then, as an afterthought, 'tell the coxswain to be ready with his old rope, sailcloth and empty tins in case we find ourselves on detached duty. Gray mullet are best; they have a flavour like none other.'

With Alexandria over the horizon the merchant ships tooted their farewells on their sirens and the escorts parted company. Commander Sykes hoisted '*Order 1, G–18*,' the ships under his command to form line ahead and increase to eighteen knots. He turned southwards towards Alexandria while the convoy continued its stately progress toward Port Said, only a few hours distant. At Port Said they would turn southwards through the Suez Canal and into the Red Sea.

Within sight of the Pharos light *Minstrel* picked up a pilot and led the way into the inner harbour where the ships refuelled and took on fresh water. Two hours later they moved to their berths alongside the jetty, all four together as they had been at Gibraltar. Leave was granted to half the ships' companies until midnight.

There followed several days of uncertainty because the naval officer ashore could give commander Sykes no information about their future movements. Presumably they would escort another convoy westwards, presumably the ships that were to make up the convoy were by then in the Red Sea or the Canal, but for security reasons or because it wasn't known, no firm date could be given. The ships, therefore, were kept at twelve hours' notice for steam which meant that sightseeing could only be undertaken in Alexandria or on a one-day schedule to Cairo.

Edmund and Marko had wanted, beyond anything, to see Upper Egypt, Luxor and the Valley of the Kings, but had to make do with a train trip to Cairo, a brief look at the Cairo Museum followed by lunch and an afternoon car ride to Giza and Sakkara. It was an interesting day and their guide was excellent, but it fell short of satisfying the full range of their curiosity. They wanted to see more, to ponder and ask questions, to immerse themselves in the astonishing beauty and complexity of ancient Egypt.

The return train journey during the late afternoon was a memorable conclusion to their day. The countryside came alive at that hour with the activities of the farmers and their domestic animals. The water wheels turned, the sluiceways were opened and smoke from the evening fires rose into a darkening sky. The date palms stood as they had stood in the days of the pharaohs; the villages bestirred themselves for a brief hour to rejoice in the long unaltered continuity of Egyptian life.

'The land of Goshen, the Old Testament calls it. How much did the Hebrews learn from being here when they had to make bricks without straw?' Edmund asked. 'How were they affected by this and how much of it filtered through to us?'

'One thing I know,' Marko said as he watched from the train window, 'King Balshazzar couldn't read the writing on the wall because it was written in Egyptian hieroglyphics. Egyptians are the ones who write on walls, other people write in books. His clerks hadn't learned their Egyptian ABCs.'

They dined at a hotel in Alexandria and returned to the ship to find Reece in the wardroom. He seemed upset and in reply to Edmund's question he told his story.

'I was supposed to be duty officer to-day, but Pemberton was staying aboard and the captain wanted me to accompany a party from the other ships. He said I'd learn something. Someone had arranged a cabaret performance in a run-down quarter of town. We went there in taxis and had to pay to get in.'

'I heard them talking about it,' Marko broke in. '*Harp*'s navigator was involved.'

'It was so awful I'd never have believed it. The first act was donkey-fuck-lady. I felt like being sick.'

Edmund looked at Marko and then back to Reece.

'Braithwaite was there?' Edmund asked quietly.

'Yes, and Dobreiner, but none of the other captains or first lieutenants. There was a sub-lieutenant from *Harp*, one from *Chorister* and half a dozen petty officers.'

'What did you do?' Edmund asked. 'You could have walked out.'

'That's what I did, so they insulted me. I was offered a girl, free, and was told that if I didn't seduce her she'd be beaten. And they'd be standing over me to see I did.'

Reece hesitated and took a few moments to pull himself together.

'She was a child of about thirteen and she had no proper

clothes on. The worst of it was she looked so much like my sister. I don't think I'll ever forget the look on her face. She was a slave. I'd never seen the look on a slave's face.'

'God', Edmund said, 'and our esteemed captain, lieutenant-commander Braithwaite, Royal Naval Reserve, had persuaded you to be there.'

'The bastard,' Marko said in an undertone.

'But you left all right?'

'Yes, after a lot of fuss they unlocked the door and I left with Dobreiner and a couple of petty officers. We found a taxi. One of the petty officers was sick out the window.'

'Oh yes,' he ended by saying, 'that was the first act, but there was more.'

An embarrassed silence was broken by Edmund.

'We had such a wonderful day in Cairo. Our guide was a young Egyptian from the university and he tried hard to answer our questions. We had lunch together, a very French meal. They're not all like what you . . . saw this evening.'

'Is the captain back on board?' Edmund asked suddenly.

Reece shook his head. 'I would have heard him.'

'There's something else,' Marko said. 'Whose idea was it to form a combined party of officers and non-commissioned officers? An all-ranks group may be O.K. if you're sightseeing, but for going ashore in the evening it's a bloody mistake.'

He turned to Reece. 'Aboard *Troubadour* you're treated like any other officer; navigation, a watch on the bridge and officer-of-the-day in harbour, but you say you were insulted.'

'Some of them, certainly . . .'

'And the captain didn't do anything?'

Reece shook his head.

'I can't understand him,' Marko continued. 'He has a high opinion of you; the other day he told me to look up the rules for accelerated promotion.'

Edmund stood up and looked out the open scuttle.

'I have a very special dislike for those of us who insult these people, call them names and pretend to be so superior. These are poor folk who need a bit of money to feed and clothe their children, at least that's what I choose to think. And why do we pay to witness the kind of thing you saw? I think the morality of the spectators is worse than that of the performers.'

There was a step on the steel ladder and they stiffened. There followed a muffled but familiar curse followed by an irregular footfall, and a few moments later Braithwaite entered the wardroom on unsteady legs. Marko and Reece stood up and Edmund turned to face him.

'What you all doing here?' he demanded; 'is the bar open?'

'No, sir. The bar closed at ten o'clock,' Edmund replied. 'We're talking.'

'What about?'

'Cyr and I have been to Cairo. We've had an interesting day. We saw the Pyramids, the Sphinx, the tomb of Ti, the step pyramid of Sakkara . . .'

'How you make out with the wogs?'

'Fine, sir. They speak French, the educated ones. Our guide was first rate . . .'

'Yes, yes. All right.'

If Braithwaite had been sober and very perceptive he might have noticed the looks on the faces of his three officers.

'Where's Pemberton?'

'Turned in, sir; bit of gyppy tummy.'

'Very well, you can carry on talking about the bloody pyramids and the goddam gypos to your heart's content.' He turned and stumbled out.

They waited until his cabin door slammed and then trooped out of the wardroom to their own cabins. The captain's cabin had a bathroom of its own and they knew that he wouldn't be seen again until morning.

'Bedtime,' Cyr announced. 'It's been quite a day.'

The four ships lay alongside for almost three weeks. Alexandria was a beautiful city which combined Egyptian, French, English and Greek influences. The shopping was good, the bars and restaurants varied and as fast as Edmund paid the ship's company the money was spent. A favourite purchase was rose-petal jam with its delicate pink colour and distinctive flavour. Another favourite was the boxes of large, sweet dates. The mess deck tables became laden with locally grown oranges and bananas which Pemberton encouraged as a useful supplement to the standard ship's diet. Fish was also obtained and a fishing boat that tied up alongside was relieved of its cargo in exchange for the coxswain's old rope and empty tins. The beer which was to be had in the local bars, however, did not win much approval and the more enterprising tried out the cheap, dark wine from Algeria which they drank as though it were beer and soon regretted it.

When the time came to raise steam and put to sea the ships' companies were rested and ready to return to work. It seemed strange that they had been kept idle when the North Atlantic was starved of ships. However, a westbound convoy of eight ships had assembled and it was assumed that the escorts would lead them through the straits of Gibraltar and northwards to England. They were fast, modern ships, one of which was still painted in its peacetime livery of white and mauve. They sailed westwards the length of the Mediterranean and only five days later the Rock again loomed up ahead of them.

The passage had been uneventful and Edmund and Marko found time to discuss the events which had taken place in Alexandria. Braithwaite, they concluded, had some perversity of character that made him vulnerable when he was ashore; less so when at sea. Ashore he could be devious and unpredictable, as though he had been removed from his proper element and could not adjust to the demands of terrestrial life. At sea he was at home, surrounded by the things he knew and cherished, a craftsman within reach of the comforting tools of his trade.

And speaking of a double life, sea and land, Edmund's mind went back to his own past existence, the life of a student and an aspiring clergyman. Things had seemed so serene in those days, so shorn of the coarse hair of masculinity. He had gone to chapel twice a day, attended lectures and spent long hours working at his desk. His release from this bondage had begun with his participation in athletics; yes, his father had been right in saying that it led him astray. But if sports had unlocked the door, the naval reserve had opened it wide. He began to see the university from the outside, from the standpoint of those who had never been to one, the Braithwaites and Dobreiners of the world. To them the university was like an island cut off from the great mass of mankind, a self-perpetuating juggernaut borne on the rusty wheels of classical scholarship. What sense did it make from their point of view? What justification could be found for idle and ill-disciplined students, professors who never wrote a book that anyone could understand?

His isolated world of divinity had been at a far remove from the verities of *Troubadour* and he asked himself if he could have learned as much in six years of study as he had learned in six months of sea service. It had been a sanitized world that he had lived in, not the real world of flesh and blood. It was all very well to be 'called', as Daniel had been called, to study the Old Testament under creaking professors who looked like prophets themselves, or systematic theology with tutors whose object was to confuse and obfuscate, but it was removed from life, a step away from the reek of humanity. Even the music of the Church, thought by many to be one of its great glories, sounded contrived when compared against the pure chant of wind and sea.

When they cleared Gibraltar and entered the Atlantic their expectations were shattered once again. Instead of turning to starboard, to the north, they hugged the coast of Africa on a southwesterly course, escorting a fast convoy bound for Capetown. In a couple of days they were in white uniforms and the sun became warmer so that Pemberton had to warn the ship's company against sunburn. If a man became seriously sunburned and unable to do his work it was taken to be a self-inflicted injury which was punishable under naval discipline.

At Freetown, a few degrees north of the equator, the flotilla put in for fuel and water and learned that they would not be sailing south to the Cape of Good Hope. Commerce raiders were the enemy in these waters, not U-boats, and the cruisers knew how to handle them, in fact wanted nothing better than an encounter.

The flotilla remained in Freetown for two days, ample time for unanimous agreement to be reached that Freetown was the dullest place they had ever put in. The clubs and bars were frightful, the food unpalatable, the shops empty. It was hot and uninteresting, devoid of all that makes a seaman's life worth living. They looked forward to returning up the coast of Africa and the familiar sight of Gibraltar, at which point they would be halfway home. But again some perverse consideration intervened and they found themselves escorting a motley of ships to Georgetown in Guyana. They set sail westwards toward the coast of South America.

'Pity,' Marko said as he came up for his watch. 'I wanted to try some of those South African wines. I always look at the small print on the backs of wine bottles and the Paarl Valley claims to equal the best Alsacian wines. Paarl means 'pearl' and refers to a rock in the centre of the valley that shines in the rain.'

He looked back at the convoy.

'Damn those blighters. Why do they want to go to a miserable dump like Georgetown? I'll bet you a bottle of wine it's worse than Freetown.'

The westbound convoy contained a chronic laggard. It fell astern regularly and without warning, and no advice or encouragement from *Chorister* could persuade it to maintain proper station. It was a small merchantman with three holds, which probably meant it was of six thousand tons burden. It had derricks above each hold and its bridge was aft so that one wondered how captain or officer of the watch could see forward at all. It ignored signals made by flag or light and it had no lookouts on the wings of the bridge or in the eyes of the ship. There was, however, a man in a bowler hat to be seen in the vicinity of the wheelhouse. To get his attention *Chorister* had to steam alongside and address him on the loud-hailer.

The name painted across her stern was *Ho Chi*, registered in Hong Kong, and to add credibility to this information there was always a group of Chinese gathered along the taffrail. They scarcely moved or looked up when *Chorister* closed and told her that she was a mile astern of station and would be reported to the Board of Trade.

'We know you can steam at convoy speed because we've seen you do it,' the captain of *Chorister* said in as kindly a tone as he could summon. 'Earlier you were doing twelve knots. Why can't you do that now?'

His voice echoed back at him from the rusty sides of *Ho Chi*.

'If you fall astern and get torpedoed we can't guarantee to come back and pick up survivors,' was his parting shot. 'Go faster and stay out of trouble.'

Braithwaite studied *Ho Chi* and then *Chorister* with his binoculars, put them down, scratched his chin and paced the bridge. The stockiness of his figure, which was of medium height, was more evident, Edmund noticed, when he was in tropical rig; white shorts, white sleeveless shirt and the faded gold stripes of a lieutenant-commander on black epaulettes. He had the upper body of a fighter or a gymnast but his legs seemed to belong to a man of sedentary occupation.

'Make a signal to *Chorister*,' he called out finally, 'and I think it would be helpful if *Minstrel* were included. Begin. *"For your information I learned about Ho Chi in the Far East a few years ago. She was under command of a captain-owner who had his Chinese wife aboard. She arranged cargoes through numerous relatives. I need not say that an ocean-going merchantman owned by the captain is rare and creates a feeling of independence and resentment against authority. His name is Picton, commonly known as Rice Bowl Picton. In 1936 he became celebrated in the Far East for riding out a typhoon with his midships hold breached. His ship was caught in a beam sea and rolled sixty degrees, which caused a steam locomotive at the bottom of the hold to break its restraining chains and plunge through the side of the ship. Somehow his vessel did not break in half and he brought her to Hong Kong under power.*

'I apologize for length of this signal but it's a quiet day, the signalman has nothing to do and this information may be of assistance in dealing with old Rice Bowl who in fact is a capable seaman".'

He turned to Edmund.

'All right, Casswell, I'm going down. Let me know if there's any reply to that. I'll be in my cabin.'

The signalman tapped it out and almost immediately *'thank you'* came from *Chorister* and *'most helpful'* from *Minstrel* which Edmund passed to Braithwaite by voicepipe.

A locomotive, Edmund found himself repeating, which must have weighed sixty or seventy tons, breaks free of its chains and goes through the side of the ship, yet somehow . . .

'Sir,' a young lookout shouted, 'something I seen broke surface over there,' and he pointed away to the port side, to the south.

'Listen for torpedo noises,' Edmund told the asdic operator, but he wasn't unduly concerned. They were steaming west only a few degrees north of the equator and the sea was a flat, glassy calm. Sea creatures were always breaking surface and a disturbance in the water could be seen for miles. When there was wave action or even a ripple only the whales and dolphins could be seen, but with a sea like glass you became aware of how much life existed in the ocean.

Edmund crossed over to the port side of the bridge where the lookout had his binoculars to his eyes.

'You're quite right to report what you saw, but there's a better way of saying it,' Edmund began. 'I'm going to tell the leading seaman to explain it to you, all right?'

This was the boy who had replaced ordinary seaman Crouch and somehow had escaped the training which he should have received from one of the leading seamen. 'Something I seen broke surface over there . . .' It was just as well Braithwaite hadn't heard it.

Not much schooling, some of these eighteen-year-olds who were given a bare three months' training ashore and then sent to ships. They were a different lot from the men who had come aboard on the day that war was declared. Those had been reservists trained at weekends, evenings and during their holidays and many possessed excellent experience and a real love of the sea. The new ones, some of them at least, were fed up with the tedious grind of civvy life and ready for a bit of adventure. The navy was better than sweeping floors or running errands and in fine weather it was pure pleasure to stand on the bridge with a pair of navy binoculars and watch sea and sky.

Edmund wondered what Pemberton would do about the men who had asked permission to sleep on the upper deck. It seemed reasonable when the weather was warm and the sea calm to let them sling their hammocks wherever they could find space or else lie down directly on the teak deck using the 'donkey's breakfast' inside their hammock as a mattress. There were difficulties, all the same. If there were some kind of emergency the upper deck would become a confusion of prostrate forms, hammocks secured to every available handhold and men on duty trying to fight fires, lower a boat or whatever the emergency called for. There was also the possibility of a *tsunami*, a rogue wave which could roll the ship unexpectedly and throw men overboard. Braithwaite had spoken of one he encountered on passage between Manila and Osaka which seemed to have originated with a deep-sea earthquake. The wave came at great speed and left a calm sea behind it. There was something inexplicable, he had said, something ghostly about a wave from an unseen source which made the ship roll and then passed on silently.

The issue was settled by consulting *Minstrel*. It was learned that commander Sykes had no objection to the practice provided it could be administered 'without the upper deck becoming cluttered and without danger to the men involved.'

Troubadour and her sister ships escorted the convoy to Georgetown in Guyana, which was, as predicted, as dull as Freetown had been. Thereafter the flotilla seemed destined for odd and rather pointless duties in the Caribbean, seemingly at the beck and call of planners who had little idea of the realities of war. They went in and out of Belize, Kingston and Nassau, then finally northwards to New York and Halifax.

When they were approaching Nassau with Andros Island away on the port side Braithwaite suddenly turned to Edmund and asked, 'do you know the name of a familiar public figure who tried to grow sisal plants on that island?'

'No, sir, no idea,' Edmund replied.

'Well it was the prime minister, the man with the umbrella, the fool who spoke of "Peace in our Time". He wasted years of his life trying to grow a crop that wouldn't grow and which makes second-rate cordage if he'd succeeded.'

As the days lengthened into summer the war at sea was extended to the coasts of Norway. Commander Sykes' flotilla played no part in the battles that raged in the fjords and waterways of Trondheim and Namsos, but the news of losses, the allied lack of air power and inadequate planning came through to the crews of *Minstrel*, *Troubadour* and their sister ships. There were daring exploits by individual ships and great deeds were performed individually, but at the end of it the battles fought in Norway ended in defeat, and the long and strategically valuable Norwegian coast fell into German hands. Britain had lacked aircraft and anti-aircraft guns.

Braithwaite railed at the fact that under the likes of Chamberlain the inventiveness and wealth of Great Britain had been squandered during the preceding years. They had never come to grips, for instance, with the need for an effective anti-aircraft weapon for close defence of ships. A dribble of bofors and oerlikon guns were coming from Sweden whose government sold them to both sides. But why, with the example of the Spanish Civil War from which to learn the power and danger of aircraft, had we not produced our own? The principle of the machine gun had been mastered in the previous century; could not British inventiveness come up with something of one-inch bore with a high rate of fire and an explosive projectile weighing about a pound? But then how do you expect a political gentleman who couldn't even grow a crop of sisal to understand that?

Braithwaite was much given to criticizing high authority and most of his strictures were justified. He was old enough to know what life had been like between the wars, to have experienced the Depression, seen politicians stumbling about the corridors of power perplexed by the enormity of their tasks. There was much to deplore, and for Braithwaite there was the added dimension that he had seen and admired the German alternative. Deep in his heart he respected Hitler's ruthless country and like many others at that time he did not comprehend its cost in human freedom. Criticism had reached almost epidemic proportions in consequence of the navy's losses during the early part of the war. All ranks indulged to the point where respect for high authority was non-existent. Ordinary day-to-day discipline was maintained and there continued to be great love of country, but few at that time would have given the Admiralty credit for anything.

If Braithwaite was a critic, tedious at times, he was also a teacher. A few officers and non-commissioned officers were gifted in this way and the bogus captain McCormick came instantly to mind. Petty officer Clancey was another and 'Lofty' Fenway the best among the leading seamen. There were some, however, who took no trouble to help or explain, who would curse a subordinate who did something amiss but not bother to show him what he had done wrong or how to put it right.

Edmund wondered if the ability to teach subordinates was even regarded as a virtue. Visions conjured up by the traditional icons, 'the silent service', 'the old sea dog' seemed far removed from the idea of a patient instructor striving to pass on his knowledge. The navy's officer report form made specific mention of an officer's sobriety, but no mention of whether he had been successful in raising his subordinates to a higher standard of performance. This was a glaring omission in a service where every man was supposed to be capable of performing at a level higher than his own.

The complexity of Braithwaite's character and his ability as an instructor had been demonstrated in an incident that occurred when the ship was alongside. Two seamen were painting the ship's side, working from a wooden stage that was secured round the guard-rail stanchions. The paint pot was also suspended from the deck above on a lanyard. They painted downwards to the water-line and sat waiting for the leading seaman on deck to pull up the paint pot and take their brushes. At this point a harbour seal, appearing large and belligerent at such close quarters, surfaced under the stage and stared with an unblinking eye at the two men, one of whom, able seaman Rogers, fell in the water and lost his paint brush. He was hauled out by his companion but naval discipline decreed that he appear before Pemberton charged with negligently losing one paint brush, the property of His Majesty, valued at ninepence halfpenny.

When he heard the story, Pemberton was hard put to suppress laughter as he dismissed the offence, but Braithwaite was not satisfied. He paid the ninepence halfpenny from his own pocket so that the books would not show a discrepancy and sent for leading seaman Fenway.

'Why do you suppose,' he asked, 'a navy paintbrush has a hole at the end of the handle?'

'Oh yessir, I see, sir. So it can be tied with a lanyard from above, sir.'

'So it was your fault, Fenway, that the paintbrush was lost, not Rogers' at all.'

Fenway was on the point of placing some of the blame on the

grey harbour seal. With Pemberton he could have got away with it, but the unsmiling look on Braithwaite's face persuaded him to silence.

On another occasion Reece came to the door of the ship's office and asked Edmund for a sheet of plain paper. He had not seen Braithwaite in the other chair.

'What do you want it for?' Braithwaite demanded.

'Oh, it's just something private, sir.'

'Well, if it's private you can't have it. That would be theft of government stores, wouldn't it?'

Reece looked at him in bewilderment.

'A sheet of paper, sir?'

'I don't care whether you steal a sheet of paper or a whole bloody aircraft carrier. It's still theft.'

A side glance from Edmund persuaded Reece that there was nothing more to be said. Both Edmund and Reece, however, could have been excused for wondering in their minds how this punctilious regard for a sheet of paper or a navy paintbrush was to be weighed in the balance against the obscenities of an Alexandrine night club.

CHAPTER 11

THE FLOTILLA, weary of the sea, sailed eastwards from Halifax with a convoy of over a hundred ships. It was a slow crossing, but the sea was moderate and when U-boats attacked they did so with little perseverance. The Irish coast came in sight and two days later *Troubadour* and her sister ships lay in the Mersey preparing to enter dry-dock. The hulls were to be scraped of marine growth, the boilers cleaned and minor defects made good.

There was talk about getting fitted with RDF, standing for Radio Direction Finding, a new device which would help to locate U-boats on the surface at night. They learned, however, that euipment was in short supply and not enough operators had been trained. Three men would be needed for each ship so that the set could be run on a twenty-four-hour basis which meant twelve operators for the flotilla. The trained men, they were told, were not available.

The ships' companies were to be granted twenty-one days' leave. Stores and ammunition were landed, even the charts removed from the chartroom and placed ashore for safekeeping. The ships, in consequence, took on the bleak look of an unoccupied house; flags hauled down, cutlery and crockery put away, clothes lockers open and empty. Harbour tugs came alongside and jostled them into drydock. With baulks of timber in place to keep them steady and in perfect alignment, the gates were closed and the level lowered until they rested, dripping and forlorn, on their keels.

As the ships' companies prepared for their leave, planned what they would do and adjusted their thoughts to a brief return to life on shore, apprehension filled the minds of many. The war was only eight months old and battle had scarcely been joined, yet two separate and conflicting viewpoints had begun to emerge. Some people couldn't grasp the enormity of the conflict and made pretence of keeping things as they had been before the war. Not even the miseries of the blackout could jolt them into an acceptance of desperate reality. They wished only that it would all go away so their lives could be resumed without breaking step with the past. The other view was that the damage would be irreversible and England would never recover. Their thoughts returned to the bloodshed of twenty years before which had deprived the country of a generation of men. Their cry was, 'Not again, we cannot abide it'. Among this group suicide was all too frequent. It was, therefore, toward a confused and unsettled country that the sailors, stokers, petty officers and officers turned their eyes. An absence of a few months was not an eternity, but it was the first step of the war and for the men of those four small ships it had been a harsh beginning.

Edmund had invited Marko to spend his leave in the bishop's palace which, he hastened to add, was not much of a palace. They had decided to pack all their belongings and take time and trouble to get their clothes washed and repaired. Their uniforms would go to the cleaners, their shirts to a proper laundry and they would stock up on seagoing kit. They would also ask the dean of the cathedral to appeal for clothes for the seamen; not just a few odds and ends but in quantity. If the Admiralty couldn't supply warm clothing for its sailors then the cathedral congregation must be prevailed upon. At the same time they would try for a small piano, musical instruments, sheet music and song books.

Edmund paid the ship's company and issued railway warrants while Pemberton impressed on them the date by which they must be back on board. Edmund, Marko, Pemberton and Reece were crowded into the ship's office discussing the final details.

'We don't need to worry about buses,' Pemberton was saying. '*Minstrel* has it organized.'

Braithwaite suddenly appeared at the door and his voice was raised in anger.

'Rape! I don't bloody well believe it.'

He had a paper in his hand and his eyes flashed at the four officers.

Edmund stood up; the others were already standing.

'Not this man. There's been a mistake. Here Pemberton, look at this. They want us to hand over Knatchbull on a charge of rape.'

'Oh no; not Knatchbull,' Pemberton said.

A man in civilian clothes, evidently a police officer, was behind Braithwaite. One could not quarrel with his north-country accent, but there was a hint of smugness about him which was irritating.

'Good morning, gentlemen. I am sorry to disturb you like this, but I am here to execute this warrant of arrest.'

'Now, just a minute, what's this about?' Marko snapped.

It was as though the policeman had learned it by heart.

'A complaint was sworn by the prosecutrix in consequence of which this seaman Knatchbull was apprehended whilst he were on shore. He were told of the circumstances of the complaint against him, informed of his rights and he thereupon elected to make a voluntary statement. This statement is in the nature of a confession of guilt and it is on this basis that his arrest has been ordered. If I may say so, I doubt whether bail will be granted. You may not appreciate . . .'

'Did he have a lawyer present when he made the statement?' Marko cut him off.

'That's hardly for me to say.'

'This is the oldest trick in the world,' Marko snapped. 'He isn't allowed to call a lawyer, and they con him into making a statement on the promise that he'll be released when he has said what they want him to say. I'll have to get the statement retracted and ask the court to forgo bail on the understanding that we produce him when called upon.' He spoke to Braithwaite. 'May I proceed along those lines?'

'Yes, indeed,' Braithwaite said. 'You know what you're doing.'

Marko ignored the police officer and turned to Reece.

'Go to the petty officers' mess and tell the coxswain what's happening. Knatchbull must be discharged into the hands of the civil authorities. He's to be ready in twenty minutes with his kit-bag. We'll accompany him to the police station.'

'May I assume you are his lawyer?' the man enquired.

'You can assume what you like,' Marko shot back. 'Now get off the ship and wait by the gangway.'

He left and Braithwaite sat down in the clerk's chair.

'What a hell of a situation.' He paused. 'Look, Cyr, you're not to spend all your time dealing with this. You need your leave as much as any of us.'

'Yessir, but I'm not going to let Knatchbull get screwed. I don't like this sod of a policeman. He thinks he knows a lot about the law. We'll see.'

As the moment drew closer for Edmund to walk through the door of the five-hundred-year-old stone house that was called the Bishop's Palace he tried to focus his mind on what lay ahead. He realised that his father would be displeased with him, so he determined to stay in the background, work in the garden or go fishing, and cause the least amount of disturbance. Marko would follow as soon as he had done his best for able seaman Knatchbull. He worried that Marko with his exuberance might not see eye to eye with his parents. His directness might jar their sensibilities, but it was a risk that had to be taken. Marko was a man of character and he hoped his parents would realise it and acknowledge his contribution to the allied war effort. Besides that, he himself wanted to know Marko better. They had never spoken about his Canadian upbringing; how he had acquired his practicality and resourcefulness, his uncommon sense.

Edmund's mother met him at the door, her usual perfumed and effusive self, with Tom not far behind. His father had decided to take a walk after supper, which gave Edmund a few minutes to deal with his and Marko's luggage and speak to his mother. He explained that Marko might not arrive for two or three days and finally he asked about his father.

'Edmund, darling, you're so incredibly tanned; what on earth have you been doing? You're the colour of a . . .' She jolted her mind back to the more significant problem. 'Your father is afraid you may fall from the pedestal . . . You do understand that, don't you?'

'I've grown up a lot,' he said quietly. 'I could scarcely have gone through the past six months without being affected.'

'It's your future in the Church he's worried about. After all, Edmund, you are . . . special. When you joined the navy it raised doubts in his mind. Will you reassure him?'

'Mother, I'll do my best and I want you to be the perfect hostess where my friend is concerned. He's a dedicated man, a lawyer; a bit rough and ready, and I don't think he has kept up his connection with the Catholic Church. He picked up his English in the street, but try to see the good in him. I don't want father to be . . . stuffy, pontifical.'

'Edmund!'

'Yes, mother, I know.' He decided on a quick change of direction.

'I brought a box of provisions from New York. I'd like to go and help Amy open it. Will you come?'

Edmund had changed out of uniform and was wearing flannel trousers and an open shirt while he unpacked in what for many years had been his room. His mother sat on a chair and talked. The door was ajar and at half past nine his father appeared in the doorway, consulting his gold pocket watch as he did so.

'How good to see you, Edmund. You mother has offered you your old room?'

'Good evening, father,' Edmund said, straightening up from his task. 'I hope it's convenient to use this room. I'll only be here for a few days.' He seemed to be apologising for being there at all.

His father mumbled some sort of assent.

'I take it you've had something to eat?'

'No, but it's too late now.'

'How remiss of us not to kill the fatted calf.' He gave his wife a sidelong glance.

Edmund wanted to say that he had been at war, not sharing his portion with harlots or however it was that the prodigal son spent his time, but he remembered his good intentions and said nothing. His mother was on her feet and took her husband's arm.

'We must leave Edmund to get on with his work,' she said, the nervousness apparent in her voice, 'I want to tell you of some wonderful ideas he has.'

The bishop paid scant attention.

'I thought you were bringing a friend?'

'He couldn't come. Perhaps in a day or two when he has the problem under control.'

'Is he in trouble of some sort?'

'One of our sailors has been accused of assault and Marko is doing his best for the man.'

'His name is Marko? I've never heard that name. I've heard of Mark or Marcus. And your friend is of the Roman Catholic persuasion?'

'Yes, I think so.'

'I see. I trust he will not indulge his Romish practices under my roof.'

'Of course not, father.'

'Do I take it from what you say that he is a lapsed Catholic?'

'I've never questioned him about his religious beliefs. I respect his right to privacy.'

'Does he know of your circumstances? That your life is dedicated?'

'I told him that you were a bishop and he knows that I was studying at Cambridge. Beyond that I can't say what he knows.'

His father looked up at the ceiling and then left the room. He had not embraced Edmund or even shaken him by the hand. He had, however, regarded him as though displeased. Their conversation had been what conversations usually were, like lawyers jousting on a field of pure malice. Why should he apologise, Edmund asked himself, for using his old room? Why should he be on the defensive?

The next morning at breakfast his father was in the same mood. Edmund asked if he might approach the dean of the cathedral and ask that a prayer be said for ordinary seaman Crouch. It didn't seem an unreasonable request since the boy had died almost at Edmund's feet, but it was refused on the grounds that the dean could not be sure that Crouch had been baptised and confirmed in the Church of England. He might be a pagan for all the dean knew. And almost certainly was, Edmund thought to himself.

Next came his appeal for musical instruments and sheet music, but difficulties existed there because members of the congregation had a duty to withhold an old flute or violin unless they were assured that the instrument would be used solely for sacred purposes. Any song that was not specifically Christian was profane, and the donor had a duty to be outraged at the prospect of his instrument, which hitherto had been used only to sing God's praises, being debased by playing a mere song.

Edmund took a deep breath and finished his breakfast. His father, he thought, had never gone that far. He decided to say nothing about the old clothes because it occurred to him that the former owners would feel righteous Christian indignation if anyone used improper language while wearing their castoffs.

Edmund changed into garden clothes and went outside. There was a vegetable patch at the rear of the house sheltered by a brick wall and he stood for a full minute contemplating its decay during the time he had been at sea. Here it was in the month of April and no effort had been made to dig or plant. An appeal had gone out from the Ministry of Food that those who had land should bend their backs to bring it under cultivation, yet this potentially productive garden was lying derelict. He pushed his way into the shed, took a digging fork, rake and wheelbarrow and applied himself to the task.

He was a perfectionist where gardening was concerned. He pulled up the weeds and threw them in the wheelbarrow, brought manure from a nearby stable and spread it on the surface. There followed the actual digging which he accomplished with the fork, working in neat rows. At each plunge of the tines he lifted the soil and turned it over so that the manure was submerged under the soil. He never trod on the garden once it was dug but raked until it was as smooth and level as a carpet. Finally he laid walk-boards across in parallel lines, each line three feet apart.

His walk-boards were the secret of a tidy garden. He had salvaged them when an old barn was being demolished; foot-wide oak planks which he had cut into manageable lengths. The trick was to tread on the walk-boards for planting, weeding and all the manifold operations of gardening and never on the soft earth. His garden, therefore, never had footprints on it, never that miserable trodden-down look.

Edmund possessed a characteristic that set him apart from most of his friends at Cambridge, being able to turn his mind to small, practical matters which he didn't consider beneath his dignity. The young men with whom he attended lectures would have been contemptuous of his simplistic ideas; the garden pegs made from old broom handles cut in two-foot lengths, the cord which was stretched so that the lines of plants would be straight; even the ink marks on the cord so that seedlings could be spaced exactly. He was the equal of any of them when wrestling with great philosophical concepts, but he also liked to grapple with small things which made all the difference to an orderly life. The thoughts of Saint Paul, the first Christian theologian, were as familiar to him as they were to his brother students, but he possessed another side to his character which could be summarized as Paul the tentmaker, the practical man who knew how to work with his hands.

He wondered why his father had never felt drawn to create anything practical. It didn't seem perverse to Edmund's mind that as the Creator created us, we stood in a special relationship to Him when we turned our hands to some creative act. Nor did it matter if the act were trivial in the great scheme of things; a well-planted garden or a lovingly cooked supper were surely as worthy as a large and ill-conceived piece of pretentious art. What was it that one of those marvellous women saints had said, something about God preferring the faithful performance of the most trifling duty given to us rather than the frantic pursuit of objects that were really none of our damn business. Something like that.

When it was lunch time he took off his rubber boots and entered the house. He washed his hands in the kitchen sink, asked what was for lunch and walked through to the dining room. The dean of the cathedral had been invited and was in conversation with his father. He was a robust man in his mid-fifties and Edmund had known him since boyhood, secretly calling him 'the corporal', because if his father had been a general that would have best described their relative status.

'The dean has refused a glass of sherry,' were his father's opening words, 'would you care to help yourself?'

'No, thank you, father, but I'm looking forward to my lunch. Good day, dean. I hope you are well; and Mrs. Potter.'

'Thank you, Edmund, yes. You've been working in the garden?'

'It's been rather neglected. I've made a start and I'll get some seeds this afternoon and do the planting. Ah, here's mother; I must know her preference where vegetables are concerned.'

His mother swept in shook hands with the dean.

'I heard what you said. I'd like to go with you, Edmund, and we can choose the seeds. And now, shall we go in to lunch? It's not much, I'm afraid.'

During the meal the dean made efforts to bring the conversation round to the war and, more specifically, to Edmund's part in it. Edmund, however, would not be drawn in that direction and brushed aside all attempts to get him to speak of his experiences.

'I'm sure,' his father said, 'that Edmund is ashamed of what he's doing and cannot speak of it without embarrassment.'

His father's words struck him like a blow. All good intentions were forgotten and there surged up a tidal wave of anger.

'No, father. You are mistaken,' Edmund shot back. 'I'm proud of what I'm doing. It's a difficult life, but I love it. I wouldn't choose to be anywhere else on this earth.'

The three of them stared at him. How can anyone enjoy a war, they seemed to be asking.

'We had expected you to say that it was a living hell; that you longed for a return to your true vocation . . .' The dean put his fork down on his plate and seemed to be about to say more, but Edmund interrupted him.

'Yes, in one way I feel embarrassment, a deep sense of shame at the memory of those foolish years I spent at Cambridge. My fellow students were conceited, spoiled and tiresome. The teaching staff were pompous and opinionated, they would gladly answer questions we had not asked, but danced around the matters that they could not or would not address. It was a world that was vacuous and unreal.'

He paused.

'My brother officers and the men aboard *Troubadour* are the best of comrades. It's a pleasure to serve with them and suffer the same hardships. I'm proud of my ship, proud of my captain, despite his faults, and proud of the sailors despite their lack of education.'

He looked defiantly at his father.

'For the first time in my life I am not ashamed of what I'm doing.'

'I can see,' his father replied icily, 'that we need to have a little talk.'

He said it as though he were speaking to a child and thereafter lapsed into a moody silence.

His mother appeared on the verge of tears and the dean looked stunned. Recovering quickly from his anger it was Edmund's chance to direct the course of the conversation and he chose to speak about gardening, which he did with massive sarcasm. The dean was an easy target so he reproached him for his failure to contribute to the nation's food supply by toiling in his vineyard; 'the workman,' he intoned, 'is worthy of his hire.' He pointed an accusing finger, 'by the sweat of thy brow shalt thou eat.'

No churchman, Edmund had discovered, had any response when biblical strictures were taken out of context and thrown at them. Besides, the dean had the reputation of being lazy and alcoholic, a fact well known to the choir, if not to the congregation. It was said in the choir that at matins he was irreproachable, at evening prayer guided by the spirit and at compline incomprehensible. His reason for having refused a sherry before lunch was, as Edmund knew, because with only one sip he'd be gone for the rest of the day. He would have returned home and polished off a half bottle of gin. One had to be sorry for the man, but being sorry didn't prohibit a few jests on a safe subject like gardening.

That afternoon Edmund lay down on his bed and slept an agreeable and light-hearted sleep. It was not dark or prehistoric but close to the surface; he dreamed only of plants and green things upon the earth. When his mother called him to go shopping he emerged, not as from a cave, but as though he had only closed his eyes lightly on a summer's day.

Later she walked with him in the cathedral grounds and reminded him of the years when he had sung in the choir and been the soloist. It had not been a happy time, because he could never sing with joy nor without feeling his father's critical eye on him. His voice had attracted the love and admiration of the congregation, but his pleasure was always spoiled by his father's faint praise and admonition to be humble. He was glad when his voice broke at twelve years of age; and it was all over suddenly, like a death.

His mother turned to him. 'Edmund, I've so much to say but I don't know where to begin.'

'Let's begin with girls,' Edmund suggested. 'I was thinking about a certain girl while I was at sea. It saddens me because I don't believe anything will come of it. She's French and her name is Marguerite. I met her when I was with uncle Philippe.'

'You've never told me about her,' his mother reproached him.

'She'll be nineteen now, and not what English people expect a French girl to be. She's not dark and vivacious; rather tall and quiet.'

'Do you know her well?'

'Not really. We met when uncle Philippe was tasting the Bordeaux wines; she lives near Pauillac; her mother has a vineyard.'

'And her English?'

'Like my French; we get along perfectly well, but France is suddenly very far away. I haven't seen her for months.'

'There are other girls, more available,' his mother said.

'Yes, I've heard about the girls in every port. But they're not the same. Marguerite is . . .'

He hesitated to find the word and a car turned into the driveway.

'Good heavens, here's Marko.'

Edmund ran forward.

'Marko; good to see you. Welcome to the palace. Meet my mother.'

'*Enchanté*, madame.' Marko said, bending over her hand.

Later, after his return to *Troubadour*, Edmund would recall his leave as a series of memorable but disconnected episodes. He would remember his mother playing the part of the desperate hostess who chattered about trivialities as though fearing to allow the briefest lapse into silence or reflection. His father was withdrawn and morose, giving the impression of a Russian aristocrat who finds himself cast accidentally into the company of his own serfs. He would remember the vegetable garden with its earthy smells where he worked for an hour in the early mornings before the others were up. He gained pleasure in its orderliness, which he likened in his mind to the upper deck of a ship. The tomato seedlings were planted in straight lines; so straight that a mathematician could scarcely have found fault. Coloured pegs marked the rows of peas, beans and a dozen other varieties of vegetable. When he was finished he faced his handiwork and stood to attention. 'Sir, God, Sir,' he said, 'remind Tom to water them, and it's up to You to make them grow.'

Then there was the woman friend of his mother's who sat on the edge of the sofa and cried. She owned a kennel of exceptionally fine mastiff dogs, huge animals that could not survive without their diet of meat. The butcher, however, was at his wits' end; in wartime he couldn't supply enough scraps to keep them alive. She wanted to send them to America but knew in her heart that it couldn't be done and they would have to be put down. Superlative animals in their prime; put down; killed; slaughtered.

The tone of the holiday, however, was set by two conversations. First, it had been Edmund's angry outburst when dean Potter had been present; second, when Marko spoke about his religious upbringing. It had begun innocently with Marko answering Mrs Casswell's questions about his legal studies.

He had obtained his law degree in Canada, he explained, and although he never intended to practice, being more inclined toward a career in business and politics, he had been offered the opportunity to do post-graduate work in England; in the quaint phraseology of the bar, 'to eat his dinners' at the Inns of Court. Most of all, he said, he wanted to get away from home and from the narrow perspective of small-town life. It was an opportunity that he couldn't pass up.

'You have so much history and so little geography,' he said; 'for us it's the other way. I'm told that a man can walk the length of England and Scotland in less than two weeks; the same thing in Canada would take months and months. Here the very walls groan under the burden of history; in Canada our history is so brief we have to invent most of it. Nor do we have a mythology to sustain us in troubled times; no Magna Carta being forced on a reluctant king; nor England's little admiral who wore his heart on his sleeve and was struck down at the moment of triumph. No saint prodding dragons in the ribs; no round table; no idiot allowing the cakes to burn.

'I wanted to find out how the French-English problem is handled, how you live with your Gallic neighbours. Well, a play I saw in London, which had a long run, was partly in English and partly in French. It was hilarious in a self-deprecating way and both languages were understood because the audience laughed in the right places. Something like that wouldn't have gone down in Canada. I can't imagine the stuffy Toronto people pretending to rule the world and the French-speaking folks in Quebec claiming to be the only civilised people in it.'

A question from Mrs Casswell, and Marko was off again.

'What I like most about the English is the crazy customs which are cherished in full knowledge of their absurdity. To chase after a fox you need a huge collection of identical dogs, a regiment of horses and people sitting on them wearing a spectacular uniform of red coats and white pants. Pound for pound the fox is outweighed fifty million to one by its pursuers.'

'Isn't it strange,' Edmund interjected, 'we can wear any old clothes aboard ship to chase the king's enemies, but to chase a little red fox you have to be in ceremonial outfit.'

The bishop shot him a swift glance then asked Marko whether he was a practising Catholic. The answer was stunningly direct.

'No, I left the Church in disgust because I don't believe a word of its teachings. I'm put off by its worldliness and angered by its grip on politics and family life. When I was a child I was an altar boy until an assistant to the priest tried to commit an act of . . . let's call it *gross indecency*. I ran out of the vestry and told my dad who admonished me not to say a word or the family business would be jeopardised. Next I told my grandfather, the judge, who shook his head and said it was only my word against his.

'Soon I began to ponder the teachings of the Church and later, at university, I thought about the history of catholicism over the centuries; the religious wars, intolerance on a massive scale, the Inquisition, people like the Aztecs wiped out, greed and self-aggrandisement; no thank you, not for me, I wanted nothing to do with it.'

Thinking to be on safer ground Mrs Casswell tried again. 'You must have a lovely family, Mr Cyr; do tell me about them.'

'Well then, my parents are both from what we call the North Shore; the river St Lawrence, that is. For the first two years of their marriage they were childless, but not from want of trying. They confided to the priest and eventually the congregation got to praying for them, so when I came along I was baptised Rogation Marcus, the child they had prayed for. At school I was Rogey, which I didn't like, so I changed it to Marko, which goes better with Cyr. To be truly French it would have to be Marc with a *c*, but *Marc Cyr* is not easy to pronounce like *Marko Cyr*. It was a relative of mine, Louis Cyr, who is in the record books as having been the strongest man in the world.

'My dad didn't get too much education and he runs the family business; a dozen fishing vessels each crewed by six or seven men. Of course that's where I learned my seamanship; specially from one of the skippers who was a petty officer at the battle of Jutland. His ship was astern of the *Queen Mary* when she blew up. They didn't stop to pick up survivors, because there weren't any survivors.'

'I have four sisters and a brother, all younger than me and my mum, she looks after them. She keeps the account books for my dad and pays the men, because dad can't read and write. And she makes the girls' dresses.'

'Good heavens,' Mrs Casswell exclaimed, 'she must be run off her feet.'

'My mum says it's getting better all the time, because the girls are growing up and helping her. No daughter of hers is going to get married who can't keep house, cook for a dozen people and sew her own clothes. And if they've been through university and have professional training, so much the better.'

Mrs Casswell looked at him in amazement.

'And all this without servants?'

Marko shook his head.

'We managed because the children were expected to help. It made for a solid family.'

'And what did the boys do to contribute?' Mrs Casswell asked.

'In winter I'd hitch up the horse, cut firewood in the forest with my little brother and haul it back to the house on a sled, and of course we cleared the snow from the driveway and paths. We looked after the garden in the summer, made repairs around the house, went hunting for deer in the fall and fished just about any time.'

That answers my question, Edmund thought, and explains so much about Marko. How different from his own upbringing as an only child in a household where there were servants. Neither his father nor mother had been a true parent to him, the task having been shared by uncle Philippe, captain Watts, the household servants and the various schoolmasters at Winchester. His father had been a distant, shadowy figure whose influence had only counted during the last two or three years. How, he asked himself, could a family be a rock-solid team as long as boys were sent to boarding school for nearly three-quarters of the year? Try as it might, no school could duplicate the experience of family life, but seemed rather to encourage perversity.

'And one question from me,' Edmund said at last. 'You never really told us how you came to join the Royal Naval Volunteer Reserve and cast your lot with us aboard *Troubadour*.'

'You're going to think me crazy,' Marko replied. 'I was in a London pub, oh, about eighteen months ago, and I got talking to a very decent fellow who suggested we play a game of darts. I thought myself quite passable at darts and at first this guy didn't seem good at all. We didn't play for money, but on our last game he made an offer I couldn't refuse; he'd pay me a hundred pounds if I won the game; join the RNVR if I lost. They say I'm a fast learner and I learned pretty quick that day. I swear he was the best darts player in London and his name was de Bongard Percival Sykes, Order of the British Empire, Royal Naval Reserve.'

Edmund let out a hoot of glee. 'Our flotilla leader!'

'Well, I went in front of a navy selection board,' Marko went on, 'you know what they ask me? Whether I play cricket. I swallowed and said, "yes, and darts as well." I hoped they wouldn't want anyone who played silly games. Anyhow I was wrong and they took me. Mind you, they made sure I knew my seamanship and navigation.

'In June I finished at the Inns of Court and was sent on training courses, including a month at Whale Island, where they teach gunnery. That's where Edmund and I first bumped into each other. I said to myself that I can always resign if I don't like it, but that was before they posted me to *Troubadour*. Now there's nothing would make me resign, unless the Canadian navy wanted me. That might be different.'

The bishop, Mrs Casswell and Edmund let out a sort of collective sigh.

'What an extraordinary story,' the bishop said, 'is that how they recruit for the navy?'

'I don't know how they do it officially, but I met up with Johnny Pearl, the yachtsman who sailed half around the world single-handed. One board member asked him if he was the pearl of great price, but he'd heard all that before and said, "no, I'm the one that got cast in front of the swine." They made him a lieutenant-commander and put him in charge of a torpedo-boat flotilla.'

Even the bishop smiled and it seemed that the moment had come for Mrs Casswell to change the conversation.

'Now don't forget, everyone, we're invited to the choir party. There's a buffet supper with dancing and singing.'

'If I sing they'll throw me out,' Marko said.

'That's where you're wrong, they only throw people out if they don't sing,' Edmund retorted.

Edmund recalled that a few years earlier the controversy about admitting women to the cathedral choir had rocked the clergy and congregation. Boy sopranos, like Edmund himself, had served until that time, but boys with good voices were hard to find and it seemed that they were losing their voices at increasingly young ages. The time had been reached when the choirmaster simply couldn't manage the difficult music without women sopranos whose presence, however, created a furore. Saint Paul, had he not written that no woman's voice should be raised in church? The bickering and ill-will of which the Church was capable on this as on many other topics was a sad reflection on the Church and the small-mindedness of churchgoers. Oh well, Edmund thought, with women in the choir the music is better and they do organise a good party.

Later, bathed, shaved and in uniform he and Marko went downstairs where Tom served them drinks.

'What about the girls?' Marko asked as he sipped his whisky and soda.

'If I may suggest, sir,' Tom broke into the discussion, 'based on a considerable understanding of these things, I would say the redhead soprano is your best bet. She has a big voice, rather coloratura, and she's powerful in the upper register. She has passion in her voice and indeed elsewhere. If she don't come through, then it has to be the dark-haired contralto with the big 'uns, you know what I mean. A splash more soda, sir?'

'Which reminds me,' Edmund said, 'you won't forget to splash water on the garden, will you, Tom?'

'Oh no, sir. And if I may add another word, there's an absolute smasher of a blonde just joined the choir; shy, mind you, and probably needs a bit of careful cultivation . . .'

'Oh good, you're having a drink.' It was Mrs Casswell at the door. 'I hope Tom is looking after you . . .'

'Our every need,' from Marko.

'Still talking about gardening? I heard the word "cultivation". How magnificent you both look in your uniforms.'

'Anything for you, madam? A sherry?'

'No thanks, Tom.'

Mrs Casswell was wearing a silver-grey evening gown of austere cut, trimmed very sparsely with blue and with a small diamond brooch. It looked stunning in a restrained way and Marko used the French language to express his compliments.

Later that evening, the bishop and Mrs Casswell having departed after the buffet dinner, Edmund and Marko found themselves at a large table near the dance floor. Both were tolerable dancers, Edmund a good average, Marko better than that, and being in naval uniform they were the object of much attention. Everyone remembered Edmund from his days in the choir and while the tenors and bases clamoured to shake his hand the sopranos wanted a dance with him. How strange, he found himself saying, that at a navy party you are categorised by the gold on your sleeve; at a choir party by the register of your voice.

Tom had been right, absolutely right, about the red-headed soprano. She sang *O for the Wings of a Dove* with feeling, but Marko's intuition told him that it wasn't the wings of a dove that turned her on. They danced several times together, then slipped away unobtrusively. 'I'll see the back door's left open,' Edmund whispered.

Tom's 'smashing blonde' caught Edmund's eye almost immediately. She sang with a pleasant but rather juvenile voice that needed training and discipline. She had studied music, she said, and hoped to become a teacher. Her conversation, however, was pitiful. She was one of the world's innocent bystanders; beautiful and uncomprehending. By the time she had asked him which psalm he liked his eyes had become glazed and he realized that the robust world of *Troubadour* had washed away his youth and innocence. A year or two before the answer might have been the one about being glad when they said *Let us go up to the House of the Lord*. Now the only psalm he could relate to was where you go down to the sea in ships and occupy yourself in great waters. Oh well, he thought, Tom did his best; he was right about the need for ample cultivation. Which reminded him of Marko and the redhead who by this time would doubtless be lying down in some variant of a green pasture.

The next day Edmund introduced Marko to the mysteries of fly-fishing. They studied the stream, collected samples of the flies which the trout were rising to, then tied artificial flies which were meant to resemble them. Edmund showed Marko how to cast the fly over a likely spot and let it drift downstream for a few yards. It had never occurred to Marko that fishing could be so like hunting. You creep up on your quarry and outwit him by dropping a fly a few feet from his nose. If he doesn't take your offering you put on another and present him with a change of diet. Until that time Marko had though of fishing either as scooping them up in nets, or sport fishing as waiting till the fish decided to come to you.

The days passed pleasantly enough and the bishop began to

understand, a little at a time, the kind of life that Edmund and Marko had been living and the attachment they had conceived for their comrades and their ship. One evening Edmund judged the moment opportune and spoke about their daily lives on board and the great convoys of ships which crossed the ocean under their care. He spoke of the men who worked below the waterline in the engine room and boiler rooms, of those who laboured in the ammunition and depth-charge magazines when the ship went into action. He also recounted the needy circumstances in which many of them had been raised, emphasizing that they were still in their teens and early twenties but had learned to accept the harsh demands of seagoing in time of war.

The bishop listened and did not interrupt. His brow furrowed when Edmund spoke of their moody and strange captain whose seamanship was of such a high order, but who was so erratic when he went ashore. He spoke of the minesweepers they had encountered in Gibraltar which had attracted no buyers between the wars at a hundred and fifty pounds and which the captain had described as being out-of-date at the beginning of the last war, never mind this one. Finally he spoke of the incomprehension of those in high places who could not accept the need for small vessels as a valid part of the navy and the price they had paid for their obtuseness at the time of the Dardanelles.

Edmund was careful not to place the blame for England's predicament where he knew it belonged, upon the unrepentant shoulders of his father's generation, but the bishop would have been uncomprehending indeed if he had failed to perceive the implication. For a long time he remained silent, then rose and crossed the room. Mrs Casswell and Marko were playing bridge with the dean and Mrs Potter in another room. He finally turned to Edmund and said something that struck Edmund as being a total withdrawal from reality, an example of wishful thinking on the grand scale.

'The war is not going to last; you have my word on it. It is not our war and I'm at a loss to know how we became involved. All this belligerence will soon be a thing of the past.'

'Well,' Edmund replied, 'in case it doesn't end as soon as you think, there's just one matter I want to mention. It would distress me to think of mother having to deal with my belongings if I were reported missing, so I've decided to take all my old clothes to the ship and what I don't need I'll give away. There'll be nothing here except my bicycle and with petrol rationing on the horizon someone might find it useful.'

His father looked at him.

'I hope and pray that it will not come to that.'

In the weeks and months that followed Edmund's mind would return many times to that conversation. A quick end to the war? It made absolutely no sense. What had his father heard or read?

It occurred to Edmund that he might try again to get a supply of warm clothes from the cathedral congregation. A few castoffs, surely that's not asking much. But he knew what difficulties would be raised; 'approval from the appropriate committee', 'dean and chapter', 'people's wardens . . .' No, the Church wasn't organised for efficiency or even for good deeds. It would take days, weeks; there are times when you might as well not bother and if his father thought the war would soon be over they would use it as an excuse for doing nothing.

A shadow crossed Edmund's mind. Was this the organization for which he himself had been destined? A Church that can't say a prayer for a poor dead sailor, a dean who's drunk half the time, a congregation that can't be expected to rouse itself and part with a few old clothes? Was that to have been the arena in which his life was to have been lived?

Chapter 12

'WOULD YOU GENTLEMEN happen to be for one of the following ships?' the ticket collector asked as Edmund and Marko passed through the barrier at Lime Street Station; '*Harp, Minstrel, Troubadour, Chorister?*'

'Yes, we are,' Edmund replied.

'Then kindly report to the desk over there manned by naval personnel.'

They found a chief petty officer of the Regulating Branch seated at a table near the main entrance.

'There's been a delay,' he began. 'Officers are to proceed to this address. Your names and ships, please?'

'Casswell and Cyr; *Troubadour.*'

He found their names and ticked them off.

'Are we the first to arrive?'

'No, sir. Mr Dobreiner arrived two hours ago. He took a taxi to the hotel seeing as how I can't send a bus unless there's a full load.'

'We'll do the same. With all this kit we're going to need two taxis.'

'Where will the ship's company be quartered?' Edmund asked.

'We've taken over a hotel,' was the reply. 'It'll only be a couple of days, as I understand.'

'Not serious,' were Dobreiner's first words, 'new starboard propellor for *Chorister* and asdic dome replacement for *Harp*. We were still hoping for RDF sets, but the answer is negative; no sets, no operators.'

They settled into their rooms, then went downstairs.

'What do we do for two days in this place?' Edmund asked.

'For me, it's work on the Knatchbull case,' Marko replied. 'The petty officers can help me.'

'What do they know about law?'

'Nothing, but there's work all the same. I want them out investigating, asking questions.'

An hour later a bus pulled up and Pemberton and Reece arrived with some twenty officers from the other ships, commander Sykes among them.

'Where's our captain?' Marko asked.

'Come to my room for a minute,' Pemberton replied. 'Braithwaite's been delayed,' he began when the door was closed. 'He phoned me at home and told me to take command of the ship until he gets there. Commander Sykes knows about it.'

'Sick?' Edmund asked.

'Nothing so simple. It seems that he and Lucinda Braithwaite went to the cinema near where they lived. Lucinda got held up in the ladies' room and Braithwaite went outside and waited. He was in civilian clothes and two girls accosted him and said he ought to be ashamed for not being in uniform. He told them what they could do, as you might expect, and it seems that a third person got involved who shoved Braithwaite. He didn't like that and punched him.'

'Wouldn't you know it,' Marko said.

'Lucinda came out to find our esteemed captain shouting at an angry crowd; two girls screaming their heads off and mister whoever-he-was groaning in the gutter. Now he has to appear in court. All this about a week ago.'

'Sounds like there was provocation,' Marko said. 'I wouldn't mind defending him.'

'One other thing,' Pemberton went on. 'My wife Nancy called Lucinda Braithwaite on a sympathetic woman-to-woman basis and it seems that Braithwaite told the two girls that he was the captain of a bloody fine ship and that to insult him was to insult the men under his command.'

'And me, I ask myself what the film was about,' Marko said shaking his head. 'Did the good guys clobber the bad guys?'

Two days later *Troubadour* and her sister ships were refloated and taken by tug to their berths. Normal shipboard life returned, the ships were cleaned up, *Troubadour* under Edmund's direction since he was now acting first lieutenant. Pemberton had not been officially appointed in command and according to custom Edmund and Marko did not address him as 'sir' but continued to call him 'first lieutenant'. He did, however, attend a captain's meeting in *Minstrel* and was met by questioning glances from the captains of *Chorister* and *Harp.*

'Are we to congratulate you?' one of them asked.

'No, not at all,' Pemberton replied.

Marko, meanwhile, had not been idle. He prevailed on the court to have Knatchbull released from detention and brought under naval guard to *Troubadour* where he was officially confined to the ship. No date had been set for the trial, but the few days before the ship was due to sail were used to good effect. The engine room staff were not fully occupied as long as the boilers were cold so Marko set the three stoker petty officers to work as detectives.

'The surprising thing,' Marko said, 'is how well they do it. In two days they turned up the names and addresses of half a dozen men who slept with her; the record of her being pregnant once before and having a miscarriage, and right here on board we have a telegraphist who was at the dance and saw her messing around with Knatchbull. This doesn't prove that he did nor didn't rape her, but it sure as hell is going to influence the jury.

'And talking about influencing the jury, I'm having the two youngest seamen in the ship, plus the midshipman, to sit in front of the jury in their best uniforms; right slap in front of them. They can carry papers and run errands for me, but the point is that they'll be there in full view; innocent, disciplined and very young. All of them on that jury, man or woman, will secretly wish they had boys like that. Then another thought will come to them and they'll ask themselves why we put children in uniform and send them to war. Is this a children's crusade? How did the country get in this mess? It's going to make the rape case look stupid and we'll send them to the jury room with other things on their minds.'

Marko went on to say that he felt confident of an acquittal if he were handling the case on his own, but thought the court-appointed lawyer was only half committed to Knatchbull's interests and too old for the work. The difficulty was Knatchbull's admission that he used some force. He claimed to have had experience with other women and concluded that there's a type of girl who doesn't want to be thought of as 'easy'. She puts up a show of resistance and expects to have it opposed; indeed she seems to enjoy an element of struggle. The questions that would be asked in court would concentrate on the amount of struggle and whether it was serious or playful. Marko thought that there was no menace in Knatchbull's actions and that he could obtain an acquittal on that ground. However, he was going to be careful to leave nothing to chance and would keep Knatchbull from giving evidence on his own behalf. Like all honest people Knatchbull thought that all he had to do was enter the box and speak the truth, which would give the prosecution the right to cross-examine. He had already said too much in his statement to police and was bound to make a fool of himself if he was allowed to give his testimony and expose himself to questions.

'What surprises do they have?' Marko asked. 'What are they holding back? I can't believe that the case is as straightforward as this.'

The mood aboard *Troubadour* was one of perplexity during the days that followed. Rumours that the captain was facing criminal charges swirled about the lower deck and while details were lacking it was rumoured that he had stood up for the reputation of the ship. That was what they wanted to believe; their captain, temperamental but solid as a rock, wouldn't let them down when it came to dealing with the outside world. But it did seem strange that he had been detained. What was the Admiralty doing? The first lord? Didn't they care about the captains of their ships?

As soon as *Troubadour* and her sister ships were out of dockyard hands the depth charges were reloaded, ammunition, stores and supplies taken back on board and the ship prepared for sea. On a Friday in mid-April they were ordered to raise steam. As the moment approached for them to sail there was still no sign of Braithwaite so Pemberton remained in command.

'Hands to stations for leaving harbour,' he told Edmund. 'Single up to a backspring,' and Edmund passed it on to Harding on the forecastle and Fenway aft.

'Shall I take in the gangway?' Edmund asked.

'No, hold it a minute,' Pemberton replied. 'Wait till *Minstrel's* clear.'

Minstrel was alongside. She slipped her lines and began to move, a jet of water thrusting out from beneath her transom. Commander Sykes on *Minstrel's* bridge was only a few feet away.

'Good luck,' he said to Pemberton and leaned down to the voicepipe.

Pemberton went to the after end of the bridge.

'All right Casswell, you can . . .' but he stopped in mid-sentence. A car was hurtling down the jetty towards the ship, bumping crazily over the rail lines and cobblestones. It came to a stop a few feet from the gangway and out stepped Braithwaite one side and Lucinda the other. Braithwaite shouted to the men on the upper deck and half a dozen ran across the gangway and seized his luggage from the car. In seconds they were back on board with Braithwaite behind them.

'Take in the gangway,' Edmund called out, 'stand by to let go.' A seaman took turns off the bollard and stood waiting.

Braithwaite ran up to the bridge and Pemberton saluted.

'Engine room ready to obey telegraphs. Order one, sir. Speed eight knots.'

'Thank you. Let go. Slow ahead; port ten. Where's the wind?'

'Offshore.'

Braithwaite moved across the bridge and waved to Lucinda. It was a brief motion, more like a salute, and she returned it with a small gloved hand. Both doors of the car had remained open, which she ignored; she just stood there waving, her eyes fixed upward at the bridge. Braithwaite wanted to tell her to close the car doors, to make it look ship-shape and seamanlike, but he said nothing and the distance between them began to increase.

'May I leave the bridge; I'll send Casswell up,' Pemberton asked.

'Yes, very good. Thank you. Does anyone know where we're going?'

'Commander Sykes didn't say.'

A moment later Edmund was on the bridge.

'Casswell on the bridge, sir. Have we signalled *Minstrel* that you have resumed command?'

'Do so,' Braithwaite said.

'Leading signalman. To *Minstrel, commanding officer aboard 1159 hours.*'

He turned to Braithwaite again. 'May I have the keys of your luggage? Your cabin was cleaned thoroughly when we got out of the dockyard. I'll have someone unpack your gear.'

'Thank you, Casswell.' He took keys from his pocket and handed them to Edmund then looked toward his wife still standing on the jetty and the car doors, still open. The distance was increasing.

'Get my binoculars,' he said, and a seaman slid down the handrails to the deck below.

With engine and helm orders he turned the ship and came in astern of *Minstrel. Chorister* and *Harp* were slipping from the jetty upriver. Lucinda Braithwaite would have been uncomprehending indeed had she not been struck by the controlled activity and sense of purpose of the four ships as they put to sea. Perhaps she would also have seen beauty in the scene, the fine spring day, the gray ships and white seagulls wheeling above.

'Your cabin's going to be ready in half an hour. The steward says he doesn't know where you want everything, but he'll do his best.'

'Thank you, Casswell. That's the thing about the navy; it's so like a family.'

'Yessir; and if I may say so, your wife looked very striking as she stood on the jetty. It's something you'll want to remember.'

'I hope she remembered to pack my chilli peppers.'

Edmund smiled to himself. 'Shall I take the ship?'

'Yes, you have her. The quartermaster is following *Minstrel*. I wonder where it'll be this time.'

Edmund stepped up to the compass. 'Merchantmen have been putting to sea all morning. North Atlantic, I expect, right across, the way we did last time. None of this Western Approaches stuff.'

Within an hour they had picked up a large convoy outside Liverpool. Ships of all shapes and descriptions dotted the sea;

tankers, merchantmen, even a couple of small liners. *Minstrel* ordered *Chorister* to remain at the rear of the convoy, then led *Troubadour* and *Harp* to open water ahead. *Troubadour* took her usual station a thousand yards on *Minstrel*'s port hand. The course was westerly, which meant that the commodore, acting on instructions from the Admiralty, was taking the southerly route through St George's channel and round the south coast of Ireland.

One of the merchant ships dropped astern of the convoy in spite of pleas and threats from *Chorister*. During the night she continued to lose ground and was out of sight by morning. Her last cry, like that of an innocent creature struck down by predators was picked up by the wireless operator. 'Hit by torpedoes; crew . . .' and the rest was silence.

So we're back to work, Edmund said to himself. The ship is as good as new, the men are experienced and we've just had some leave; all except able seaman Knatchbull. Why does this ship get itself into all these tangles? Braithwaite in trouble, although he seems to be over it; Knatchbull turning a supposed act of love into an accumulation of sordid legalities. Is *Troubadour* an unlucky ship? What we need is a quiet crossing so we can get back in stride. No U-boats, no ships sunk and New York please, not Halifax.

It was the third day out with Reece on the bridge and Braithwaite sitting in the captain's chair with his eyes closed that a torpedo struck a merchantman at the rear of the convoy. A few minutes later *Harp* dropped a pattern of depth charges which exploded with a rumble like distant thunder.

'We'll go to action stations in two minutes,' Braithwaite ordered.

'*Go to Harp's assistance*,' *Minstrel* signalled.

'Acknowledge,' Braithwaite called out. He turned to Reece. 'Put that in the log, first the exact time, . . .'

'Ping-ding, ping-ding.'

Braithwaite stiffened, his attention focussed on the asdic.

'Hold that echo,' he ordered.

'Ping-ding, ping-ding.'

'Action stations.'

The signalman jumped forward and pressed the alarm bell and

the men who were not on duty leaped to life, pulled on coats and boots and ran for their battle stations.

Edmund had been in his cabin. He took his cap and binoculars and was on the bridge in seconds. He seized his asdic headphone and listened.

'U-boat,' he said. 'Echo high.'

The bridge suddenly filled. The leading signalman and both signalmen, two more lookouts, a communications rating and the spare asdic operator.

'One-five-four revolutions. Attacking.' Braithwaite called down the voicepipe. 'Steer two-seven-five degrees.' Then to the leading signalman, 'hoist large red flag to indicate we have a contact. Signal *Minstrel "Have U-boat contact thousand yards ahead . . ."*'

'Coxswain on the wheel, sir,' came a reassuring voice from the wheelhouse. 'One-five-four revolutions. Course two-seven-five degrees.'

'Echo high,' Edmund reported. 'She's moving towards us. The depth charges are set for standard emergency pattern. Distance six hundred yards.'

Reece, very composed, called up from the chartroom, 'I've started plotting and it looks like a head-on attack.'

Braithwaite spoke to Edmund. 'I expect she'll turn one way or the other; tell me as soon as you know.' Then he picked up the phone to the first lieutenant's position, 'we have a U-boat contact and we'll be firing a full pattern of charges in one minute.'

'Echo high,' Edmund said. 'Operating conditions good. Range four hundred yards.'

'Lookouts,' Braithwaite shouted, 'keep watch ahead. U-boat.'

'Sir,' Edmund called out, 'we might pass directly over on this attack. Tell Reece to switch on the echo-sounder and get her depth.'

'Switch on echo-sounder,' Braithwaite ordered.

'Enemy coming straight on. Echo high. Range three hundred,' Edmund reported.

'Ding-ding, ding-ding' from the asdic. The decreasing distance made the return 'ding' sound closer to the outgoing.

'She's not turning. Go straight over.'

'Dingding, dingding,' the range was closing.

'Range one hundred.'

A few seconds later Edmund began pressing the firing button and a pattern of ten depth charges sailed out from the throwers and fell from the stern chutes. The explosions came with a numbing, shattering effect and cones of water were thrust upward from the surface of the sea.

'I picked her up,' Reece called out; 'somewhere between eighty and a hundred feet.'

Damn, Edmund thought. If they had been set for a hundred feet then the submarine would have been surrounded by explosions within a few feet of its hull. As it was, they were a few feet too high.

Braithwaite turned the ship to starboard and opened the distance to four hundred yards. At that point he stopped engines and went astern to take way off and told Edmund to search for the U-boat as soon as the explosions were dissipated.

'Ping,' went the asdic, but no answering 'ding'.

'Cut left,' Edmund ordered. 'Cut left again.'

'Ping-ding, ping-ding.'

'We have it,' he shouted. 'Hold that echo.'

'Ping-ding,' it went again.

'Captain sir,' the leading signalman called out, 'convoy closing.'

Braithwaite looked toward the convoy and sure enough it was maintaining its course. A line of four ships was bearing down on *Troubadour*.

'Four blasts on the siren,' Braithwaite ordered. 'Signal the leading ship to give me a wide berth. Can't they see my red flag?'

'Aye aye, sir,' from the leading signalman, and he jumped toward an Aldis lamp and began tapping it out. The leading ship, however, a ten-thousand-ton vessel, ploughed on towards them.

'Ping-ding', went the asdic.

'Range four hundred,' Edmund reported. 'Echo same. I think she's diving deeper.'

'Very well.'

A pause.

'She doesn't reply,' said the leading signalman. 'They're all dead aboard that ship.'

'Fire a red rocket,' shouted Braithwaite, 'and switch on fighting lights.'

The leading signalman did so and the merchant vessel, now a scant six hundred yards distant, bore down on them relentlessly, a huge bow wave ahead of her. Astern of her the other ships had turned away.

'Casswell,' Braithwaite yelled, 'go down to the depth charge deck and fire one from the thrower. Get the bastards to turn.'

'Aye aye, sir,' and Edmund tore off his headset, leaped to the ladder, slid down on his hands, then the ladder below and raced down the deck to the depth charge throwers.

'Captain's orders,' he shouted, 'fire a depth charge and wake up this bastard.' He pointed at the ship which looked as though it was trying to cut them in half.

The torpedomen were reloading and had started with the throwers on the starboard side.

'Set this charge for two hundred feet,' he ordered, and a torpedoman thrust his hand into the depth charge and set the depth.

'Set for two hundred. Ready to fire.'

Edmund grabbed the firing lanyard and then looked back at the ship which was now no more than four hundred yards away. If she maintained her present course she'd hit and sink *Troubadour*; nothing could save her from that huge ship, ten times her size. He pulled the lanyard and the depth charge sailed off the thrower and struck the sea somewhere between *Troubadour* and the merchant ship. For a few seconds it sank and then exploded with a roar.

'Reload,' Edmund shouted, and ran back to the bridge where he resumed his headset and listened intently.

'I think we've found it, but not very clear,' reported the operator.

'Ding-unch' went the asdic. 'Ding-unch.'

'Cut right,' Edmund ordered.

'Ding-unch,' went the asdic again.

'Right again.'

'Ding-shinn.'

'Hold that one.'

For the next few seconds the men on *Troubadour*'s bridge watched in horrified silence as the merchant vessel came relentlessly on. There was nothing Braithwaite could do to get clear, because it would have taken *Troubadour* almost a minute for the power on the ship's screws to overcome inertia and get her moving through the water. She was condemned to remain where she was and watch the bows of a ten-thousand-ton ship lunge toward her.

Braithwaite knew he had done everything that naval regulation and ancient custom required. He had hoisted the large red flag which means 'I am hunting a U-boat, keep clear of me'. He had sounded four blasts on the siren which means 'get out of my way because I cannot get out of yours'. He had fired a rocket to call attention to his predicament and switched on his fighting lights, an array of lights on the mast and yard-arm which added one more exclamation mark.

If this had occurred at night, he thought, it might be attributed to ignorance, poor seamanship, inefficient lookouts, an officer on watch who deserved immediate court martial and a captain who was unfit to command, but this was broad daylight, which made it worse. *Troubadour*'s depth charges, a ton and a half of high explosive, should have alerted the fools and given them all the time needed to turn away.

'Sound four blasts again,' Braithwaite called to the signalman who, glad to have something to do, pulled the lever four times, making the steam whistle on the funnel scream out its message.

'Her stern is swinging to port, sir,' Edmund called out at last. 'She's making a starboard turn. Let's hope she takes wheel off quickly or she'll hit us broadside.'

Braithwaite was thinking the same and seemed to be helping the merchant captain to give the correct order. 'Midships, midships, you arsehole. Now put ten degrees of port wheel on and swing your stern clear of me.'

The merchantman missed *Troubadour* by less than twenty feet. High above *Troubadour* as they passed someone looked down at them and shook his fist, actually shook his fist at them.

Braithwaite was at the side of the bridge and shouted up, 'I hope the U-boats...' then *Troubadour* was hit by the bow wave and he grabbed the rail to steady himself. Suddenly it became pointless even to shout as the black side of the ship slipped past. As the stern went by Edmund could smell cooking from the after deckhouse.

Braithwaite turned away in utter disgust and Edmund attempted to relocate the U-boat, but the merchantman had left a huge wake of turbulence between *Troubadour* and the enemy which the asdic couldn't penetrate. What was worse, they were now inside the phalanx of ships and the U-boat, at its best speed of seven knots, would hear the ships above and make its escape.

'I'm sorry, sir, I've lost it,' Edmund said, 'and it's not much use searching with all these ships round us.'

Braithwaite was white and shaking. 'Casswell,' he said, 'prepare a signal to *Minstrel* repeated to the commodore and tell them what happened. Use any language you please and try to convey the extent of my frustration.' He paused. 'Haul down large red flag. Switch off fighting lights. We're still under orders to go to the assistance of *Harp*.'

'You know, sir, we are supposed to be a security for those who pass on the seas on their lawful occasions; at least that's what the navy prayer says. Some of them don't make it easy for us. I hope you'll press a formal complaint.'

'Imagine how I feel. I'm a professional seaman,' Braithwaite mumbled.

He took the ship up to twenty-two knots and steamed toward *Harp*, which had lost contact. The stricken merchant ship lay over on its side and *Harp* was now moving in to pick-up survivors. She signalled *Troubadour* to circle her in case the U-boat was still in the area. They watched as the torpedoed ship rolled over and plunged downward leaving a thin whisp of white smoke in the air. Boats, debris and swimming men littered the sea.

For the next three days and nights, until the convoy reached the mid-Atlantic mark, they came under continuous attack from U-boats. At one point the commodore made a course alteration to the south and then west again, but the U-boats, thought to have been five in number, were not deterred. Four merchant ships were sunk, but one other, although torpedoed, was able to continue under its own power. All the ships of *Minstrel's* flotilla had made asdic contact at one time or another and twelve patterns of depth charges had been dropped. *Harp* claimed a 'possible' kill. The ships were continuously at action stations and on the upper deck officers and men alike were so tired that food and drink seemed unimportant while a sleep of four hours was an unbelievable luxury. Below decks it was easier because men working the ammunition hoists, the fire and damage control parties could sit or lie on the steel decks and sleep fitfully.

On the sixteenth day out from Liverpool the convoy entered New York and the four escort vessels broke away from their charges and steamed into the watery heart of the great city. The men were dirty and bearded, their ships foul-smelling, low on fuel and provisions, but those were defects which could be remedied in a few hours. The malaise in their minds would be harder to put aside. The long wastes of ocean, the torpedo tracks and the stricken ships; the oil-covered men whom they rescued from the sea and the merchantman that almost rammed *Troubadour;* such were the stark memories that could not easily be banished. A sleep, a good meal and a drink would help, long moments spent in the oblivion of hot water and then clothes that smelled clean, anything but the stench of sweat and death. Yes, these would salve the pain and perhaps the great city would ease their minds with its traffic and teeming people, its light and its wonders. The cure was to be here or nowhere; it was May Day, and New York was at peace, a city not of joy but of plenty.

Yet, even as they came alongside the jetty and secured their ships, all four together, they learned that the world was on the brink of catastrophe. They received the BBC on the ship's wireless, but the long days and nights at battle stations, the fatigue and preoccupation with their own concerns meant that they didn't concentrate their minds on outside news. The phoney war, it seemed, was over, and the Germans had begun the rape of Europe.

'You know something?' Edmund said as he stared into the depths of his wineglass, 'the Norwegian campaign has encouraged the Germans. Now they have Swedish iron ore and Norwegian naval bases and they aren't going to stop. They've got their maps on the table; what we've seen so far is only the beginning. My uncle with his business interests in France says the French are in no mood to fight. They're not cowards, but they're fed up; lost their confidence.'

'What about the Maginot line?' Reece asked. 'They claim it'll stop anything.'

'If I was the German army I'd go round it,' Pemberton said.

Braithwaite looked down the table at his officers. Whatever he may have thought of them eight months earlier when the ship commissioned, whatever reservations he may have harboured about their competence and dedication, he trusted them now and even enjoyed their company. These young men from different backgrounds had formed a team as dependable as he could have wished for. Only Gus Dobreiner had been specifically trained for a career at sea and he had 'come up the hawse pipe' or whatever the engine room equivalent was. He had begun as a stoker and worked his way to warrant officer rank. He had been wrong about the others, thought they lacked stamina, were sissy. Now that he knew them he felt himself lucky and well served. He leaned back in his chair and changed the subject.

'Did you let Knatchbull go ashore?'

'Yessir,' Pemberton replied. 'There's not the least chance he'll desert. Coxswain warned him to stay with his messmates and not go off by himself.'

'When are they going to hear his case?'

'No date set,' Marko answered. 'When we return to Liverpool I'll be in touch with the prosecution and tell them about the evidence I've collected. Unless they have some surprise for us; something I don't know about; it should blow the case away. The sickening thing is that the court-appointed lawyer would never have discovered what we discovered. He's too old and stupid and besides appearing in court and collecting his fee he wasn't going to do anything.'

Braithwaite had said nothing about his own case, and as they sat round the wardroom table Marko sensed that the moment had come when he could tactfully raise the subject.

'Sir, may I ask a question?' Marko began. 'We were worried when we heard you'd got involved in some trouble ashore and were going to be delayed.'

He looked at Pemberton. 'Maybe the first lieutenant knows more than the rest of us, but I think we all want to be assured that it ended up all right.'

'Very well, I'll tell you about it,' Braithwaite said, 'although I'm damned if it's any of your business.

'I was in civvies outside the cinema waiting for my wife. She can spend a bloody age in the ladies room; I often wonder what she finds to do in there. A couple of tarts saw me and came barging up with a long harangue about my not being much of a man and that I should be in the army. I told them I commanded a ship and was serving my country as well as the next. I suggested they mind their own business and it was bloody obvious what their business was.

'One of them said something along the lines "some rotten ship you've got" and called me a dirty liar. I told her she could insult me if it gave her any pleasure, but I was damned if she was going to insult my ship or the brave men who served in it. At about this point I gave her a good slap in the face.

'It was then that an employee of the cinema in a green uniform marched up and grabbed me by the collar. He was large, fat and officious and he probably thought his size would be the deciding factor. I broke free and gave him a very good one precisely on the jaw.

'My wife Lucinda was next to arrive on the scene and I told her that if she'd gone a bit faster in the ladies poop-house none of this would have happened. The two women were screaming, the fat usher had concussion and a crowd had collected. You know what she said, "Really, I can't leave you alone for a moment." '

They tried to stifle their laughter.

'I was hauled in front of the local magistrates for causing a disturbance and hitting the usher. Of course by that time I was in uniform and told them what *Troubadour* had been doing since war was declared; the places we'd been, the weather in the North Atlantic during the winter, the battles we'd fought, the convoys we'd protected. I told them how proud I was of the ship and the men who served in it and, as captain, I wasn't going to be pushed around by some jackass who wasn't a quarter as good as any of my men. They didn't even bother to go outside and consider their verdict, they just looked at each other, nodded and the chairman told me I was acquitted. On the way out I told Flabby Joe to get off his arse and join the navy.'

It was as though a dam had broken and they roared with laughter.

The flotilla was almost a week in New York and then sailed for Halifax where an eastbound convoy was being assembled. The days became longer as they sailed northwards and the news from Europe continued to draw every man to the wireless set. The German armies were slicing into Belgium and Holland.

Halifax was their least favoured port of call. It was a dreary place which had nothing to offer; no entertainment, deplorable beer, and girls, as a species, seemed to have gone extinct. Even sailors with money in their pockets saw no reason to walk ashore and the officers couldn't find a decent restaurant that served wine so they stayed in their wardrooms.

In mid-May they were at sea again with an eastbound convoy. Two old destroyers, *Venice* and *Vane*, were with them and came under commander Sykes' orders. He decided that there would be no change in the dispositions that had worked well up to that point, himself in *Minstrel* directly ahead of the convoy, *Troubadour* on his port hand, *Harp* away to starboard and *Chorister* astern. The two newcomers would be on the wings to protect from flank attack.

Wardroom conversation in *Troubadour* turned briefly to the two destroyers which were more than twenty years old. Their torpedoes had been taken out and replaced by small-calibre guns, but even with the weight reduction on the upper deck they rolled abominably due to their absurdly rounded hulls.

'I served in one of that class on the China station,' Dobreiner said. 'They're scarcely fit to go to sea. They need fifty tons of concrete in the double bottoms to stop the roll, bilge keels and a modern gun armament. And while you're at it, build up the bows so they go over the waves and not through them.'

'In other words you might as well scrap them and start again,' someone said.

The convoy took a northerly route past Iceland and was not

attacked until the seventh day. *Vane* got a contact and dropped two patterns, then a tanker was torpedoed. These were the preliminaries to a sustained attack by U-boats which were, however, deterred by the six escort ships. Then, almost within sight of the coast of Ireland, *Chorister* was hit by a single torpedo. It was night and she never obtained asdic contact. *Venice* went alongside and took off survivors. *Chorister* sank in minutes with her stern blown off. *Minstrel* and *Harp* hunted the U-boat for an hour but failed to make contact.

On *Troubadour*'s bridge they talked about it quietly and Edmund wrote in the log "*0035 Chorister sunk by torpedo. Venice alongside for survivors.*"

'If we'd had that bloody RDF set, it might have been different,' someone said. 'The U-boat must have surfaced.'

The ship's company went about their duties with renewed vigilance. It might so easily have been us, they all seemed to be saying, but it was not until *Minstrel* hoisted *Order 1* to bring the ships in line to enter the Mersey that they realised the extent of their loss. *Harp* came in astern of *Troubadour* and the two destroyers followed. If there had been such a thing as a black flag all ships would have wanted to hoist it. They had left *Chorister* behind at the bottom of the Atlantic.

As they came within sight of the Liver building, a signal was being flashed from the tower, '*Immediately on completion of refuelling and replenishment of fresh water return to sea and proceed with all despatch to the Nore.*'

'The army's being taken off at Dunkirk,' someone said. 'I heard it on the wireless.'

Refuelling took about three hours. When *Venice* came alongside she discharged the survivors of *Chorister* who stood on the jetty waiting for 'Soapy' Hudson to come and take charge. The injured would be driven to the naval hospital, others would receive leave passes and clothing allowances.

They learned that *Chorister*'s captain, the London stockbroker, had remained with the severely wounded on the upper deck of his ship. He could have saved himself by jumping across to *Venice*'s forecastle, but he chose otherwise.

A story later circulated about *Chorister*'s sub-lieutenant. As he sat in a railway compartment on his way home, wearing frayed survivor's clothing and pained by burns, he was assumed to be drunk and asked by an elderly lady to vacate his seat. He refused and another passenger extended something toward him. In his tired and befuddled condition he thought he was being offered something to eat. The passenger had concluded that he was an objectionable civilian who had shirked war service so he handed him a white feather as an imputation of cowardice.

CHAPTER 13

DURING THE LAST days of May, 1940, the condition of the British Expeditionary Force in France had become precarious. The Belgian army capitulated on 28th May, exposing the British flank and leaving no alternative but a retreat to the sea. Unless the navy could come to their rescue the soldiers were doomed to captivity for the remainder of the war. As a point of embarkation there could have been worse places than Dunkirk. It possessed a substantial harbour capable of receiving large vessels, was sheltered to the northern side by sandbanks off the coasts of France and Belgium while the beaches themselves were sandy with dunes set back from the shoreline.

Having steamed up the English channel at his best speed, commander Sykes and his flotilla refuelled at Dover and joined the armada that was being assembled for the rescue operation. Destroyers were the navy's most potent ships present and these were supported by minesweepers, trawlers, tugs and dozens of smaller craft. When *Troubadour* came on the scene the short summer night of 28th May was falling. *Venice* and *Vane* were detached and ordered to join one of the destroyer flotillas.

As Edmund turned his binoculars toward the coast of France, the army, what he could see of it, was waiting in lines, bereft of its weapons and possessed of only a shred of hope. In the town of Dunkirk there were thousands of soldiers, while many more had assembled on the sand dunes to the north of the harbour. They had been under air attack for much of the day and were within range of German guns.

Edmund tried to grasp the situation. This, he said to himself, is what an army looks like in retreat. He was gripped by a feeling of frustration, not against the king's enemies but against a whole generation of smug, self-satisfied pacifists, supposedly friends, whose voices had been heard, whose opinions were respected and who had somehow condoned the primrose path which had led to the beaches of Dunkirk. They had spoken of disarmament, of a phoney war, a war that was not worth fighting: they had announced that the enemy were reasonable, and that the Versailles Treaty was at fault and had compelled Germany to stand up for itself in a few small matters.

Germany had meanwhile turned Europe into an arsenal and armed itself with tanks, guns and aircraft to an extent that was astonishing to the powers that opposed it. It had also armed itself with an additional weapon that outreached the others, an armoury of lies. They lied about themselves, about others, about their intentions. It was as though they elevated their lies and distortions, like their swastika flag, and were proud to have deceived. Damn them, he thought, and damn the people who were taken in. Damn the slobbering fools who preach love and brotherhood; who propose that everyone become as little children. Well, here's our army and they look like little children. They stand abjectly at the bus stop waiting to be taken home.

'What do you see?' Braithwaite asked.

'A bloody mess, sir; a bloody disgrace.'

They entered astern of *Minstrel* and the firing seemed to intensify. Gun flashes and shell bursts which could not be seen in daylight now lit up the horizon and the growling, whining and complaining of weaponry, the full orchestra of battle, increased in volume. The darkness was slow in coming, but did not hide the beached ships, the shell craters, the soldiers milling about.

A naval launch came to within hailing distance of *Troubadour* and an officer with a megaphone called out, 'Captain, your orders are to go alongside the jetty *there*, and take as many soldiers on board as is safe for your ship. Your decision in this matter is final. As soon as they are aboard you are to sail for Dover at your best speed. Is that clear?'

'Yes, perfectly clear,' Braithwaite called back in level tones.

'Thank you. Admiral Wake-Walker hopes to see you again in a

matter of hours. One other thing, the ship astern of you will come in alongside you. What's its name?'

'*Harp*,' someone shouted.

Braithwaite turned to Edmund. 'We have an admiral here, Wake-Walker. I know him. Nothing wrong with him; nothing.'

As Braithwaite took the ship alongside Edmund asked if there was any advice to be given to Pemberton about loading the ship with its human cargo.

'No, he can decide.'

The ship eased alongside a jetty that had just been vacated by a Hunt Class destroyer. Heaving lines sailed through the air and were caught by soldiers who seemed unsure of what they should do with them. Marko, in charge of the forecastle, cupped his hands and called out in his most affected English accent, 'Pull on the rope, you chaps; that's it. The loop at the end fits over the funny metal thing; you got it. Well done.'

The coxswain called up the voicepipe, 'I'll help the first lieutenant, sir. Able seaman McVane standing by for me.'

'Very well, coxswain,' Braithwaite called back.

The gangway was pushed out and attention was focussed on the soldiers marching down the jetty. There seemed to be hundreds of them, a line three-deep that extended back into the darkness. *Harp* came alongside and secured up in silence and Braithwaite crossed the bridge to exchange brief greetings with *Harp*'s captain.

'Very well,' he said to the lieutenant-commander a few feet away on the other bridge. 'So far, so good. When you have your passengers, slip and proceed and I'll overtake you outside the harbour.'

He crossed back to where he could see the jetty and picked up his megaphone. The first company of soldiers halted and a sergeant was dressing them by the right while Pemberton was talking to a group of officers. He called up to the bridge, 'The colonel wants me to convey his compliments and asks if you wish to inspect . . .'

'Get them on board at the double,' Braithwaite bellowed. 'Fill up *Harp* first. Ask the colonel how much his men weigh; how many men make a ton?'

Edmund smiled. Somehow Braithwaite had reduced the idiocy

of a time-wasting inspection in the dark to the mundane question of how much soldiers weigh.

'My guess is about ten to the ton, sir. They don't have much equipment with them; not even rifles.'

'So let's say a hundred men is ten tons,' Braithwaite mumbled. 'I think we can take five hundred but they must be stowed well down in the ship. Only men with rifles and ammunition on the upper deck.'

A steady stream of khaki-clad soldiers was coming over the gangway. By this time it was too dark for Edmund to see their faces but their stumbling movements said it all. The coxswain had teamed up with a sergeant-major and they stood together and kept up a flow of encouragement.

'All right lads, step lively. Sooner you're on board, sooner you'll be 'ome. This ain't the *Queen Mary*, but it'll 'ave to do. Go across to the next ship and don't bump yer heads.'

'Our captain thinks we can take five hundred men provided they are stowed well down in the ship,' Pemberton said to *Harp*'s first lieutenant.

'I'll try four hundred for a start,' he replied.

A few minutes later *Harp* slipped and sailed with well over four hundred, while *Troubadour*, with almost five hundred, was only a few minutes astern of her. A message had come from *Minstrel* that they would be delayed and that *Troubadour* and *Harp* were to proceed to Dover under *Troubadour*'s command.

They steamed out through the breakwater at slow speed out of considerion for the many small craft, then turned westward threading their way between the armada of yachts, lifeboats and tugs. Braithwaite went to the chartroom.

'Warn the lookouts,' he told Edmund, his foot on the ladder, 'enemy E-boats. And keep a sharp eye for our own craft. They're darkened and they're all over the place.'

Edmund could see *Harp* two miles ahead and a little to the north. A yacht was dead ahead so he turned to starboard, made a sweep round it and resumed course to the west. In a few minutes they would overtake *Harp* and could proceed in company. If they found themselves in action against enemy E-boats it would be an advantage for the two ships to combine their firepower. He heard firing to the north-east and saw gun flashes on the horizon, but *Troubadour* was already at action stations and there was nothing more to be done.

Edmund tried to visualise what the situation was like below decks with five hundred soldiers huddled on the steel decks, packed in by their officers and sergeants. If they had been mined or torpedoed it would have been a disaster and he wondered whether Pemberton had ordered them to remove their boots to make it easier if they found themselves in the water. Braithwaite must have known the risk he was taking, but at least the sea was calm and the motion on the ship was slight.

As action officer of the watch Edmund would remain on the bridge as long as the ship was at battle stations. Some captains almost never left the bridges of their ships and insisted on giving every helm and engine order themselves. Braithwaite, however, allowed Edmund to do much of the ship handling and liked to go down to the chartroom which left Edmund on his own.

He leaned down to the voicepipe. 'Who's on the wheel?'

'Kirk, sir,' came a voice.

'Send someone to my cabin and get my coat. My old sea coat in the cupboard.'

A few minutes later a very young seaman was thrusting the coat toward him in the darkness.

'Thank you.'

'It weren't easy,' the boy said, 'there's twelve army gents in your cabin; I counted them. I didn't know where to put me feet and I couldn't open the cupboard door.'

'I hope none of them are smoking or being sick.'

'No sir. First lieutenant has been very strict about that. No naked lights and they can pewk in their 'elmets.'

Twelve of them, Edmund mused. That's almost impossible. It sounds like one of those silly undergraduate pranks, twelve people in a space eight feet by eight. And that ordinary seaman, what was his name, Clegg? He was one of the two chosen by Marko to play 'innocent boy' at Knatchbull's trial. Yes, Marko was going to make fools of the prosecution. Pity the jury couldn't see what was going on aboard *Troubadour*; what Knatchbull and the rest of them were doing at this moment.

Edmund had never locked his cabin door nor even his clothes cupboard, but he did lock his desk where the men's personal files were stored. It seemed to him that he could trust his shipmates where his own property was concerned, but official documents which belonged to the navy were not his to risk. Braithwaite, he knew, was less trusting and kept everything under lock and key. Yet surely it was sad if a captain, or any officer for that matter, had no confidence in the honesty of his men. However, these soldiers were unknown to him and he decided that he would go below and lock everything at the next opportunity.

'Captain on the bridge,' came a voice from the darkness. Edmund lowered his binoculars and moved aside.

'*Harp* is three cables ahead. I'm overtaking on her port side so we can semaphore. There's enough light if we pass close.'

'Yes, go ahead,' Braithwaite replied. Then to the leading signalman, 'When we're abeam make *Order 1, ships in line ahead, speed twenty-two knots.* Use semaphore and execute immediately.'

'You know,' Braithwaite said, turning to Edmund, 'I've been speaking to the colonel of this regiment. He says the army is trying to form a perimeter and hold the Germans back while we take them off. If they break through it's over. Trouble is they have armoured divisions in the neighbourhood and we have no way of stopping armour. The bombing will start again at daybreak.'

At one o'clock in the morning of the 29th *Troubadour* led *Harp* into the small, crowded harbour of Dover. Action stations were stood down and the seamen prepared for coming alongside. Officers, navy and army, were waiting on the jetty and came on board as soon as the gangway was in place. A navy captain hurried up the ladder to the bridge.

'Commanding Officer?' he said, saluting. His four gold rings could be seen in the dark, although the tattered insignia on Braithwaite's shoulders was scarcely visible.

'Yessir,' said Braithwaite.

'Compliments of admiral Ramsay; these are your orders. After unloading, return at your best speed to Dunkirk and bring off one more full load before daybreak. You are senior to *Harp*, so *Harp* will be under your orders. How many men did you bring this time?'

'Just under five hundred, sir.'

'That's good. Any difficulties?'

'Not really. We had a refit recently. I'd like to top up on fuel sometime to-morrow; I mean to-day. Steaming at high speed uses it up.'

'Very well, I'll see that you get alongside the fuel jetty during daylight. Meanwhile, good luck and I'm putting two or three officers on board for passage to Dunkirk. Admiral Wake-Walker has asked for them.'

It took *Troubadour* and *Harp* only a few minutes to disembark their passengers and steam out through the breakwater. Edmund had gone down to his cabin, taken a quick look round and locked his clothes cupboard and the drawers under the bunk. The only article missing was his small, leather picture-frame which had been on the desk. If someone wanted to steal the frame, he asked himself, why couldn't he pull out the pictures and leave them there? Why does some army gent need a picture of my mum and dad and my girlfriend?

Two hours later they were off Dunkirk again and were ordered to a position half a mile offshore to the north of the harbour. Small boats of all descriptions, including lifeboats from the ships in London docks, were being used to ferry soldiers from the beaches to *Troubadour* and *Harp*, but it was a more cumbersome process than having them march on board and daylight came before the two ships had their full quota. Enemy aircraft began to appear, but their bombs, falling in the sand dunes, caused less damage than would have been the case if the ground had been hard.

Edmund turned his binoculars toward the beaches and could see the long lines of men filing across the sand. Poor bastards, he thought; no food, no anti-aircraft weapons, their lives reduced to waiting and hoping. Their discipline at least, had not broken; there's no panic. These, he discovered, were men of the Third Corps which had been engaged in previous days against the German onslaught.

About a dozen aircraft came over, none of them British, and bombs were dropped on Dunkirk town and along the beaches. A few rifles were fired at them and one swung out over the sea and dropped a bomb near *Harp*. It fell out of the aircraft and curved downwards, appearing to increase in size, and hit the sea with a splash and explosion. *Harp*'s four-inch gun and her two oerlikon guns were firing and the plane flew off with smoke pouring from one of its engines.

'I wonder where the Spitfires and Hurricanes are,' Edmund said to no one in particular.

'Their airfields are fifty miles away in Kent,' Braithwaite snapped. 'How do you expect them to be overhead all the time? It would take thousands to put continuous cover over this area. A full squadron would have to take off every few minutes.'

Pemberton appeared on the bridge and reported that they had a full load of soldiers and again the two ships shaped course for Dover. As they gathered speed another air attack developed and six twin-engined bombers flew towards them. Braithwaite leaned over the forward end of the bridge and shouted to Marko to keep firing as long as they were in range. At two thousand yards Marko ordered the first shot and a puff of smoke appeared below the leading aircraft. *Harp* joined the firing, then a trawler some way off to seaward. In a few seconds the oerlikon machine guns were pouring out streams of 20–millimetre tracer and it seemed as though the black, twin-engined aircraft must be hit, but it flew on and released its bomb, aimed at *Troubadour*. Soldiers on the upper deck fired their rifles.

Edmund had his binoculars to his eyes and watched the bomb fall.

'Good Lord,' he said, 'it's painted green.'

The bomb sailed over *Troubadour*'s mast and hit the sea a ship's length on the other side. But the aircraft seemed to falter in the air and a wing suddenly folded upwards. It turned on its side and plunged into the sea. There was a ragged cheer from the men on *Troubadour*'s upper deck. The remaining aircraft turned toward land to find easier targets.

'Well done, gun's crews,' Braithwaite called out.

On 28th May, *Troubadour* and *Harp* had made one round trip from Dover to Dunkirk and return, and on the 29th, their best day, they did three. On the 30th and 31st the difficulties were mounting, ships were sunk or damaged in Dunkirk harbour, air raids and shelling increased and soldiers who had been embarked aboard ships that were sunk had to be rescued a second time. On 1st and 2nd June they were down to one round trip. During all this time *Minstrel* had been operating independently and, according to her instructions, had been conveying her passengers, not to Dover, but to Chatham.

Between them *Troubadour* and *Harp* had rescued six thousand soldiers and had been constantly at action stations. They had suffered some damage, but any pleasure they may have derived from their achievements was crushed when they heard that *Minstrel* had been lost on 1st June. She had received a direct hit from a bomb and lay with her back broken in shallow water. There had been no soldiers on board, but commander Sykes and twenty of his crew were dead.

Commander the Honorable de Bongard Percival Sykes, Edmund said to himself; what a decent, civilised man. He had led his little ships through ten months of war. First to go had been *Chorister*, torpedoed off the north coast of Ireland; now it was *Minstrel*'s turn; a direct hit from a German bomb. *Troubadour* and *Harp* would be left to sail alone and Braithwaite would be in command.

It was not uncommon in wartime for junior officers to respect and admire their commanding officers more than their own fathers. The very circumstances of command often showed an officer at his best; he would rise to the challenge and his years of training and preparation would flower. He became the embodiment of what junior officers hoped they would live long enough to become. Not all captains of ships were like that to be sure, there were a few utter bastards, but many were greatly loved and admired, de Bongard Sykes among them. Edmund turned his binoculars on the corpse of *Minstrel*, beached, broken and helpless.

Again the tired, red-eyed crews of *Troubadour* and *Harp* readied themselves for a final run across the English Channel on the evening of 2nd June. It was to have been their last mission. The Dunkirk perimeter had shrunk to the point where ships and soldiers were under constant artillery attack and aerial bombardment. The harbour was strewn with sunken ships, and the flow of soldiers to be taken off had shrunk to a trickle.

By this time the two ships were dirty and low on provisions and ammunition. Brass cartridge cases littered the upper deck; the lower decks, part covered with linoleum, were pock-marked by the nailed boots of soldiers. Below decks the smell of dirt and defeat was overpowering.

Being ordered to return one final time, the men of *Troubadour* and *Harp* roused themselves for the final effort. As they sailed eastwards that night they passed a stream of small ships sailing west to England. To his amazement Edmund recognised *La Belle Poule*. He wondered if captain Watts was aboard or whether they had installed navy crews. *La Belle Poule*, his old ship, his first love where the sea was concerned.

On the upper deck they scarcely bothered to wave to those closest, they merely shaped course toward the gunflashes, realising that gunfire indicated that resistance was continuing. If the gunfire ceased then resistance had ceased and the port and beaches would fall into enemy hands. A destroyer was ahead of her, so *Troubadour* followed her in and went alongside among a jumble of wrecked ships.

Their passengers this time were mostly French soldiers and the British rearguard. The French were not returning to their country or their homes as were the British soldiers, but leaving France for an unknown destination. On Braithwaite's order, Marko left his position forward and joined Pemberton to welcome them in their own language. Suddenly there were none left and the jetty was deserted except for the naval officer who had acted as loading master.

'Go round to the beaches,' he called to Braithwaite. 'Collect the stragglers. On your return, keep a lookout for boats that may have broken down and take them in tow. If you get too many, take off the men and sink the boats.'

'Understood, but what about you?' Braithwaite called back.

'As long as the rearguard is in action I'll stay here,' came the reply.

The men whom they found on the beaches were mostly wounded so *Troubadour* and *Harp* took them on board as carefully as they could. Finally their task finished, and with dawn rising they shaped course for the Nore. By the time they reached the

Thames estuary they had an assortment of smaller vessels in tow which had broken down or run out of fuel. In one, which had been attacked by an aircraft, the men had been machine-gunned and were all dead, although the vessel itself, surprisingly, had not foundered.

In bright sunlight on a beautiful June afternoon they secured up in their old billet in the Medway and Braithwaite called down, 'Finished with engines.' The gangway was being pushed out, the soldiers were coming up on deck while ambulances, lorries, liaison officers and curious crowds were gathered on the jetty.

Edmund turned to Braithwaite. He didn't salute, he just said very quietly, 'Well done, sir.'

CHAPTER 14

TIRED AND LIGHT-HEADED, Edmund went ashore and found a telephone. His mother answered.

'Edmund, how nice to hear your voice. So you haven't forgotten us. From where do you call?'

'I'm in the south of England. Can't say exactly.'

'Oh, those silly regulations,' she said. 'I don't know what the world is coming to.'

'Mother, it would make no difference if you knew. Please try to understand. I'm terribly tired and I thought you'd want to hear I'm safe, for the time being, at least. Are you and father all right?'

'Safe; what do you mean? You haven't been doing anything foolish have you? I hope you're being careful.'

'Mother, haven't you been reading the papers and listening to the BBC? The war situation is frightful. The French army is falling to pieces. France is being overrun.'

'Oh dear, that's a shame. Your father said that church attendance was up on Sunday because of the war. He thinks the new prime minister is an adventurer who'll take risks. He had a better opinion of Mr Chamberlain.'

'Mother, please listen. Mr Chamberlain has done more than any other man in England to get us in our present state. We're well rid of him. Tell father I called. I must get off the line because other people are waiting for the telephone. I'm rather exhausted.'

'Really, Edmund,' she said angrily, 'you're not the only one who can't sleep. We have our worries which you don't seem to appreciate. Please don't feel you can neglect us.'

Edmund shook his head, 'Bye, mother,' and hung up. He walked back to the ship and decided that in the morning he would phone

Marguerite. The French telephone system was a joke and he'd probably never get through, but at least he'd try.

Edmund often thought of Marguerite these days and wrote to her frequently, hoping against all hope that she was planning to leave France. They had last spoken months before as they walked together among the vines on the family estate. Her mother, a relentless woman, ran the family business which centred on a beautiful and historic vineyard. By the standards of the Bordeaux region it was a large property, but it was going through hard times and the vines were diseased and unproductive. Uncle Philippe had often visited them because at some point in the past Marguerite's mother had been one of his lovers and he showed no hesitation in knocking on doors, whether of château or chalet, where he had eaten, drunk or bedded down. His business, as Edmund knew, combined the purchase of wine, the joys of the table and those of lovemaking with equal dedication.

Marguerite was tall and serious and while perhaps not a stunning beauty as the world judges these things, Edmund was deeply in love with her. Her height, for one thing, was no disadvantage to Edmund who himself was tall, and her seriousness was what he most admired. There was no silliness in her makeup, she was not a little girl but possessed a quiet, no-nonsense maturity. Most of all he admired her ability to express herself; to say a simple thing in a beautiful way. She didn't mumble, chatter or speak in silly clichés or smart expressions and her French was faultless, the result of a classical education. She laughed at his whimsical humour but not at his French, nor did she even correct him, preferring to call attention to something he might have said awkwardly by working it into her own conversation. She and Edmund were a serious couple who loved each other's company and wanted, most of all, to live and grow side by side. Sex, they knew, was to be part of it, and a part to be cherished, but not the whole.

Sex, he mused; the word 'six' in Latin. As a child he had been the proud owner of a Sunday-school reader that contained pictures of God's six fateful days of Creation. It was in Latin so that God would understand. He would open it in expectation that all Creation would be revealed to him. I, it began, *Dies Unum*, Light and Darkness. Half the page was black and half white. Very well then, turn to II, the second day, Land and Water. So it went on via Seas, Green Things, Planets, Stars and Living Creatures, all the way to day six, shown as VI, *Dies Sex*. The illustration showed Adam and Eve, modestly taking refuge in the shrubbery. Thus the numeral VI had come via the good offices of the Sunday School *Illustrated Reader For Obedient Children* to acquire an unexpected significance vis-à-vis Adam and Eve. To Edmund it seemed careless of the Church to allow Latin numerals to get out of control like that; surely in the whole length and breadth of the English language another word could be found to describe human reproductive activity. He couldn't imagine the sailors going ashore and looking around for a girl to have VI with.

Nor could he imagine himself married to Marguerite unless the ceremony was conducted in the ancient and approved manner by his father who would stand in for God. He wanted to hear his father pronounce the sumptuous words, the robust and unequivocal phrases of the marriage service. He wanted it to be performed with due ceremony, for surely such a love as theirs, which was eternal and God-given, merited the embrace of the great cathedral under whose shadow he had lived for so much of his life.

But how could he think of marriage? His chances were so slender and the obstacles so overwhelming. He was living in a dream; deceiving himself; she was in France, aligned by family affection, patriotism, friends and language with her own cultural magnetic pole while he was a naval officer far away. A war separated them; it was no earthly use attempting the impossible or hoping for simple solutions. Wearily he went back on board and was told by the quartermaster that he was wanted in the wardroom. Braithwaite had taken his place at the head of the table, Pemberton and Dobreiner at each side. Marko and Edmund faced each other lower down, while Reece sat at the end.

'I know we are all tired,' Braithwaite began, 'but we ought to plan for next week. It seems we'll be here for three or four days. After that I expect we'll go back to Liverpool for more convoy duty. I think we're in fair shape, but our guests have left us with a dirty ship.'

'Looks worse than it is,' Pemberton said. 'Two or three days; I want to paint the whole ship.'

'Very well,' Braithwaite continued. 'You can grant overnight leave, starting to-morrow. This evening we simply go to bed and leave things as they are.'

He looked at the five young men sitting round. They were unshaven, bedraggled, slouched in their chairs; the very opposite of what a naval officer is meant to be.

'Thank you,' he said. 'You've done an excellent job; and the whole ship's company. Steward,' he called out, 'drinks! Oh yes, a signal from Admiralty. Sub-lieutenant Cyr, RNVR, promoted to lieutenant.'

'Terrific,' Pemberton said, and the others added congratulations of their own.

'What was our final score of soldiers rescued?' Reece asked.

'Three thousand, four hundred and fourteen, give or take half a dozen. One died on the way back; a few slipped across between *Troubadour* and *Harp* when no one was looking and may have been counted twice or not counted at all.'

Edmund found himself talking in a disconnected way.

'So the plan is to concentrate during the next few days on getting the ship ready for sea again. I'll get cash and pay the men. May I suggest a formal parade and some words from the captain commending them on their conduct?'

'Bloody good idea,' from Braithwaite. 'Now let's have a drink and some supper and then most of us will be ready to turn in.'

Pemberton went forward to the mess decks to pass on the information about leave. Reece fell asleep in his chair and Marko became drunk after two small glasses. No one was at his best.

Edmund was a morning person and he usually awoke early. He liked to put on his track suit and go out on the jetty for exercise before showering and getting dressed for the day. On this day, however, his first thought was to get his cabin clean so he took his two blankets out on the sunlit deck and shook them, rolled soiled sheets and pillow cases with his other washing and found a bucket of hot water, a scrubber and a bar of Sunlight soap.

As he scrubbed, washed and wiped the paint and linoleum

surfaces in his cabin he thought back on those seven days and nights that had become crowded together in his mind in a confused blur. Seven days in which his world had changed; *Minstrel* lost, commander Sykes killed, and his little picture-holder taken from his cabin. He could visualise the ships in Dunkirk harbour on fire, hear the bomb bursts and smell the columns of smoke from the burning oil-tanks.

He pulled out the mattress, took it on deck and laid it in the sun, then washed the gray metal surfaces with soap the smell of which was reminiscent of childhood; nursemaids and starched aprons. He could hear the scream of diving aircraft, the shuddering crump of bombs which took your breath away when they struck sea or sand, and the noise of enemy artillery shells, like trains in tunnels.

These he tried to obliterate with his scrubbing brush, to expunge every last trace of battle with the circular motion of his hands and see only the cleanness that his cloth left in its wake. But the cordite fumes from *Troubadour's* guns persisted, the clatter of empty brass cartridge cases, the small craft going about their frantic business in the shallows as the waves rolled toward the beach and hundreds of men lined up to wait their turn. He saw the haunted, spectral look of the soldiers, not daring to believe that their deliverance was at hand; their uniforms caked in dirt and those awkward, badly designed helmets which they wore at different angles on their heads. He took his black shoes outside and polished them with a practised hand, then went for more hot water and washed his socks and underclothes. He wondered what it would do to him, that raucous experience of war, what residue it would leave in the private recesses of his mind.

He remembered how tired he had been, tired to the point of dementia, but no worse than the others. He had seen Braithwaite with his head on the flat dish of the gyroscopic compass, the lookouts asleep as they stood, leading seaman Harding and his men draped about the gun in fantastic postures. They had been asked to do what men were not capable of doing, to serve at their places of duty without respite for a week.

Carefully, Edmund restored his bunk to its proper condition, put on clean sheets and pillowcase and tucked in the blankets. He had slept for ten hours and beyond a feeling of light-headedness he was ready for the day.

Having paid the ship's company and dealt with the papers in the ship's office, Edmund and Marko decided to go to London. Braithwaite raised no objection; indeed he had spent the night ashore with Lucinda who had booked into a nearby hotel. Nancy Pemberton had a job and was therefore more restricted in her movements, but planned to join her husband at the weekend when Marko would prepare a special dinner on board for the officers and their ladies.

Central London bore unmistakable signs of introspection and resolve. Barrage balloons floated overhead; air-raid wardens, the corporals of civil intrusion, rode their bicycles from one trivial duty to the next, and air-raid shelters were prominently signposted. There were more uniforms on the street than there had been a few weeks before and government notices to the effect that *Careless Talk Costs Lives* were posted everywhere. The mood of the people was also changing. The crowds were chastened but not humiliated and wore the demeanour of revellers who now face the judge and are told they must suffer for their intemperance.

Groups stood about the newspaper stands, hesitating to accept what they saw, resentment mounting against the measured drumbeat of events that had suddenly proved so many of them to have been so totally wrong. 'Evacuation Complete,' 'French Army Encircled,' read the notices, 'Germans Continue Advance.' They stood in groups at bus stops, in shops and arcades, at last accepting the fact that their world had been breached, that Czechoslovakia was not an insignificant, distant country over whose plight they could shrug and disclaim responsibility as one politician had urged. These were people who had never believed the worst about Hitler or Mussolini, who had cherished delusions as to Britain's power and who now were seeing the lights of Europe darken like a theatre before the curtain. It was a time when a lot of peoples' bowels felt heavier than before.

Edmund and Marko had decided that their day in London would be memorable and it proved to be so in ways that neither of them could have predicted. They began at Gieves, the naval tailor; indeed, more than a tailor, Gieves was almost a part of the navy. New uniforms had to be ordered and old ones refitted, a process that was not financially as painful as it might have been, because they had each been making an allotment to Gieves and had built up credit against the sudden onslaught of a shopping spree. The Gieves staff went about their work on the heavily carpeted floor with subdued voices and an air of sumptuous self-abnegation. From Gieves they walked to Trumpers to have their hair cut. For lunch they found a pub in a back street, but instead of being allowed to sit quietly they were surrounded by patrons, polite in the extreme, who asked them if they knew what was happening in France. Why is France collapsing? What went wrong?

Edmund answered as best he could and the ring of serious faces round him hung on his every word.

'And was you there sir, at Dunkirk?' a man in a long leather apron asked.

'Yes, we were. We rescued more than three thousand soldiers in our ship.'

'Bloody hell,' someone else said. 'We're going to need them soldiers.'

'It looks like we're on our own; backs to the wall; don't it?' from a small man with a wizened face.

'It's Napoleon all over again,' observed another.

An hour later they threaded their way through the crowds on Shaftsbury Avenue to the theatre which they entered a minute or two before curtain time. There had only been two seats left and they were well forward, and the usher led them to the row where the seats were located. At that moment the unexpected happened. The audience somehow became aware of them, noticed them, and provoked perhaps by the excitement of the moment, expressed themselves by standing up and clapping. Women smiled, men extended their hands, some strange telepathy having persuaded them that Edmund and Marko had been at Dunkirk. It was another moment of embarrassment for both, not so easy to handle as the situation in the pub where they only had to answer a few simple questions and listen to peoples' comments.

They looked about them in confusion, not comprehending the sentiments which underlay the sudden demonstration, and totally unused to being the centre of so much attention. It continued for half a minute and then broke off as quickly as it had begun. They stood together in silence and sat down when the others did.

'I thought the English were reserved and unemotional,' Marko whispered.

After that, the play was an anti-climax and when the curtain fell the two of them went out into the cool afternoon air.

'Have you heard of Quaglino's?' Edmund asked. 'I've only been there once. It's rather old-fashioned but the food is incredibly good. Let's walk; it's not all that far.'

They fell into step and Marko was silent until they reached Piccadilly.

'You know, I don't think we should mention it; I mean what happened in the theatre. It wouldn't sound right, would it?'

'No, but we can say that the people in the pub were friendly and asked a lot of questions. I hope no one asks me what the play was about.'

The mess dinner aboard *Troubadour* was a success, not only because Marko was a passable cook and knowledgeable where wines were concerned, but because the party as a whole never faltered. He had chosen a menu that was not difficult to serve in the crowded wardroom, a beef stew accompanied by a Burgundy. There followed a salad, fresh fruits, cheese, coffee and a vintage port. It was not extravagant and although rationing was in force, some things remained unrationed, such as fruits and vegetables. The beef was navy issue, part of the food saved during the Dunkirk week when the officers were either too busy or too tired to eat.

It was Nancy Pemberton who raised the subject of Italy entering the war and Braithwaite who pointed out that if Italy came in on the German side the situation in the Mediterranean would be disastrous. We would be fighting Germans in the Atlantic and the North Sea and Italians in the Mediterranean, the only thing worse would be for the French fleet to be seized by Germany and turned against us, an intolerable thought which would have to be opposed at all costs.

Marko thought that French resistance would stiffen if they had to fight the Italians whom they hated more than the Germans. His girlfriend, a fashion model of considerable beauty but restricted intellect, thought that Italians should stick with the things they were good at like being gigolos and making spaghetti. Edmund thought that Churchill, having become prime minister the month before, had inherited a horrifying situation. His speeches were flawless, but was he up to the task?

'I heard,' Dobreiner said, 'that the soldiers we took off at Dunkirk were granted a week's leave, so things can't be too desperate or they'd have kept them in barracks.'

Talk turned to the fear of spies and saboteurs and the possibility that enemy agents had infiltrated the returning soldiers. Reece noted that the B.B.C. announcers were now giving their names, which had not been done up to that time. Listeners would be able to recognise the individual voices of Bruce Belfrage or Alvar Liddell and if the Germans landed and took over a broadcasting station they wouldn't be able to issue false instructions in the name of the government. In France the Germans had persuaded thousands of French civilians to flee their homes and take to the roads so that French army columns were immobilised. Indeed, the French army couldn't use the roads without mowing down their own women and children.

There was much to ponder on that June night and they remained in their chairs until late. Pemberton, in his own gentle manner, ended on a lighthearted note. He told the story of a senior civil servant in Whitehall, a man who wore the respected uniform of a black bowler hat, pin-striped trousers and stiff wing collar who had aroused the suspicion of his neighbours and even of those whom he supervised in a large government department. His furtive behaviour, guilty looks and the way he clung to his briefcase had, in spite of his long record of exemplary service and the high award which he had received at the hands of the king, compelled the conclusion that he was a traitor. What was in his briefcase? Government secrets? Battle plans? The detailed design of Britain's RDF? He was fingered and two policemen in size fourteen boots grabbed him and pushed him and his briefcase into an unmarked car. At the police station he was led to a dingy room and invited to be seated on a wooden chair. Without preliminaries an officer opened the briefcase to expose its nefarious contents. It was full of horse manure.

The senior civil servant had been too young for the first war and too old for the second. The banners under which he marched, his patriotism and dedication to the work of his Department had left unfulfilled his craving to make some tangible contribution to the war effort. He wanted to get his hands dirty in his country's cause, to sweat and perhaps to suffer, and the only thing he could think of was to dig the flowers out of his modest suburban plot and plant vegetables. On his way to and from work he collected horse manure from the streets, having first lined a large government briefcase with suitable material, and conveyed it to his other Eden, demi-paradise, where he worked it into the soil. His fear that this small intrigue would be discovered to his embarrassment, even though it was compelled by the most virtuous motives, produced the furtive demeanour to which the attention of his neighbours had been drawn.

Exactly the sort of story, Marko thought, that the English love to tell about themselves. Everyone had laughed, but it was not funny, it was touching and deadly serious. Who was it, he asked himself, who said that in time of war things are so terrible you can only joke about them?

When the party finally broke up Edmund went to his cabin and wrote a long letter to Marguerite and there were tears in his eyes as he ended by assuring her of his undying love. In the morning he put stamps on it, pulled on his track suit and ran down the jetty and out of the dockyard with his long, loping stride. As he dropped it in the pillar box he raised his hand to a coal deliveryman atop his horse-drawn cart. The short summer night had purified the air so that he could smell both the coal dust and the horse, even though he was at a distance across the road. He ran on through the quiet streets, nodded to a solitary policeman and thanked God, even as he ran, for his strong body and primitive enjoyment of the morning.

That afternoon *Troubadour*'s officers were again summoned to the wardroom. This time they sat straight in their chairs, their uniforms were clean, they were shaved, barbered and their shoes shined. Braithwaite wasted no time.

'*Harp* and ourselves will raise steam and sail at 0800. I am prepared to inform you of our destination on the clear understanding that it is not mentioned outside this wardroom. Reece, you will not leave any charts lying on the chartroom table. We will be crossing to France. It seems that certain members of the French government have left Paris and gone to Bordeaux. Our job will be to carry them to England or North Africa. The prime minister is aware of this. It was his idea. When I told the commander-in-chief that I had two officers who spoke French, lieutenants Casswell and Cyr, he said he knew it perfectly well. I confess I was astonished.'

'Bordeaux,' Edmund repeated, 'Bordeaux.' His heart was pounding and he didn't dare believe what he heard.

'Casswell,' Braithwaite barked at him. 'You've been there before. What's it like to get in?'

'Not difficult, sir. It's a long haul up the Gironde river, fifty or sixty miles from the coast to the port of Bordeaux. Quite large seagoing ships go up. It's tidal all the way. If we don't get a pilot we can follow the chart and use the echo-sounder.'

'Very well, I don't need to tell you that diplomacy may be needed in our dealings with the French government.'

'Oh,' Pemberton said, 'if we're going to carry members of the French government then I presume our seagoing dress will have to be smartened up.'

'Yes, you're right. We've always allowed any old clothes to be worn at sea, but this is different. Proper blue rig for everyone.'

'One more thing,' Braithwaite continued. 'I haven't the faintest idea how many passengers we'll have on board the two ships, and whether they'll be men, women or children. How we'll feed them I can't imagine, but lieutenant Cyr will go ashore in Bordeaux and buy food and fresh milk. In France there isn't any rationing. All right Cyr?'

'*Mais oui, mon capitaine.*'

They laughed and the meeting broke up.

10th June was the day on which Italy formally entered the war on the side of Germany and was also the day on which *Troubadour* and *Harp*, refreshed by their week in harbour, steamed into the broad estuary of the Thames. Their crews were veterans now, confident in their seamanlike abilities, sober in their assessment of the war and its demands. Braithwaite ordered eighteen knots, rounded the north Foreland within two hours and was off Dover in three. In the chartroom Reece bent over his charts with dividers and parallel rulers, the Admiralty tide tables open in front of him. He called up the voicepipe to Edmund to alter course to two-two-zero until they were off Dungeness when he would set a new course for the Cherbourg peninsula and Alderney Island. It was a warm, clear day and the coasts of Britain and France lay on each side of them. The seaman on the wheel steered easily, almost without concentration, knowing that *Troubadour* held her course well at that speed.

Edmund kept the forenoon watch. He looked back at *Harp* following a cable and a half astern in *Troubadour*'s wake, then at the coastline of France that disappeared in the mist toward the mouth of the Somme. To the north lay the coast of England; Winchelsea, Hastings and Eastbourne, and the white cliffs which gave it the name Albion, white, the little country with a mighty heart. Like so many of his contemporaries Edmund was devoted to the Bard of Avon, whose voice had sounded down the centuries and given pride and courage to a dozen generations of Englishmen. At moments like these Edmund's private universe of hope and despair was keeping a lonely vigil while nations clashed and civilization faltered; at moments like these it was the Bard whose words hovered in his mind.

'Floating mine at red six-o.'

He turned his binoculars to the port side and saw it bobbing in the sea a hundred yards distant; its black horns projecting at obscene angles. He crossed to the port side of the bridge, loaded an anti-tank rifle, fired and missed. He reloaded and tried again, this time the bullet hit the mine casing.

'You got it,' said the lookout.

'Captain, sir,' Edmund called down the voicepipe. 'Floating mine. Sank it.'

A noise from Braithwaite's cabin.

'Can you imagine,' Marko said when he came up at midday, 'those stupid pop guns being expected to stop enemy tanks? Half-inch calibre, single shot and useless against armour.'

'They're all right for sinking mines. How many did we get?' Edmund asked.

'Just two and about a dozen rounds. We can't afford to miss too often. Some colonel told Pemberton he could have the bloody things.'

At midnight the two ships were off Alderney. Braithwaite was on the bridge and Reece still in the chartroom. They passed Guernsey at 0400 and when Pemberton came up for his watch the dawn was rising. Edmund went to his cabin and decided he would sleep through breakfast and into the forenoon. When he returned to the bridge they were steaming southwards and the indented coast of Brittany lay on their port hand. All afternoon and evening they steamed, now in the Bay of Biscay with its compressed, bumpy waves. Midnight found them off La Rochelle and nearing 0200 they sighted Pointe de la Coubre.

'We'll go straight in,' Braithwaite ordered.

They turned to port and the dark hills of Médoc rose up to starboard on the southern side. The slopes of Saintonge, the holy angel, lay to port. At Pauillac, where the river narrowed, Braithwaite reduced from eighteen knots to twelve. It was moving towards 0500 and Edmund wondered if Marguerite was there, a mile or two distant. Where the river forks and the Garonne meets the Dordogne they turned southward along the Garonne. Other ships appeared and with a burst of joy the sun came over the horizon.

Braithwaite brought *Troubadour* alongside and heaving lines were cast shorewards from fore and aft. When they were secure and the gangway in place *Harp* came in and nudged against them.

'As soon as we've refuelled,' Braithwaite called out to *Harp*'s captain, 'I'll go ashore with Cyr and find out what's happening.'

Dobreiner appeared on the bridge in engineer's overalls and an officer's cap.

'You'll have to keep steam up,' Braithwaite told him. 'Let's go for breakfast,' he added, 'an English breakfast, not a French one.'

'I'd like to go ashore, sir, and find a telephone,' Edmund said.

'Have you got French money?'

'Yessir. I changed five hundred pounds before we left London. It seemed best to have enough.'

Braithwaite waved at the river and the town beyond. 'Recognise this?' he asked.

'I do, sir. It's an old and historic town. Those warehouses are where the wine is stored before being shipped. They call it *La Porte de la Lune* because it's crescent-shaped. What sailors like is that it's only a stroll from the jetty to the centre of town so they can have a meal and a drink within sight of their ships.'

When Edmund went ashore a little later he entered a café, bought coffee and a newspaper and asked if he could use the telephone. His hand was shaking as it had not shaken during the week of Dunkirk. To his relief and surprise he found himself talking to Marguerite. He knew that her mother would not answer the phone because of her deafness.

'Where are you?' she asked, her preliminary surprise overcome.

'Here in Bordeaux, in my ship. I've come to take you back to England. My father will marry us.'

'Edmund,' said said, 'my mother needs me to stay. You should have told me you were coming, then I could have . . .'

'No, no,' he pleaded. 'The Germans are in Paris and they'll be here in a few days. Your mother will be safe, but not you. It's only a matter of days before the French government surrenders. I want you to come with me and start a new life.'

'Can you come here and speak to my mother?' she asked.

'No, because we might be ordered out at a moment's notice. Don't throw away this opportunity. Pack what you need and come to the ship. Bring your birth certificate and passport. I can look after you. It's our last chance; our only chance. It's now or never.'

'Very well,' she said, and hung up, and Edmund said a more fervent prayer than he had ever said in his life before.

He hurried back to *Troubadour* and was told that the captain and Marko had gone ashore to contact the civil authorities. Pemberton was on the upper deck speaking with a French officer.

'We have limited space,' he was saying. 'We must give first choice to our own nationals.'

'How many can you accommodate?' The officer looked round him contemptuously at the upper decks of the two ships.

'It would depend on the baggage and the arms they carried. Say two hundred in each.'

'I see,' the officer replied.

'But if you want my advice,' Pemberton went on, 'you'll seize that ship over there; yes, just take it. She's five thousand tons at least, and you can carry the entire regiment.'

The officer seemed stunned by the idea.

Pemberton turned to Edmund. 'Your French is better than mine. Tell him that we rescued large numbers of French troops at Dunkirk with the approval of the French high command. The Germans are advancing everywhere and we're now taking off our own troops to be regrouped and rearmed in England. This is not running away; rather avoiding capture. One day he and his men will be back and he'll be part of a victorious army.'

Edmund did his best and as he finished a car drew up and an unmistakably English family came across the gangway.

'Can we get a lift with you?' they asked. 'We're tourists.'

'Why don't you drive to Biarritz and then into Spain?' Pemberton replied. 'I can't tell you when we'll be leaving, how many passengers we'll have aboard or what our destination will be. The only thing I'm sure of is that you'll be thoroughly uncomfortable and seasick all the way.'

The quartermaster, able seaman Kirk, turned away with a smile on his face and Edmund marvelled at Pemberton's mastery of the situation. He was not the quiet, reserved yachtsman he had been less than a year ago; somewhere along the way he had grown in self-confidence and authority.

As the morning passed Edmund was reminded of a play, an opera. French officers in their uniforms came across *Troubadour*'s gangway, made impassioned speeches, saluted and went away again. Civilians did the same only with more vehemence and hand waving. A messenger on a bicycle delivered a telegram from the French Ministry of Marine which made no sense and which they thought best to ignore. A stream of people arrived, told their stories and took their leave. Pemberton dealt with each as best he could.

'Up spirits,' was piped at six bells and Braithwaite came aboard a few minutes later.

'Some British soldiers and French civilians,' he said when he had been piped aboard. 'After that we can use our discretion and take whom we like.' He looked down the jetty; 'those must be some of our British soldiers.'

A group of khaki-clad men were alighting from an army vehicle. They threw out their kit and climbed down, then lit cigarettes and stood or sat with no one apparently in charge. Pemberton and the coxswain were supervising rum issue, Braithwaite was talking to *Harp*'s captain and Edmund was by the gangway. He walked across and spoke to the nearest soldier who made only the weakest effort to stand to attention and hide his cigarette.

'Who's in charge here?' Edmund demanded.

'Dunno. We was told to go on board some tub called "Troubledoor".' He sniggered and took a pull on his cigarette. Edmund was furious.

'Stand to attention, all of you,' he shouted.

'Fukkinell,' one of them said.

'If you think you're taking passage aboard His Majesty's Ship *Troubadour* you'd better smarten up. Line up your kit and fall in facing me.' He paused while they grudgingly complied.

'A straight line,' he shouted, 'not in front of the gangway; to one side of it. Two ranks and dress by the right.' He glared at the ten men.

'I don't like your language and I don't like your comportment. Before you come aboard there's going to be an improvement. Quartermaster,' he shouted over his shoulder, 'I want leading seaman Harding here at the double.'

'Aye aye, sir,' from able seaman Kirk.

'Leading seaman Harding is a non-commissioned officer,' Edmund continued with a rasp in his voice. 'He'll drill you up and down this jetty until I'm satisfied. We are a very disciplined ship and some of it is going to rub off on you.'

Harding appeared a few moments later, ran across the gangway and saluted. 'Sir?'

'I am not satisfied that these soldiers are fit to come aboard *Troubadour*,' Edmund said. 'They are undisciplined and they use insulting language. You are to drill them on this jetty; small arms drill, marching and at the double. Understood?'

'Yessir.'

'The slightest insubordination and you will take the man in front of the captain.'

'Aye aye, sir.'

Harding saluted, faced the men and looked them over while Edmund walked away.

Thank God for the Hardings of the navy, he said to himself, they're disciplined and competent. Fenway wouldn't do it so well, he's too kind, almost gracious. He'd listen to backchat and try to reason with them.

He looked down the jetty and his heart missed a complete beat. Marguerite was approaching on her horse. It wasn't the photo, no, it was the real thing.

Chapter 15

IF EDMUND CASSWELL had lived for a thousand years he would not have forgotten that moment. The young woman whom he loved, who was to become his wife, whom he treasured as much as his own parents was, after a long separation, approaching down the ancient cobbled jetty of Bordeaux. She sat astride the same horse she had ridden when he took her picture so many months before. Behind her was one of the estate employees driving a cart and it was the cart's contents which confirmed Edmund's highest hopes. On it was an old-fashioned cabin trunk and other luggage which rejoiced his heart and told him that she would go with him to England.

He stood with his hand on the rail as though to steady himself.

'Thank You,' he said quietly. 'Thank You very much.'

'Good heavens,' able seaman Kirk intoned, ''ere comes a lady on a 'orse. That's one we 'aven't seen before.'

'And she will become my wife,' Edmund said quietly.

He hurried towards her as she reined in, kicked her feet free of the stirrups and slid to the ground. Then for a long moment, hidden partly by the horse, he held her in his strong arms.

'My mother has agreed,' were Marguerite's first words. 'She has given us the blessing.'

Edmund couldn't speak, he stood holding her while the horse breathed heavily at his side.

'And she asks you to take care of me.'

'I shall take good care of you. I'm so happy. We'll go to England and be married. Did you get my letters? I numbered them so you would know if any were missing.'

'Yes, I am up to number 26. There was a lot of love in 26.'

'And grammatical mistakes?'

'A few.'

'Your English is better. Have you been practising?'

She nodded.

'And you look so smart in your uniform.'

'I am a nurse in the French army,' she said simply. 'The army is being rescued by the British, so I must go with the army.' She gave him a sly look.

Marko was approaching over the gangway.

'May I have the honour of being introduced?' he asked with a broad smile on his face.

'But I know you already,' Marguerite said. She had collected herself more quickly than Edmund. 'You are the gallant officer from New France. My fiancé has told me about lieutenant Marko Cyr who entered the Royal Navy because he could not play well at some absurd game in the bistro.'

Marko laughed and took her hand.

'I wish you all the good fortune it's possible to have, and as for my friend Edmund, I say he is the world's luckiest man.'

They conversed easily for a few minutes, then Marko called able seaman Kirk and some others to unload the cart.

'We will store your trunk deep down in the ship. It will keep company with the wine that I have bought, the cheese and the chicken from Bresse,' Marko explained. 'If you'll tell me what you need for the next couple of days, the good able seaman Kirk will see that it goes in your cabin. All the rest can be stowed below.'

Kirk's hand went to his mouth to hide an embarrassed smile.

She indicated a suitcase and a small toilet case.

'May I be the one to tell you this,' Marko went on, becoming suddenly serious, 'aboard *Troubadour* you have nothing to fear. We are all friends and brothers.'

'Now,' Edmund said, 'let's find the captain.'

Braithwaite was on the upper deck with Pemberton and Dalzell-Paul, captain of *Harp*.

'May I introduce *Marguerite de Tilly*,' Edmund began, 'nurse of the French army. She is my fiancée.' And to Marguerite he said, 'this is lieutenant-commander Braithwaite, my commanding officer. And lieutenant-commander Dalzell-Paul, captain of *Harp*, and lieutenant Pemberton, our first lieutenant.'

They shook hands and Braithwaite spoke for all of them. '*Enchanté, mademoiselle.*' He bowed as he must have done many times to ladies aboard passenger liners before the war. It was not an obsequious bow, rather an inclination of the head, a small gesture, but replete with nuance.

'Your fiancée?' he said to Edmund, 'how splendid. I congratulate you. And you, *mademoiselle*, are most welcome in the wardroom of my ship. I take it you will accompany us to England. We'll do our best to make you comfortable.'

'Thank you, captain, you are kind. And if, as a nurse, I can care for any sick or injured, please accept my service.'

'How thoughtful of you,' Braithwaite replied with genuine feeling. 'I gladly accept. Edmund will show you first to our little sick bay, as we call it, then to his cabin. Edmund, you'll have to find other accommodation while we're on passage.'

'You notice,' Edmund said in an undertone as they went forward past the lightly smoking funnel, 'the sick room comes first and I show you to my cabin afterwards. I don't know how we appear, but we are very disciplined. Your place of duty is the sick bay, so that's where we go before we think of personal comfort.'

They went forward to the sick bay which was on the port side by the canteen. Curious eyes followed them and watched as Marguerite stepped over the sill and into the little white-painted compartment where Jennings was bandaging a stoker's hand.

'Good morning, Jennings,' Edmund began, 'this is Miss de Tilly, our passenger. She is a nurse and the captain has ordered that she assist you if needed.'

'Very glad to have you,' he said, hesitating in his work.

'No, please go on. What was this, a burn?'

'Yes miss. We have a burn lotion but they're slow to heal at sea. This man was thrown against a steam pipe.'

The bandaging finished, Jennings showed her his small stock of medicines and bandages. He pointed to the fact that the two bunks, one above the other, were suspended from the deckhead, rather like hammocks, to minimise the motion of the ship and make it more comfortable for the patient. The bunks themselves were in the centre of the compartment so the patient could be approached from all sides.

'It's not much,' he said apologetically, 'but they're a healthy lot. Just cuts, burns and headache. Most of my afternoons are spent cutting the men's hair on the upper deck.'

Edmund smiled. He had often seen Jennings at work which reminded him of the barber-surgeons of the Middle Ages.

They went on deck again and Edmund excused himself while he stepped out on the jetty.

'Order arms,' Harding shouted; 'slope arms.'

'Leading seaman Harding,' he called out. Harding turned and faced him.

'Do you find any improvement?'

'Yessir. They are obeying their orders smartly, sir.'

'Thank you, Harding. Stand them at ease.'

He took a few steps toward them and looked them over.

'Listen to me,' he said. 'This is His Majesty's Ship *Troubadour* and beyond her is *Harp*. You will not be the first British soldiers we have carried as passengers. During the eight days of the Dunkirk evacuation we rescued, between the two ships, over six thousand soldiers from the harbour and the open beaches. We took them to England. They were not taken prisoner by the Germans.'

He paused to let his words sink in. 'When you speak to *Troubadour*'s officers and non-commissioned officers you don't smoke cigarettes or use dirty language. I hope that is very clear.'

He spat the words out decisively and then turned to Harding.

'Thank you, Harding. March them on board and report to the first lieutenant. They will be taken on strength and assigned to battle stations and a mess deck.'

'Aye aye, sir. Thank you, sir.'

He rejoined Marguerite who was standing with a group of *Troubadour*'s seamen surrounding the two horses. One of them held a bucket of water, the others patted them and rubbed their coats.

'What's his name?' one of them asked, hugging the saddle horse.

'Bellerophon,' Marguerite replied.

'Can we 'ave 'im on board?' the man asked mischievously.

'No,' she replied, 'we'll send him back to his home where he has green fields and plenty of space.'

'But 'ere in France they eat 'orses don't they? He might be better off in England.'

Edmund wondered if the man spoke wholly in jest or whether there was not a hint of worry in his voice.

Marguerite answered with a simple directness.

'We'll send him home and I'll always be grateful to him for bringing me here to your ship.'

She patted Bellerophon for the last time while the driver unsaddled him, lifted the saddle into the cart and tied the reins beside his seat. He turned to Marguerite and spoke only two words, *'Adieu, mademoiselle,'* then he looked away. The sailors stood silent while the driver picked up his reins and a couple of them pushed the cart to get it started. It was a simple act, somehow typical of sailors. Bellerophon shook his massive head and followed, his hoofs clattering on the cobbles. Marguerite took Edmund's hand. He realised that she was close to tears.

How is it, Edmund asked himself, that life's most devastating moments are made more poignant when shared with our beloved animals? At a state funeral the riderless horse led by the bridle, boots reversed in the stirrups, speaks to the hearts of the onlookers as passionately as the marching men and the black-draped gun carriage. The horse seems to add a deeper layer of sorrow as though the animal itself was grief-stricken at being deprived of its accustomed burden.

Together they went on board and down to his cabin where she cried openly. For Marguerite the first twenty years of her life were over. She had committed herself to a new life, new friends and loyalties. She clung to Edmund for long minutes and he tasted the salt tear on her face.

'Why Bellerophon?' he asked. 'Why not the car?'

A pause.

'It was taken by the military.'

Then suddenly he smiled and she felt a change in the muscles of his face.

'It's a silly thing to be thinking of,' he said, 'but never before has the captain called me Edmund. Even in private I've always been lieutenant Casswell. You have the power to change people, to make them,' he said it in French, '*plus agréable.*'

A little later, washed, brushed and ready for lunch, they went to the wardroom and joined the other officers. It was 14th June and on the radio they heard that Paris had fallen to the German army.

If Marguerite did not see it at that moment she would later recognise that this was the last day of her old life and the first day of the new. Her parting from her mother, coming aboard *Troubadour* and the fall of Paris was the exact point of transition. She had cried, but only Edmund, her future husband, had seen her, and now she was ready to put away childish things and step across the threshold into a different world. She knew that Bellerophon would be ridden by one of her brothers, and for many years to come his hard hooves would leave their imprint in the dark soil of France.

Edmund introduced her to Dobreiner and Reece while the steward approached and asked if she would like something to drink.

'Our steward has a nice dry sherry,' Marko said, joining them. 'The English have no drinks of their own; they drink sherry from Spain, port from Portugal, whisky from Scotland and gin which came originally from Holland.'

'And wine from France,' said Reece.

'I would like to try a small sherry, please. What do you drink, monsieur Cyr? Something from New France?'

'No; Quebec has no drink of its own; at least nothing that's legal. I'm having gin and tonic.'

'And monsieur Reece takes mineral water; is that because you are a cadet?'

'Not really; I'm allowed to spend five shillings a month at the bar and the captain hasn't placed any restriction on what I drink. Sometimes I have beer, but not at lunch time.'

'Forgive my asking, monsieur Reece, but is it usual for a cadet of your age to be at sea?'

'Well, I'm eighteen,' he said defensively.

Marguerite smiled with a hint of disbelief while Marko led the conversation into other pastures.

Edmund stood back and watched Marguerite with unconcealed admiration. She didn't have the flamboyant gaiety, the effeminate gestures, the exhibitionism that attracted some men, but rather a quiet and graceful serenity. She stood very straight, a slight smile on her face, her sparkling eyes on the person who was speaking. In ancient times swords would have sprung from their scabbards in her defence, courageous men would have dared the dragons of war in her honour, and yet she was not a great beauty but only a simple and charming lady. She was not cowed by these men that stood round her, nor overwhelmed, nor did she try to act as though she were one of them. She was herself; unspokenly declaring that she was equal but different.

He marvelled at the devious whims of providence that had brought them together, placed them beside each other at her mother's table, a table always resplendent with the products of farm and vineyard. Uncle Philippe had been a frequent and welcome guest; garrulous, borne upon a surge of wine and words, buying vintages that he might not have bought if quality had been his sole criterion. And beyond the stone walls of the ancient château were the rows of vines where they had walked, held hands and declared, in faulty French and English, their eternal love.

They had realised from the outset, from the first touch and the first stirrings of affection, that their future together was ill-assured. A sea divided them, they were surrounded by Europe in convulsions and on both sides there were cautious elders who would, when confronted, raise all the traditional obstacles. Yet it was the war itself that had finally become the arbiter and had routed those same difficulties which it seemed to have created. It was the war that had carried Edmund to Bordeaux; it would be in a ship of war that Marguerite would be borne away to England and it was the prospect of German occupation that had persuaded madame de Tilly to hope for a safe haven for her daughter across the sea.

Suddenly Edmund's own words returned to him, spoken when he had last been on leave. 'No, father, you are mistaken. I'm rather enjoying the war.' It had visibly shocked his father, but it was true; for him the war had been a release from bondage, a blessed relief. The focus of his life was changing and what his father would have called *the world* in deprecating tones he now desired only to embrace.

Edmund's parents can have known nothing of what had taken place that morning in Bordeaux. Neither the early telephone call, Marguerite's hasty packing with her mother's help, nor her ride from the château to the dockside. Nor could they have known that the week before she had received a telegram requiring her to report to a military hospital at Lille and her mother's refusal to let her go because Lille was already in German hands. She had sought confirmation and received no reply so she delayed and her waiting had been interrupted by Edmund's voice.

Able seaman Kirk appeared at the door with a civilian behind him and both Pemberton and Braithwaite hastened to greet him. Rotund and perspiring, the man put down his briefcase and was introduced as the British consul in Bordeaux. He shook hands all round and hardly seemed to remark on Marguerite's presence. She was, after all, in a dark blue uniform and must have seemed at first glance not to be out of place.

Braithwaite was anxious to get on with lunch so he asked if everyone was ready and motioned the consul to the seat at his right. They all listened as the consul spoke of the official passengers who were to come aboard that afternoon. There would be at least one senior French government official, more British soldiers and an undetermined number of French civilians.

'In truth,' he confessed, 'the situation with regard to the French government is rather, er . . . fluid. They were supposed to keep me informed, but what has come through is either contradictory or hedged with doubt.'

'What about the British residents in Bordeaux?' Pemberton asked. 'I imagine there are others in the wine trade.'

'Most of them will close up their establishments and move south,' he replied. 'Quite a number of the bigger houses have offices in Madrid and Lisbon. Spain is uncommitted and Portugal has always been a friend.'

Conversation became general and the consul spoke of an agreement which he believed the French government would try to negotiate with the Germans. The idea, as he understood it, was that southern France would be declared a neutral zone where the existing French government would continue its authority.

'That's interesting,' Braithwaite said. 'The French Mediterranean fleet is based at Toulon and by that arrangement it would continue under French control. Our main concern is not to let French ships fall into German hands.'

'Oh, by the way, all of you,' Braithwaite went on in his most decisive manner, 'we are at immediate notice and we'll sail when we get our passengers. I don't want to place myself in the position of having to turn people away, so the moment our official guests are on board we'll sail.'

Edmund smiled to himself; it sounded as though Braithwaite was trying to keep pace with the consul, to sound important and use intimidating words.

'For an overnight passage like this,' he went on, 'two nights at sea, I've decided that a hundred passengers are enough, a hundred and twenty the absolute limit. British and French soldiers get priority, then civilians. I think that *Harp*'s captain will agree.' He sat back.

'I don't need to say that the first lieutenant has a difficult job of organising the sleeping accommodation and meals. Fresh water is another problem. Our water tanks are full, but passengers are not trained as we are and can be careless. There's to be no bathing or showers and passengers are to be put on their honour to use no more than one gallon a day for personal use.'

He had abandoned any attempt to keep matters relevant to the consul's presence.

Conversation drifted into other areas and the consul resumed his status as the centre of interest. They didn't linger after the meal and as the officers dispersed he turned suddenly to Marguerite. 'I apologise for not recognising you. Of course I know the wine from your vineyard.'

That afternoon Marguerite sat at Edmund's desk and wrote a letter to her mother, then took it to the ship's office. Next she went to the sick bay, but found it deserted and concluded that there were no duties there. She had been well trained and knew the value of resting when opportunity offered, so she lay on Edmund's bunk, pulled a coat over her and slept.

As she did so a contingent of British soldiers arrived on the jetty in army vehicles, this time under the command of their officers. They had large quantities of kit and equipment and it took time to get it stowed away and more time before Pemberton and the coxswain had taken the men's names and assigned them to mess decks. Each soldier was given an action station, told to stay well clear of the depth charges when the ship was at sea, warned to be careful not to fall overboard when being seasick, lectured about not wasting fresh water, and finally told to take his boots off below decks.

A group of French government personnel came on board, talking a great deal, found the arrangements unsatisfactory and went ashore again, leaving only two of their party. The older was a *sous ministre* of some government Department, a sour individual in his sixties who had been ordered aboard by his minister.

Other French civilians came and went in a mood of pessimism and indecision. Their morale, like the morale of France, had been shattered and a twilight had enveloped them bordering on insanity. Their world had long been jeopardised by want of confidence in their own institutions, but now the whole country was collapsing before the hammer blows of the German invader. Can this be happening to France, they asked themselves, where is the glory now?

Militarily, France had become moribund. The air force had not taken to the air; the army was ill-trained, ill-equipped and led by a coterie of ancient generals who had failed in every aspect of military leadership. Even soldiers in barracks did not salute their officers or shine their boots; it was reported that a detachment of élite troops who had been given the order 'Eyes Right' to show respect to their divisional general had steadfastly continued to face the front. Officers at the lower levels had become dispirited, and the non-commissioned officers, the true professionals in every army, were as disillusioned as any. It was France's most tragic hour, a time of muttered curses and reproaches, of theories endlessly repeated as to why it had all gone wrong.

On *Troubadour*'s upper deck Marko Cyr, from New France,

witnessed the agony of the older France. He stood with Pemberton at the gangway and as he listened to the complaints, pleadings and fulminations of those who came aboard he was struck by the clean, efficient appearance of the two ships when contrasted against the confusion and agony that prevailed ashore. It was as though he had been thrust into the centre of a heated parliamentary debate in a country whose problems were incomprehensible to him and although he understood the words he could not appreciate the passion that underlay them.

'What is this gentleman saying?' Pemberton asked.

'He is appealing to heaven to be his witness,' Marko replied, 'and he wants to go to North Africa.'

'Our advice is that he proceed to Marseilles and find a passenger ship.'

'His wife is sick; his business will be ruined and his son in the army will be captured. For years he has known that some politicians were on the side of the communists.'

'Thank you. Tell him we can't help him. What about this fellow?'

'I've spoken to him. He has known all along that *Hélène LaPorte* was the very devil, worse than *Marie-Antoinette*.'

'Who's *Hélène LaPorte*?'

'If I've got the story right, she's the President's mistress. Military officers trying to report to the President get interviewed by her first. If the news isn't good they're sent away.'

'And what about that lot over there?'

'I told them to wait on the jetty. They're American newspaper correspondents and therefore neutral, so I don't know why we should give them passage. Something tells me they want a free ride so they can do a story about us.'

'They're out of luck,' Pemberton said. 'No ride, no story.'

There were more than a hundred people milling about on the jetty and Pemberton realised that excitement was mounting.

'Put a guard of six armed men on the gangway,' he ordered. 'I don't want things out of control. Three sailors and three soldiers under the orders of one of the army officers.'

'Aye aye, sir.'

'Midshipman Reece,' he went on; 'my compliments to the army

captain. I want an officer and three of his men. Armed; at the double; no questions.'

A group of French marines appeared and Marko spoke to one of them.

'This bunch seems all right,' he reported to Pemberton. 'They're from the depot and they want to go to England. Their officer told them they'd be shot if they left barracks, so here they are, no kit, nothing.'

'Very well, get them across to *Harp* and out of sight.'

'John,' he called out to *Harp*'s first lieutenant. 'This lot over to you.'

Evening was approaching as the consul returned on board and hurried to Braithwaite's cabin, led there by Pemberton. It was decided that they had done what they were sent to do, they had their passengers and could carry no more. Dalzell-Paul agreed and Braithwaite ended the conversation. He and the consul wished each other luck.

'I'll leave when the Germans get a bit closer,' he said. 'I have a good car and I'll drive to Spain.'

'It's been an interesting twelve hours,' Braithwaite added as he bade him goodbye.

He turned to Pemberton. 'Hands to stations for leaving harbour.' He reached for his uniform cap.

Edmund was in the office with Marguerite and explained that now he had to go on the bridge. He left her standing on the flag deck from which she could see both sides of the ship.

Pemberton hurried aft with the consul and saluted as he stepped ashore, then ordered the guard to come aboard and the gangway to be pulled in.

'Are we all aboard?' he asked the quartermaster, and being assured that no one remained ashore he told Harding and Fenway to single up to a backspring. Then he looked up to the bridge and when Braithwaite made an upward motion with his hands he ordered the backspring to be let go. In minutes, *Troubadour* and *Harp* were under way. It was 1730 and Edmund wrote the time in the log followed by 'Obey engine room telegraphs. Slip and proceed.'

He wanted to add, 'and Marguerite is on board.'

Chapter 16

'EIGHT KNOTS,' BRAITHWAITE told the leading signalman; then to Reece, 'tide is going out, so we'll get ten or twelve over the ground. Lookouts,' he went on, 'report buoys and channel markers.'

He felt suddenly relieved. Before all else he was a seaman who rejoiced in the throb of the ship under his feet and the knowledge that his orders were being meticulously obeyed. The hours spent in Bordeaux had not been to his liking; he wanted to shake them off and return to a situation where he was in control.

'Coxswain,' he called down the voicepipe. 'I want you to stay on the wheel 'till we're in open water. Tell me if she doesn't seem to be steering well.' He paused. 'Casswell, take the ship. Remember we're going downstream and the current can sweep you out of the channel. Now,' he continued, 'let's get an idea who we have on board.'

Braithwaite glanced at the green slopes of the hills covered with a patchwork of vineyards, mile after mile, but he didn't see their fragile beauty as the shadows fell. When Pemberton came on the bridge he asked, 'what about the passengers; they all right?'

'We'll manage,' Pemberton replied. 'I've got the volunteers I need as extra cooks and stewards. These army people settle in quickly.'

'How about the wardroom?'

'Twenty-three to feed at a table that seats eight. We're doing it in three sittings and keeping the bar open for passengers.'

'And one other thing,' Pemberton continued, 'I've stationed two soldiers as lifebelt watch.'

'Good idea,' Braithwaite conceded, 'and you've told them what to do?'

'Yessir.'

Braithwaite had already indicated that he didn't object to having two or three wardroom passengers on the bridge while *Troubadour* was at sea, but he decided that on the way downriver there were too many of them and they'd be in the way. In truth he enjoyed showing off his authority and would have liked the French government people to see the unruffled efficiency of the officers and men under his command. Accordingly he told Pemberton to allow them on the flag deck immediately below the bridge. A few passengers, including Marguerite, had come up to catch their last glimpse of France as the river widened and darkness fell.

Standing there, she remembered how her father had spoken to her as a child and recounted the stories of France's heroes. The chieftain Vercingetorix had been conquered by Caesar's legions but held his head high when made a laughing stock in the streets of Rome. Charles Martel had routed the Saracens and Charlemagne assembled France into a unity. Then there was Joan of Arc and her devotion to God and the monarchy; Napoleon who tried in his misguided way to unite Europe by force. Where were they now, the Capetian horsemen, the Valois kings? From Reims cathedral to the grotto of Massabielle the ancient land of France now seemed bereft of the men and women about whom her father had spoken. She wanted to talk to Edmund, to share her doubts about her country's future, to wonder aloud whether they would ever again walk in the ancestral vineyards of Pauillac which were so near to where she stood.

Occupied as he was, Edmund nevertheless kept a close watch on the shoreline, knowing that the château de Tilly lay in a hollow about five kilometers from Pauillac. Darkness had set in and a mist was gathering, but the old château suddenly came into view among the trees. It was hardly visible to the naked eye, but he went to the after end of the bridge and pointed it out.

'Leading signalman,' Braithwaite suddenly interrupted him, 'we'll go up to twelve knots.'

'Aye aye, sir,' and the leading signalman leaned over the bridge rail and called out 'G twelve, hoist,' to the signalman below. With the passengers watching, the signalman took G from its pigeonhole, the brown and white flag, bent it on the halyard with an Inglefield clip and added pennants one and two. Within seconds it was at the yardarm and even in darkness alert eyes in *Harp* saw it and hoisted the answering pennant.

'Answering pennant up,' the leading signalman reported.

'Execute,' Braithwaite ordered, and while *Troubadour*'s signal and *Harp*'s answering pennant came down together Edmund leaned toward the voicepipe and ordered an increase in engine revolutions.

Reece was bent over his chart with dividers in hand. 'Next channel marker a quarter of a mile ahead and fine to starboard,' he called up.

'I see it,' from Edmund. 'Very fine to starboard. How close do you want me to pass?'

'Leave it fifty yards to starboard,' Reece replied.

'Coxswain, steer three-one-o.'

'Three-one-o, sir. Course is now three-one-zero.'

Braithwaite moved about the bridge and watched the officers but rarely interfered. He studied the shoreline and the river ahead, looked back at *Harp* in *Troubadour*'s wake and then went to the chart table where Reece would point to the spot on the pencilled line where he estimated *Troubadour*'s position to be.

At 2000 hours, two and a half hours after they had slipped from Bordeaux and having made numerous course alterations to follow the channel, they passed Pauillac and the channel widened. Marko came up to take over the watch and Edmund went down the ladder and joined Marguerite.

'Aren't you cold?'

She shook her head.

'Supper?'

'I'm not really hungry.'

'Nor me, I'm too much in love; but I think we should try and eat something.'

They found places at the end of the wardroom table and their water glasses were filled by a soldier. Edmund explained to the minister and his party that the captain would be taking his meal on the bridge since the ship was in pilotage waters. In answer to their questions he said they would increase speed as the river opened toward the sea and the town of Royan would be passed within two hours. After that they would be in the Bay of Biscay.

'And when do we view England?' the minister asked.

'The day after to-morrow, before midday,' Edmund replied. 'We have two nights at sea, three if we are ordered to the port of London.'

The minister thanked him, rather dismissively, and resumed conversation with his friends. At that moment Reece came in and seated himself beside Marguerite.

'Golly,' he said, 'roast chicken.'

Out on deck again Edmund told Marguerite that he would have to go back on duty at midnight. They would be out of the estuary by that time and there would be nothing much to do unless things went wrong. Meanwhile he would lie down in the chartroom and get three hours' sleep. They went down to his cabin and bade each other goodnight.

'Don't get up in the morning if you don't feel well,' he said, 'and wear my track suit over your night clothes so you'll be presentable if you have to leave the cabin. Here's an empty paint pot, in case.'

Edmund felt as though he had only been asleep for a few minutes when he was awakened. He put on his cap and greatcoat and hung his binoculars round his neck. He found Marko propped against the binnacle. Marko handed over and went below, leaving Edmund to take stock. The coast of France lay in mist to the east; the sea was choppy with a gentle breeze from the south-west. Their course would carry them within sight of the Brest peninsula some time later that day. Their speed was still twelve knots, which gave *Troubadour* some pitch but little roll. The leading seaman came up to check the lookouts and report. He listened to the relentless sound of the asdic and told Edmund that two soldiers were on lifebelt watch and had been instructed in their duties.

At one in the morning Edmund filled in the log book and then turned his binoculars on *Harp* and watched her for long minutes. She rose and fell with a white bow wave casting back from the forefoot and occasionally the white of her wake could be seen when a wave lifted her stern. She was a graceful ship, dark and ghostly, shrouded in white veils, plunging at the waves which looked like English hedgerows, rank upon rank, ready to challenge her.

At 0200 he repeated the routine, then settled back to await the passing of another hour. He was leaning against the compass binnacle, one arm draped round it to steady himself against the motion of the ship when he became aware that someone was behind him, someone unaccustomed to the sea who staggered uncertainly the few steps from the top of the ladder to where he stood. A hand was on his arm and Marguerite was beside him in the dark.

'I couldn't sleep,' she said.

It was the perfect setting for them to talk about the future; how she would report to French army headquarters in England and they would marry on his next leave. He told her that the photograph which he had kept in his cabin had been stolen but now had been replaced a millionfold.

'As my father would say, the ways of man are small and devious, but the ways of God . . .'

'Man overboard,' came a shout from somewhere aft, and again, 'man overboard.' The voice seemed to come from the port side, so Edmund leaned down to the voicepipe and ordered hard-a-port and full astern on the port engine. Seconds later a soldier scrambled up the ladder, saluted and repeated 'man overboard.'

'Which side?' Edmund asked.

'This side.' The soldier indicated port.

'How close to him was the lifebelt?'

'Very close. No more than a few feet.'

'That's fine; stay on the bridge.'

'Hoist the letter O,' he ordered the signalman, 'I want *Harp* to know what's going on.' Then into the captain's voicepipe, 'come up, sir. We've lost a man overboard.'

As the ship swung to port he called the starboard lookout to the port side and told both lookouts to locate the lifebelt and not lose sight of it; then he told Marguerite to do the same, giving her his binoculars.

'Who's on the wheel?' he called down.

'McVane, sir. Wheel hard-a-port. Port engine full astern.'

The ship was swinging fast.

'Stop port,' he ordered. 'Both engines half ahead. Steady the ship at one-one-five degrees.'

McVane repeated the order as a lookout reported, 'I see the lifebelt.'

'Very well, don't put your binoculars down; keep it in view. Make a guess at the distance.'

'Must be a quarter mile, sir.'

Edmund looked past the man's shoulder and decided it was at one-two-zero degrees, judged by the line of his binoculars.

'I see the *sauvetage* also,' Marguerite said.

'I 'ave it,' from the other lookout; 'but I don't see no man in it.'

'What's going on?' It was Braithwaite who had bounded up the ladder and stood for a moment, his eyes not fully accustomed to the dark.

'Man overboard, sir. I've turned the ship through a hundred and eighty degrees and the lookouts have their binoculars on the lifebelt.'

'*Harp* sees our signal; she's turning,' the signalman reported.

'All right, I have control of the ship,' Braithwaite said. 'What's the distance?'

'Down to three hundred yards.'

Suddenly Marguerite spoke up again. 'I can see the man in the water.'

'Yes; lady's right, sir,' a lookout said.

'Stop engines,' Braithwaite ordered. 'Call the first lieutenant.'

He turned to Reece who had appeared. 'I don't want a lot of people on deck. I'm putting the ship beside him. Tell the first lieutenant to use the scrambling net on the starboard side.'

Reece plunged down the ladder.

Braithwaite noticed the soldier and asked, 'did you see who it was?'

'Well, sir, he didn't look like a soldier or a sailor. It must have been one of them French civvies and I'd say he done it deliberate.'

'How do you mean, deliberate?'

'It was dark but from what I saw he climbed over the railing and jumped. He'd been standing there for more than an hour.'

'Oh God,' Braithwaite mumbled.

'The lifebelt is less than half a cable ahead and slightly to starboard,' Edmund reported. Braithwaite went astern on both engines.

'Commandant,' Marguerite said. 'I have been watching the man in the water. He did not try to be rescued. Now he is gone.'

'Damn,' from Braithwaite.

He brought *Troubadour* up to the lifebelt and a sailor with a boathook leaned over the rail and plucked it from the water.

'What time was it when the man went over?' Braithwaite asked.

'Two-sixteen,' Edmund replied.

'That's only about four minutes ago and the sea isn't really cold.'

Half a dozen pairs of binoculars searched the water while *Harp* moved at slow speed round *Troubadour*.

'You saw him disappear?' Braithwaite asked Marguerite.

'Yes, commandant. One moment he was there, next moment he was not.'

'I'd agree with that, sir,' from the lookout. 'He were lifted up on a wave and I saw his head; then he were carried down and he weren't there no more.'

'Dammit, we've lost him.'

Braithwaite turned away and a few minutes later he said, 'There's nothing more to be done. Make a signal to *Harp* to resume course and speed. Use flags, not light.'

The people gathered on *Troubadour*'s bridge were reluctant to take their binoculars from their eyes, but as Edmund turned the ship to the north-west and *Troubadour* picked up speed they quietly resumed their duties. It seemed strange to Marguerite that so many of *Troubadour*'s officers and men had appeared from nowhere. There had been no alarm bells, nothing to rouse them from sleep, yet clues that would have passed unnoticed by an inexperienced person such as the change in motion of the ship and the sound of voices on deck had alerted them. The officers had gathered on the bridge, the coxswain was in the wheelhouse; Harding, Fenway and half a dozen seamen were on the main deck.

Pemberton came up the bridge ladder with Marko behind him.

'It was the deputy minister,' he said, 'Jean-Pierre Duval; he's not in his bunk and the minister says he heard him go out some time after midnight. He didn't say anything because he assumed he wanted to be sick. All other passengers are accounted for.'

'Hell,' Braithwaite said. 'What do we do now?'

There was a pause while they thought about it and the darkness seemed only to intensify the silence.

'Hold an inquiry,' Marko finally blurted out. 'At least *you* don't; you order it to be held by the first lieutenant with myself as secretary. My job will be to call the witnesses and take down their statements. The first lieutenant can ask the questions. The main thing is to start to-morrow, I mean to-day, and get the information while it's fresh in everyone's mind. And there's no objection to having the minister sit on the inquiry.'

'Why him?' Reece asked.

'Because this guy who went for a swim was a French national. There can never be accusations of negligence if we get the facts down quickly and Pemberton and the minister sign it.'

'Good idea; you can use my cabin. How do I appoint you?' Braithwaite asked.

'Just write it in the ship's log,' Marko said.

'What do I say?'

'Make it a bit pompous. *I have, at this very hour, instructed lieutenant David Pemberton to conduct an inquiry into the apparent suicide of Monsieur J. P. Duval.* Next you mention that the minister is requested to join the inquiry and that lieutenant Cyr will act as secretary. That's all there is to it.'

Braithwaite bent over the log book and said something about a captain having to be a lawyer these days, then straightened up and asked who was officer of the watch.

'I am, sir,' Edmund retorted.

'Yes, but I'm due for the morning watch in an hour,' Pemberton said, 'I might as well stay here and let Edmund go below. He can sleep in my bunk.'

They trooped off the bridge in the darkness and Marguerite, who had been watching *Harp* through Edmund's binoculars, joined him without a word.

'Now you can have a long sleep,' he said, 'unless you want to get up for breakfast.'

In the cabin he slumped down on the chair while she took her coat off and sat on the edge of the bunk. She was wearing his track suit and a pair of tennis shoes.

'I began by feeling a bit unwell; but with all the excitement . . .' she hesitated. 'Edmund, you did what you could to save him. I had no idea that in the middle of the night people would appear from nowhere and there would be such perfect discipline; no, I mean working together, co-ordination. Nor did I know that with the binoculars I could see so much, almost like day.'

'You must have wonderful eyesight and the ability to concentrate on what you are looking at. Some people find that if you look a little away from an object, just a fraction, you see it better.'

He realised he was lecturing and changed the subject.

'I'm sorry you had to experience this; to see the man the moment before he drowned. Thanks for coming up in the first place.'

He looked at her across the small cabin which was lit only by a night light and the blood rushed through his body. It seemed to force him toward her, counselling abandonment and surrender to his instincts. Her presence in his small cabin, the cool night on the bridge and the emotion of an attempted rescue had conspired to dispel his inhibitions and reduce him to a different, more primitive creature. He was in a cloud of forgetfulness, held captive by the present, oblivious to all else. The deck swayed beneath their feet and he told her many times how much he loved her. Then gradually his arms loosened and he sighed. 'No, not now. We have promised that we will do everything perfectly in our lives and this would not be perfect.' Sadly he left her and went to Pemberton's cabin where he lay down and slept.

Seven hours later, at ten in the forenoon, Edmund awoke. There was an unkind motion on the ship; the roll and pitch was more pronounced than the night before. He tip-toed into his cabin to find Marguerite asleep, so he took his towel, soap and other toilet articles and went to the bathroom. Careful to use a minimum of water he shaved and washed, brushed his teeth and even rubbed himself down with a wet cloth. Feeling better, he returned to the cabin, put on a clean shirt and went to the wardroom for an early lunch.

His head was still buzzing and inner voices were persistent in telling him he was a weaker man than he had thought himself. He had gone to the very edge and would have been deeply ashamed if he had gone further. Coarser minds would have called it strength to go on, but to Edmund and Marguerite it would have lacked decency and honour, been more barnyard than château; the sordid lust of uncle Philippe all over again, a gross departure from the tradition of the original troubadours who extolled courtly love. What would Marguerite's feelings have been if he had taken advantage of her? Marko's words, that she had nothing to fear aboard *Troubadour*, would have turned to ashes. She would have learned that she had much to fear and that the man for whom she had left everything was a hypocrite.

When Edmund entered the wardroom he found the table had not been set and two of the military officers were sprawled on the settee armed with drinks. The weather had worsened and *Troubadour* was labouring in a crossing sea. There was a jerkiness in her roll and pitch, a motion that made one think the sea was trying to shake her as a predator would shake a carcass. The sky had become overcast and the light turned to a steely grey which reflected down from the sky and created a troubled atmosphere. The two military men had not yet succumbed, but they clung in silent determination to their glasses.

'Suppose you're used to this,' one of them said, hoping he wouldn't have to listen to an answer. Edmund nodded and made his way to the hatch. The steward was propped in a corner of the pantry and his face brightened when he saw Edmund.

'Going up for the afternoon watch?' he asked, and Edmund nodded again. 'Well, it's mutton stew, sir. Looks good; lots of everything.'

Meals in these circumstances were a well-tested ritual. The steward took a metal serving dish from the rack, put in two scoops of stew and passed it through to Edmund who had taken a slice of bread and a spoon which he stuck in his top pocket. He then made his way to a chair, hooked his feet round the table legs and with the steel bowl under his chin he ladled the food into his mouth. The army officers watched the performance without betraying the slightest desire to try it. When Edmund went back for another scoop, one of them excused himself and staggered to the door.

On the bridge Edmund found Reece making the midday entries in the log book. *Harp* was still in station a thousand yards to the west and the asdic voiced its search for the elusive U-boats.

'Sea and swell?' Reece asked.

'Four and four,' Edmund replied.

'Not five and five?'

'Can't be five and five,' Edmund insisted, 'I ate my lunch sitting on a chair.'

'Could be five and five,' Reece came back, 'judging by the amount of suffering among the passengers.'

They looked at the chart and estimated that *Belle Ile* was over the horizon to the east and that the Brest peninsula would come up in four hours at their present speed.

'All right, I have it,' Edmund said. 'Where's the captain?'

'Giving his evidence.'

Reece's tone changed. 'How's your lady, your future wife?'

'Sleeping.'

'And she was up here when it happened?'

'Yes, she saw the whole thing; she saw him go down.'

'Braithwaite told Pemberton that you handled it perfectly. When he reached the bridge there was really nothing left for him to do.'

'Just an empty lifebelt,' Edmund replied. 'This is the second time on my watch that the Lord hath taken away.'

Edmund wondered what had impelled the man, a deputy minister in the French civil service at the pinnacle of his career to commit his body to the deep and his soul to God. According to the soldier he had stood for an hour contemplating the dark sea and had then climbed over the rail and stepped to his doom. What had passed through his mind? Did he leave a widow, grown-up children? And Marguerite, with binoculars to her eyes, had seen him near the lifebelt.

He looked down at the binoculars which hung at his chest. 'Zeiss,' he read. '10 × 50. Made in Germany.'

The war, he said to himself, seemed to affect people differently. A few were ennobled by it, made more mature, offered challenges they would never have encountered in time of peace. Others seemed cowed and shrunk, their lives blighted, their moral fibre shredded by its demands. These were the fearful ones, the cowards who died a thousand deaths, the limp personalities who would not stand up or let themselves be counted. A third group seemed unaffected by it all. Marko was one of these robust people who would always be the same, rain or shine, peace or war, good fortune or bad.

Where did the deputy minister stand? The second group, a coward? What could he not face; the past, the present or the future? Let's give him the benefit of every doubt, Edmund thought; perhaps he was suffering from an incurable disease, or his wife of many years had deserted him, or his life's work had been shattered before his eyes. Here was a man who must have made many decisions affecting others and now makes the final decision which affects himself.

Braithwaite had spoken of a captain in peace time whose ship had been rammed and almost sunk. The vessel that struck her, still seaworthy, stood off while the crew took to the boats. The captain, however, remained on his bridge. So long as his vessel was afloat he refused to abandon the one object whose care had been entrusted to him, together with its valuable cargo. She took on a dangerous list and for a week his lonely figure, without food or comfort, was to be seen clinging to a corner of the bridge. The other ship did not abandon her sister in agony and stood off a cable or two distant. Someone had a camera and took photographs and a week later a deep-sea tug appeared in response to radio calls, took the damaged ship in tow and brought her to safety.

The pictures that had been taken captivated the nation. They were technically inferior, but combined with the story of the captain's heroism there was something almost religious about them; the wounded ship, the faithful captain. The King of England summoned him to Buckingham Palace and hung about his neck the insignia of a Commander of the British Empire.

'I knew the captain,' Braithwaite said. 'Proper bastard. He couldn't abandon his ship because he was carrying his own private cargo from the poppy fields of South America. If he had left her and another ship had taken her in he would have been imprisoned, lost his master's ticket, lost everything.'

He had also spoken of people falling overboard from passenger liners. It was not uncommon, and while the captain always put the ship about, the proportion rescued was small. Sometimes the word was not given until minutes or hours after, and even if the interval was short the turning circle of the ship was wide and in rough weather you couldn't see a coloured lifebelt in the water, never mind a human head.

When a search was abandoned the passengers became emotional and many would be in tears when course was resumed. At this point a flagrant untruth would be spread to the effect that a man falling overboard would almost certainly be killed instantly. No one, to Braithwaite's knowledge, had ever seen this happen and most knowledgeable seamen cancelled it off as improbable, but it made it a little easier for the captain to face his passengers.

Pemberton had told a story about a passenger who fell overboard in the Indian Ocean and it occurred to Edmund that Pemberton's stories were of a different style. The man staggered from the ship's bar and fell into a fairly calm sea when attempting to obey a simple call of nature. He was not a person of deep religious conviction, but on this occasion, as he spat out a mouthful of sea water and surveyed the departing ship, he addressed his Creator, 'As you probably know, Sir, I'm a betting man and I'll lay you a thousand pounds you can't get me out of this mess.'

At that moment a giant sea turtle surfaced beside him and he scrambled on its back. An hour later he was picked up and his first words when re-entering the bar were not to order a drink but to ask for the purser's cheque-book. He wrote a cheque for a thousand pounds to the Distressed Seamens' Benevolent Fund and signed it. In other words he was prompt in paying up and one likes to think that God was not dissatisfied with the outcome of the wager. A lady passenger took the pen from his hand and drew a cartoon at the top of the cheque; a man seated on the back of a huge deep sea turtle. For many years thereafter the framed cheque hung in the office of the Distressed Seaman's Benevolent Fund.

'They've finished with me.' It was Braithwaite's voice behind him. 'I'll take the ship while you give evidence.'

Edmund went down to Braithwaite's cabin and found Pemberton at the table with the French minister of state on one side and Marko on the other. He took off his cap, sat down and began to answer Pemberton's questions.

'My name is lieutenant Edmund Casswell. It was my turn to keep the middle watch, midnight until four o'clock on the morning of the June 15th.'

Pemberton asked him the course and speed of the ship and the weather conditions.

'That information was entered in the ship's log at hourly intervals.'

Pemberton smiled. 'Of course. What happened?'

'I heard the cry, *Man overboard* at 0216 and thought that it was from the port side, so I ordered the ship turned to port. A soldier came up and reported exactly that; a man had gone over the port side.'

Pemberton asked why he had not waited for the captain to give him permission to turn the ship, and Edmund thought for a moment.

'The captain trusts his officers and allows us the freedom to act as we think best. It was inconceivable that he would do other than put the ship about and try to rescue the man. At that point I had no idea who he was. What I knew was that minutes, even seconds, could make a difference, so I ordered the wheel put hard over and went full astern on the port engine. This has the effect of swinging the ship rapidly.'

'And you ordered a signal to be hoisted?'

'Yes, I ordered the signalman to hoist the letter O, which means *Man overboard*. *Harp* must have seen us, read our signal and turned immediately. *Harp* is experienced and didn't need to be told what to do; she closed and helped with the search.'

'Then the captain came up and took over?'

'Yes. I went to the log book and began by recording the time, 0216. A few minutes later I added other details.'

Marko was translating into French for the benefit of the minister and Pemberton continued to ask questions.

'I believe that your fiancée, mademoiselle de Tilly, was on the bridge when it happened. Are you sure that her presence did not delay you?'

'Certainly not. As soon as I heard the cry I gave the helm order. I was standing by the voicepipe and the interval was less than five seconds.'

Edmund realised that Pemberton had asked the question because he wanted the minister to hear the answer. Marko translated and the minister nodded.

'Do you have any questions?' Pemberton asked the minister. He shook his head. 'Very well, we'll read it back to lieutenant Casswell and ask him to sign it.'

Pemberton sat back and looked at the papers in front of him.

'All right, we've heard from the captain, the officer of the watch, both lookouts, the soldiers, the quartermaster who was steering the ship, the signalman, and I've given my evidence. Does that cover it?'

'No,' Marko said, 'not at all. We must interview the people to whom the deceased spoke at supper and get some evidence as to his state of mind.'

Edmund was excused and went back to the bridge. He wanted to go and see Marguerite, but decided that she was probably still sleeping and would prefer to be left alone. He wondered how much longer the inquiry would take and realised that until it was concluded he would have to keep watch-and-watch-about with Reece.

'So you're going to be married?' Braithwaite said.

'Yessir; next leave.'

'It won't be much of a life for the two of you. Wartime; the long separations; food shortages.'

'We know that, sir, but we'll count our blessings. It was miraculous that we were ordered to Bordeaux and that I was able to reach her by telephone.'

Braithwaite turned and looked at him.

'You know, Casswell, you've learned a lot in the past year. You don't hesitate any more. I wonder if your fiancée understands that. Pemberton told me yesterday that you were annoyed by some army pongoes who insulted the ship or insulted you, I don't know which, and you called leading seaman Harding to give them some square-bashing. What you did was probably illegal and I thoroughly approve of it. Last night you handled the ship to perfection and never put a foot wrong. The war has been your teacher and I congratulate you, but I hope, for your sake, the young lady is able to accept it.'

'I think so, sir. She was to have gone back to a finishing school in Switzerland but chose army nursing instead. Surely that says something.'

As though to confirm Edmund's judgement, Marguerite came on the bridge later that evening. The board of inquiry was still at work and Edmund had remained on watch. Reece should have relieved him but had fallen asleep in the chartroom and Edmund refused to let him be roused.

'What have you been up to?' he asked.

'Well, monsieur Clancey, whom you call Coxswain, and the *sous-officiers*, how do you say, petty officers? invited me to have tea in their quarters. I was sure you would not object and I was touched by their kindness. Did you know that when monsieur Clancey was a young sailor he served *pour sauver les esclaves . . .*'

'Anti-slavery patrols,' Edmund prompted her.

'Yes, in the Red Sea. I could not imagine it in recent years; wicked men taking slaves in Africa and transporting them across the sea.' She was excited and tripped over the words.

'Your mother would think it a strange tea-time conversation. Not what the nuns teach you in finishing school.'

She smiled. 'That's over now. I'm ready to start a new life. Perhaps it will be possible to invite monsieur Clancey to our wedding. The man who spent his youth helping to free slaves. I would be deeply honoured.'

Chapter 17

THE ADMIRALTY HAD signalled *Troubadour* to proceed to Chatham which meant an extra few hours on board for the passengers. The weather, however, in the English Channel was calm and Braithwaite was able to increase speed to twenty knots. As they passed Margate and entered the Thames estuary he sent a signal disclosing the name of the minister and other officials. A welcoming party was on the jetty.

Arrangements had been made for Marguerite to be taken under the wing of the minister. She said goodbye to Edmund in the seclusion of his cabin and they went on deck carrying her hand luggage. She found herself being helped into an official government car. Newspaper reporters and photographers crowded round, but the minister waved them away and the car drove off. She had promised to write the moment she had a permanent address.

As Edmund returned on board he was elated that Marguerite was safe on English soil, but perplexed at the uncertainties that appeared before them. Southern England was preparing for invasion and during the last days of June the military situation in France deteriorated towards a French surrender. The French government emerged as an assortment of collaborators and pacifists who had taken refuge in the very city of Bordeaux where *Troubadour* and *Harp* had so recently played their small part.

The Admiralty had meanwhile assembled a great armada of ships on the south coast of England with the object of frustrating the enemy's attempted invasion. There were hundreds of vessels involved which meant that at this most dangerous time in England's history the individual ships were often less than fully occupied. It seemed perverse that at such a moment *Troubadour* and *Harp*, which had been recklessly engaged during the proceeding ten months of war, should now have time to spare.

News from Marguerite was quick to arrive. A fledgling organization was being assembled in London to manage the affairs of the French military units that had been evacuated. Later it would be called the Free French and would be headed by General de Gaulle, but at this stage it was loosely organised and in process of establishing itself. Marguerite found herself drawn into it, was given a desk and a chair and an assortment of duties.

Her name, de Tilly, stood her in good stead. It was an illustrious name in France and while her father, Antoine de Tilly, had inherited the headship of only a cadet branch of the family, he was remembered for his exploits in the First World War. He had risen from captain to major-general in five years, had been twice wounded and escaped from captivity. The recollection of such men strengthened the hearts of the new organization that was taking shape in London.

Finding a room with an English family was not difficult because many Londoners had moved away, particularly the elderly who had no reason to remain in the city. The bombing had not started in the last days of June, 1940, but it was expected and many people decided that the country held irresistible attractions. Edmund telephoned immediately; he was able to take the train to central London, then the Underground and be at her side in an hour. It was summer and they could mingle with the crowds or walk alone in the park; they could join Marko and his lady at the theatre or go to a quiet restaurant. As the battle raged and France capitulated Germany opened her aerial attack across the few miles of water that gave England her blessed immunity from the German armoured divisions. At this moment, however, the sheer folly of Britain's wartime leaders cast a long shadow over Britain's relations with France. It could not shake the love which Edmund and Marguerite had for each other, but their two countries passed from brotherhood and promises of eternal amity to a level that was only a step away from open hostility.

During the German advance Churchill had made visits to France to confer with his French counterparts and keep abreast of the military situation. He had proposed, during one of his visits, a unity of citizenship between the French and British peoples, a last-minute espousal of causes that would give comfort to both partners in their terrible adversity. It had not come to fruition because it was scarcely practical, but it cheered the hearts of French and English alike. It was the idea that counted, the offer of partnership and the expression of brotherly affection. Yet within days the author of this beatific proposal had ordered the guns of the Royal Navy to fire upon the French fleet.

During the first five days of July *Troubadour* and *Harp* had been at sea, returning to Chatham on the evening of the fifth. Edmund called Marguerite as she was preparing for bed.

'Have you heard?' Marguerite's voice was agitated. 'The most terrible thing.'

Edmund stood in the phone booth with the receiver to his ear. He was aghast at the sound of her voice.

'No,' he said quietly. 'I've been at sea. Is everything all right?'

'God, it's terrible,' she went on. 'The British government has made war against the French.'

'Against France?' Edmund repeated incredulously. 'Against France?'

'There has been talk all day at French headquarters. Our fleet was attacked at its base. They call it Mers el Kebir. More than a thousand Frenchmen are dead.'

'Oh no,' Edmund whispered.

Thoughts crowded his mind. The French fleet in the Mediterranean and the need to prevent it from falling into German hands; was that it?

As though reading his mind, Marguerite went on. 'They are saying that the fleet would never have gone over to the Germans or Italians. Most of them wanted to continue the fight against Germany. The admirals gave assurances to your admirals; this is what I heard today.'

'And we attacked them, with the sanction of the British government?'

Edmund still couldn't imagine in his mind how Royal Navy gunners could put their crosswires on French ships.

'War,' he repeated. 'I can't understand.'

'For my part,' Marguerite continued, 'I told the officers about my escape from Bordeaux and the kindness I received. I told them about the *sous-ministre*, Jean-Pierre Duval, how you tried to save him; the perfect discipline. I told of the inquiry ordered by your *commandant* and the meticulous way it was undertaken by lieutenants Pemberton and Cyr. I said that after what I had seen I couldn't believe that our navy had been fired on unless there was terrible misunderstanding.'

'You're right,' Edmund said, 'but what's happening now?'

'The Free French,' she replied, 'will come to an end. The soldiers and sailors are asking to be repatriated; to go back to France. There will be none left here. General de Gaulle is at his wit's end. And you,' she said finally, 'my dear Edmund, I must forbid you to come to my office in your uniform. It would be deeply resented. Please understand the passion . . . they were fired on by those who had promised to be their friends.'

Edmund sighed, then realised that others were waiting to use the phone.

'I'm sorry,' he said, 'deeply sorry. I'll call again to-morrow.'

He walked back along the jetty to *Troubadour* more distressed in mind than he had ever been. What on earth had happened, he kept asking himself, what had the Navy done to reach such a point, to antagonise the entire French nation, to dissuade a million French soldiers and sailors from joining the fight against the common enemy?

Answers came gradually over a period of days and weeks. However much the navy coveted the sobriquet 'the silent service', it was as much a gossip mill as any parish committee. Stories flowed from ship to ship, from mess deck to mess deck and one ocean to another. There emerged two separate pictures, one from Alexandria at the eastern end of the Mediterranean where *Troubadour* had so recently been, the other from Mers el Kebir in Algeria, a mere half day's steaming from Gibraltar.

In Alexandria, admiral Cunningham, whose fleet had been strongly reinforced at the time of Italy's entry into the war; persuaded the French admiral to disarm his ships. Cunningham himself had made slow headway in discussions with vice-admiral

Godfroy, so he entrusted his message to the captains of British ships who boarded their French counterparts and spoke personally to the French officers. It worked; no shots were fired and the French ships were disarmed.

At Oran, where lay the bulk of the French fleet, it was different. Negotiations were entrusted to captain Holland, a distinguished officer who had previously served in Paris as naval attaché at the British embassy. He was the perfect choice because the French admirals knew him personally, or at least knew his name and reputation. Captain Holland found himself dealing with admiral Gensoul, who was not to be rushed and requested more time to reach a decision from among the alternatives that captain Holland laid before him.

At this point, lacking patience and unable to leave matters in the hands of officers on the spot, the British government panicked and ordered admiral Somerville to fire on the French fleet. There followed the melancholy action at Oran in which the French ships were bombarded at their anchorage, only five destroyers and a battleship being able to escape. The death toll in the final count was thirteen hundred men.

Both captain Holland and admiral Somerville insisted in their reports that the tragedy need not have happened if they had been permitted to deal with the French officers in their own way and in their own time. The French were honourable men and their word should have been accepted. They were convinced that the French fleet would have sided with the British there being no enmity between them until the British guns spoke at Oran.

After Oran the British found that France was no longer a friend or ally. French opinion was outraged, the French navy in particular, and men deserted the allied cause in their thousands. In the days that followed Oran, a hundred thousand Frenchmen in Britain who had been rescued by *Troubadour* and many other ships from the coastal ports of France, demanded repatriation. General de Gaulle was left with a handful of supporters, to be numbered in hundreds rather than thousands. The majority streamed back to France to face shame and servitude rather than fight beside the British.

Worst of all was the effect which Oran created in the minds

and hearts of the French in North Africa, in the other French colonies and in France itself. The British had demonstrated by one outrageous act that they were devious and untrustworthy and for the remainder of the war the French played only a minuscule part in displacing the Nazis from their homeland. Within days the Vichy government broke off diplomatic relations with Britain and admiral Somerville informed his staff that it had been 'a bloody business', the most obscene diplomatic foul-up of modern times.

The navy, alert to the nuances of parliamentary government, were aghast at the final insult. Not content with having been the chief author of the Oran outrage, the prime minister sought to make personal capital from the incident in the House of Commons. Having told less than the truth about the circumstances leading towards it, he was roundly applauded by members when he proposed himself as a ruthless leader, harshly capable of decisive action against a former ally and therefore fit to lead the nation in the struggle that lay ahead.

Edmund and Marguerite spoke of Oran many times and always with sorrow. To Edmund it seemed that the world in which he would play his part, the world shaped by his parents' generation contained a measure of hypocrisy in whatever direction one searched. There were the lazy and improvident pacifists on the one hand who could not rouse themselves to the national emergency, yet the only alternative seemed to be a bloated orator whose interference in every military and naval operation ensured its failure. Many feared him as a dangerous adventurer; a mind brimming with fine phrases and eloquent pronouncements but incapable of leaving military decisions to those who were qualified to make them.

From his friends at the Admiralty Braithwaite had learned of a scheme that Churchill hatched during the early months of the war involving a breakthrough into the Baltic by British ships. It was foolish beyond belief, because it failed to take account of the existence of enemy land-based aircraft. The admirals who were supposed to be planning the enterprise were relieved when it was overtaken by events and never carried out.

The battle which had begun in the skies over southern England came to be known as the Battle of Britain. German aircraft first attacked RDF stations along the coast but grew tired of this disciplined form of war and began to drop their bombs on London. They could be seen almost daily crossing the Kent coast and were greeted by the men of the Royal Air Force. The German losses were invariably greater than those of Britain. In *Troubadour* and *Harp* they watched the conflict from Chatham dockyard, from the Thames estuary, the Channel, or wherever they happened to be. They wished devoutly that they could help those who flew the Spitfires and Hurricanes, but in truth there was nothing they could do but look upwards and marvel. The Germans knew that they could not invade England without first achieving aerial mastery. Their invasion fleet couldn't prevail against the hundreds of warships that were mustered under the white ensign unless the air above was dominated by black crosses. They came not even close to success, but in their vile Germanic way they afforded themselves the satisfaction of bombing the dwellings of London's poor.

It was because of this that Edmund's father, Bishop Casswell, was ordered south by his superiors and presented with a large portfolio of responsibilities. The physical resources of the Church were enormous; it had property of many kinds; dwelling houses, churches, rectories and more. A guiding hand unhampered by other ecclesiastical duties was needed to oversee and control the many uses to which the Church and its resources were now committed by the sad progress of the war. Without so much as a chance to inform his son, the bishop packed a suitcase and travelled to Lambeth palace where, for a few days, he was to stay as a guest of the archbishop of Canterbury. Mrs Casswell remained behind in the north, employed a firm of removers and was to join her husband when the matter of their future accommodation had been settled.

Thus it was during the first week of August, when *Troubadour* returned from patrol in the Channel that Edmund found a letter awaiting him. His father rarely wrote so the London postmark, combined with his father's handwriting, surprised him.

'My dear son,' it began. 'It hath pleased Almighty God and

the archbishop to appoint me to special duties in the metropolis. My work will involve the provision of shelter, clothing, consolation and much else to the unfortunates who have lost their worldly possessions by bombing. You will understand that I have only been here for a day or two and have scarcely found my feet. It will be administrative and pastoral work and although I remonstrated with my superiors in both Church and State that my gifts, such as they are, lay in other directions, I was abruptly overruled. Your mother will join me when she and Carter Patterson's have packed our belongings. It is a terrible blow for her to leave the house in which we have lived happily for so many years; the garden, of course, is beautiful at this time of year and the vegetables you planted . . .'

There was more, but Edmund put the letter down, got up from his desk and went on deck. It was a warm August afternoon and he wanted to be on his feet, walk for a moment and come to terms with what had happened.

His father, so untouchable, so rooted in the very stones of his great cathedral and so secure in his authority was now reduced to mortal status. It was exactly the appointment his father would have detested. He was a theologian, not an administrator; his was the abstruse realm of theological speculation, his mind fine-tuned to the delicacies of esoteric argument, so why would they choose him for such a mundane task?

Edmund didn't dare to believe what his intuition was telling him. Someone at the pinnacle of power was putting bishop Casswell to the test; not the test of faith but the test of works. Someone had said to himself that he had become too comfortable, that he needed to be cast down in the dust like Paul of Tarsus. How would his father respond? Would he rise to the occasion and illuminate the performance of his new duties with efficiency and goodwill, or would he be overwhelmed, leave them unloved and only half done?

Edmund went to a telephone and called Marguerite, finding her at her desk.

'My love, my darling,' he began when he heard her voice, 'my beautiful lady of France, my life and my heart's desire; guess what's happened?'

'Well, obviously *Troubadour* has returned you safely to the unconquerable country of your birth.'

These florid openings had become a game in which they meant every word of what they said although Marguerite, when she thought of a good phrase, jotted it on the blotting paper. They arranged to meet that evening and would present themselves to the bishop. Lambeth, he knew, was not hard to reach from central London. A few minutes later he was talking to a clerk in the archdiocesan secretariat.

'Will you tell bishop Casswell,' Edmund said slowly, 'that his son, lieutenant Edmund Casswell, will come to Lambeth and will hope to see him this evening at about six. With him will be his fiancée, Margaret de Tilly.' To make it easier he pronounced 'Margaret' in the English manner.

'I'll write that down,' came a voice from the other end. 'Wait and I'll find a pencil.'

How can anyone in a secretariat be without a pencil, Edmund wondered. He had seen a good deal of church organization and they never seemed able to get the small things right. Presumably that was what his father would be up against; people in a secretariat who had to walk across the room to find a pencil, only on a far larger scale.

It was a warm August evening when he and Marguerite travelled to Lambeth. Edmund was grateful for all such time which he could spend with her; it was God-given time whether they were walking side by side or with their arms touching in bus or train. The noise of the Underground and the stale odours mattered not, so happy were they to be together. They were in the dreamland that pure lovers inhabit; each step was light; theirs an aura not quite of this world.

On arrival at Lambeth they were shown into a reception room and asked to wait. There was no sofa in the room and the place had an austere, unattractive look with a table in the centre and chairs round the walls. On the table was a vase of dusty artificial flowers. The pictures were standard religious fare; Victorian and overblown. In one, Jesus and the disciples looked English, prosperous and middle-class. Seed was being cast around and fell in all the wrong places while the disciples gave the appearance of being headed for a fancy dress party. In another, the fishing boat on Lake Galillee was fitted with a single mast and no proper rigging; distinctly unhandy in a tempest.

That story about Jesus falling asleep had always bothered Edmund. He was supposed to have been a carpenter, a practical man who would have had a grasp of practical matters, yet the boat was in peril and Jesus fell asleep with his head on the 'pillow', a poor translation of the Greek word which described a device used by the steersman to brace himself when handling the heavy rudder. It wasn't really a pillow and if Jesus chose to prop himself against it he must have been insensitive to the labours of those about him. A practical man? It was the worst spot he could have chosen.

'Ah, my dear Edmund.' The door opened and the bishop, older and a little more stooped, was framed in the doorway. Edmund released Marguerite's hand and stood up, but then took it again and helped her to her feet.

'Father,' he said, 'it's good to see you. May I introduce Marguerite de Tilly.'

They advanced toward each other but the table with its vase of dusty flowers was in the way. Marguerite went round it, shook the bishop by the hand, curtsied lightly and stood aside for Edmund.

'Marguerite, yes. My dear wife mentioned your name, but I had no idea you were in England. How did you travel?'

'I came in Edmund's ship, my lord.'

The bishop looked from one to the other. 'I am truly astonished,' he said; then after a moment's pause, 'but you are wearing a uniform, are you not?'

'Yes. I have taken my training as a nurse, but my superiors have directed me to the French organization here in London. I think they are going to call it the Free French.'

The bishop looked perplexed.

'We have so much to discuss. May we sit and talk for a little while. I regret I have no refreshment to offer.'

Edmund and Marguerite resumed their chairs. Their gas masks were set on the table with Edmund's uniform cap and Marguerite's white gloves. The bishop was aware of how handsome they were, but more than that, there was something deeper. Sensing it, he took a seat opposite and cleared his throat.

'My dear children, what a pleasure. So it seems we are all now subject to worldly discipline. Will you tell me your story?'

'Yes father, and I hope you will tell us yours.'

They sat and talked for more than an hour and reviewed their lives and the progress of the war. The bishop was forthright about himself and expressed his anguish at being moved suddenly and against his will. He felt that there must be others, 'men of affairs' he called them, more qualified than he for the Church's worldly tasks, and was afraid that his hitherto unblemished career would become spotted by controversy.

'I had not wanted this war,' he said, 'and now I am cast into the very centre of it.' He continued with even more bitterness, 'the records and registers of the Church's property have been wretchedly kept; there's no accounting, no record of any audit that I can comprehend, and for myself I have little experience in such matters. I fear that I have entered a maze and whichever way I turn will be the wrong way.'

It seemed to Edmund that he should offer consolation.

'Father, years ago, during the days of sailing ships, men of great courage and skill were employed at the most dangerous tasks high on the mast. Are they not asserting that you are the only bishop who can do this?'

'I take your point and I will even accept the implied rebuke, but I feel as though the decision was made with motives that were not strictly impartial.'

'Come, father; in times of national emergency we cannot delve too deeply into the motives of those who make decisions.'

The bishop looked from Edmund to Marguerite who said rather quietly, 'I am so proud that my future father-in-law will be engaged on important war work.'

'Oh my dear, are you planning an early marriage? I had not realised. There must be formidable obstacles?'

'Yes father, there are formidable obstacles.'

'We hope,' Marguerite said, 'that you will marry us when Edmund is next granted leave. We know of a small residence which is near my work. I myself will continue at my job.'

'I didn't know your plans were so advanced. Your mother and I, Edmund, will want time to consider. You have chosen, if I may say so, a difficult moment.'

The bishop seemed to be warming to his subject.

'I don't know what you have discussed between yourselves, but I hope and pray that you will delay marriage for the present. I know you have money of your own from your mother's side of the family, but I can predict no comfort for you until some sanity is restored to the world.'

Very well, Edmund thought to himself, if he's going to pronounce a long litany of difficulties then it's time to change the subject.

'Father,' he said. 'May we turn to the here and now; is there anything that Marguerite and I can do to help you?'

The bishop seemed at a loss and thanked them both, but was unsure of where he would reside.

'I have never before lived in a flat,' he said, 'but for what I trust will be a temporary residence it might be the best. There are rectories available but they are large and drafty and would need upkeep. Your mother will help me decide.'

When Edmund and Marguerite took their leave it was nearly eight o'clock. They made their way to a small restaurant while the air-raid sirens wailed and a few bombs fell randomly as the city subsided into twilight. The streets cleared of traffic; pedestrians quickened their pace and glanced upwards. The barrage balloons, pathetic but defiant, were extended to the full scope of their cables. The war had come to London and while the wardens fumed at the reckless disregard of danger by many citizens, the London Underground stations had been supplied with bunk-type beds and were ideal for the more cautious. Along the shopping streets the plate glass windows had been boarded up or criss-crossed with adhesive tape to control the flying glass. Blackout curtains shrouded every doorway.

Edmund took Marguerite's hand.

'We younger people have an advantage,' he nodded toward the sound of a distant bomb blast, 'we take it more in stride. I'm sorry for my father. I've never seen him so out of his element. I can't make matters worse by . . .'

'Telling him your mind is changing?'

'He'll take it as a terrible reproach. He still wants me to resign from the navy, which of course is ridiculous. Can you imagine, in wartime?'

It was midnight when Edmund stepped back on board. He found a note in Marko's handwriting on his desk. 'New officer joining to-morrow. Pemberton met him and thinks he's first rate. I'll be there with Little Brother and a few others for exercise class at 0630,' which had been crossed out and '0700' substituted. 'Don't go too fast, your legs are longer than mine.'

The following morning when Edmund came out on the upper deck he found Marko, Reece and a dozen sailors waiting on the jetty. They spread themselves out and Edmund started with simple bending and stretching exercises for ten minutes, then led off at a gentle pace for what he called his 'two-mile circuit'. As he rounded a corner they came on a company of Home Guard, two hundred strong, mustered on a side street. The men were at ease while officers checked equipment and rifles. There was good-natured banter on both sides; 'lost yer ship, 'ave yer mate?' Edmund waved but almost immediately heard the sound of a distant air-raid siren borne on the clear morning air. Another started closer and he turned to the men behind him and called out, 'back to the ship. Uncover the guns.'

The air raid lasted for much of the morning and while it was in progress sub-lieutenant Jardine, RNVR, *Troubadour*'s new officer, came aboard. He was in his late twenties, had some sailing experience and had joined the navy on the lower deck seven or eight months before. He had spent his prior working life in Barclays Bank and had expected to be posted abroad as a junior manager after gaining the necessary experience.

'We're lucky to have sub-lieutenant Jardine,' Braithwaite said by way of introduction. 'He passed out in the top ten of his class. Speaking for myself I was expecting a youngster straight from school or university, but Jardine brings experience with him.'

Edmund's questioning look made Braithwaite pause. 'How would you sum up the kind of things you've been doing, Jardine?'

'Apart from the financial and accounting work which you'd expect in a bank, we were involved in markets, the stock exchange and estate work. One of my interests has been in overseas markets, which I expected to be dealing with in a place like Singapore. My father was in Singapore.'

'What about the navy training you received?' Pemberton asked. 'Any good?'

Jardine smiled. 'I only finished a couple of weeks ago and I don't want to be hasty, but I'd say it was pretty awful. They didn't know what they were trying to teach so they kept us on the parade ground. There was a bit of navigation, signals and gunnery, but not much. In six months I'll be able to answer your question better.'

'Interesting,' Braithwaite said. 'I can assure you that aboard this ship we'll take your training seriously. I want you to learn watchkeeping from all the officers and get their differing points of view; besides that you can work with Reece in the chartroom, Casswell in the office, and I want you to take the miscellaneous division. Your action station will be on the bridge. So now we'll turn you over to lieutenant Pemberton who'll get down to details.'

The officers stood as Braithwaite left, then gathered round Jardine.

'We seem to be telling you,' Pemberton said, 'that you're to be congratulated for being appointed to *Troubadour*. Sit down everyone.'

'You notice that the captain didn't mention the discipline and behaviour of the officers. In the ten or eleven months we've been together he's never had to mention it; never. We'd be insulted if he did.'

Jardine nodded.

'Who's officer of the day?'

'I am,' Reece replied.

'And you two are going ashore this evening with your ladies?' He looked down the table at Edmund and Marko.

'Yes, dinner and a movie,' Marko replied. 'I mean *cinema*.'

Excellent, Edmund said to himself as he walked to the ship's office along the upper deck. Jardine seems sensible and Marko can be trusted to welcome him, show him round and make him feel at home. With Jardine we can share the work and things are going to be easier.

That evening Edmund made his way to Marguerite's lodgings; a pleasant old house near Cadogan Square. Marguerite had a lower floor room with her own bathroom which, in former years, had been the servants' quarters. The owner, Mr Wreford Hay, opened the door and invited him into the hall. Edmund thanked him and put his cap and gas mask on a chair.

'This is really quite an honour, Mr Casswell,' Hay began. 'My wife Lucy and I want you to know that we're so happy to have Miss Margaret, when you're away at sea, I mean. Please understand that we want to treat her as though she were our own daughter.' There was a catch in his voice. 'You see, we never had children of our own and we've heard her say that she has no relatives in this country; except yourself, of course. Mind you, we'd have given her a room on the first floor, but Lucy wanted her to be in the safest place; what with the bombing. The air-raid warden was emphatic about the basement being best. And Lucy scolds her when she makes her own bed or helps in the kitchen.'

'You mustn't spoil her,' Edmund said, although secretly he was delighted that Marguerite was among such kind people.

They were joined by Lucy Hay who came bustling in with a measuring tape round her neck.

'How nice to see you, Mr Casswell. Margaret's been telling me all about your wonderful father; what a distinction to be the son of such a man. I do hope you'll be very happy. She'll be ready in a minute. I've been helping with a little sewing.'

'Really, Mrs Hay; you're very kind.'

'No, Mr Casswell. This is wartime as you know better than any of us. The way I can hold my head high is by helping my husband who's foreman in the arsenal, yourself who's serving at sea and Margaret who works for the French army. She's given up so much to be here. It's the least I can do.'

Her husband broke in, 'And when you get married, Mr Casswell, I hope you'll come and live here when you're on leave. It's a big house; you could have a whole floor.'

'Thank you, Mr Hay. Thank you both very much.'

At that moment Marguerite came into the hall and Edmund went toward her. In front of the Hays he could embrace her openly.

'So what did we think of the film?' Marko asked as the four of them sat down at a restaurant later that evening.

'Well, it was entertainment,' his girlfriend said, shrugging.

'But is life really like that?' Marguerite asked. 'Artificial, free of problems except those which selfish people create for themselves. How can one sympathise, how can one feel involved?'

Edmund took Marguerite's hand under the table.

'I've been thinking the same. Before the film I was talking to Mr and Mrs Hay, Marguerite's landlord couple, and they were so kind and generous; they brought a lump to my throat; it was higher than drama, higher than church, it made you wonder about those Germans. How can they ever prevail against the sheer goodness of Wreford Hay, man and wife? The war brings out the best in some people. They rise to heights that make a film like this look . . .' he searched for the word, 'squalid. I agree with Marguerite, what shallow people; what dishonesty, what false heroics, trivality'.

'Yes,' Marko said, 'it was rather frightful if you analyse it, but you're saying something else, which is that we are caught up in the times in which we live and are spoiled for anything small and mean.'

'Exactly,' Edmund broke in. 'Never again will we swallow nonsense churned out by the entertainment industry. It won't pass the test and for the whole of our lives we're going to look back and say that this was when our judgements and opinions changed.'

'Gosh, Edmund, you should have been a lawyer.'

'What do you expect?' Marguerite asked. 'The hot blood of France runs in his veins.'

'Which reminds me,' Marko continued. 'It's my turn to choose the wine; a Burgundy, perhaps.'

'What a perverse world,' Edmund mused. 'We go to the theatre to be entertained by an American movie that has done nothing more than irritate us. We drink Burgundy while our enemies march in the vineyards where it was grown. We don't listen to music with our meal, but the sound of the air-raid sirens is clear enough. And my dad, a doctor of Divinity and a noted theologian spent the day in a warehouse filled with old clothes.'

'And your prime minister,' Marguerite continued the train of thought, 'orders you to fire on your only ally so now you have no allies left.'

'Yes, we're alone,' Edmund sighed, 'and we live with the sins of the fathers.'

Chapter 18

BRAITHWAITE WAS IN his usual place at the head of the table and called for the attention of his officers. He told the steward to stay in the pantry and allow no one into the wardroom.

'I was talking to *Harp*'s captain,' he began, 'lieutenant-commander Dalzell-Paul. You all know him and you've probably heard something of his background. Before the war he was on the staff of the Royal Greenwich Observatory. He's a brilliant man and a first-rate seaman; been in the RNVR for ten years; promoted lieutenant-commander when he got *Harp*. It wouldn't surprise me if he ended up with a fleet destroyer. Well, today he made a decision which could conceivably mess up his career.'

Braithwaite paused and looked down the table.

'You know that sub-lieutenant in *Harp* with the loud voice and the disgusting manners.'

'Donkin,' someone said, 'Dirty Donkin.'

'Yes, he was given twenty minutes to pack his kit, pay his mess bill and get off the ship.'

'Crumbs, what did he do?' Marko asked.

'Dalzell-Paul had warned him a couple of times about his behaviour by logging him; you know, having him entered in the log book. I saw one of the entries. 'I have this day warned sub-lieutenant Donkin for carelessness in allowing the whaleboat to be lost . . .' or something of the sort. Another was for failing to report a torpedoed ship when he was on watch. Anyway, his latest offence was something rather different. It seems that Donkin was given some letters to censor, one of which was written by a man in the engine room department to his newly married wife. The man wrote that he was sorry he had not performed well on their wedding night and asked her to be patient. Donkin thought the whole thing a big joke, spoke openly about it and taunted the engineer with the suggestion that the engine room staff were impotent. The engineer went straight to the captain who listened to the story, including the evidence of the officers who had been in the wardroom, then told him to get off the ship. When it was done Dalzell-Paul came and reported to me as flotilla leader. Oh yes, he had Donkin escorted to the barracks by a lieutenant.'

'So what's the problem?' Marko asked.

'I've never heard of this being done in the Royal Navy,' Braithwaite looked down at his hands, 'and I don't even know if it's legal. Look at it this way; Donkin was sent to *Harp* by order of the Admiralty. It was intended that he serve aboard *Harp* and it seems to me that the captain can't just push him out. Doesn't that add up to a form of insubordination on the captain's part? Anyway, I'm asking your views and I won't hide the fact that I count a lot on Cyr's legal opinions.'

Marko sat back in his chair. 'All right, then, let's consider the facts. Donkin's behaviour was disgraceful. It cut deeply into the trust which men must have in their officers if discipline is to be maintained. As far as censorship is concerned, an officer has an obligation to read the men's letters, but such an obligation doesn't alter the individual man's right to privacy. A man's home life can't be invaded and those of us who censor letters keep this in mind. Donkin read something of a personal and private nature and he did so legally, but then he took it to the wardroom and used it to insult the man and cast the engineering branch into contempt. It makes you wonder how he got to be an officer at all.'

Pemberton nodded his agreement.

'Very well, let's take another step and ask ourselves what harm could have been done. I think it can be argued that his conduct was so repugnant that it could have led to a breakdown of discipline. The captain as entitled to take drastic action.'

'Why couldn't he choose an orthodox punishment? Why this?' Braithwaite asked.

'Well, he may have considered a court martial, but decided it was too lengthy and cumbersome. He may also have decided that further warnings in the log book were a waste of time. After all, from what you say there had been two already.'

Reece put his hand up and Braithwaite nodded to him.

'I want to know whether Donkin's remarks were picked up by anyone else. Were they overheard by the steward, for instance? It seems to me that Donkin's offence is not so bad if it was only the officers who heard what he said.'

Marko shook his head. 'No. He spoke, as I understand it, to anyone who would listen, and part of it was intentionally directed toward the engineer. It was pure chance as to who else may have heard and I don't think it alters the case.'

Edmund had been silent up to this moment, but now he pointed out that Donkin had been given no opportunity to consult a brother officer or make his defence. He was punished without trial.

'Not really,' Marko replied. 'It was a hasty decision to put him ashore, and he had no chance to defend himself, but I question whether it was in fact a punishment. Punishments are set out in the Articles of War; 'dismissal from the service with disgrace,' all that; but I don't believe that being told to pack your kit and go back to barracks can be classed as punishment. It could be argued that he has suffered nothing from this, and that he'll be given another appointment in a more suitable type of ship.'

Marko hesitated then went on. 'So, what I'm saying is that while Donkin's actions were repugnant and a danger to the discipline of the ship, he hasn't suffered any punishment as the navy defines it.'

'But in point of fact it must have been devastating to be ordered off the ship at short notice. I can't imagine anything more degrading.' Edmund looked round the table as he spoke.

'You may have a point there,' Marko continued, 'but he didn't lose pay or seniority. In a technical sense he's no worse off. There's nothing on his record except what the captain may have written in his annual report.'

Pemberton nodded. 'I suppose it would have been worse if Donkin had been kept on board. The captain could have cancelled his duties so that he had nothing to do. He could have confined him to his cabin and allowed him on deck only if he had no communication with anyone. He could have revoked his bar privileges and ordered the other officers to speak to him only when necessary. I read of this being done in the old days; it's far worse than being put ashore.'

'That's right,' Marko agreed, 'but there's another matter which the captain has to consider. If he puts an officer ashore, I don't see how he can ask for a replacement. He must be prepared to sail without him and the others will have to keep extra watches and do his work.'

'I heard from a friend in a battleship,' Pemberton mused, 'that they had so many officers that a lieutenant could expect to keep two four-hour watches a week; not a day, a week! In other words, if they got rid of someone at a junior level without replacement it would make scarcely any difference. But not in a ship like this.'

'Very well,' Braithwaite said. 'Let's sum up. The captain decides he has an officer on board who's a danger to the discipline of the ship. Warnings have proved useless. The court martial procedure is lengthy and the captain considers that he must act on the spot. He puts the officer ashore, not to punish him but for the sake of the ship. He's saying that he is prepared to do without a replacement even though it imposes a burden on the others.'

'Let's be absolutely clear,' Marko added, 'the officer's presence in the ship is worse than his absence. The captain can manage without him, but he can't stand having him.'

'One other thing,' from Pemberton. 'It would scarcely do to put someone ashore in Tristan de Cunha. The place itself must be on a trade route, as they say. In this case he sent him in a taxi with an escort to ensure that he arrived in barracks.'

'One last question,' Braithwaite looked round at them. 'Knowing what we know, was the captain of *Harp* justified? Midshipman?'

'Justified, sir.'
'Dobreiner?'
'Fully justified.'
'And the rest of you?'
A chorus of agreement.

'You're a moralistic group and you demand high standards. I've known plenty of officers who would have considered this a borderline case. They would have said it was a joke gone wrong, not very funny, but not worth making a fuss about.'

The meeting broke up and Braithwaite went to his cabin and sat at his desk. He took out paper and fountain pen and began to make notes. Never before, he thought, had he served aboard ship with an officer who had legal qualifications and who was able to apply them in a commonsense way. Cyr seemed able to see inside a problem after he had taken it apart piece by piece. Other lawyers made things complicated and unintelligible; Marko Cyr, well, at least you could understand what he was talking about.

Edmund and Marko were meanwhile discussing it quietly between themselves. What surprised both of them was that Braithwaite had called the meeting at all. It seemed out of character that he should ask for opinions instead of pretending to know the answers. Few captains ever consulted with their officers and Braithwaite was no exception. However, in this instance he had tacitly admitted being out of his depth.

It made them smile to think that on the lower deck a captain, about whom little is really known, is often thought of in relation to some trivial characteristic. This was true in Braithwaite's case; the one thing the entire ship was sure about was his predilection for hot Mexican peppers. The wardroom steward had not exaggerated when he said that he placed them on the table at every meal. One of the stoker petty officers who had been on the East Africa station knew a word for red peppers, *pilli-pilli*, with the result that this became the captain's nickname. In truth he liked his food spicy and always told the officers to help themselves from his ample supply.

The following day Braithwaite and Dalzell-Paul were summoned to the office of a staff officer, a full captain with the faded gold lace of many years on his sleeve and on his chest the ribbons of other wars. The meeting was not as difficult as either of them had anticipated and Braithwaite's well rehearsed lines were accepted with a resigned look. The captain didn't find fault with what Dalzell-Paul had done and airily cancelled off Donkin with the words, 'I think I'll send him back to the merchant navy. That's where he came from. We'll put him about and fill his sails with a different wind.'

From there the conversation moved to staffing generally, beginning with the officers. The captain explained that a steady flow of newly-minted reserve sub-lieutenants had become available and within the past few weeks *Troubadour* and *Harp* had both received one. Neither would have had much experience, but they had survived a demanding course of study following some months on the lower deck. The object was to train them, the captain said, not curse them, and in six months or a year they'd be useful officers.

He picked up another file from his desk and looked at Braithwaite.

'Midshipman Reece,' he said. 'Tell me about him; how's he doing?'

'Well, sir. I've made him navigator and he keeps the forenoon watch. He behaves himself, learns fast and he's on his way to becoming, as you said, a useful officer. Of course he was at Pangbourne.'

Braithwaite allowed himself a smile before he went on.

'I know Pangbourne quite well. I taught there.'

The captain picked up his pipe, held it for a moment and put it aside.

'And you say he's satisfactory?'

'Better than satisfactory and the first lieutenant would agree with me. I'm inclined to say he's an outstanding young officer.'

'Well, isn't that interesting. The Admiralty has discovered that he's too young; he misrepresented his age and got into the navy before he should have done.'

Braithwaite and Dalzell-Paul both laughed.

'You may think it's funny, but the Admiralty is taking it seriously. They point out that he made a false declaration.'

'Oh come, sir, in wartime? All the best youngsters are doing it. What does a month or two matter?'

'It wasn't a month or two,' the captain suppressed a smile, 'he got in at the age of fifteen.'

Braithwaite shrugged in disbelief. 'How the hell did he pull it off?'

'Surprisingly simple,' the captain said. 'His elder brother was also at Pangbourne and, would you believe, he joined the Royal Air Force. Due to sloppy office work the RAF people, instead of holding his records, gave them all back so your boy borrowed his brother's papers and took them to the navy recruiting office. He'd been two years at Pangbourne and our people, thinking he'd been there five years, accepted him as a midshipman without question. Not that it really matters, his name isn't Gerald, it's Frederick.'

'Well, I say good luck to him. He's a strong boy and I never heard a word of complaint from him, not even during that awful crossing last winter. I've seen men of twenty or twenty-five who couldn't take it half as well. I ask you, sir, don't let them throw him out.'

Braithwaite was annoyed and took little trouble to hide it. It was time for Dalzell-Paul to say something.

'You must think us strange, sir. One minute we want to see the last of Donkin, next minute we want to keep Reece. If I may ask a facetious question, how old was Lord Nelson when he went to sea?'

'Yes, of course,' the captain said, 'in those days it was standard practice for a young gentleman to go to sea at twelve or thirteen, but in this instance Reece misrepresented himself; he told a rather elaborate lie. If he wants to stay in the navy he's going to lose six months' seniority which means he can't become a sub-lieutenant until he's eighteen and a half. It sounds a bit perverse to punish him for showing patriotism and serving faithfully, which you say he's doing. If it had been my decision I'd have given him his promotion a year ahead of time.'

The captain reached for his pipe and began to fill it.

'You'll have to tell him, Braithwaite, that he's been found out. If he wants to say something on his own behalf, he can. My advice is that he keep quiet and I'll tell the Admiralty that the silliest thing they can do is throw him out because it's sure to be in all the newspapers. It's the kind of patriotic story which the country loves to hear.

Dalzell-Paul gave the captain a quick glance.

'Sir, in view of Reece's excellent performance it seems possible that his commanding officer will recommend him strenuously for six months or a year's accelerated promotion.'

'Entirely possible,' the captain agreed as he finally struck a match and lit his pipe.

Chapter 19

THE MONTH OF August slipped past and in September the German onslaught in the skies over Southern England took on a desperate intensity. Hundreds of aircraft were cast into the battle; the destruction on both sides was terrifying yet the Royal Air Force continued to sustain fewer losses and maintain its ascendancy. Realization came to the watchers below that if the enemy was to have prevailed they would have had to do so during the early stages of the battle. The fact they had not become masters of the sky meant that their chance of invasion had been lost. The Royal Air Force had the measure of its opponents and needed only to continue its defence into the winter after which any German attack by sea would be impossible.

There were reports of great numbers of barges along the Dutch, Belgian and French coasts, but the Royal Navy was ready and waiting. Indeed there were many aboard the British ships who would have welcomed an opportunity to meet them when they were crowded with German soldiers. *Troubadour* and *Harp* continued to be based at Chatham within a few miles of London. They patrolled the narrow seas and escorted convoys, but were essentially spectators in the great drama that was being enacted in the sky overhead.

On a warm day in early September, Christopher Jardine, the newly arrived sub-lieutenant, went to sea for the first time as an officer. His cap badge was shiny and he toyed nervously with the binoculars which hung at his chest by a leather strap. Braithwaite was not yet on the bridge, but Jardine wanted to be sure that the log book had been brought up from the gangway. His station for entering and leaving harbour was the bridge and his specific duty was to maintain the log, not an arduous duty but one that he was determined to perform correctly. He possessed good handwriting and ample experience of making ledger entries in the bank where he had previously worked. That morning Reece, conscious that he was instructing an officer ten years older than himself and technically senior, had shown him the log book and gone over the details that had to be entered.

'On this side,' he had said, 'is the standard information; the date, the hour, the weather conditions, amount of sea and swell, course and speed. Over here are the "remarks". When things are happening there's never enough space, when it's quiet there's too much.'

'When the captain comes up on the bridge you always salute, and his first words are likely to be, 'Obey Engine Room Telegraphs.' In the wheelhouse a seaman grasps the two levers on the telegraph and runs them at least twice from *Full Ahead* to *Full Astern*, then puts them back to *Stop*. Bells ring in the wheelhouse and engine room and draw the attention of the engineer to the fact that an order is about to be given. You then call the engine room on the red telephone and say, 'Obey Engine Room Telegraphs'. Note the time and write it in the log. By the way, if you have a reliable watch, accurate to within a few seconds, you can use it. Otherwise you must use the ship's official chronometer which is in my care and is brought up to the bridge when we're going to sea.'

'Is there any set language for entering remarks in the log?' Jardine asked.

'Not really; but keep it short and to the point. What the captain can't stand is bombs, mines, sinking ships and heaven knows what with nothing recorded at all. Oh yes, I think he disapproves of humour. The only time he got pissed off with the first lieutenant was when Pemberton wrote: 'Entertained a pretty little wren on the bridge during the morning watch.' The captain wanted to know what the hell he meant and was not amused when Pemberton explained that it was not a Womens Royal Naval Service girl, always called a Wren, but a little bird that got blown out to sea and landed exhausted on the bridge. One of the seamen caught it, put it in a box and let it go in Hyde Park. When the log was taken down to the gangway every sailor in the ship crowded round to see the entry. It's a good ship and a happy ship, as you'll discover, and the captain knows it, but I suppose he has to draw the line somewhere.'

Jardine's battle station was to be on the bridge as 'communication officer.' He would be responsible for answering the telephones and conveying messages quickly and accurately and passing the captain's orders to the various positions. For this, Edmund had taken over from Reece as his instructor, and his meticulous approach, his determination that Jardine would master every detail was more than he had expected. Jardine stood rather in awe of Edmund, but was grateful for the painstaking way he had gone about it. Edmund had tested him thoroughly at the end of the morning and only when Edmund declared himself satisfied, which meant that Jardine scored a hundred percent, did they leave the bridge.

'Sound action stations,' Edmund ordered, and Jardine immediately pointed to the appropriate button. 'Short-long, short-long for aircraft, long-long for anything else, including anti-submarine.'

'Good. Now tell the engine room that I'm going to manoeuvre. Yes, that's the right phone. Now, order the four-inch gun to train to green five-o, enemy aircraft. Yes, all right, but what have you forgotten?'

'I don't know, sir. Oh yes, of course, look over the fore end of the bridge and see if the gun has in fact been trained to green five-o.'

Edmund went on relentlessly. 'Depth charge crew, stand by.' 'Sound four blasts on the siren.' 'Ask the first lieutenant if I'm clear aft.' 'Switch on fighting lights.' 'Tell the steward I'll be down for supper in five minutes and to make sure the chilli peppers are on the table.' He had been standing near the voicepipe and a laugh came up from Reece.

It was almost sailing time so Jardine toured the bridge one last time and reminded himself of the whereabouts of every voicepipe, telephone and button. Overhead were vapour trails, too distant to determine whether made by enemy or friendly aircraft. Guns were firing a few miles away, probably in the Ramsgate and

Margate area, and sirens were wailing from a dozen locations in London to the west.

Meanwhile, as the fate of great nations was being decided in the skies above *Troubadour*, the fate of a single individual was to be determined during the next few moments. Dobreiner had been unusually vigilant since being told some months earlier by a petty officer that one of his men, stoker Rostron, had tried to sabotage the ship. Dobreiner had not a jot of evidence that would stand up in a court martial and he had discussed it with no one save the petty officer who had found sand in the main bearings and reported his suspicions.

Dobreiner had spent the afternoon in the engine room and boiler rooms while steam was being raised and now went to Braithwaite's cabin to report that the engines were ready to deliver power. A few moments later he was back in his own domain of heat and noise and took his place beside the engine room artificer of the watch. He looked over the dials with a steady eye.

The engine room was poorly lit, but out of the corner of his eye Dobreiner saw a figure approaching from the direction of the boiler rooms. The man stopped by the main bearings, looked in Dobreiner's direction and his hand went to his pocket. Dobreiner turned and faced him and his sudden movement made the man draw back. He slipped and partly fell on the greasy steel walkway. Gathering himself he ran toward the watertight door through which he had passed moments before. As he did so he let fall a small container.

On the other side of the watertight door in the air-lock compartment between engine room and boiler room an invisible hand had slammed it shut, as it should have been at that moment, and was in process of securing the heavy metal clips. These were, in effect, levers which jammed the door and could be operated from either side. The fugitive drew back against the door as the six clips relentlessly moved into the secure position. He glanced over his shoulder at Dobreiner and there was a look of ultimate desperation in his face.

The engine room telegraph sounded and the pointer turned to 'slow ahead' on the starboard engine. The artificer, who was the only other occupant of the engine room, opened the valve to allow steam to pass and watched the shaft as it began to turn.

Dobreiner stooped and picked up the small cardboard container, satisfied himself as to its contents and advanced toward his victim. The man's hand was on one of the clips and he was trying to move it but his strength failed him. A length of hollow pipe was nearby, used for that very purpose which he was trying to achieve. It was fitted over the six-inch clips to give extra leverage when opening or closing them. Dobreiner seized it from its accustomed place and dealt the man a crushing blow on the head. He sank to the ground and with absolute composure Dobreiner slipped the pipe on the lever and left it in place. He then found an oil can and put it beside the body which he examined carefully for the first time. It was Rostron and it was obvious that he was dead.

Dobreiner was not naturally a violent person, but the sight of one of his own men trying to sabotage the ship as it put to sea had raised a fury in him which he had not know until that moment that he possessed. All his adult life he had been in the navy. He had come up the hard way and had one inflexible idea in his mind, that the engines entrusted to his care would be kept running in all circumstances and at all costs. The captain, high up on the bridge, was to be obeyed meticulously or the ship would be imperilled. Any failure, loss of power, breakdown or malfunction was not acceptable in war or in peace. An act of sabotage was punishable by death. If lovesick stokers could prevent ships from going to sea and performing their appointed tasks, then the war would be lost and the dark age of Nazi rule would settle over the world.

Dobreiner returned to the control position and found half speed ahead on one shaft and half astern on the other. The ship is out in the stream, he said to himself, turning downriver toward the sea. Soon it would be half ahead on both engines and a buildup of power as they gained open water. The artificer on watch had seen nothing of the incident by the watertight door. Dobreiner watched the dials for a few moments then picked up the bridge telephone and turned the handle.

'Bridge,' a voice came back.

'Will you send Jennings to the engine room. There seems to have been an accident near the watertight door.'

Jardine was not experienced enough to ask what sort of accident and it didn't sound serious. He replaced the phone and informed Edmund who bent over the wheelhouse voicepipe and said, 'someone go and find the sick berth attendant. Tell him to report to the engine room.'

Jardine had been watching as Braithwaite brought *Troubadour* into the stream and turned her while *Harp* took station astern. The seamen lined the ship's rail and the muddy banks of the river slipped away. It was daylight and clear enough to see for miles but Reece stood by the chart and called out the information which it provided.

'Can you see the next buoy on the south side?' he asked. 'Green two-o.'

'Yes, got it,' Edmund replied.

'Course due east, then.'

Midshipman Reece, the secret of his age having at last been revealed, was now held in high esteem by his brother officers and the ship's company. He had been admitted at the age of fifteen, was only sixteen now, and had got the better of the navy recruitment procedures. In an earlier age the likes of Reece would have gone to sea at twelve or thirteen. If he had survived accident, disease and war he would have been a lieutenant at eighteen and a captain at thirty. He was a good navigator, a skill which he had learned at Pangbourne, the merchant navy training school. Being a natural mathematician he made it look easy, but more than that his preparatory work was meticulous. When he had learned the ship's destination that morning he had taken out the chart, pencilled in the courses and looked up the tides that would be running.

Jardine had heard stories about the treatment meted out to midshipmen in cruisers and battleships and seen some of it when he had been on the lower deck. Every derogatory epithet was applied to them, they were 'snotties', 'dogsbodies', 'the lowest form of animal life'. The officer appointed to instruct them was called the 'the snotties' nurse' and usually contented himself with a string of rebukes and insults toward his charges.

The midshipman who assisted the officer of the watch when a

capital ship was in harbour was supposed to carry a telescope under his left arm. Binoculars would have been more appropriate, but the antiquated stupidity of a telescope appealed to the mentality of the big ship navy. In addition, a midshipman who allowed the angle of his telescope to vary in the slightest degree from the horizontal could be rebuked instantly and satisfyingly with the order, 'Correct the angle of your telescope.' This phrase gained colour and momentum in the wartime navy. It came to imply the mindless ritualism of the peacetime navy, the pathological need felt by some individuals to emphasize rank and superordination, to assert themselves and fill in time by saying things that didn't need saying. The phrase 'Correct the angle of your telescope' carried an undertone, therefore, which the navy of reservists and volunteers felt towards their peacetime counterparts. It also implied that carrying a telescope was about all that could be entrusted to a midshipman.

In *Troubadour*, however, Reece was doing an officer's job and was treated accordingly. He chatted easily with the officers in the wardroom and was a part of their councils and discussions. His manner was faultless and Braithwaite's words were soon round the messdecks to the effect that during the preceding winter in the North Atlantic he had endured the conditions as well as anyone. There was one aspect of his character, however, which surprised Jardine. Reece, whose rate of pay as a midshipman was wretched, nevertheless made an allotment on a monthly basis to his mother. It was a pitifully small sum and she had no need of it, but it gave him a feeling of triumph that he was now contributing to the family that had raised him. Money earned aboard ship in wartime had about it an almost sacramental quality; he was thanking his parents and honouring them.

Dobreiner came up the bridge ladder and looked round him.

'Captain, sir, I'm afraid the accident's worse than I thought. We strapped him to a stretcher and got him to the sick bay but Jennings says he's dead.'

A weary and resigned look came over Braithwaite.

'Have you got the ship, Casswell?'

'Yessir,' Edmund replied.

Braithwaite turned back to Dobreiner.

'How the hell did it happen?'

'Looks like a freak accident, sir; but it wouldn't have happened if my orders had been obeyed. It seems that when we were casting off from the jetty he came from the boiler room to the engine room. He didn't close the watertight door but searched around for his oil can and left the iron pipe stuck on one of the door clips. The clips on that door have always been a bit stiff, never mind the grease that goes on, so we keep iron pipes handy on both sides of the door.'

'Yes, yes, I understand that,' Braithwaite said. 'The pipe is placed over the clip to give purchase.'

'Yessir. Well, what this lad did was to leave the pipe on the clip. On the other side the stoker petty officer sees the clips are not fastened and didn't know that a stoker was in the engine room. He uses the pipe on the boiler-room side to wrench down on the clip, which brought the pipe on the engine room side down on the stoker's head. The petty officer did absolutely right and he couldn't have known that a man was on the other side of the door. They've been told many times not to leave the pipe like that, irregardless of how short a time.'

'That's exactly what happened in the P & O line,' Braithwaite said. 'Years ago. Oh shit.'

He looked back toward the convoy.

'We've had more than our fair share. Tell the first lieutenant I want to see him.'

Edmund turned to Jardine and without saying anything he pointed at the log book. Jardine looked at his watch, picked up a pencil and began to write 'Chief Engineer reports . . .'

Pemberton already knew about the accident, had been down to the engine room and talked to Jennings in the sick bay. There was nothing to be added to the chief engineer's report, it was one of those accidents which occur when instructions are not followed.

Pemberton ordered that the man be sewn in his hammock by his messmates and placed in the steering compartment. The coxswain would go through the process of discharging him from the navy and the letters DD would appear after his name; Discharged Dead. The body would not be buried at sea but carried to the Forth and put ashore. If time allowed an officer and a firing party would go to the cemetery and he'd be interred with proper ceremony.

'All because of an oil can,' Pemberton grumbled. He seemed resigned and determined not to allow the incident to harm *Troubadour*'s efficiency as they sailed on another wartime operation.

'Married, was he?' Pemberton asked.

'No, but I think he had a girl and from what I heard his parents are still living.'

Dobreiner turned to go and Pemberton spoke to Jardine. 'As soon as we reach the Forth you'll be shown the kind of letters of condolence that have to be sent. There's quite a routine to be followed when someone gets killed. We auction off his possessions and the money goes to his family.'

Marko came up as the afternoon watch ended. Edmund didn't just leave the bridge but spent a full ten minutes handing over. The course and speed, the twenty-ship convoy astern, *Harp* a thousand yards to the west, a clumsy-looking gun-ship astern, two armed yachts and a torpedo boat. Enemy aircraft were the danger, but it was a clear evening and the lookouts could see for miles. Jardine took it all in.

Something that seemed odd and faintly embarrassing to Jardine was when the captain's orders were passed from one officer to another within the captain's hearing. Braithwaite sat in his raised chair on the starboard side of the bridge within easy earshot and Edmund said, 'the captain warned me to be extra vigilant for low-flying aircraft.' Next, 'the captain mentioned that the two yachts and the torpedo boat have only one signalman who can't be on the bridge all the time so there may be some delay in answering signals.'

Jardine would soon come to realise that a ship was a small place and conversations overheard were common. Later that evening he came on the bridge for the first night watch and Edmund called down, 'Reece, old chap, when the captain comes up he'll probably ask you for the time of moonrise.'

There was a momentary pause, then Reece replied, 'the captain's here and he just did.'

After only a few watches on the bridge it was evident to Jardine that his training ashore had prepared him inadequately for his new duties. The officer instruction had been unimaginative, time had been wasted on non-essentials and whole areas like astro-navigation had been omitted. He could hardly have expected, however, that the ship would be jolted by a fatal accident on his first trip. He resolved to put the incident out of his mind and concentrate on what was taking place round him. The sombre mood of his brother officers, however, contrasted with the mood that had prevailed at the lunch table a few hours earlier. Braithwaite had called a meeting during the morning which had been attended by the captains of the various escort vessels and he had come back with a story about the luxurious accommodation on board one of the yachts in which all the men had bunks with curtains and reading lights. The officers' bathroom had a bidet which they unscrewed and used for serving food. Jardine hadn't been sure whether he should laugh or not, but Reece laughed after which the smiled faded from his face. 'What's a bee-day?' he asked.

Jardine realised that *Troubadour* was better built and more comfortable than ships that had been constructed under navy contract, although perhaps not up to the standard of a millionaire's yacht. The navy was realistic about its ships, knowing that in wartime many would be lost and that even in peacetime there could be accidents. The purpose, therefore, was to build the greatest number of ships and accord workmanship, finish and habitability a low priority. Offence, defence and speed were at the top, along with sea-keeping qualities. What they were like to live in came last in order of importance. The navy would have had three or four ships for the price of *Troubadour* and *Harp*. They would have been faster, with less beam, and would have packed more guns and torpedo tubes. The accommodation would have been miserable, and his mind went back to the cruiser in which he had served; crowded, wet and crammed with armament.

There was something else they had not taught him which was that in a good ship there is a lot of mutual respect. Edmund Casswell and Marko Cyr, for instance, both of them reserve lieutenants but very different, were obviously the best of friends. Cyr was Canadian, tough and outgoing but not a bully. They called him 'the Gallant Officer from New France' and Reece told a story about him being tricked into joining the navy in a London pub. He was a practical, confident man who would make a joke about anything and, if he had been a businessman, would have driven a hard bargain. The word had got around that he was to be best man at Edmund's wedding.

Edmund was scholarly and intense, a perfectionist who would leave nothing to chance. He was a natural teacher, and Jardine wondered why such a person had not been selected to teach aspiring officers. How long would it take the Admiralty to find him and put him in a position where he could influence hundreds of others? Reece had said of him that his head was among the stars, his wife-to-be was a beautiful French girl and his father was a bishop. Reece seemed genuinely moved. 'He's the most efficient officer in the navy. Well, almost,' he conceded. 'He walks with God and his God is very demanding. You could have done worse than fall into his hands.'

These officers, Jardine realised, had been together since the start of the war. They had suffered disappointments and achieved some modest success, and month by month they had gained in strength and unity. Sadly they could be blown apart in seconds by bomb, mine or torpedo. *Minstrel* and *Chorister* were gone and it would be foolish to believe that *Troubadour* enjoyed the special favour of Providence.

When he had been on the lower deck he had heard unflattering comments about the officers, but his own opinion had been formed when his ship had been in Scapa Flow and a lieutenant asked him if he wanted to go sailing. He jumped at the chance and demonstrated in minutes that he knew how to handle a boat and was later called to the officer's cabin for an hour of discussion. A month later his naval rating's cap bore the white ribbon of the officer training school. He never discovered the officer's name, but was grateful that he had gone out of his way to be of help.

What he had heard about officers being heavy drinkers was patently untrue as far as *Troubadour* was concerned. Braithwaite obviously drank, but Dobreiner was a teetotaler and the others contented themselves with a glass of wine in the evenings. There was no drinking at all when the ship was at sea. The 'no-treating' rule was strictly applied so that everyone paid for what he consumed and this made sense of the captain's rule that Reece should expend no more than five shillings a month at the bar, and he, a sub-lieutenant, could spend ten shillings. At duty-free prices it was ample.

Reece had mentioned that before the fall of France they had been at Bordeaux and bought a consignment of wines and brandies. In consequence an evening in harbour would not have been complete without wine on the wardroom table. The bottle would be opened with ceremony, tasted with anticipation and discussed in florid prose.

'Pretentious,' Cyr might say, 'the balance is there, but it's trying to be something it really isn't.'

'Not a lot of depth or complexity when you think about it,' Edmund might add, 'although it stands up well to the food.'

The captain would smile and shake his head, Reece would take a small sip and would admit he didn't know what they were talking about. Jardine had a feeling that he had to be careful not to put a foot wrong in this unusual company.

Jardine was aware that his own circumstances gave no cause for rejoicing. His marriage had been hasty and ill-considered, entered into for the wrong reasons to a woman whose irresponsible behaviour, far from being cured by marriage, had grown worse with the passage of time. She complained endlessly, was extravagant and a wretched homemaker. Housekeeping money was spent on clothes and cosmetics. She couldn't cook, refused to clean house and wanted to eat out every night of the week. In bed she was uninspired and so far as the future was concerned she vowed that she would not accompany her husband if he were posted overseas.

One of her more annoying characteristics was the repeated complaint that by marrying Chris she had been forced to abandon a successful career as a dress designer. In fact she had worked in a ladies' shop and had advised customers who were unsure of their own preferences, but to describe this as dress design was being very economical with the truth. When she married, just before the outbreak of war, she gave up her job so that she could devote full time to her marriage.

At first Chris had wanted children, but had learned from the family doctor that it was out of the question. When a woman does everything badly it seemed pointless to assume that she would do any better in the demanding role of parent, so he came to regard her screwed-up insides as a blessing. He cooked the evening meal, cleaned their small house and went shopping on Saturdays, having also to work long hours at Barclays Bank. He was physically strong and took these exertions in stride, but his life changed when he was advised that his job at the bank was not to be a reserved occupation and the War Office planned to call him up for the Army Pay Corps. With his small yachting experience, which could have been measured more appropriately in hours than days, he joined the navy as an ordinary seaman.

Chris Jardine had gained sufficient experience in his eight years at the bank to settle his own affairs so that his assets were beyond the clumsy reach of his wife. He took steps to prevent her from selling or disposing of the small house which he had inherited and made over his savings to his sister who lived in Vancouver. He left some money in the joint account and made an allotment from his pay which was available to his wife, at the same time telling her to return to her old job so that she would have an added income.

Mabel Jardine possessed a small roomful of clothes and was, therefore, well placed to face the severe clothing rationing which lay ahead. Her choice tended, however, toward the bizarre, verging on the outlandish, impelled by her desire to stand out in a crowd. Clothes were her life; not family, nor house, nor food, nor conversation. When he returned from sea, however, he was not prepared for what he found. His wife had not written to him, but a neighbour disclosed that police had been at the house. Some of her clothes had been loaded into a police van and had been used as exhibits in court. Mabel was lucky to have been placed on probation. She had lost her job and had a police record. When he entered his house Chris was confronted by a young woman, sad and complaining, who sat smoking in a kitchen where none of the dishes were washed.

On his second leave, as an officer, things were only slightly better. The probation officer was doing her best and enlisted

Chris as an ally in her attempts to bring Mabel to her senses. She had shown her that rage and petulance would not do, that the path ahead would be an uphill struggle. It had been a dismal two weeks' leave.

That evening, the day of stoker Rostron's death, Jardine found himself alone with Dobreiner in the wardroom. There was little motion on the ship because the sea was calm and the engines beneath them hummed in a purposeful way. Whatever thoughts may have occupied Dobreiner's mind he was outwardly quiet and composed, seemingly resigned to the vicissitudes of life and the chances that befall a seagoing ship in time of war. He did not much care to talk with Jardine at that moment nor with anyone else for that matter, but wardroom proprieties demanded that he make some pretence of discussing the events of the day. Jardine's saving grace was that he had been on the lower deck for a few months and had not walked directly into the wardroom from Cowes Regatta or Bond Street.

'That stoker wasn't much use.' Dobreiner said quietly. 'Couldn't follow simple instructions. Truth is he got what he asked for.'

'A bash on the head and a fractured skull,' Jardine said. 'It must have been an awful blow.'

'You know how it is,' Dobreiner went on. 'My petty officer was annoyed at seeing the door open when it should have been shut. He bore down on that clip with all his weight and he's a big man.'

'And he'll remember to the end of his days that he inadvertently caused a man's death, a man who in fact was standing only inches away from him.'

'A half inch of steel separated them.' Dobreiner stifled a yawn. 'I don't think the petty officer is going to lose a lot of sleep over it. I know I won't.'

Troubadour was escorting a convoy from the Nore to the Forth, London to Edinburgh, so Edmund slipped into the routine of life at sea and rejoiced as he performed the small duties of his daily existence. It was summer, the weather was warm, the days long and the nights short. *Harp* rose and fell a thousand yards on

Troubadour's beam while the businesslike black shapes of coastal vessels came up astern, pushing their white bow waves.

Jardine had been keeping watches with Pemberton, Edmund and Marko in turn. He was an intense man, rather humourless, but a hard worker. He came from an existence governed by paper, regulation and fixed procedure and found himself in a world where chance, common sense and the captain's judgement prevailed.

'Very well,' Edmund said. 'Let's say aircraft are reported approaching from the east, that's Germany. What are you going to do?'

'Call the captain. Sound action stations,' was the reply.

'And it never hurts to check the time and if it's daylight and a flag signal will be seen, then hoist . . .'

'Starboard lookout – bridge.'

Edmund spun round.

'Bridge.'

'Looks like a lifeboat, sir. Green nine-o.'

'Yes, I have it, well done. Do you see it, Jardine?' He crossed to the captain's voicepipe.

'Captain, sir. Lifeboat away to starboard. Three to four miles. May have survivors in it.'

'Very well, I'm coming up.'

'Jardine, take a compass bearing so that if fog comes down we can steam towards it. Now write in the log the time and the compass bearing. And tell the lookout, able seaman McVane, to keep his binoculars on it.'

'Whereaway?' Braithwaite called out as he ran up the ladder.

'Just past the beam, sir, bearing o-nine-five.'

'Funny, I don't see it.'

'I lost it in the fog,' McVane said. 'Can't see it no more.'

'Turn towards,' Braithwaite ordered.

'Aye aye, sir. Starboard twenty', Edmund called down the voicepipe. 'Can I go up to twenty knots?'

'Go up to twenty-four knots.'

'Two-six-five revolutions. Steady at o-nine-five.'

Edmund turned to Jardine.

'Stop and think. First, the engine room. Call them and say we are going to investigate what looks like a lifeboat. After that, call the first lieutenant. He needs to know what's happening. Third, make sure Reece is in the chart room. He'll want to mark our position on the chart.'

Edmund paused.

'We're going to pass ahead of the trawler, the *Mary Something-or-other*. Have the signalman stand by in case the captain wants to make a signal for him to get out of our way. Or perhaps four blasts on the siren would do.'

'Now, stop and think some more,' Edmund went on. 'The captain may want to signal *Harp* to continue course and speed, but then again we haven't ordered an alteration so that's what she'll do anyway. They'll see us going off at high speed, assume we're suspicious and are going to take a look. In wartime we try to avoid unnecessary signalling.'

'Next problem,' Edmund went on relentlessly, 'why didn't *Mary-Something* see it from her position a thousand yards closer.'

'Not keeping such a good lookout, a peculiarity of the fog, we only saw it a few seconds,' Jardine replied.

'All right. Now tell me why the captain chose to go and investigate and didn't tell *Mary* to go.'

Jardine thought for a moment. 'Because we saw it, we took a compass bearing and we're faster.'

'Much faster. Their top speed is probably twelve or fourteen knots; ours is twenty-four or twenty-five. It's not going to take us all day to get back to our station ahead of the convoy.'

They searched the sea and Edmund suddenly said; 'Captain, sir, I see it. Dead ahead.'

He turned to Jardine. 'We're still thinking, aren't we? Could it be some sort of booby trap? Is the boat filled with explosives? Are there a couple of E-boats hiding in the fog waiting to torpedo us? All right then, tell the lookouts to do an all-round search.'

Troubadour approached the boat whose two occupants waved clothing, indeed continued to do so long after it must have been obvious that they had been seen. It was not a lifeboat but looked more like a small fishing craft. Braithwaite put *Troubadour* alongside and a heaving line coiled out from *Troubadour*'s upper deck. Two young men scrambled on board.

'Tell the first lieutenant to cast off and sink it with gunfire.'

Braithwaite spoke to no one in particular, but Edmund pointed to Jardine who hurried off the bridge.

'Rejoin the convoy,' he said to Edmund. 'I wonder who they are.'

'Half ahead together,' Edmund called down. 'Two-six-five revolutions; port twenty.'

Troubadour shook as the screws gripped and shot a jet of white water astern. The boat floated away from her side and a seaman fired a short burst from the port oerlikon gun which ripped it to shreds. Jardine was back on the bridge.

'Sir, they claim to be Danish boys running away from the Germans. They've been rowing for three days. They're only eighteen.'

'Very good, I'd like to talk to them,' Braithwaite said. 'I can speak German after a fashion. They'll probably understand.'

'Have you written all this in the log book?' Edmund asked Jardine. 'Put in sufficient detail that it makes sense if it has to be referred to later. And enter the names of the two young fellows as soon as the Coxswain finds out who they are.'

'One other thing,' he went on. 'Ask the captain if you may record in the log book the name of the starboard lookout, able seaman McVane, together with an expression of the captain's approval.'

Braithwaite turned and said, 'Do so, I'll sign it.'

'And what is the first thing the Coxswain will do with the two men after they've had any medical treatment they need?'

'A good meal, I should think.'

'Wrong. Their battle stations. Where they go when the alarm bells sound, and what is expected of them. After that they can eat and sleep. Have you learned anything from this, Jardine?'

'Gosh yes. Thank you.'

That night Edmund came up for the middle watch at midnight, relieving Marko. He was content to have the watch to himself, four hours during which he would be interrupted in his thoughts only for the routine matters of the ship. He passed Harding as he came up and asked him. 'Coming on or going off?'

'On, sir,' Harding said.

That meant fewer worries for him. Harding was methodical

and rarely had to be told anything; he'd be a petty officer within a few months. *Troubadour* had twenty or more men who had been identified for promotion, able seaman to leading seaman, leading seaman to petty officer. Clancy, the coxwain, would go to a destroyer as a chief petty officer and the leading signalman was ready to become a yeoman of signals. Yes, they all had a foot on the next rung and there would be promotions when *Troubadour* went in for her next refit.

He looked in the log book and read what Jardine had said about the rescue of the two Danish boys. They were from a fishing village on the coast of Denmark and had taken their uncle's boat from the harbour and sailed westwards. They hadn't done badly, almost three hundred miles in three days. They were smart enough to carry food, water and a compass and they even had some identity with them; school passes and membership in a football club. One of them could speak a few words of English, and when Pemberton told him to come up to the bridge to be interviewed by the captain the boy had asked if they could first go below, shave and get themselves presentable. They had a certain style, in other words, and in these desperate times the navy would take them with no questions asked.

'The captain has commented favourably on the alertness of able seaman McVane for having sighted the boat in conditions of poor visibility.' Yes, that would do; it must have made McVane feel pretty good, especially when he went below and the coxswain had introduced him to the two Danish boys.

He wondered what Jardine had thought about his first few days aboard *Troubadour*. 'A succession of small happenings,' he had told him. 'The main thing is to get the small things right and don't let them develop into problems.' But why had Jardine volunteered for the navy and gone on the lower deck? He was in his late twenties, could almost certainly have been exempted from service on the grounds that Barclays Bank had to carry on as a worldwide organization. Everywhere that ships put in or there was an airfield or a brigade of troops there was a Barclays Bank where officers like himself could go and pick up money to pay the men. Running a bank was war service of a sort, probably well remunerated, and he could have been living with his wife. So why the navy? True, he was an officer now, but his ten years' experience in the banking business was not being put to much use. The ship's office didn't call for the sort of skill and experience that Jardine possessed.

Edmund had a simple office system in place, correspondence one side; pay the other. It hadn't taken him fifteen minutes to explain it and the speed at which Jardine mastered the work, counted money and did mental arithmetic was astonishing. Oh well, he thought, Marko would find out more about him. Marko was good at asking questions, it didn't seem to embarrass him as it did Edmund. Somewhere in Jardine's life there was a blot on the paper, a tragedy, and he had probably joined the navy to put it behind him.

Chapter 20

IN LATE SEPTEMBER *Troubadour* and *Harp* led their charges into the broad estuary of the Forth. Unknown to the men aboard the two ships they would not be returning to Chatham but would be sailing once more in the stormy North Atlantic. For a start they were due to escort a cruiser, HMS *Daphne*, as far as Scapa Flow in the Orkneys. The islands, off Scotland's north coast, lay two hundred and fifty sea miles distant, a mere twelve or fifteen hours' steaming, assuming *Daphne* ordered a speed somewhere between fifteen and twenty knots.

The weather was fine as they put to sea once again. The hills of Scotland stood out in their harsh and triumphant splendour, the muted shades of red, brown and grey a feast for the eyes of the two lookouts whose binoculars brought them seemingly within touching distance of the shore. White clouds, like disconnected thoughts, dotted the eastern horizon, and there was a stillness in the air broken only by the seagulls that followed wheeling and plunging above *Troubadour*'s wake. The rich scents of the land, redolent of honey and ripe fruit, were carried on the breeze. These were not the dream-laden perfumes of tropical countries, but told of the robust character of a northern people who had gone outward from this wilful place and in their quiet, industrious way had left their mark upon half the world.

'What makes them leave?' Edmund asked, knowing that Braithwaite would understand him.

'Not big enough; the lure of vast acres across the sea.'

'And they carry with them the sound of the pipes, their pagan dances and their mournful songs to the ends of the earth, and it ends up that there are more Scotsmen outside Scotland than in it. You know, sir,' Edmund went on, 'I've never had a Scottish boy in my division who couldn't read and write. Their education, whatever it lacks, sends them out from here a basically literate people.'

Like so many conversations on the bridge of a warship this one was destined to be cut short. The cruiser, HMS *Daphne*, was astern and *Troubadour* assumed her station a thousand yards on her port bow, *Harp* the same distance on her starboard bow.

'Signalling,' reported the lookout.

'*What is your best speed?*' flashed from *Daphne*'s bridge.

'Reply twenty-four knots,' from Braithwaite.

G-21 went up *Daphne*'s halyards and Braithwaite groaned. 'Why does he have to choose twenty-one? Hell, we've been lying within spitting distance all day. He could have called me over and discussed his proposed course, speed, and formation. He turned to the signalman.

'*Regret twenty-one knots unsatisfactory for this class of ship. Shuddering occurs which reduces effectiveness of asdic. Respectfully request reduction by one or two knots.*'

The signalman wrote it on his pad, aimed his Aldis lamp over the quarter and began to spell it out. The leading signalman was beside him reading from the pad. 'Shuddering, two Ds, occurs, one R,' he said in an undertone.

There was a pause, then *Daphne* negated the signal and hoisted a fresh one, *twenty knots.*

'Execute,' from the signalman.

Edmund leaned toward the voicepipe and ordered an increase in engine revolutions and a puff of smoke emerged from *Troubadour*'s funnel, a common occurrence when there's a change of speed.

'*Why are you making smoke?*' *Daphne* signalled. '*Such carelessness is not to be tolerated in wartime.*'

Braithwaite looked back at the cruiser with a look of disgust on his face. A small puff of smoke which would dissipate in seconds was not worth making a signal about.

'Casswell, do you think he expects a reply?'

'I doubt it, sir.'

Daphne was now signalling *Harp*.

'Read it,' Braithwaite told the signalman. 'Even if it's not meant for us.'

'*You are out of station by one degree and your boat rope is too slack. Make necessary corrections.*'

Braithwaite stared round the horizon with a stunned look, but nothing could have prepared him for the next signal.

'*How do you dispose of your gash without attracting U-boats?*'

Yes, there were rules about not throwing crates or boxes overboard, or anything that would float and possibly be seen by a U-boat. The men in *Troubadour* and *Harp* knew this and were strict in compliance. It was a dubious rule, because the chances of a U-boat seeing a waterlogged object in an expanse of ocean were negligible and even less of knowing which direction a ship or convoy had taken or how long ago. But to worry about gash, the navy word for kitchen scraps, was bordering on stupidity. Anything edible that didn't sink would be grabbed by the seagulls.

'What do we say to that?' Braithwaite asked. 'The man's off his rocker. What the hell does he think we do with our gash?'

'Then perhaps we could reply that crates and boxes are put ashore while gash is disposed of in the time-honoured manner,' Edmund suggested.

'Yes, that'll do,' Braithwaite replied; then, 'O God, here comes another.'

'*Commence zig-zag number 8,*' the signalman said. 'Execute.'

'Reece, bring the zig-zag book,' Edmund called down to the chart room. Then to Jardine, 'Station-keeping is more difficult when we're zig-zagging.'

Reece ran up the bridge ladder with the zig-zag book and opened it to number 8.

'It's now 1923 hours and the next turn is twelve degrees to port at 1925. We'll be on that course for five minutes. Your new course,' Reece was using the compass to help with the calculation, 'will be 034 degrees.'

'That bastard deliberately gave us less than two minutes to make the first turn,' Braithwaite said. 'What's he trying to do?' He hesitated. 'What percentage of loss is there in this one?'

'Sixteen percent,' Reece read off the top of the page.

'On passage from here to Cape Town sixteen percent would be a thousand miles lost.'

Braithwaite had an extraordinary faculty for mental arithmetic.

'If he were more considerate he'd start the zig-zag on the hour and give us ten minutes' warning. In a cruiser he has an officer of the watch, probably two, and all the midshipmen he needs.' Braithwaite stamped his feet as he did when he was angry, but the captain of the cruiser wasn't finished.

'*You turned too rapidly and are now out of station by a quarter of a cable. Do not escort vessels know the importance of accurate station keeping?*'

Edmund checked the cruisers' compass bearing and range.

'My fault,' he said. 'I forgot that *Daphne* is larger and makes a slower turn. Instead of using twenty degrees of rudder I should have used ten. I'll go round more slowly on the next turn.'

'*There's a floating mine four thousand yards to the east. Why has it not been reported?*' was the cruiser's next signal.

'*We don't report floating mines unless they present immediate danger,*' Braithwaite shot back. Then, as an aside he went on, 'after a storm we see dozens of the bloody things in the North Sea. It's a waste of time to make signals about mines to senior officers who can see them just as well as we can.'

'Shall I pass all that, sir?' the signalman asked.

Braithwaite didn't answer but put his binoculars up to his eyes and took a long look at HMS *Daphne*.

'You know, sir,' Edmund began, 'that captain, whoever he is, wants to harass us. I suggest brief replies.'

'*Harp* evidently thought the same. In reply to a signal, '*Explain why I can see washing drying on your boat deck*,' Dalzell-Paul signalled back, '*because it's wet.*'

'*How am I to know*,' Daphne was flashing again, '*that by morning I will have an anti-submarine escort ahead of me?*'

'That's a damnable insult,' Braithwaite blurted out. 'I'm not letting that one pass. *Troubadour* and *Harp* have served faithfully since war began. Two of our sister ships have been sunk. God knows we have nothing to be ashamed of.'

He stamped around the bridge for a full minute, then stopped and glared back at *Daphne*. His annoyance had reached the point where he was prepared to risk the consequences of insubordination.

'*Do I have your permission to place your signals and our war record before the commander-in-chief?*' he signalled.

There was no reply. No light shone from HMS *Daphne*, no blinking Aldis lamp.

Five minutes passed, then ten.

'He's probably gone down for supper,' Reece suggested.

'Anyone know that ship?' Braithwaite asked.

'Only by reputation,' Jardine replied. 'She's an unlucky ship; steamed all over the South Atlantic with two other cruisers trying to find commerce raiders. Always missed them; never in the right place at the right time. They call the captain Kali Charley; you know, Kali, the Indian god of waste and destruction. I don't know that her sister ships have done any better; *Delta, Dayspring, Deptford*. They have no anti-aircraft armament; just six-inch guns and a few torpedoes.'

'Know the captain's name?' Braithwaite asked.

'No sir, but I could find out when we get to Scapa Flow.'

Braithwaite took a last look round and went to the bridge ladder.

'Well, if captain Talkative of the Silent Service has gone down for supper I'm doing the same.' He turned to the signalman. 'Make copies of all signals passed since we left harbour.'

'Now, stop and consider, Jardine, what have you learned from this?' Edmund asked.

'Well, sir, I get the impression that the captain of *Daphne* doesn't appreciate escort vessels, probably because they're commanded and manned by reservists.'

'Very well and did we do anything to provoke him?'

'Only that we couldn't steam at a certain speed, twenty-one knots to be precise.'

'And what about his signals?'

'I suppose he's allowed to make what signals he likes.'

'I doubt that,' Edmund replied. 'I'm not sure if there's anything in writing about foolish and unnecessary signals, but it's well known that at sea things should be short, to the point and confined to operational matters. The navy prides itself on its ability to say a simple thing in a simple way. Grace before meals properly consists of two words, *Thank God*.'

'We're coming to another turn.' Jardine had his eye on the chronometer. 'Twenty seconds; now turn to starboard; your new course will be . . .'

He used the compass to work it out, as Reece had done.

The turn complete, Edmund resumed.

'Our captain was right. There was all day to call a conference on board the cruiser; speed, zig-zag, other details, so why didn't he?'

'He wanted to spring some surprises on us, and make us look foolish if we got it wrong.'

'Yes, I'm afraid so, but I like to think this is unusual,' Edmund continued. 'In the first year of the war we've never seen anything like it; no, I'm wrong. There was an incident in St John's harbour in Newfoundland. A flag officer, or more likely one of his staff, ordered us to go back to sea because the men on the upper deck were a bit disreputable. We refused.'

The memory of that crossing made Edmund turn away and pull up his coat collar.

'What about the signals themselves?' he asked.

'Well, if I may say so, he makes a stupid signal and he gets a stupid answer. All that stuff about throwing gash overboard.'

'Very well, and are you clear that there can be no signalling by Aldis lamp during darkness? The U-boats will be on the surface; they can see us more easily than we can see them because they have a low silhouette. If it's absolutely necessary, pencil-light can be used but it's better to use flag signals and the surprising thing is that even on a dark night they can usually be seen. With good binoculars and a lot of experience the signalman can do wonders.'

'And if you simply can't read it?' Jardine asked.

'Then it's up to the captain; but in some circumstances it might be reasonable to increase to full speed, close the ship until his flags are visible, then go back to your place on the screen. You know that if a ship is beyond you on the screen you repeat the flag signal so the more distant ship can see it.'

What Edmund did not tell Jardine was that he worried about Braithwaite when incidents of this kind occurred. Braithwaite didn't stand up well to reproach; he took things personally and took them hard. He was a vulnerable man who couldn't keep in mind that by to-morrow midday they'd be in Scapa Flow and probably would never again see or hear of HMS *Daphne* and its talkative, critical captain. What did they call him? Kali Charley?

'Anyway, think over what's been happening,' Edmund ended by saying, 'and reach your own conclusions. This has been quite a day even by *Troubadour*'s standards.'

At 2000 Marko came up for his watch. 'So far as the war is concerned,' Edmund told him, 'it's uneventful and even the cruiser has quietened down. It looks as though we'll be on this zig-zag all night.'

Edmund waited a few minutes for Marko to get his bearings. 'By the way,' he added, 'make your turns rather gently with ten degrees of rudder because the cruiser turns more slowly than we do.'

As he passed the wheelhouse on the way down he put his head through the door and addressed the seamen who were grouped round the wheel.

'Someone please give me a shake at fifteen minutes to midnight, Mr Jardine as well.'

'Yessir, Mr Casswell,' the reply came back.

'Thanks, Kirk,' he said, recognising the voice.

'Are you from this part of Scotland by any chance?'

'Few miles north, sir, Aberdeen.'

'We'll be sailing past Aberdeen. What a pity. I'd love to go ashore. You too, I expect.'

'Oh aye, sir.'

Edmund and Jardine went down to the main deck and turned aft to the wardroom.

'Fine man, Kirk; ablest of the able. Been with us since we commissioned. He ought to be a leading seaman.'

'You'll excuse my saying so,' Jardine replied, 'but I've never heard you say other than a good word about every man on board.'

'We're lucky,' Edmund replied. 'These men give everything and get so little.'

He and Jardine joined Braithwaite and Pemberton in the wardroom and sat down to a quiet supper. Just after nine Edmund rose and said he was going to his cabin and as he did so the wardroom telephone sounded.

'Captain there?' Marko asked.

'Yes.'

'Ask him to come up on the bridge. There's something wrong with *Daphne*.'

Edmund spun round.

'Captain, sir. Cyr wants you on the bridge, something wrong with the cruiser; didn't say what.'

They all grabbed their caps and binoculars and Edmund stood aside for the captain to leave first. In moments they were on the bridge.

'There was a kind of muffled explosion from the cruiser. She made a lot of smoke and now she's lying stopped in the water. I've turned through a hundred and eighty degrees, so has *Harp*.'

'Very good, Cyr. I'll take the ship. Go to action stations.'

Jardine's hand was on the alarm button and he pressed long blasts. There was a moment of silence in the ship and then a rumble as the men stopped what they were doing and ran for their battle stations.

'Reece, did you note the time of the explosion?' Edmund asked.

'Twenty-one-o-seven.'

'Thank you. Work out the position of the ship.'

'Very strange,' Braithwaite said almost to himself. 'I don't see fire and she's not listing. What do you make of it, Casswell?'

HMS *Daphne* lay in the extreme twilight of late summer. A trail of smoke emerged from her funnel but there seemed to be no unusual movement on the upper deck. Her six-inch guns were trained fore and aft; she lay stopped and scarcely rolled on the light swell.

Troubadour and *Harp* had both assumed that she had been torpedoed although this theory was soon set aside because the asdic operator said he had not heard torpedo sounds. A mine, then? One of those magnetics?

'Reece, what's the depth of water?' Braithwaite called down.

'Sixty fathoms, sir.'

'Well, that settles it. Too deep for a magnetic and a contact mine would hit forward, which doesn't seem to have happened.'

Braithwaite was speaking half to himself and half to Edmund. Suddenly he reached a decision.

'Casswell, I'm going within hailing distance.'

Edmund took *Troubadour* in a circle to starboard, reduced speed and went astern on the engines within fifty yards of *Daphne*. A signalman produced a loud hailer and set it on the bridge rail.

By this time seamen had taken shape on the upper deck of the cruiser. Her bridge was crowded and fire parties could be seen on the main deck with their hoses and extinguishers. Two black balls, one above the other, hung from her yard arm, signifying that she was not under control.

Braithwaite sounded composed. 'Ahoy there. May I be of assistance?'

There was a pause. 'Not at the moment.' It was an officer's voice but it didn't sound like the captain.

'What is amiss?' Braithwaite asked. 'I assume it was not a torpedo.'

There was another pause.

'Trouble in the boiler room,' the voice came back. 'A boiler has primed and the steam joints blown.'

'Good Lord!' escaped from Braithwaite. 'That's bloody serious.' He collected himself. 'I can do one of two things; either stand off and wait your orders, or join *Harp* in a standard anti-submarine search.'

'We are carrying out repairs. You will conduct an anti-submarine search until we are ready to proceed.'

'Aye aye, sir,' Braithwaite replied. He turned to Edmund. 'Take her away.'

Edmund ordered half ahead on both engines and steamed away from the cruiser. He could see *Harp* a thousand yards to the west, the Scotland side, and could tell by her bow-wave that she was doing twelve knots. She was conducting a search anti-clockwise, so Edmund took *Troubadour* to the opposite side of the square and told the asdic operators to be vigilant.

'I want to see the chief engineer,' Braithwaite called down the voicepipe, and a minute later Dobreiner was on the bridge. He saluted and said, 'Yes sir, I heard your exchange with the cruiser. It's serious all right.'

'What do you think happened, chief?'

'It sounds like a severe case of what we call "condenseritis" which caused the boilers to prime. This blew the steam joints: the main steam-pipe joint, by the sound of things.'

'But chief, that's the sort of thing that happens in a tramp steamer when the engine room crew isn't properly trained.' He shot a swift glance at *Daphne*. 'Could it be sabotage?'

'Sabotage, sir?' Dobreiner's face paled in the darkness. 'Oh no, not sabotage, sir. But these D-class cruisers are twenty years old and they weren't constructed very well in the first place. A primed boiler isn't impossible. There was one back in 1931.'

'Look, chief, here's a ship that has sailed all over the South Atlantic, probably at high speeds and in bad weather. She's probably steamed far enough in the past year to take her three times round the world and now on a calm evening, at twenty knots, a few miles off the coast of Scotland, her boilers prime. How do you explain it?'

Dobreiner pulled off his leather glove. 'I can only suggest that she was due for a refit; not just due but overdue. Her boilers and steampipes were probably worn to the limit. Perhaps a steam gauge got stuck and gave a wrong reading. A stoker petty officer, inattentive, new to ship, doesn't notice anything. That's all I can suggest.'

'Is there any chance of getting it repaired?'

'I haven't seen the damage and I'm only guessing. They'll have to wait till the steam pipes cool off, but if it's the main steam joint they don't stand a chance.'

'Casualties?'

'Almost certainly. You can't have that happen without casualties.'

Braithwaite looked back at the dark outline of HMS *Daphne*.

'Dammit,' he said. 'Poor bastards. Unlucky ship. *Daphne*'s a stupid name for a cruiser.'

He walked round the bridge and Jardine stepped out of his way.

'Thanks, chief.'

Dobreiner saluted and left, and Braithwaite picked up the telephone and spoke to Pemberton.

'We'll have to stay at action stations,' he said. 'A cruiser lying stopped is asking for trouble. I'm not discounting the possibility of taking her in tow. Aberdeen is only a few miles away and we could do it if the weather holds.'

'What about a fleet tug?' Pemberton asked. 'Any sort of tug. Be here in a couple of hours.'

'It would mean breaking wireless silence to get it.' Braithwaite replied. 'Unless he sends *Harp* with orders to come back with a tug. That's a possibility.'

There was another pause. 'I still think he'll choose to manage on his own,' Braithwaite persisted. 'One of us will have to take him in tow while the other does the anti-submarine search. We might manage three knots, perhaps four.'

'Do you really think so, sir? A six-thousand-ton cruiser. Take it in tow?'

'Well, I want you to prepare the tow. Oh, and another thing; put extra lookouts on the bridge.'

'Aye aye, sir,' from Pemberton.

'Were you listening to that?' Edmund asked Jardine.

'Yes, I was. Shouldn't I have been?'

'Yes, of course. The captain didn't lower his voice and people like you and me listen and then think about what was said. The captain isn't just waiting for the next order from Kali Charley over there, he's working out the various options and trying to anticipate.

'First, we admit this is a dangerous situation. A cruiser is lying stopped at sea. If a patrolling U-boat comes on the scene, and remember that Aberdeen is a large port, then it could approach to within three or four miles and we'd be lucky to see it. Our asdic range at absolute best is fifteen hundred yards. So it manoeuvres round to get *Daphne* broadside and fires torpedoes. What do we do? We post extra lookouts on the bridge.'

Edmund turned *Troubadour* through ninety degrees and when she was steady on her new course he continued. 'I think the first lieutenant favoured trying to get a tug from Aberdeen, assuming that *Daphne* won't be able to get under way. A decent-sized tug might tow her at six knots, possibly more, which would leave *Harp* and ourselves free to do what we're doing now, providing anti-submarine protection. The captain, however, is thinking that Kali Charley is impatient and would rather be moving through the water than lying stopped.'

'One question,' Jardine said. 'Why do we search in a square pattern rather than a round one? I would have thought a circular course would be geometrically more efficient.'

'Because there's no helm order I can give the quartermaster that's going to keep the ship moving in a circle with a radius of a thousand yards. If I were to order two or three degrees of port rudder I wouldn't have control and the ship wouldn't swing in a true circle. Going into the wind she'd turn slowly; falling off the wind she'd turn faster. I'd be continuously making silly little corrections. Much better a box formation so the quartermaster is on a straight course for two thousand yards and then I can turn the ship with a proper helm order through ninety degrees. The worst thing is to give idiotic helm orders like "a little bit less". In the days of sail they'd sometimes order "one spoke to starboard", meaning a spoke of the wheel, but not nowadays.'

Edmund made the next course alteration, then asked Braithwaite's permission for Jardine to leave the bridge and see how the tow was prepared.

'Yes, all right,' Braithwaite said. 'Remember the ship being towed has to supply the towing line. Our problem is to secure it, distributing the strain. It can be difficult in a ship like this because the whole quarter-deck is cluttered with depth charge racks. Yes, go ahead; see how it's done.'

'How's he making out?' Braithwaite asked when Jardine was off the bridge.

'Learning fast, sir. He asks questions and he's trying his best. I rather enjoy teaching him. They say you don't really understand a thing yourself until you've explained it to someone else. You know that, sir, you've been a teacher.'

They chatted quietly until Jardine returned to the bridge and explained that the heaviest wire rope in the ship had been secured on the midship bollards on the port side, led aft to where a turn had been made on the after bollards and then out the port quarter fairlead, loosely round the stern and in again on the starboard quarter. There followed a turn on the starboard after bollards and then forward to the midship bollards. The wire rope was long enough to repeat the whole process in reverse so that in the result the strain would be taken by all four sets of bollards. The point of tow would be outside the ship, not inboard, about three feet abaft the transom. Chafing gear had been rigged at the points where the wires passed through the fairleads; old rags, sailcloth and the like, and neatly fastened. Where the doubled wire circled round the stern it had been fastened with yarn and brought back to the ship's rail.

'And all this was done in the dark in a matter of minutes with no noise,' he reported, then added. 'Fenders are in place but not so they'll interfere with the depth charges and the shackle can't fall overboard because it's secured with a lanyard.'

'That's what I would have expected,' Braithwaite replied. 'Thank you, Jardine.'

A moment later Pemberton called Braithwaite and reported, 'ready to tow, sir.'

At midnight Braithwaite told Edmund to change the seamen about, lookouts to the wheelhouse, wheelhouse crew to act as lookouts. Edmund did so and then took a long look at *Daphne*. In the darkness he thought he could see activity on her forecastle.

'Sir, I think something's happened on her forward deck. She must be preparing a tow. There's nothing else she'd be doing on the forecastle.'

'You're right,' Braithwaite said. 'What they've done is to unshackle the starboard anchor and suspend it from the cathead, which gets it out of the way and makes it easier to pass the tow. Very well, watch for signals.'

A few minutes later a flag hoist went up her halyards and *Troubadour* turned toward.

'*Take me in tow*,' the leading signalman called out.

'Very well, Casswell. I'll take the ship from here. I'm going to pass down her starboard side then stop with our stern under her bows and pick up the tow. You go to the after deck and keep me informed of my distance from her. Remember that I can't really see aft from here. Jardine will be on the telephone.' He turned to the leading signalman, 'I'll need the loud hailer.'

How satisfying to be right, Edmund thought as he went down

the ladder and hurried aft. Whatever one might say about Braithwaite he possessed a basic common sense, an instinct that rarely led him astray where seamanship was concerned. He'd been correct in his assessment and instead of a last minute dash to prepare the tow, Pemberton, Fenway and some men were quietly looking over the preparations.

Braithwaite handled the ship to perfection. He brought *Troubadour* alongside within easy hailing distance and waited for *Daphne* to open the conversation.

'You will take me in tow using my starboard anchor cable. Are you ready?'

It was Kali Charley himself this time. He was close enough to see the gold lace on his cap and he sounded irritated.

'Yes, sir. Perfectly ready. I observed that your anchor was catted.'

Braithwaite allowed the slightest hint of condescension to enter his voice.

'I take it you'll pay out cable as I go ahead. Where do you wish me to steer for?'

'Aberdeen.'

Edmund hoped that able seaman Kirk was listening.

'Do you know at what speed you can tow me?'

That's a stupid question, Edmund thought. We don't get much practice towing cruisers around.

'I'm sorry, sir,' from Braithwaite. 'I really can't say. Perhaps three knots. A fleet tug would do six.'

Braithwaite brought *Troubadour* to a stop with her stern a few feet from the cruiser's bow.

'You're ten feet away from her cable, sir,' Edmund spoke into the phone. 'If you go dead slow ahead on the port engine and dead slow astern starboard you'll put the cable over our transom.'

'We're doing that,' from Jardine.

'Well done. We've taken the cable and it's being shackled on. Secure, sir. Go dead slow ahead. All clear aft and fenders are in. Perfect.'

Pemberton called across to the commander on the cruiser's foredeck. 'Tow secured.'

It seemed strange to Edmund that for hours *Daphne* had been a grey shape a thousand yards distant but was now suddenly a few feet away with men talking to each other.

'You've had some back luck,' Pemberton was saying to the commander. 'I'm sorry there's so little we can do.' The commander thanked him and hoped they'd meet again in more agreeable circumstances. The seamen were also chatting across the few feet of water and learned that *Daphne* had suffered numerous casualties and her sick bay was full of injured. The phrase 'severe burns' kept being repeated.

Braithwaite moved *Troubadour* ahead and the gap between the two ships widened. *Daphne* paid out cable so that there were no sudden jerks and she even began moving through the water at very slow speed. Edmund returned to the bridge and found Braithwaite concentrating on the task of increasing speed infinitely slowly so as not to put any sudden strain on the tow. *Daphne*'s anchor cable was just under the surface of the water between the two ships. Jardine had the hand-held range-finder and was calling out the distance every few seconds.

'She's supposed to be six thousand tons,' Braithwaite was saying. 'We're one thousand. The breaking strain of the tow is around two hundred tons. That's how careful we have to be.'

'I wonder how much cable she has,' Edmund asked.

'There's your answer,' from Braithwaite as a man on *Daphne*'s forecastle faced *Troubadour* with his arms crossed in an X. It was that most ubiquitous signal known to seamen and meant that a rope, in this case her cable, was secured and made fast.

'Two hundred yards,' Jardine was saying.

The tow came slowly out of the sea, but retained a slight curve and never became bar taut, then gradually sank back until it touched the water.

'Got you,' said Braithwaite, 'that's the difficult part.' He then built up the engine speed until *Troubadour* was doing revolutions for twelve knots. Their speed through the water was no more than three. Reece calculated a course of 285 degrees for Aberdeen and the unlucky cruiser steered in their wake.

The dawn rose slowly and disclosed weary men aboard *Troubadour* and *Daphne*. Reece took morning stars, fixed the ship's position and having studied the tide tables proposed a five-degree alteration of course. As it became light a mood of cheerfulness took hold. It always happened that way; an upsurge of the human spirit to greet the rising sun. Sailors at their guns, torpedomen at the depth charges, lookouts searching sea and sky stirred and stretched their limbs. They began talking again, joking and hoping for a cup of tea.

The same thing often happened at a dinner party, Edmund recalled. The conversation might be sedate and serious during the main course but when some sugared frivolity appeared, some improbable rising-sun of fruit, cream and cake, the conversation followed suit and became lighthearted. There was no explanation for it other than the obvious one that people imagined the main course to be serious business while the sweet things that followed could provoke laughter. Perhaps sweet flavours were a memory of childhood.

When it was daylight Braithwaite ordered action stations relaxed because the danger from U-boats had diminished. An aircraft approached from the direction of Aberdeen, obviously sent to look for them. It circled a couple of times and the pilot waved and went back in the direction from which he had come. An hour later the Scottish hills rose above the sea.

A signal came from *Daphne*, '*what orders did you last give Harp?*'

Braithwaite thought for a moment then replied, '*No orders. At this slow speed Harp would automatically conduct a box search at about sixteen knots.*'

Braithwaite turned to Edmund. 'What I'm trying to tell Kali Charley is that during the past year we've learned to do our work with a minimum of signals.'

They all looked back at *Daphne*, following obediently like a dog on a lead. There were four or five men on her forecastle watching the tow; others could be seen on the bridge.

'I'm going to give an order,' Braithwaite said suddenly with surprising vehemence.

'Yesterday the captain of that ship made some signals which were thoughtless and unnecessary. Among other things he said that he hoped the escorts would still be ahead of him in the morning. Well, we are ahead of him all right, but not as he would have wished. His ship has suffered an accident and men are dead and injured. This being so, we will say nothing about his foolish signals and we're going to be discreet if we find ourselves in conversation with his officers. Do I make myself clear?'

'Yessir, perfectly clear.'

'Good, then pass it round the whole ship.'

By mid-morning a fleet tug was approaching and Kali Charley ordered *Troubadour* to slip the tow. Braithwaite stopped engines while Pemberton on the after deck had his men take turns off the bollards. Gradually the wire rope released itself and was hauled in together with the shackle still attached to its lanyard. Only when Pemberton reported that all was inboard and nothing could foul the screws did Braithwaite go ahead on the engines. It was then the turn of the fleet tug to take *Daphne* in tow. *Troubadour* and *Harp* were ordered to proceed independently and enter Aberdeen.

As *Harp* took station astern a signal flashed from *Daphne*, the last they were to receive from her. '*Manoeuvre well executed. I repeat, well executed.*'

'My God,' Braithwaite mumbled. 'The man's human after all.'

Chapter 21

FROM ABERDEEN, WHERE they remained only a few hours, *Troubadour* and *Harp* were ordered to Scapa Flow. This was Britain's great naval base lying at fifty-nine degrees north latitude and surrounded by low-lying, treeless islands. Ten miles across, the Flow could shelter a huge fleet of ships, yet beneath its steely surface its deep waters hid many secrets. It was here that surrendered German submarines had scuttled themselves after the First War; here that *Royal Oak* had been torpedoed at her moorings in 1939. In spite of its northern location, however, it remained ice-free throughout the year, being sufficiently influenced by the warm waters of the Gulf Stream.

At Scapa Flow the two ships refuelled and then led a small convoy into the Pentland Firth. *Troubadour*'s first cruise after commissioning had taken her through these same seas, westwards until Cape Wrath was passed and south through the Minches, the dangerous passage between the Outer Hebrides and the west coast of Scotland. Skirting Tiree they entered the North Channel, as they had done a year earlier, passed the Isle of Man and sailed south-eastwards for Liverpool and the river Mersey.

Although *Troubadour* and *Harp* had been commissioned as Chatham ships and were manned by Londoners they had been transferred to Liverpool months earlier for service in the Atlantic. Their records and accounts were held in Liverpool and they had expected to return there when the invasion threat had passed.

By this time, the autumn of 1940, the great concourse of ships that had been assembled to stem the German tide across the straits of Dover, the Channel and the North Sea was being disbanded. The bombing of London and the southern counties continued, but the enemy had given up any immediate hope of launching their armies upon the shores of England. The destroyers and larger escort vessels were despatched to duties in other seas, attention being focussed on the threat by the Italian fleet in the Mediterranean and the submarine menace in the North Atlantic.

The invasion threat had begun, Edmund recalled, with that dash down the Channel at the end of June led by commander Sykes in *Minstrel*. The seven days and nights of the Dunkirk evacuation had rescued most of the British army and no sooner had *Troubadour* recovered from the ordeal than they were away again to Bordeaux. Months later Edmund could still not think of Bordeaux without a pounding heart and racing blood. Bordeaux's every scene and every word spoken were etched on his memory. It was where Marguerite had truly entered his life.

After Bordeaux they had spent three months in the North Sea and the English Channel during which time he had seen Marguerite many times, their relationship deepening as they tried to plan their future lives. Now they were separated once again, but in two months *Troubadour* and *Harp* would be in need of docking and refit. A mere two months and he would be granted leave and he and Marguerite would be together.

They sailed from Liverpool with a westbound convoy and Edmund came on duty for the middle watch. The wheelhouse voicepipe came suddenly alive.

'Cuppa kai for you, sir?'

'Yes, if it's hot,' Edmund replied.

He didn't much like navy cocoa; 'kai', as the sailors called it, but it would do well enough on a cold night. A minute later it was in his hands, black, bitter and slightly greasy. Cocoa, he recalled from his reading, had appeared in Europe in the latter Middle Ages, but had been denied to pregnant women because it was feared that their babies would be born black.

Troubadour was in mid-Atlantic. There were three old destroyers and a converted trawler on the screen, *Harp* having been sent to Reykjavik in Iceland on some other duty. The senior officer of the escort was a commander who had placed *Troubadour* on the southern side of the convoy with orders to guard the flank and rear.

September turned to November while they were at sea and the winter weather began in earnest. A hundred merchant ships were set out like toys on the ocean; dark and mysterious in their silence, purposeful in their westward migration.

Jardine had been aboard for almost three months and would soon be keeping watches on his own. As Edmund had explained, U-boats were now the enemy and until he had heard the answering 'ding' of the asdic when it struck a U-boat hull he had not heard it all. 'Where asdic is concerned,' Edmund had said, 'you are a kind of whale. You don't see what lies ahead, you only hear. You cast your sound into the water and listen for it to strike an object and return with information. When you hear your first U-boat it will stop your heart, your mind will go blank and you'll wish the captain were beside you.'

Jardine was learning astro-navigation from Reece. His training had been too slapdash to include this most necessary and basic requirement, but with his orderly mind and grasp of mathematics he soon found himself mastering it. Edmund, for his part, taught him to identify the stars, a necessary first step. Edmund didn't use a star chart or any other aid to star recognition, he carried the map in his head and started by saying, 'let's make the stars our friends. Form an idea of where to find the first magnitude stars, then learn their names and characteristics. Arcturus, the red star; Spica, orange like our sun; Vega, ice blue.' He hesitated and then went on. 'Don't be fooled by the planet Mars. Just now it happens to be close to Regulus, but Mars is rust-coloured and doesn't shine with its own light.'

From star identification their conversation had groped deeper into space, into the mysteries of stars, galaxies and the universe. They had moved outward from planet earth into those reaches where the human mind falters and fades into incomprehension, ending by seeking refuge in religious simplicities.

Jardine was discovering that Edmund had read widely and thought deeply on subjects which seemed to him almost beyond the range of human enquiry; the creation of the universe and of life; the origins of man, the mind; speech and learning; faith and its antique claims. Jardine could not have known, as he kept a night watch with Edmund, of the turmoil that the war had created in Edmund's life. Three or four years earlier he had entered upon his theological studies without having given the world any serious thought. True, he had sailed in *La Belle Poule* and had travelled every year in the wine-growing countries of Europe, but realization had washed over him slowly that the world of ordinary people, the world of business, love and marriage, of children and simple pleasures was a world worth considering and not beneath his dignity. Until that time people had told him that he was destined for the Church and Edmund had consented without demur.

It now seemed to him to have been far in the past, in the days when he had been a choir boy, that he had been blinded by the panoply of the Church as represented by his father. He saw him only surrounded by respectful acolytes, the whole scene enacted against soaring arches, stained glass and ancient gothic stone. Edmund had craved the authority which his father wielded, the respect accorded him, the aura of sanctity which hung about his voice. He wanted to be privy to those sacred and memorable moments in the lives of his flock at the centre of which were birth, marriage and death. He wanted to participate in the ancient rituals, dispensing comfort to the faithful, reproach to the wicked and hope to the timid.

Edmund had been brought up in the belief that the real world was not real at all, but that reality lay elsewhere and was not seen by human eyes. The war, however, had taught him a different lesson; to rejoice in simple pleasures and see in life a sacredness which was not confined to the precincts of religion. He looked forward now with honest anticipation to marriage and he had gained immeasurably from his friendship with Marko Cyr and David Pemberton. Edmund had not entirely cast aside his earlier beliefs, but now he thanked God for the earth, its riches and its promise. He was grateful that he had life and intelligence, that he could appreciate beauty, rejoice in the sight of ships, the sunrise and the stars.

'Why do you never speak about religion?' Jardine asked, 'when you've studied it so much?'

Edmund thought for a moment.

'Because I would be subject to the uninformed opinions of those who have not studied it, which, I'm sorry to say, I find tiresome. I can't tolerate theological baby talk. If someone, on the other hand, who knows nothing about wine starts holding forth I don't seem to care but, as I say, theological clap-trap brings out the worst in me. I have patience with wine fools and perhaps with a hundred other kinds of fools and can suffer them more or less gladly, but not with religious fools.'

Edmund called attention to a long, black cloud ahead, of sharp definition, like a cliff rising from the sea.

'A linesquall,' he said. 'Textbook example. The weather could change dramatically when we're inside it. As officer of the watch are you going to take any precautions?'

'Call the captain?' Jardine asked.

'No, not yet. When visibility is reduced and we lost sight of the convoy will be soon enough. Meantime, call the leading seaman of the watch, show him what we're up against and he'll warn the men who need to be warned. For a start the lookouts are going to need their oilskins.'

'And put it in the log,' Edmund continued. 'There's a code for linesquall, I think it's KQ, and watch the barometer.'

'Damn the linesquall,' Jardine said to himself. 'Just as it was getting interesting.'

Troubadour butted into the linesquall a few minutes later. From the outside it looked solid and monolithic; inside was dark, rainy and confused. The convoy faded and disappeared from sight and Edmund went to the captains' voicepipe. Spray began to fly over the bridge from a choppy sea that seemed undecided as to what direction it should take.

'Captain, sir,' Edmund began, but then the lookout reported that he could make out a merchantmen, a sixteen-thousand tonner high in the water.

'We're passing through a linesquall and for a minute I lost the convoy.' A pause.

'No, don't come up. It's getting colder, which is normal. I'm not worried.'

He straightened up and searched the northern horizon with

his binoculars but the overcast had again blotted out the merchantmen. Minutes later they reappeared and Jardine reported that the barometer was rising.

'We're through it. What were we talking about?'

'Religious baby talk,' Jardine replied.

'Yes, of course. And the first question usually asked is whether the Bible is true, to which a theology student would reply with another question, 'what do you mean by true, the ancient definition or ours?' Much of the Bible was thought to be true in the context of those who wrote it but comes nowhere close to truth in the sense we understand. Pontius Pilate was right to ask 'what is truth?''

Edmund leaned his back against the compass and took a long look around the dark horizon.

'The gospel writers' notion of truth was the fulfilment of ancient prophecy. They saw what we would say was not there, they believed things for which we would find no shred of evidence. According to their lights they were not untruthful. Western theologians have tried to lay aside the tall tales and exaggerations of those early writers and search for the real Jesus underneath the layers of paint and varnish.

'This process usually gets back to faith, that most prized Christian virtue, over which so much ink has been spilt. What it all gets down to is that faith enables you to believe things that run counter to the dictates of reason. Nowhere in the New Testament will you find a word in favour of reason or intelligence; rather the reverse; we are told we must become as little children who have blind faith and not much reason. So, the student asks, 'how can we worship a God who creates in mankind a soaring intelligence and then tells him that he's not encouraged to use it?'

'For myself,' Edmund went on, 'God has given me a small measure of intelligence to probe and question, and I choose to study where my mind leads me, whether it be heaven or earth, sacred or profane. I am not persuaded that there are limitations on what I may think, and no one can tell me that Jesus himself is not to be studied historically, because the gospels themselves claim to be historical.

'Take that passage early in Luke's gospel relating to the nativity.

Augustus Caesar orders taxation on the whole world. This is established precisely in time, as any historian might do; Herod was king of Judaea and Quirinius governor of Syria.

'Ah, but wait a minute. There was no such taxation during the Augustan era; in Herod's incumbency Quirinius was not governor of Syria and Herod had died at least four years earlier. This is one minuscule example of what we are up against. I could relate dozens more.

'So if we can't even get the birth date straight, how sure are we that he was born in Bethlehem, and scholarly opinion says that he almost certainly was not. So why the emphatic assertion, with embellishments, that he was? Because they turned up an ancient document which said that a messiah ought to be born there. For them, the ancient document constituted truth.

'I could go on like this for hours. I am not a particularly original thinker but I read a lot, listened to the professors at university and tried to sort it out in my mind. And remember that the work of biblical comment and criticism is not being done by scoundrels in back-rooms, but by accredited scholars in the great universities.

'If it hadn't been for the war I would have gone headlong into the Church, propelled by a combination of family tradition, some scholarly aptitude and a conceited belief that I had been called. So you can see how grateful I feel to all this,' Edmund patted the gyroscopic compass and his eyes swept the northern horizon with its hundred plodding ships, 'for giving me time to reconsider.'

Jardine looked at Edmund's tall outline in the darkness, bundled up against the night wind.

'But does that mean you've kicked over the whole thing, become an unbeliever?'

'Oh no,' Edmund replied. 'What I'm trying to do is to separate fiction from fact, draw a line in the sand, with exaggeration, embellishment and myth on one side and historical certainties on the other.

'I'm not opposed to myths as long as we know they are myths and don't expect anyone but small children to take them literally. Myths can have power and a real claim on the affections of mankind, but let's remember that for every one who's attracted by Christian mythology a dozen others are put off and say that it's silly and unbelievable. Virgin birth, rising from the dead, walking on water; no thank you, they say. Somehow I have to come to terms with this and not be angry that myths have been preached as truth to gullible people, myself included.'

'But you're not going back?'

'It's a decision which has taken *Troubadour* and me a long time to reach, but no, I won't return to my theological studies.'

'Marriage, a family and all that?'

'Why not? God was said to have ordered the human race to go forth, increase and multiply.'

'So why wasn't Jesus married?'

'I think he obviously was. He was a rabbi or teacher, and in the century in which he lived it was unheard of for a rabbi to be unmarried. One of my professors thinks he was married to a Levite woman at Cana of Galilee.'

'Where the water was changed . . .'

'Yes, someone said it was changed to wine. Quite a party they had. Of course you'll come to our wedding.'

'Nothing I'd like better.'

'And your wife?'

'I don't know if she'll attend.'

Edmund felt a lot of sympathy for Jardine. His home life was a mess, that was obvious. He didn't speak of his wife with affection or respect and when asked to join the other officers and their ladies he always declined, saying that it could not be arranged.

There came the distant thud of an explosion and both Edmund and Jardine turned together. The lookout began his report but was interrupted by Edmund.

'Thank you. I see it.'

A red sheet of flame appeared for a moment at the far side of the convoy and died down.

'Captain, sir,' Edmund called into the captain's voicepipe 'A ship torpedoed about three thousand yards on the far side. Can't make out the details.'

'I'll come up.' Braithwaite said.

'One minute to three,' Edmund sighed. 'I'd hoped for a quiet watch.'

He went to the dimly-lit asdic compartment on the starboard side of the bridge.

'Operator, who is it? Hounsom? A ship torpedoed on the other wing. What are conditions like?'

Hounsom didn't turn or hesitate.

'Clear. Good operating conditions.'

Braithwaite came up the bridge ladder.

'What did you see?'

'Not much. Just a red glow. Seems to have died down. The Admiralty trawler's on that side of the convoy.'

Braithwaite spent long minutes searching with his binoculars.

'I don't think there's any point in going to action stations,' he said finally. 'I can see two of the destroyers ahead of the convoy, the other must have turned back.'

He was interrupted by flashes and the sound of gunfire.

'That's the destroyer firing. Must be a U-boat on the surface. Damn difficult target, U-boat. Nothing to aim at.'

A few minutes later the destroyer had fallen astern and, by the sound of the dull explosions, was attacking with depth charges. Even when the distance had opened to four or five miles the sound could be heard, not so much across the surface of the sea but upwards through the hull of *Troubadour*. Edmund found himself hoping that the destroyer's attack had been successful, that the U-boat was on the bottom, a mile down, her crew dead.

The remainder of the night was quiet. Pemberton came up for the morning watch and Edmund went to his cabin and lay down. He wondered why he had been so honest in reply to Jardine's questions; Marko was the person in whom he would normally confide. What he had not told Jardine was that he felt relieved at having made the decision not to go on with his studies; it was as though a load had fallen from his shoulders. He couldn't have faced the moment when he would have to preach doctrines that he did not believe or make a pretence of faith that he no longer possessed.

Three days later the convoy sailed into New York. It seemed to Edmund and Marko, as they went ashore, that America was at a far remove from entering the war on the allied side. Even the fall of France, the German conquest of Poland and the rape of most of central Europe had not changed their minds. Germans, they said, were an orderly people who would give Europe the discipline and organization it needed. 'Too much artistic crap and too little production,' was how a taxi driver described it and, after all, German and Italian immigrants were at the very heart of American life which seemed, at that moment, to be exceedingly pleased with itself.

'What do you want for a wedding present?' Marko asked as they entered a department store.

'A decent set of pots and pans for the kitchen. You can't get them in England now.'

'That's what it's going to be. Let's go and look for them.'

Troubadour spent a week in New York and was soon joined by *Harp*. Sailors went ashore from the two ships, spent their money and returned on board broke but impressed with the vitality and delights of the city. Macy's department store was a favourite, also Radio City and Times Square. On a seaman's pay the pleasures, however, were of short duration. Wearily, the men stepped back aboard to face the long return to the Mersey.

How different, Edmund thought, from the tedious existence that gripped his own country. England was in shadow, groping and stumbling as it armed itself for a long and bloody war. It was illuminated by no more than a spark of hope, many thought it a forlorn hope, a bet against all the odds. But here was a people bent on the pursuit of happiness, their towns ablaze with light, their minds drugged by the incessant dance music which drowned the cries of anguish from afar. Europe was not their business, they had traversed an ocean to cast off its ancient affliction. They lived as they chose in the delusion that their shallow joys would last a lifetime.

Troubadour sailed on a windy and desolate day. A convoy was being assembled and the escorts were to be the three old battle-weary destroyers which would form the forward screen, *Troubadour* and *Harp* on the wings and the Admiralty trawler in rear. The senior officer of the escort was by rank a commander who called a meeting and discussed his plans with the other captains.

'Let's hope it's a peaceful one,' he had said as the four captains left his cabin.

Seagoing discipline returned to *Troubadour* as she cast off her lines and proceeded down river. Braithwaite's commands took on a sharpness, the officers became models of efficiency and the men hurried about their tasks. Even the most practised crew acquire an urgency as they put to sea on a long or dangerous voyage; an apprehension prevails, a quickening of the pulse in face of the unknown.

Off Long Island they picked up their forty-ship convoy and the commodore shaped course north-eastwards so as to leave Nantucket Island to the west. The escorts took up their stations and the asdic sets became the focus of attention. *Troubadour* was again on the left of the convoy, the landward side. *Harp* lay two or three miles to the east.

Sub-lieutenant Jardine was to keep watch by himself, so Edmund handed over to him as soon as *Troubadour* was in proper station. He looked at the chart room on his way down and Reece answered his question before he asked it.

'At this speed, three days to Halifax.'

When Edmund entered the wardroom he found Marko with a cup of coffee in one hand and an Admiralty signal in the other.

'Would you believe it?' Marko flourished the signal. 'After all this time, they've dropped the charges against Knatchbull. They had no case; we could have demolished them, but why did it take them months and bloody months?'

'Waiting for the baby to be born?' Edmund asked.

Marko handed him the signal paper.

'No, the rape charge isn't affected by the birth of the baby. Of course she only started yelling when she discovered she was pregnant. I'm sorry for the baby if it looks anything like Knatchbull.'

'Have you told him?'

'No, because you're his divisional officer.' Marko smiled.

'But if he has legal questions you should be on hand to answer them.' It was Edmund's turn for a small joke.

When Edmund told him that the case against him had been dropped, Knatchbull showed no emotion.

'Yessir; thank you, sir.'

'You must be relieved it's behind you, and of course you have no record with the police.'

'Stands to reason, sir. I didn't do nothing wrong.'

'You gave lieutenant Cyr a lot of work and trouble.'

'Yes, I know that, sir. I were glad to have him on my side.'

That afternoon Edmund lay down and slept but was awakened by an explosion followed by the alarm bells. He seized cap, binoculars and coat and ran for the bridge.

'Ship torpedoed right next to us,' someone said, and even as he looked over the starboard side of the bridge, another torpedo hit a five-thousand tonner a mile distant. He checked the asdic operators, all three of whom were crouched over the set.

'Torpedo noises?' he asked.

'Very slight, but conditions aren't good. It's like soup.'

'Captain, sir,' he said to Braithwaite. 'Poor operating conditions.'

'I'm increasing to sixteen knots and I'll make a wide circle to port,' Braithwaite said. 'The trawler can help these two.'

Edmund took off his cap and put on the asdic headphones.

'Signal the senior officer of the escort,' Braithwaite called out. '*Two ships torpedoed. No contacts. Am searching further out.*'

He turned *Troubadour* to the westward, but the asdic found nothing.

'*Go to assistance of Panama City,*' signalled the escort commander. '*U-boat reported inside the convoy.*'

'Inside the bloody convoy,' Braithwaite repeated. 'How the hell did it get there with three destroyers up ahead? They must have gone right over it.'

'Poor conditions,' Edmund replied. 'I think there's a thermocline; a level where the water temperature changes. It produces false echoes, or no echo at all.'

Braithwaite turned *Troubadour* back to the south and increased to twenty knots.

'The convoy ought to be a hundred miles further east,' he groaned. 'This is where they expect us.'

When they reached *Panama City* they found her lying over on her side and the trawler, *Northern Harvest*, picking up her crew who had crowded into a boat. *Troubadour* swept past toward a bulk carrier, an ungainly-looking ship that was stopped in the water a mile distant.

'*What's your condition?*' Braithwaite signalled. There was a delay of a minute or more after which a light came on her bridge and the one word *No* was passed. Another delay and the word *U-boat.*'

'So what does that tell us?' Braithwaite wondered. 'They don't have a signalman and they can't speak English. Are they trying to say a U-boat's in the area? Try this, leading signalman; make it very slowly, *Where is the U-boat?*'

Troubadour circled the ship and studied her.

'They've abandoned the engine room; I can see engine room staff on the upper deck,' Edmund said.

'She's a bulk ore carrier. Flag of convenience; none of the officers knows enough to reply to a simple signal.' Braithwaite was losing his patience.

'She's hoisted *Not Under Control*,' the leading signalman called out.

'And turned out a lifeboat,' from Edmund.

'Very well,' Braithwaite said. 'If he's going to abandon I'll risk stopping and pick them up.'

He took *Troubadour* to within half a cable of the ore carrier and went astern on the engines.

'Jardine, tell the first lieutenant to take them aboard and sink the lifeboat.'

The ore carrier lowered her boat and men began sliding down the falls. When the upper deck was deserted they readied their oars and began pulling toward *Troubadour*. There was a lot of splashing and progress was slow.

'Look at that,' Braithwaite said in a low voice. 'They call themselves seamen.'

The crew of the ore carrier pulled alongside as though they had never before handled a boat, and a few minutes later Pemberton called the bridge to say that twenty-three survivors were on *Troubadour*'s deck and all was clear. Braithwaite went ahead on the engines and told Edmund to rejoin the convoy at twenty knots.

'Aye aye, sir. Twenty knots.'

'Jardine. Prepare a signal which we'll pass when we get a bit closer. To the senior officer of the escort. *We've taken off survivors from whatever its name is, Silas P. Fennimore. Say she's low in the water but looks salvageable. Her captain has chosen to abandon.*

'Aye aye, sir,' from Jardine.

Edmund was bent over the wheelhouse voicepipe and Braithwaite searched through his binoculars for the convoy, now hull down on the horizon. *Northern Harvest* was two or three miles ahead.

'Hear that, sir?'

'Hear what?' Braithwaite's eye went to the asdic compartment on the starboard side of the bridge.

'Depth charges. A full pattern. *Harp* or one of the destroyers.'

'How did you hear it? I didn't.'

Unseen to both Braithwaite and Edmund the captain of the *Silas P. Fennimore* had climbed the bridge ladder and was standing behind them. He was a bulky man in an ill-fitting uniform with the four stripes of a captain on each epaulette.

He wore his cap at an angle and had binoculars round his neck. There followed an exchange which Edmund would not have believed if he hadn't heard it.

'S'cuse, captain.'

Braithwaite turned and stared at him.

'S'cuse, captain. What happen to my ship?'

'What the hell are you talking about?' Braithwaite shot back. 'You've abandoned your ship.'

He turned to Jardine. 'Get this man away from here. He'll come on the bridge only at my invitation.'

Jardine took him by the arm and tried to lead him to the bridge ladder.

'Come on, old fellow. Captain says you shouldn't be here. We're at battle stations.'

'What happen to my ship?' he persisted.

'You have abandoned your ship.' Braithwaite spoke slowly. 'Once you abandon ship that's the end of it. It isn't your ship any more.'

'But wounded on board.'

'Wounded?' Braithwaite repeated. 'How many wounded?'

'Two men, sick.'

'And you left them and didn't bring them off?'

'I think your business go back and find wounded.'

'Did you hear that, Casswell? Did you really hear that? This arsehole doesn't understand that I'm captain of this ship, not that one.'

Braithwaite's arm pointed aft past *Troubadour*'s funnel, down the white wake towards the *Silas P. Fennimore*, but before he spoke again Edmund had interrupted.

'Captain, sir. Another pattern of depth charges.'

'Thank you, Casswell.'

Braithwaite had become calmer. He turned to the captain of the ore carrier and his words were slow and carefully chosen.

'I have a war to fight. I'm not putting my ship about which would waste time and place us in danger while she's stopped. You should have brought your wounded with you. And I want you to be very sure in your dirty little mind that your conduct will be fully reported when we get to Halifax.'

Jardine still had his hand on the man's arm.

'Now Jardine, get him off my bridge. Oh, and one other thing: tell the first lieutenant that this officer or is not invited to make use of my cabin.'

'Aye, aye, sir.'

Jardine was a powerful man and spun him round to face the ladder. The leading signalman also closed in and the captain of the ore carrier realised that the interview was over.

'I can't possibly go back now,' Braithwaite said with a catch in his voice, 'it's dangerous and stupid.'

Edmund tried to think of something consoling.

'We don't know what injuries they have. Perhaps they can make themselves comfortable until a tug comes out from Nantucket Island.' He paused. 'You know, sir, the great majority of merchant navy captains are competent, brave men, so why do we have to run into this?'

'Twice in one war,' Braithwaite muttered. He was thinking of the time they were nearly run down.

That night the convoy came under further attack and another ship was lost, this time a tanker. Braithwaite cursed and kept *Troubadour* at action stations all night.

At dawn they stood down, but at midday two of the destroyers hoisted red flags and began depth charging. The convoy was turned ninety degrees to starboard, to the east, and *Troubadour* was ordered to take station ahead to replace the destroyers which dropped a total of eight patterns, eighty charges. They went on for two hours, but lost contact and could claim no more than a 'possible' victory. Oil and debris had appeared which did not, however, constitute a certain kill.

At dusk it was *Troubadour*'s turn. The port lookout reported a U-boat on the surface about three miles distant and all binoculars were instantly turned toward it. At almost the same moment the asdic operator reported torpedo sounds. Braithwaite turned *Troubadour* towards the U-boat, found the torpedo tracks and went down them at full speed.

'Hoist flag 'T', torpedoes in the water,' Edmund called out. He listened for the asdic to make contact.

'Drop a full pattern where the torpedo tracks end,' Braithwaite ordered.

There was no contact and Edmund pressed his firing button when Jardine reported that the torpedo tracks had faded out. It was a poor way of making an attack, but would let the U-boat know that its presence had not passed unnoticed.

Troubadour's depth charges were flung out of the throwers, two each side of the ship, while six more slipped from the racks. They were set for a depth of fifty feet and exploded with massive detonations that shook the ship. Dead fish floated to the surface over a wide area.

Braithwaite then took the ship in a square pattern, two miles on each side of the square, but no contact was made. Edmund stood at the doorway of the asdic compartment watching the three operators, but there was no answer to the probing of the asdic.

'Damn,' Braithwaite said. 'We'll go back to our station on the convoy.'

'The tanker's sinking, sir.' Jardine had his binoculars to his eyes. '*Northern Harvest* is going alongside.'

All eyes turned to the tanker, low in the water and on fire, with *Northern Harvest* approaching from astern. She was a ship's length distant when a huge sheet of flame erupted over the tanker, followed by a boom. Even at two miles they felt the concussion and saw debris flung into the air.

'God, the poor bastards,' Braithwaite said it for all of them. 'I wonder what that did to *Northern Harvest*.'

'A lot of flaming debris came down on her,' Jardine reported.

Braithwaite leaned down to the voicepipe. 'Full ahead. I'm going alongside *Northern Harvest*. Tell the first lieutenant to stand by with fire hoses and extinguishers. I'll try and hold the ship a few feet off, but we'd better have fenders out.'

Braithwaite took *Troubadour* alongside. Fires were raging on *Northern Harvest*'s upper deck which was a shambles of black twisted metal that had rained down from the explosion of the tanker. Her captain had survived the blast, protected by the fore part of the bridge, but the after part of the bridge was wrecked and the dead and injured lay in grotesque heaps. Worse still was the forward deck where the gun's crew had assembled with grappling lines and fenders. Their intention had been to hold the tanker for the few seconds needed to let the crew scramble across to safety. All had received the full force of the explosion and either died or were thrown in the sea.

Braithwaite surveyed the damage. He had the loud hailer in his hand.

'Captain?' he said.

A blackened figure with no cap and blood running down his face put his hand up. It was like a boy in school, Edmund thought; he was a short man who could hardly be seen over the side of the bridge.

'How bad is it?' Braithwaite asked.

The captain picked up a megaphone and tried to reply but couldn't.

Braithwaite had put *Troubadour* close alongside. A fire was raging midships, beside the funnel, and the whaler was burning, but what worried Braithwaite was a fire near the depth charges. Hoses from *Troubadour* played over it but it continued to burn. The crew of *Northern Harvest* were doing their best, but there were no officers to be seen and the men seemed shocked. Many were injured.

Pemberton called up to the bridge. 'We'll have to get rid of those depth charges.'

He knew that there would be damage to both ships in that swell as they scraped together, but fenders would be put out and it was worth the risk. Pemberton had tried calling across the few feet of water, but the survivors seemed unable to comprehend what had to be done. The depth charges on *Northern Harvest*'s stern had to be jettisoned at all costs.

'Those depth charges sir,' Edmund began, but Braithwaite cut him off.

'Jardine, my orders are that Pemberton goes aboard *Northern Harvest* and helps the captain, while Cyr gets rid of the depth charges. Williams will go with him and a couple of volunteers. We can't expect their crew to help themselves; they're out of it. I'll put the ship alongside and they'll have to jump. Go!'

'Yessir,' Jardine replied, and hurried off.

'Something else,' Braithwaite went on. 'Call Reece on the bridge; you Casswell, go down and act as first lieutenant while Pemberton's out of the ship.'

Edmund tore off his asdic headphones, grabbed his cap and slid down the bridge ladder. *Troubadour* was closing *Northern Harvest* and the heat of the fires on *Northern Harvest*'s upper deck could be felt as they drew to within a few feet. In relation to each other the ships reared wildly; up ten feet, down ten feet; there was an agonizing pause as they hung apart, too far to jump, but then suddenly seemed to be drawn together. There was a sound of screaming as the fenders, pressed to the thickness of doormats were dragged across the ship's sides. Pemberton chose his moment and jumped, then Cyr, Williams and two others. Hoses from *Troubadour* began to pour water into the fires raging on *Northern Harvest*'s upper deck.

Cyr and Williams set about the task of jettisoning the depth charges and they chose the most dangerous first, the throwers on the starboard side. With a hose playing over him Cyr plunged his hand into the hot interior of the depth charge and withdrew the pistol, throwing it into the sea. Williams then pulled back on the firing levers and the depth charges were hurled away harmlessly.

'Well done,' Pemberton shouted. 'I'll leave it to you.'

Cyr and Williams next turned their attention to the depth charge racks and having systematically pulled out the pistols they allowed them to slide into the sea.

Pemberton had gone forward, found a fire hose under the bridge ladder and soon had it in operation manned by two seamen from *Troubadour*. They went to work on the fire amidships and brought it under control. When he went up on the bridge a few minutes later he was able to report to the trawler's captain that all the fires were extinguished and the depth charges jettisoned.

Braithwaite, meanwhile, was holding *Troubadour* a few feet apart from *Northern Harvest* by engine and rudder orders, and managed to get in a few snatches of conversation with *Northern Harvest*'s captain. *Northern Harvest* was larger than *Troubadour*, about two thousand tons, and had probably been constructed for the Iceland fishing grounds. She was a handsome ship and well found, but her upper deck was littered with debris, blood and bodies.

'We saw the tanker go up,' Braithwaite said. 'Lucky you weren't closer. Do you have power on the main engines?'

'Yes,' the captain replied, mopping at his head with a blood-stained rag. 'Engine room says there's no damage below. But my upper deck's gone and I only have one officer. Think you could lend me an officer until Halifax? And half a dozen seamen?'

'Yes, of course,' Braithwaite called back. He turned to Jardine who had returned to the bridge.

'Pemberton and Cyr are to stay aboard *Northern Harvest*, also Williams, and tell the coxswain to detail six more able seamen, and a signalman.'

He turned back to the captain of *Northern Harvest*.

'Two officers and eight men; plus a signalman.'

'Thanks, old man. Thanks very much.'

The coxswain's voice came up the voicepipe.

'I heard that, sir. Six men for the trawler, sir. Right away. McVane on the wheel. Clegg and Rogers, come with me.'

Dobreiner had been directing the hoses which played across the gap between *Troubadour* and *Northern Harvest*, but the fires were now quenched and he ordered them turned off.

'Mr Dobreiner, sir,' the coxswain said. 'Captain's orders. I'm to send more men across to get her into Halifax.'

'You heard that,' Dobreiner said. 'Volunteers to go across, please.'

A chorus of 'yessir.'

'Thank you. At the double, Carlisle, Weston, Porrit. Go with the coxswain.'

Jardine was shouting across to Pemberton.

'First lieutenant, sir. Captain's orders. You, Cyr and Williams are to stay aboard where you are. Four more seamen to join you. As far as Halifax.'

Pemberton looked over his shoulder. 'Oh, all right.'

'Boarding party,' Jardine called out. 'Stand by to jump when she's close enough.'

There was a screaming noise as the weight of the two ships came together once again; the men chose their moment and jumped.

'This fire's out,' Cyr called across.

Edmund picked up the bridge telephone. 'Captain, sir. Boarding party across. All clear aft.'

'Thank you.' He turned to the captain of *Northern Harvest*.

'Sorry I can't do more. You have two capable officers and about eight of my best men. What made it blow up?'

'Aircraft fuel.'

'No survivors?' Braithwaite asked.

The captain of *Northern Harvest* shook his head. 'Look at my ship. I was best part of a hundred yards distant.'

'We'll sail in company until we rejoin the convoy or reach Halifax,' Braithwaite said. 'Build up to your best speed and I'll take station ahead of you. All right?'

The dazed, bloodstained captain of *Northern Harvest* waved and then turned to Pemberton who was beside him.

'Take my ship, will you; I'm going down for some bandages.'

'Help the captain,' Pemberton told two of *Troubadour*'s men, and they took him by the arms and guided him toward the ladder. He ordered half ahead on the engines and *Northern Harvest* shuddered into life. To another man Pemberton said, 'Find lieutenant Cyr, tell him to clean up as best he can.'

Meanwhile Braithwaite was making his own dispositions aboard *Troubadour*. He sent for Edmund and Jardine and said that although Edmund was senior he wanted Jardine to act as first lieutenant for the time it would take to reach Halifax. Edmund, he pointed out, was the asdic expert and had to be on the bridge. He turned to Jardine.

'Find the first officer of *Silas P. Fennimore*, and tell him to take over the chartroom. Line up the rest of them and ask for volunteers for full duties to replace the men we've put aboard *Northern Harvest*. They'll be paid navy wages and get a rum ration.'

'And the captain, sir?'

'I won't have that man doing anything. Keep him out of my sight. And you can relax action stations.'

Jardine saluted, shouted for the coxswain and left the bridge.

'Take the ship, Casswell,' Braithwaite went on. 'The cooks will have some dinner for us pretty soon. Oh God, I hope it isn't pork.'

Braithwaite hesitated. He was red-eyed and dazed. 'Did you see the upper deck of that ship? The dead and injured. How could one Sick Berth Attendant cope with that lot? And the captain, he couldn't have known the tanker would blow up. Burn perhaps, not blow up. He must have been protected. Poor little man; lost three of his officers, all on the upper deck. Officers who trusted him; and all those good men. Every one of the gun's crew. They'd have been all right if they'd been behind the gun shield, but they were out on the forecastle.'

Braithwaite seemed to be losing control and Edmund judged that soothing words were needed.

'Yessir, of course. It was bad, but you've sent a boarding party to get his ship into Halifax.'

'You don't know how proud I felt,' Braithwaite went on, 'when Cyr and Williams dumped those depth charges; and Pemberton on the bridge. No one slept last night. No one complained. They all volunteered.'

He trailed off and Edmund tried again.

'Sir, you've done more than anyone. Why don't you go below and get some sleep while I take the ship back to the convoy?'

'What, miss my dinner? Just as long as it isn't pork. The smell from that ship; the smell from the upper deck . . .'

'Sir, the steward's going to see that you get a nice dinner with lots of red pepper. Then you can have a sleep. I'm sure that's best, sir.'

Braithwaite seemed to weaken.

'Take the ship, Casswell,' he said again. 'That poor little man. I hope he isn't badly injured. He's got Cyr and Pemberton. We did our best, didn't we? Cyr got the depth charges away with fire all round him.'

Braithwaite walked unsteadily to the after end of the bridge, felt for the steel guardrails and went down. On the flagdeck he stopped outside the chartroom and looked in the door, saw Reece and the first officer of the bulk carrier bent over the chart and went down the next ladder to the main deck. He turned his steps aft and a group of men straightened up and faced him as he passed.

'Sir,' one of them said. 'Good work, sir.'

'Thank you,' Braithwaite mumbled.

He went to his cabin and lay down. 'God,' he said. 'What's happening to me? I can't take much more of this. First it was *Silas P. Whatever* and two wounded aboard. Then a tanker blows up and wipes out the upper deck of *Northern Harvest*.' He closed his eyes.

'Reece,' Edmund called down the voicepipe. 'You get any sleep last night?'

'Couple of hours.'

'Think you can keep the afternoon watch?'

'Sure I can.'

Edmund went to the log book and wrote in an unsteady hand, 'Station 1000 yards ahead *Northern Harvest* seems to be doing fourteen knots. Asdic conditions bloody. Convoy over horizon eastwards.'

It's somewhere about fifty miles ahead, he said to himself. We'll catch up during the night. And only a few hours ago I was standing here talking to Jardine about love and marriage, the Bible and the difficulties of faith in a rational world. Rational?

He thought about Marguerite and the time she had stood next to him on this very bridge and held his arm. Then with a sinking sensation he realised that Braithwaite was crumbling, falling apart. Braithwaite had seen his own reflection in that short, bald-headed captain covered with blood. He had smelled burning flesh and suffered at the thought of what it was like to have his officers and men killed before his eyes. Poor Braithwaite, he thought; he's not superhuman. He's not as resilient as yachtsman Pemberton or lawyer Cyr.

Edmund looked back at the oil-stained sea and tried to say a prayer for the crew of the tanker and those who had perished aboard *Northern Harvest*.

Chapter 22

As *Northern Harvest* entered Halifax all eyes were on her. Pemberton was on the bridge and Cyr had charge on the upper deck.

'I hope the captain's all right,' Braithwaite said in a whisper. 'He seemed so decent.'

The signal tower ordered them to their berths, the two destroyers alongside each other, then *Troubadour* and *Harp* outside. *Northern Harvest* was sent to a berth by herself preparatory to entering dry dock.

Pemberton waved briefly as he took her past, a bruised and fire-blackened ship manned by a weary crew.

Cyr and the men on *Northern Harvest*'s upper deck had not noticed an object that had become lodged in the starboard navigation light. It was visible to someone outboard but not evident from within the ship; a piece of seaman's blue clothing, clotted blood, and a remnant of its former owner.

'Signalman,' Edmund said; 'quickly, in semaphore. '*Object lodged in your navigation light. Suggest get rid of it.*'

The signalman took the two red and yellow semaphore flags from their stowage and held one above his head and the other horizontally to the left. *Northern Harvest* was passing at no more than half a cable's distance but the signalman, one of *Troubadour*'s, was reading a message from the signal tower which, in the overall scheme of things, was of greater importance. When *Northern Harvest* was in her berth and Pemberton stopped engines the sad relic was still there. It was a human arm.

Ambulances drove down the jetty and Pemberton on *Northern Harvest*'s bridge leaned toward the voicepipe and said, 'finished with engines,' then made his way down the ladder and knocked on the captain's door.

'We're in Halifax, sir,' he said to the bandaged figure on the bunk. 'I'll collect my men and go back to *Troubadour*. Ambulances are on the jetty and your sub-lieutenant can manage things from now on. A staff officer will be here in a few minutes.'

He took the captain's binoculars from round his neck and laid them on the table.

'Thanks, Pemberton. Thanks very much. Convey my compliments to your captain. And my thanks to the men you brought with you.'

'Yes, of course, sir.'

Pemberton closed the door quietly and nodded to the steward who had been nursing the captain. Next he found Marko and told him to round up *Troubadour*'s men and have them return. He went over the gangway and stood on the jetty for a moment looking at the fire-blackened ship which for the past few hours had been under his command. 'Oh God,' he said. 'Look at that. How did it get there?' *Northern Harvest*'s sub-lieutenant had accompanied him to the gangway and Pemberton beckoned him to the jetty. He didn't say anything but simply pointed at the outrage, the sad remnant of humanity, and patted him on the shoulder. Pemberton returned his salute and walked back towards *Troubadour* with Marko and *Troubadour*'s men. A few moments later Braithwaite was facing them, but words deserted him as he looked from one tired face to another.

'Well done, all of you,' he said at last. 'Thank you, first lieutenant; let them carry on to their mess decks. I'll have more to say to-morrow when I see the whole ship's company.'

Pemberton dismissed them and joined Braithwaite.

'You brought the ship in,' Braithwaite said. 'What about her captain?'

'He's in his bunk, sir. He'll go to hospital. Lost a lot of blood. He needs proper medical attention.'

'And *Northern Harvest*?'

'Dry dock and refit. The crew, what's left of them, are going to barracks in an hour.'

For the next few days the four small ships lay alongside in

Halifax harbour. Leave was granted, but the men had no money left in their pockets. The year was fading toward winter and there was warmth and companionship below decks. They washed their clothes, peeled potatoes carefully so as to waste nothing, tidied and rearranged their lockers and scrubbed their canvas hammocks. When *up spirits* was piped late in the forenoon they took their grog and shared it with their friends from the ships alongside.

Talk was subdued about the events on passage between New York and Halifax. Four ships had been sunk and men had been killed, but everyone thought the losses might have been worse. *Northern Harvest* was lucky to be afloat and it was conceded that Pemberton and the men who had accompanied him had done a superlative job of bringing her in. Control and confidence had been restored, the asdic had continued to sound the depths, the depth charges and gun had been manned.

Marko Cyr had taken charge on the upper deck and his first task had been to heave dead bodies and other debris overboard and hose down with sea water. He arranged the watchkeeping list so that two of *Troubadour*'s men were placed in each watch. The wounded were cared for, *up spirits* piped and a semblance of normality restored. Pemberton would write in his report that Cyr had performed in a most praiseworthy manner.

Northern Harvest, it turned out, was a modern trawler of eighteen hundred tons designed for the northern Icelandic Fisheries and, like *Troubadour* and *Harp*, had never sailed in the capacity for which it had been built, but had been taken over by the navy on the day war was declared. Asdic, depth charges and a four-inch gun had been fitted and she had sailed under the command of the skipper who was to have been her peacetime captain. Her crew were fishermen who had stepped from one role to another with a minimum of training. The sub-lieutenant who had survived the explosion was the only man on board who was an outsider and knew nothing of fishing. He had been shocked by the blast and had not been able to speak for several hours.

Rumours circulated that *Panama City* had been taken in tow and brought to Boston harbour, that the two men left on board had been found alive and that the captain would lose his master's certificate for having abandoned them. There was also a rumour that the captain of *Northern Harvest* would be decorated for his valiant effort to take off the survivors from the burning tanker. Another rumour surfaced to the effect that *Troubadour* and *Harp* were due for refit and that both ships would be decommissioned. This, if it were true, meant that the eastbound convoy would be their last voyage together.

Rumours gave way to reality, however, on a rainy forenoon when the four ships slipped their lines and sailed from the rocky embrace of Halifax. A flotilla of minesweepers of the Canadian navy shepherded the merchant ships to their stations for the long haul to the Mersey. Many of the merchantmen had come down from the north, from Montreal and Quebec City on the St Lawrence and from the ports of Nova Scotia and the Canadian Maritimes. They formed a great phalanx of more than a hundred vessels, their cargoes of raw materials, armaments and food worth millions of pounds; thousands of millions, perhaps.

Edmund brought *Troubadour* to her station on the southern flank of the convoy. A cold wind was blowing from the northwest and following seas lifted *Troubadour*'s stern, held her for a few seconds, then passed under the bridge, gun and forecastle. She wallowed until the next wave came, unsure of herself, a lack of definition in her movements. Spray didn't fly in these weather conditions, her high bow didn't slap confidently into the waves, she merely corkscrewed uneasily as the water slid past.

The convoy contained ships of differing sizes and functions. There were general purpose cargo ships, some as small as five thousand tons; also tankers and a couple of vessels which combined cargo and passenger carrying. All were painted a uniform gray and all lay deep in the water. They were destined for the west of England whence their cargoes would be carried by an overloaded railway system to the centres of population.

Edmund glanced at the chart of the North Atlantic. The long coastline of North America was its western boundary, Europe lay to the east and offshore were the British Isles, small and defiant, a glimmer of hope in a subjugated continent. The cargoes of these ships were to be her sustenance and armament. Reece had drawn a line across the chart, a tenuous pencil line that stretched in a great northward arc and plunged through the Irish Sea to the port of Liverpool. Every wave, Edmund thought, between Halifax and the Mersey could conceal an enemy periscope, every mile of sea a deadly torpedo track.

Things had not started well. One of the Canadian minesweepers had to be towed back to Halifax after colliding with another ship, either a merchant vessel or another minesweeper, it wasn't clear from the signals. How, Edmund wondered, were two ancient and creaking destroyers, plus *Troubadour* and *Harp* expected to guard this great concourse of ships for two thousand miles, two or three weeks of slow steaming? Four little ships, four asdic sets, four barrages of depth charges. If six or more U-boats attacked simultaneously it was hard to see how they would be deterred. And what about the wide rear of the convoy? How was a stern attack to be prevented; who would go to the aid of sinking ships that fell limping and wounded behind the others?

The days passed and the plodding convoy and its escort reached mid-Atlantic. So far so good, they all said to themselves; Iceland lies to the north and in a few more days we shall see the green hills of Ireland.

At that point the U-boats attacked. In their furnished and well situated bases in Norway and the Bay of Biscay they were on the threshold of the North Atlantic. They had grown confident by conquest and the spoils of earlier victories; their morale had not been dulled by the failure of their comrades to win the air battle against Britain. They looked forward with grinning anticipation to the outcome of this encounter that they would wage from under the sea. They had only to sink merchant ships which were weakly armed and scarcely able to help themselves. It was a German's fondest dream, to slaughter the defenceless.

The first torpedoes struck at night in the rear of the convoy and both *Troubadour* and *Harp* turned back to assist a merchantman that was on fire and hunt for its murderer. As *Harp* approached, the merchantman rolled over on its own lifeboat which was filled with men. Braithwaite groaned and something seemed to drain out of him. His voice became old and his hands shook.

Edmund took *Troubadour* in search of the U-boat, but made no contact and half an hour later, in the centre of the convoy, another ship was torpedoed. The U-boat had used darkness and a confused sea to thread between the lines of ships and position itself for another strike. This time the crew of the stricken vessel were more fortunate and *Harp* rescued them.

Two ships sunk and the worst was yet to come. The U-boats, like wolves, were attacking the flanks and rear of the convoy, yet *Troubadour* and *Harp* could not patrol those miles of sea, could not be everywhere at once. When the ship was at action stations nothing seemed to happen; when action stations were relaxed and they went to cruising stations there would be another alarm.

Edmund glanced at his watch. Marko was coming up the bridge ladder, but there was still half an hour before he would take over for the afternoon. He called Edmund to the after end of the bridge.

'Pemberton's bloody worried,' Marko began. 'The captain wanted to send a wireless signal to his wife. The wireless operator refused because he'd be breaking wireless silence. He took it to Pemberton who went and confronted the old boy. A row, a bloody great row. Threatened court martial. Now he's drinking.'

'Hell, we don't need this. D'you think a shot of whisky and a decent sleep will cure him?'

Marko shook his head. 'Dunno. Pemberton thinks it's better the officers know what's happening. I've told Jardine and Reece.'

Edmund turned back to his duties. He looked out towards the convoy; the ships looked sullen and reproachful, a hundred vessels guarded inadequately by a navy that wasn't capable of so vast an undertaking. Two had been lost since Halifax and the enemy knew the whereabouts of the convoy. A German long-range scouting aircraft, a Kondor, had found them and was shadowing the convoy. All this and a captain who was losing his sanity. Braithwaite had an irrational side to his nature, but this was worse than irrational, it was unthinkable to break wireless silence and give the enemy a quick and easy fix on the convoy's position. Unthinkable yes, but a captain is absolute master aboard his own ship. In this instance, however, Pemberton had been right to stop the signal.

A few moments later Braithwaite himself was on the bridge, wearing, of all things, brown golf clothes. 'Oh God,' Edmund said to himself.

'They're trying to steal my food,' Braithwaite announced. 'Will you see that I get my dinner in the gun turret?'

'I don't understand you, sir,' Edmund replied. 'When it's dinner time you'll be served in the wardroom, not in the gun turret, surely.'

'That's your trouble, Casswell. You don't understand. You're an anti-submarine officer but you allow all these bloody ships to be sunk; all these men to be killed. Signalman,' he turned to the signalman at the after end of the bridge. 'Make a signal to the flotilla leader. Say *Lieutenant Casswell is not going to become a bishop and a merry Christmas.*'

The signalman wrote it down, then faced Braithwaite. 'Is that what you want me to send, sir?'

'Yes, it is.' Braithwaite shouted back. 'There he is, commander what's-his-name. Send it.' He pointed to the distant destroyer.

The signalman shot a glance past the captain to Edmund, who nodded, and he immediately picked up his lamp and aimed it at the grey outline of the destroyer ahead of the convoy. An answering blink appeared and he began to spell it out. Edmund knew that the signalman was passing it more slowly and deliberately than he would normally have done. He was saying, in his own way, that he knew it made no sense but had been ordered to pass it.

Signalmen were selected from those who had excelled in school and were fully literate. The speed with which they had been trained to pass and read light signals was remarkable, but they had been taught more than the mere skill of good transmission, they were expected to use judgement in deciding how a message was to be sent. If Reece had signalled *Harp, 'navigator to navigator; did you get morning stars, if so, pass me your 0800 position,'* it would have been tapped out at great speed between two signalmen who knew each other and were aware of each other's capabilities. 'You' would have been passed as 'U'. The reply, however, containing co-ordinates of latitude and longitude, would have been passed more slowly and without chance of error.

Both *Troubadour* and *Harp* had a leading signalman and two signalmen who kept watches, each man four hours on duty, eight off, as long as the ship was at sea. At action stations all three would be on the bridge, also for entering or leaving harbour or when the ship was manoeuvering in company with other ships. During night watches in wartime when light could not be used it would be normal for a signalman to have no duties during his watch and he would then effectively be an extra lookout.

The two destroyers, being larger, had a petty officer signalman, known as a yeoman of signals, and three signalmen each. A yeoman was a paragon of signalling virtue, a genius of lamp and flag who had, in all probability, memorised almost every flag hoist in the book. The story was told of a yeoman who could read two light signals simultaneously although the sources were separated by a ninety degree angle. It was common for a yeoman to say of a distant signal, 'that's Jim, I know his touch.'

A yeoman, Edmund realised, could have questioned the captain's signal and said that he did not understand it. Yes, a yeoman could speak up, but scarcely an ordinary signalman. Anyway, the captain's signal was being passed in all its stupidity for the escort commander to see, which was what Edmund wanted. Edmund was in his usual position in the centre of the bridge. His shoulder was pressed against the gyroscopic compass which supported him against the roll of the ship. He paid no attention to Braithwaite who was standing by the bridge chart table.

'Very well,' Braithwaite said. 'If he won't answer my signal I'll make another one. Signalman, say "*I look forward to a meeting on the golf course this afternoon. What's your handicap?*" '

'Who to, sir?'

It was the leading signalman who had come up the ladder with a questioning look on his face.

'The commander, of course,' Braithwaite retorted. 'We'll see if he's any good.'

Braithwaite's attention was diverted by the sight of Dobreiner who had also come up on the bridge. He was in overalls with heavy gloves and an officer's cap with an oil-stained cap over.

'What d'you want, chief? We don't often see you here.'

'I came to talk to you sir. You gave an order to one of my men which can't be obeyed and I have countermanded it. If it were carried out the ship would be in danger. We don't play the fool in my engine room while the ship . . .'

Dobreiner had seen Edmund shake his head and stopped in

mid-sentence. Unseen by Braithwaite Edmund pointed at the captain, then tapped the side of his head with his index finger.

'Get off the bridge, chief, or I'll have you court-martialled.'

Edmund caught the eye of the leading signalman.

'Send it,' he said, then turned to Braithwaite.

'Nearly dinner time.' He tried to sound normal. 'Will you go to the wardroom, sir?'

Braithwaite turned to him.

'You know, Casswell, for a long time I suspected you were a ponce, but ever since I saw you with that French tart I've decided you can screw with the best of them. I hope you . . .'

Edmund turned away and closed his ears. Were these Braithwaite's unspoken thoughts about Marguerite and himself? Were these the phrases that he had stored in his mind and secretly wanted to use?

'You think you're so bloody clever and I was fool enough to trust you. Pemberton the same. Cut from the same cloth, you bastards. Never had to work for anything, never faced . . .'

'Destroyer has turned away to starboard, sir,' Edmund interrupted him.

'Hoisted red flag,' the leading signalman added. 'Must have a contact.'

There was a distant rumble of depth charges.

'Do you want me to go to action stations, sir?' Edmund asked. He stepped across to the port side of the bridge and reached for the button.

'No, certainly not. I'll be playing golf this afternoon. Did you send that signal, leading signalman?'

'Yessir, it's gone, sir.'

'Then why doesn't he reply?'

Braithwaite turned, went down the ladder, stepped over the sill into the wheelhouse and turned into the chart room. There he pulled open the drawer, gathered an armful of charts and retraced his steps to the flag deck and threw them over the side. The men in the wheelhouse watched in silent perplexity.

Next Braithwaite went down the second ladder to the main deck and hesitated as he passed the galley. The smell of food seemed to have attracted him and he stood watching the cook pulling the steel trays from the oven and handing them to the men on behalf of each mess.

'Harding,' Edmund called out. 'Did you hear him say he was going to get a revolver?'

'Yessir, we all heard it. Captain's off his rocker, sir.'

'Can you stop him from coming up on the bridge?'

'Moment he steps on the ladder he's going to need both hands on the rails, sir. He can't climb a steep ladder with no hands, or even with one hand; not when there's motion on the ship. That's when me and McVane come out of the charthouse and take him by the arms. That's if you agree, sir, you must give us the order.'

'I do so, but get more men. He's very strong. And only interfere if he's carrying a revolver in his hand or in a holster. You're right, Harding, get him when he's on the ladder.'

'Aye aye, sir, but I hate to have to do it, sir, I mean lay hands on the captain.'

Edmund went to the wardroom telephone and spun the handle.

'Jardine here,' came a voice.

'Is Pemberton there?' Edmund asked.

'Yes, everyone's here.'

'Tell him the captain is on his way down to his cabin to get his revolver and he's coming back to shoot me.'

'We've been discussing the whole situation.'

'Stop discussing it and do something.'

'If he gets better we'll be charged with mutiny.'

'If I get shot I'll never get any better.'

There was silence from the wardroom end, then Pemberton's voice.

'What's he been doing up there, Edmund?'

'Threatening to shoot me. Throwing charts overboard. He's completely mad. Now stop him and don't let him get his hands on a gun.'

'I'm hesitating at the prospect of using force.'

'Well, don't hesitate any longer and do it,' Edmund shouted.

'That's frightful,' Pemberton mumbled. 'Where's he now?'

'Last seen in the galley on his way aft. He has to pass the wardroom door. For God's sake do something. Use force.'

Edmund turned back to his duties and watched as the destroyer, two or three miles distant, dropped a pattern of depth charges. He noted the time, 1200, midday, and was relieved when leading seaman Fenton arrived in the wheelhouse and was briefed by Harding.

The captain's madness was now common knowledge throughout the ship. A few minutes earlier the coxswain had been present at the rum issue, as he always was, and there had been no other topic of conversation. The men seemed to regard it not so much as a calamity but as one of those things that happens in human life for which there are no explanations and no remedies.

Jennings, the sick berth attendant, had been told by Pemberton to find a syringe and prepare a knockout shot. It was something he had never done before and he pulled a book from the shelf and looked under the heading 'Sedatives'.

Braithwaite was walking aft down the upper deck and staggering against the roll of the ship. He raised his hand toward one of the hand-holds that slid on a wire rope between the galley and the after deckhouse, but failed to find it and went on without. He steadied himself at the port depth charge thrower, then stepped over the sill into the after deckhouse.

The depth charge watch should have been changing, but the men on duty seemed disinclined to leave in face of the drama that was unfolding. 'The captain's gone mad' was on everyone's lips. Mad, out of his mind, bonkers, they all had a word for it, but all knew that a ship with a mad captain is in mortal danger.

Was there any precedent for this, they asked themselves, had it ever happened before? If the ship had carried a medical officer it would have been easier, much easier, to reach the decision to confine the captain by force, but how does an ordinary lieutenant like Pemberton reach such a decision? What would happen if the captain recovered as quickly as he had succumbed?

Waiting outside the wardroom and barring Braithwaite's entry into his own cabin were Pemberton, Cyr, Jardine and Dobreiner. Braithwaite reached the foot of the ladder and glared at them.

'What the hell do you want?' he asked.

'Are you going to your cabin?' Pemberton asked uneasily.

'Yes, so why are you barring my way?'

They made way for him in the narrow passageway and he took

the ten or twelve steps to the door of his cabin, then leaped in and attempted to close the door behind him. It was Cyr who prevented him from doing so and who laid the first hand on him. He caught one arm and Pemberton the other, but Braithwaite was too strong for them and tore loose, making for the desk drawer where he kept his automatic pistol.

'Will you listen to me . . . ,' Pemberton was making a last desperate appeal to reason. 'You're in no state to . . . Don't you realize . . .'

'You bastards,' between clenched teeth was the only reply.

Cyr had him round the neck and Pemberton got hold of his left arm. Jardine and Dobreiner stood behind not knowing what to do. With his free arm Braithwaite pulled open a drawer, seized the weapon, turned and fired. Pemberton crumpled and fell.

It was at that moment that Edmund, high on the bridge, three decks above, pressed the alarm button. Stridently it sounded, blast after blast, shrieking at the men to go to their battle stations. Both destroyers had hoisted the large red flag and both had dropped depth charges, so Edmund decided that *Troubadour* must be at full readiness. The fact that the afternoon watch had just come on duty and the forenoon had not yet gone meant that of the men who truly fight the ship, the gun's crew, depth charge crew, asdic operators, engineers and stokers, two thirds were already in place.

In the back of his mind Edmund had sensed that Pemberton was unable to reach the decision which the circumstances compelled him to reach. Pemberton was beyond reproach when it came to playing his part within an organization, when his duties and responsibilities were clear and orderly, but when the balance was upset, the chain of authority broken, he hesitated and was confounded. He could command an escort vessel at a moment's notice because that was what he had been trained to do, but deciding how to restrain a mad captain was another thing entirely.

At this point Edmund knew nothing of the drama that was being enacted in the passageway and in the captain's cabin. As the officer of the watch he would stay on the bridge until relieved or until the captain reappeared. With the coxswain now in the wheelhouse, plus Harding, Fenway, McVane and three or four others he had little fear that the captain would make good his threat. These men were determined and with the ship at action stations he felt more confident.

Edmund paid scant attention as a message came from the senior officer of the escort.

'*Your signals not understood. Is this meant to be a joke? Explain yourself.*'

Edmund read it and handed the signal back to the leading signalman.

'We can't answer that,' he said.

Even as he said it the asdic operator turned and stuck his head out the door. 'Sir.'

Edmund grabbed the headset from its hook and put the earpiece awkwardly to his ear. For a moment he concentrated totally on the sound, then tore it away and shouted 'starboard thirty, hard-a-starboard.' The asdic operator nodded his head, 'torpedo noises.'

An icy grip seemed to take hold of Edmund's heart. To the signalman he said, 'Hoist flag "T" '. To the lookouts, 'watch the water for torpedo tracks'. His own voice sounded far away and disembodied.

'Go up to full speed,' he called down the wheelhouse voicepipe. 'Steady the ship due south.'

His next move would have been to call the captain, to get Braithwaite on the bridge as rapidly as possible, but with his hand on the voicepipe he hesitated and said nothing.

Troubadour heeled over as she turned sharply and gathered speed. Reports began to come in as the ship's company reached their action stations, but Jardine was not on the bridge and Edmund had to take them himself.

'Coxswain on the wheel,' came Clancey's voice.

'Depth charge crew closed up,' from the after deck. 'Emergency pattern set for fifty feet.'

Troubadour had turned to a southerly course when the lookout shouted, 'torpedo track on this side.'

Edmund looked over the bulwark and there it was, a torpedo passing a few yards on the port beam. It would have hit us fair and square, he thought, if I hadn't turned.

'Periscope sir,' called the lookout. 'Looks like she's approaching, with a bit of right to left.'

Edmund's binoculars went up and he saw the telltale feather of the periscope less than two thousand yards distant, the submarine's course being about zero-four-five degrees. He took a quick bearing, threw off ten degrees to port and called down, 'Coxswain, steer one-six-zero degrees.'

Edmund's confidence was building. The torpedo had not struck and he felt certain that the asdic would make contact in a few seconds.

'Coxswain,' he said again. 'I'm not going to run down the torpedo track now that I've seen the U-boat. Change the engine revolutions to one-five-four; attack speed.'

'Aye aye, sir.'

'Periscope's gone down, sir,' said the lookout.

'Asdic, search dead ahead. How are operating conditions?'

'Quite good.'

'Gun's crew closed up,' Harding reported. 'Mr Cyr isn't here.'

Edmund thought for a brief moment.

'Harding, I don't know where the officers are. Carry on by yourself. Load armour piercing and full charge. If you see the U-boat you may fire without orders.'

'Aye aye, sir.'

A sudden motion from the asdic compartment made Edmund grab at the headphones, only this time he put them on over his uniform cap.

'You got him; hold the echo,' he said to the asdic operator.

'Range fourteen hundred yards, sir.'

'I'm going to carry out the usual emergency attack,' Edmund replied, then turned to the signalman. 'Hoist red flag. We have contact.'

'Senior officer is making interrogative signal, sir.'

Reply: *'Have contact with U-boat and attacking. Ship under command of lieutenant Casswell since captain indisposed.'*

'Range one thousand, sir. Echo continues slight high.'

Edmund gave orders for a forty-degree alteration of course so that *Troubadour* would intercept the U-boat. He picked up the telephone to the quarter deck and spoke with Williams. It sounded very chatty and unofficial.

'We have a firm contact, Williams. Standard attack. I'll sound the buzzer when the time comes to start firing.'

'Yes, all right, sir. We're all ready. Er, one thing, sir. One of me mates heard a shot from the direction of the captain's cabin. Don't sound good, does it?'

'Oh God,' was all Edmund could reply.

As Pemberton lay groaning on the linoleum floor Dobreiner and Jardine entered the *mêlé*. Cyr had Braithwaite's right arm, his pistol arm, and was holding it upwards. Jardine grabbed his other arm, while Dobreiner took off the brown cloth belt from his overalls and passed it round Braithwaite's neck. He crossed it and pulled it tight with all his strength and Braithwaite's face began to turn blue. A minute later, having pulled the three men around the cabin, he fell over Pemberton's prostrate form.

Reece appeared in the doorway, Jennings behind him with a syringe. Braithwaite, forced to the floor, was given a sedative through his clothes after which they picked up his limp figure and placed him on the bunk. The livid colour drained from his face and Jennings said he was breathing. Next they turned their attention to Pemberton. He was carried to his cabin and laid on the bunk. Marko picked up the automatic pistol and put it in his coat pocket.

'We're supposed to be at action stations,' he announced. 'Jardine and Reece, you two carry on and leave this to me. Chief engineer as well.'

Jardine and Reece ran up to the bridge as the asdic reported the U-boat at four hundred yards. The interval between transmission and the return echo was diminishing, giving a life and death urgency as it spat out and returned the sound.

'Start plotting and keep the log,' Edmund said to Reece when he saw him. 'Jardine, stay here.' He was surprised at his own coolness.

'Where's the captain?' he asked.

'Sedated,' Jardine replied.

At three hundred yards Edmund judged that the U-boat was

still crossing right to left at a submerged speed of seven or eight knots. *Troubadour*'s attack speed was sixteen knots so he cast off fifty degrees to port, told the coxswain to steady on the new course and picked up the firing button in one hand and a stopwatch in the other. The U-boat was now on the starboard bow, two hundred, one hundred yards.

'*Ding-ding*,' '*ding-ding*,' the asdic persisted.

'Any last minute turn?' Edmund asked.

'No; seems to be keeping on steady,' from the asdic operator.

A few seconds later Edmund began to press the firing button, and Jardine, at the after end of the bridge, reported as each three-hundred-pound charge rolled out the chute or was flung from the throwers.

'Take off headphones,' he ordered the asdic operators, at the same time removing his own, and a second or two later the depth charges began exploding with roars that shook the ship. Ten haystacks of white water rose from the sea, hung momentarily in the air and subsided.

'Earphones back on,' Edmund called out, then to Jardine, 'I'm making a turn to port; tell Harding to train the gun on the port side, red six-o.'

'Noises, sir,' from the asdic operator. Then louder and more excited, 'blowing tanks, she's coming up.'

It seemed to Edmund that at one moment the sea was empty and the next a black and evil creature lay on the surface, shedding water from its upperworks. It was close, not more than a hundred yards distant and for agonising seconds Edmund could do no more than hope that Harding had seen it, that the gun hadn't misfired or jammed, that . . .

The gun fired and by comparison with the roar of the depth charges it made a puny and almost trivial sound. The shell struck at the base of the coming tower. Not to be outdone, the machine-guns opened fire and sprayed the submarine's conning tower with long bursts.

Edmund leaned down to the voicepipe. 'Reece, the oerlikons, go and tell them not to waste ammunition. Their job is to prevent the enemy manning his gun. Fire at the enemy's gun, not his conning tower.'

At this point in the battle *Troubadour* and the U-boat lay parallel to each other but heading in opposite directions. Edmund didn't want to pass round her stern because U-boats have stern torpedo-tubes as well as bow tubes, so he turned *Troubadour* slightly toward her and went astern on the engines. Harding had meanwhile registered two more direct hits. With the fourth, however, he missed and the shell hit the sea.

To this point Edmund had not seen any Germans and he assumed that the crew were trapped inside their vessel, but the lookout now reported that he could see men in the sea. Only the U-boat's conning tower remained above water, the upper deck was awash and as she sank Harding fired twice more at the battered upperworks.

'Cease firing,' Edmund shouted to Jardine, who relayed it to the gun.

Edmund turned to the asdic operators.

'Pick up the echo and follow as it sinks. You should be able to hear breaking-up noises at about a thousand feet.'

Edmund's next order was to Jardine to go down and organise the rescue of survivors.

Survivors, he thought, better get the coxswain in on the act. He leaned down to the wheelhouse voicepipe.

'Coxswain; hand over the wheelhouse to able seaman McVane. Survivors.'

'Aye aye, sir.'

'Half ahead together, port thirty,' he ordered when the lookout had indicated where the survivors were bobbing in the water. He took *Troubadour* towards them, stopped and went astern within a few yards of the twelve heads. Nine of them swam towards the ship, three swam away. The lookout stated the obvious.

'There's three of them that's swimming in the wrong direction, sir.'

'Yes, I see,' Edmund replied. 'Too bad.'

A moment later Jardine bounded up the ladder and saluted.

'Sir. From lieutenant Cyr. Is he to lower a boat and try to grab the three stragglers?'

'No. They've had a chance to save themselves and chosen not to. I won't waste time chasing after Germans who prefer to die.'

Jardine saluted and ran down the ladder, leaving Edmund to wonder at the ease with which he had reached such a fateful decision. It was common knowledge that some Germans had vowed not to surrender or be rescued from the sea. If they were forcibly taken aboard they would find other ways of killing themselves, so it seemed better to leave them. Marko, he knew, would be shouting at them in French and German to swim to the ship, that they had fought honourably and it was no disgrace to save themselves.

'Breaking up noises at a thousand feet,' from the asdic compartment. 'None of us ever heard a U-boat breaking up.'

'Very good,' Edmund replied. 'Recommence normal search.'

Jardine was back on the bridge.

'Nine survivors, one an officer. We're clear and ready to proceed.'

'Thank you. Half ahead together. Two-five-zero revolutions. We'll rejoin the convoy.'

The wheelhouse beneath his feet sprang into action, the engine room telegraphs sounded and were placed at 'Half Ahead,' and the revolution counter cranked up to 250, which was almost full speed.

'Leading signalman,' Edmund called out. 'What was the number painted on the conning tower?'

'I think it were 122, sir. But leading seaman Harding hit it with the first shot and it could have been 12–something else.'

'All right. Send a signalman to find out from lieutenant Cyr. He can ask the survivors.'

Edmund felt a surge of confidence.

'Reece,' he called out. 'Come up on the bridge. We don't have any charts so it's pointless your being in the chart room.'

'Take the ship back to the convoy,' he continued when Reece was at his side. 'I have to compose some signals.'

'Can you raise the senior officer of the escort by light at this distance?' he asked the leading signalman.

'Yessir, but I'll use the ten-inch lamp.'

'Very well, take this down. *U-boat forced to the surface with depth charges and sunk by gunfire. Nine survivors taken aboard. Am returning to my station at best speed.*'

'That's the happiest signal I ever made,' he said in an undertone. 'What's the time? Twelve thirty-six by my watch. It took us about half an hour.'

'Wheelhouse,' he said. 'Relax action stations. We'll go to cruising stations. Ask leading seaman Harding to come up on the bridge as soon as he's sponged out the gun.'

Edmund wondered why he was doing all the talking.

'Reece, what was the situation down aft when you last saw it?'

'Well, sir, the captain was sedated. Jennings rammed it in his backside and he went to sleep like a baby. Pemberton was shot, but it may not be fatal. Cyr and Jennings were there and Jardine sent the fire-fighting party to help them. That included the cook and two off-duty stokers, so anything could have happened. Cyr told Jardine and me to get to our action stations as soon as Braithwaite was under control. I didn't realise he threw all my charts overboard.'

'So Pemberton's all right?'

'He was breathing, but there's a lot of blood. To make matters worse they fell on him trying to hold Braithwaite. It was the most awful thing to see four men attempting to control him, yet he still managed to get at his gun and shoot. He's the one who deserved to be shot.'

'I'm not sure that I have the sequence of events perfectly straight in my mind but anyway, for all practical purposes, I seem to be in command of the ship and lieutenant Cyr is first lieutenant. This state of affairs has existed since midday today, and the ship's log can be entered to that effect.'

'Yes,' Reece conceded. 'That's about the size of it.'

'Message from the senior officer of the escort, sir,' from the leading signalman.

'*Very well done. Am passing your message to Admiralty. However, you did not provide a position.*'

'*Regret cannot indicate position where U-boat sunk,*' Edmund replied. '*All charts thrown overboard by lieutenant commander Braithwaite during rampage this forenoon of which signals to you about playing golf are but small example. He armed himself with revolver, shot and wounded lieutenant Pemberton. Is now under enforced* restraint. Ship has been under command of Casswell since midday with Cyr as first lieutenant. A full written report will be prepared.'

Troubadour's motion changed as she went up to full speed. The sea was not rough, but after the gentle and leisurely eight or nine knots of the convoy she now pitched, corkscrewed, and rolled with the increased speed.

Leading seaman Harding came on the bridge with a shy smile on his face. One would scarcely have known that he was a leading seaman gunlayer in the Royal Navy, or indeed that he was in the navy at all. He wore an old blue sweater, dungarees, rubber boots and a wool cap of a kind much favoured because headphones could be worn over the top. The navy seaman's cap, surely the most foolish headgear ever devised for men at sea, which blew off in a wind, provided no shade for the eyes, no protection against a crack on the head and could not be worn with headphones, had long ago been discarded. He dispensed with formality.

'Well done, Mr Casswell. That were a lovely job. Brought her up with the first pattern of charges.'

'You too, Harding. You hit her six out of seven. Terrific shooting.'

'The gun's crew all done well, sir. Worked like madmen . . . I mean, sir, I dunno how those lads loaded so quick. And the ship was reasonably steady for aiming.'

'Well, thank you, Harding. No one else in the navy could have done it like that.'

When Marko appeared Edmund assumed it was to report that the prisoners had been given dry clothes, their injuries attended to, and were being guarded.

'It's about Braithwaite.'

'What about him? I thought he was sleeping peacefully in his bunk.'

'He's sleeping too bloody peacefully. He's dead.'

'Oh no. How did it happen?'

'Well, as far as I can see he never really started breathing again after we got him down and Jennings administered the sedative. The chief engineer's belt was round his neck for a full minute, then three or four or us were sitting on him, and now Jennings isn't completely sure he gave him the proper sedative. And the alarm bells made it all the more difficult. I don't think we did the perfect job. Some might call it a cock-up.'

'Is Jennings sure he's dead?'

''Fraid so. After he cleaned up Pemberton's wound and made him comfortable he went back to Braithwaite's cabin and couldn't find any vital signs. He tried to resuscitate him but didn't succeed. Whatever he died of, he's dead.'

'And Pemberton, having been shot at close quarters, is still alive. All right,' Edmund went on. 'I'm going down to see for myself. Reece will be on the bridge till I get back. I suppose this means another signal to the senior officer of the escort.'

Edmund turned to the leading signalman.

'*Regret to inform you that lieutenant-commander Albert Braithwaite RNR died shortly after midday to-day apparently of injuries sustained while efforts being made to disarm him.*'

Chapter 23

IT TOOK ONLY minutes for Braithwaite's death to become common knowledge throughout the ship. The ship's company spoke openly about him as a seaman, a wartime captain and about his last sudden descent into insanity. Some said they had known it was coming over a long period and sensed that he had walked the edge of the abyss for many months until a final jolt had cast him into the depths. It was as though a knife had slashed his mind, erasing what was true, tested and tied to real experience, exposing a phantom world of false and erratic images. He had entered a chamber where God Himself could scarcely have known what it was like.

He had not been such a bad skipper, they agreed, and many of the older ones had known worse. He was harsh and a bit unpredictable, but his seamanship and navigation were superlative and he had done well to teach it to his officers. He had delegated responsibility, not grudgingly or with a closed hand, but because he trusted them to follow his example and do things the way he did.

His ideas of discipline were bizarre. He hated seeing defaulters brought before him and seemed genuinely distressed when a man did something wrong. He liked the men and they him, despite his list of foibles that would have been thought outrageous in a man of artistic inclination, never mind a supposedly disciplined wartime naval officer. They told stories about his last hour, not spitefully, but in a tone of regret and horror. He had dressed in golf clothes, he seemed disoriented, his eye no longer able to focus on grey seas, a horizon filled with ships and the petty distractions of life in a rolling, pitching escort vessel. Perhaps the boredom had been his undoing, or the feeling of helplessness as torpedoes, like the grin of a thousand sharks, carried their message of cowardly destruction. Or was it the sheer upredictability of war? The explosion of the tanker when help was within hailing distance; the ship that rolled over and sank on top of its own lifeboat. Was it the blackened misery of *Northern Harvest*; the oil, the fires; the men dazed and a captain with blood running down his face, a small man with a bald head and a voice that was shattered.

Stories began to emerge from unlikely places such as the stokers' mess and the ship's galley. He had ordered a stoker to cut the fuel lines, told the leading cook that it was unlucky to eat a sea monster. 'Throw the stew overboard,' he had shouted, 'or something terrible will happen.' The absurd tweed-clad figure retained the habit of command, but the cook, a man named Puddington, whose name so magnificently embraced his avocation, had picked up a meat cleaver and flourished it in his face. Braithwaite had presaged his own untimely death and something terrible did happen.

Some blame was placed at Pemberton's door for his reluctance to accept what could not be rejected. By midday he should have concluded that the captain was a danger to the ship and to himself. Pemberton couldn't believe it, couldn't bring himself to admit that the captain was insane and would have to be restrained. Most surprising, he hesitated in face of Marko Cyr's advice. Cyr the lawyer, an intensely practical man whose mind was uncluttered by the niceties of naval etiquette had urged him to round up the strongest men in the ship and handcuff Braithwaite with his arms round the steel stanchion in his own cabin. 'Once he's handcuffed we can let him cool off and then try talking.'

Cyr had been unconcerned at the prospect that he might recover as quickly as he had succumbed. 'We have a watertight case,' Cyr kept saying. 'No judge or jury, no court martial or Board of Admiralty could fault us for acting to ensure the safety of the ship.' Pemberton had shaken his head and clasped his hands.

'Look, old chap,' Cyr went on. 'He's ordered a man to sabotage the ship, is threatening to shoot the officer of the watch, has thrown charts overboard and God knows what else; what are we waiting for?'

It was equally agreed that Pemberton's hesitation had not warranted a serious gunshot wound. Pemberton was a gentleman, almost the relic of an earlier time, as much an anachronism in the rough and tumble of war as on the frontiers of North America or down a coal mine. He was not merely well-mannered and well-spoken, no, he went further, he was kind and thoughtful and in this instance it was his undoing. He tried to prevail by reason at a moment when brute force was the only alternative. In consequence Braithwaite had seized his loaded gun from the desk drawer and fired a shot directly at Pemberton. If Cyr had not lunged at him and held his arm, even as the shot was fired, he might have shaken free and killed every one of them, Pemberton, Cyr, Dobreiner and Jardine.

No one could blame Dobreiner for using his belt to choke Braithwaite. It was the instrument that came to hand while Cyr and Jardine attempted to restrain his arms. When a man has just been shot and is lying groaning it can hardly be urged that something round the neck of the assailant is excessive or unnecessary.

The final tragedy seemed to be compounded of misdirection and hideous ill-luck. The ship's alarm bells were sounding their call to action stations, so they placed the prostrate form on the bunk, after which Jennings announced that he was breathing. What had probably been needed was an immediate effort to resuscitate, but Jennings didn't know this, his training had been too brief to cover all such contingencies.

Since being posted to *Troubadour* many months before, Jennings had expended fifty or a hundred yards of bandages, handed out dozens of aspirin and used a jar or two of burn lotion. He had cut the men's hair, kept his little sick bay clean and tidy, but had never given an injection until the present instance. If he had been negligent it could be argued in his defence that his training had been inadequate for the tasks he faced. Whether or not he even measured out the proper dose of sedative was by no means clear.

Marko Cyr was preparing a report in his usual painstaking

manner. He took statements from witnesses, made copies of the signals that had been sent and finally put it all together in a file with a covering letter explaining how he had gone about it.

Braithwaite's body was sewn in a canvas hammock, still wearing his brown golf clothes, and was placed in the tiller flat where it would be out of the way. Jardine and Clancey brushed his uniforms and packed them in his steel uniform box, then placed the box in a corner and lashed it against the motion of the ship. Lucinda Braithwaite in her agony would unpack it at a far remove from the heaving world of *Troubadour*.

No one could deny that Edmund's attack on the U-boat had been perfectly executed. It was a standard attack, with the U-boat moving across her bows from right to left. The enemy had been sighted on the surface seconds before and was just below periscope depth as it attempted to close the convoy. A torpedo had been fired at *Troubadour*, but Edmund's rapid helm order had avoided it and it ran by harmlessly.

In a depth charge attack it is not the depth charges that are aimed at the U-boat, rather it is the attacking ship that is aimed and the depth charges released when the ship passes over. At the moment of an attack the lookouts search downwards for bubbles, oil or a water disturbance caused by the enemy below. The lookouts always claimed that in the clear and sometimes calm water of the Mediterranean it was easier to see down than in the Atlantic.

The German sub-lieutenant who was one of the survivors had spoken to Marko Cyr and been explicit about the U-boat's last moments. He had been at his battle station in the forward torpedo compartment and when *Troubadour* attacked he heard the sound of her engines and the depth charges hitting the water. There followed a kind of hammer-blow as one of them struck the steel casing of the U-boat. A fraction of a second later it exploded and inflicted mortal damage. His captain must have ordered the tanks to be blown so that the U-boat rose to the surface and he and his men escaped through the forward hatch. He had less idea what was happening elsewhere in the U-boat than the observers aboard *Troubadour*, except to say that two from the engine room had also got away. The central part of the boat had been flooded and the conning tower, which was their means of escape, had been wrecked by Harding's gunfire.

The sub-lieutenant had shrugged when asked about the three men who had swum away from *Troubadour*. He knew there were some who had taken vows not to be captured, but it was not, he thought, a policy; *une politique*, he called it, of the German government or the Kriegsmarine.

Aboard *Troubadour* the rejoicing was restrained. A U-boat sunk was an achievement, not so much because U-boats were expensive to build and manned by trained crews of selected individuals, but because more merchant ships would survive once it was gone; more cargo would reach England, more munitions enter the battle on the allied side.

Edmund himself didn't see it as a personal accomplishment, but as an honour gained by the ship. Over the months *Troubadour* had acquired a character of its own, a set of traits which made it unique and meant that one could only think of *Troubadour* in semi-human terms. The picture that came to mind was that of a goddess with a terrifying tendency to kill her children. First it was the seaman who died on the bridge, then the French deputy minister, next a stoker, and now her victims were Braithwaite and Pemberton. It was not an easy ship and it would preserve her crew from the violence of sea and the enemy only if they accepted her savage and unpredictable ways. Some might have called her a damnable mistress, demanding and selfish, a tyrant who would not forgive.

When Edmund had first set foot aboard *Troubadour* a year earlier he had possessed the mind of a student, a reader of books seated at the feet of others. That stage had passed and he had learned the harsh profession of small ships in wartime and watched as the war developed and raged around him. His war had been painful, but it was shot through with points of light, there had been moments that he would not have exchanged for anything. He had finally prevailed against all the odds and with consummate skill had guided *Troubadour* over the U-boat. Indeed, *Troubadour* seemed to have destroyed a captain and embraced another within the hour. He had assumed command, directed the attack and then without remorse had ordered the abandonment of prisoners bent on their own destruction. This was a far cry from the young man who had stepped on board the day war began.

He now stood on *Troubadour*'s bridge as her captain and for the next few days there could be no question relating to his authority. The captain was dead, the first lieutenant seriously injured and as senior surviving officer he assumed command. Cyr was a few months junior to him as a lieutenant and therefore became first lieutenant and second-in-command. No confirmation of these arrangements was needed, no blessing from higher authority; it was the time-honoured and incontestable arrangement.

He looked round the horizon and toward the convoy as he had done a thousand times, then to the two distant destroyers leading the convoy. He had met the escort commander in Halifax; Dalzell-Paul in *Harp* he knew well, but he had not met the captain of the other destroyer. By misadventure, Edmund thought to himself, he had become a member of this élite little club. On arrival in Liverpool he would go with them to report to the admiral commanding Western Approaches.

Edmund had little apprehension about his new duties. He had handled the ship frequently under Braithwaite's tutelage, commanded it in fact, and he was a 'natural' at ship handling. He had complete confidence in Marko as first lieutenant and, for that matter, the whole ship's company. They were a good lot and knew their business and he felt himself to be among friends. Yes, between them Braithwaite and Pemberton had established a high standard and passed it on.

Edmund went down to the ship's office and pulled out the forms for recommending Honours and Awards. He fingered the thick paper, then lowered a sheet into the typewriter and tapped out what he had already drafted in his handwriting. Harding, leading seaman gunlayer, Hounsom, the senior asdic operator, and Williams, leading seaman in charge of the depth charges; the three who had detected the U-boat, blasted it to the surface and shot it full of holes. In truth all the men deserved medals; the stokers far below in the boiler rooms, the signalmen, the cook; but he had to choose those who had been at the sharp point of the sword, who had contributed directly to the victory. Marko agreed that they were the most deserving.

The U-boats had fared badly in their attacks on that particular convoy. *Troubadour*'s kill was a certainty; it had been seen to be hit by shell fire, twelve survivors had been counted in the water and nine rescued. The survivors themselves confirmed that their boat had been lost and the asdic heard it break up as it plunged to a depth of a thousand feet.

The two destroyers had also claimed a 'possible' kill as witnessed by oil and dead bodies on the surface of the sea. It was known, however, that U-boats carried corpses dressed in sailor's uniforms and discharged them from the torpedo tubes while at the same time releasing oil, so that anti-submarine vessels would assume they had been successful and discontinue their attacks. The only way to be sure was for the ship to lower a boat; pick up a body and have the doctor determine how long it had been dead. If the interior of the body was still warm then it would seem likely that the U-boat had been sunk. The process, however, of lowering a boat and lying stopped for even a few minutes was dangerous and few escort captains would be inclined to take the risk. A stopped ship was too easy a target.

A third U-boat had been claimed by a merchant captain. It had surfaced, evidently by miscalculation, a short distance ahead of his vessel and he had rammed it as it tried to escape, tearing a hole in his hull and flooding a forward compartment. This, however, was by no means a certain kill; more likely a shave which the powerful construction of the U-boat could withstand. *Harp* had searched the area as the convoy steamed on, but found no evidence to confirm a sinking.

The U-boats, however, retired from the battle and left the convoy in peace for the latter part of the voyage. Against all expectation the remaining nights and days were tranquil, the moon became full and the weather cleared. By day the ships stood on a glittering sea and appeared motionless against a backdrop of high, wispy cloud. By night only their white wakes and bow waves betrayed their forward progress.

With Ireland a few hours distant over the horizon, Edmund went on the bridge in the early dawn. He had been sleeping in the charthouse and had only a dozen steps to reach the bridge. It was the morning watch and Marko was on duty.

Marko wasted no words. 'David Pemberton died during the night. About two in the morning. I didn't wake you. Reece was with him, and Jennings. I entered it in the log.' Marko paused; he was close to tears. 'Reece wrote down his last words to Nancy and promised to deliver them. It's going to be . . .' he turned aside.

'Any pain?' Edmund asked.

'According to Reece he didn't complain. He seemed composed. His words were clear and he said, "I can hear the ship," which Reece thought strange. "*Hear* the ship." '

Edmund and Marko stood without speaking for long minutes. The cool night air licked at their faces. Beyond the bows of the ship the first brush strokes of dawn touched the eastern horizon and put flecks of colour on the wave tops. Edmund's eyes went upward to the stars as though they had power to redress his grief.

'Marko,' he said 'I know we have no chart on which to plot our morning position, but I think we should make our observations because it's the right and proper thing. We have a sextant and a chronometer.'

He paused and searched the great canopy above him, his friends, the familiar stars, at the same time making a note of four or five that he would use when the horizon cleared. 'Yes, we'll take morning stars and when it gets light I'll send a signal to the escort commander.'

He sighed. '*Regret to inform you that lieutenant David Pemberton died of his wounds during the early hours of this morning.*' A pause. 'Poor Nancy. Poor girl.'

The day passed in a routine way with no enemy activity. Officers and men were affected alike at Pemberton's death and a bond seemed to have formed, a conspiracy almost, of restraint and quietness. Men spoke in hushed tones and drank their grog without pleasure. Joking and camaraderie, card games and gossip gave way to sleeping and reflection about their forthcoming leave.

Braithwaite's death had not touched them as Pemberton's did. Pemberton had been shot by his own commanding officer even as he tried to reason with him; had taken the full force of a bullet from a weapon that Braithwaite had no right to keep in his cabin. Some captains kept a firearm, but it was usually a service revolver issued to them in the same way that binoculars or a sextant would be issued. This, however, was a German automatic pistol which was Braithwaite's own property. No one knew when he got it or why, although the officers were vaguely aware that he had it somewhere among his possessions.

The one person aboard *Troubadour* who might have kept a service revolver in his cabin was Marko. He was designated as boarding officer and would lead a party of men if it became necessary to board an enemy ship. There was some advantage, possibly, in his keeping his firearm in his cabin together with his steel helmet, although Marko had thought it more trouble than it was worth. If ordered to board he said he preferred to be issued his firearm by the coxswain at the time his men were receiving theirs.

At 0800 Reece came up for the forenoon and Marko handed over the watch. 'And here are our morning stars, Little Brother,' he said, 'five of the first magnitude.'

Reece looked perplexed. 'We don't have a chart . . .'

'Exactly. We don't have a chart so we can't plot our position, but we took morning stars because . . . because we are naval officers. Here are the observations.'

Marko finished handing over and went down the ladder. Edmund yawned and remembered that he had not breakfasted. He turned to Reece.

'I'll be in the wardroom and then in the ship's office for most of the forenoon,' he said. 'One of my tasks is to write the officer's reports, yours included. Your report will recommend accelerated promotion to the rank of sub-lieutenant a full year ahead of normal time. Braithwaite told me that's what he wanted.'

Reece stammered his thanks and raised his hand in what was part salute, part gesture of acceptance.

That afternoon Edmund lay down and slept. It was not a deep sleep but close to the surface where the sounds of the ship, the hum of the machinery, the creaking and groaning of its internal construction and the water noises were not entirely absent from his brain. He slept far into the dog watches, borrowing the hours from paradise, yielding up his mortality to the cleansing power of rest. He awoke slowly, refreshed and serene in mind, and when he went on the bridge he found Jardine on watch and the hills of Ireland rising from the sea.

He decided that he would keep the watch from eight to midnight although he was not obliged to do so. A captain would not normally keep a watch, but it would be a relief for the others and he decided to have a full four hours to himself, perhaps for the last time on *Troubadour*'s bridge.

The following day they entered the Mersey and found crowds lining the shore to wave them in. It reminded Edmund of the rejoicing which, in an earlier time, would have welcomed a wagon train entering a beleagured fortress. The two destroyers plus *Troubadour* and *Harp* entered first, like outriders, responsible for the safety of the whole; then the wagons groaning beneath their burdens. Dockyard workers by the thousand were ready to unload them. After the long silent watches all seemed to be activity and noise. The rumours had been correct, and *Troubadour* and *Harp* were to be taken in for major refit. This was the word from the admiral commanding Western Approaches and soon there were civilians, unfamiliar grey-looking figures swarming over the ship.

The bodies of Braithwaite and Pemberton were landed without ceremony. Side by side they were placed in an ambulance; captain and first lieutenant; assailant and victim. Edmund, Marko and a few of the ship's company stood and watched. There was nothing more to be done; nothing to be said. The report was in the admiral's hands and the shore authorities would know how such matters were disposed of. They would contact Lucinda and Nancy and pass them the news that would shatter their lives. In a few days Edmund would call them by telephone and Reece would speak to Nancy Pemberton and pass on to her the last words uttered by her husband.

When the time came to report to the admiral Edmund was freshly shaved, bathed, and in his best uniform. He took with him the papers that had been prepared in the ship's office and joined the other captains on the jetty as they waited for a taxi. As he did so a party of Royal Marines mustered the nine German prisoners.He had not seen them until this moment, finding no reason to inspect them while the ship was at sea. He noticed that their clothes were washed and that they carried toothbrushes, soap and a few small luxuries, evidently purchased in *Troubadour*'s canteen. With his men mustered on the jetty the German sub-lieutenant faced Marko and saluted. '*Danke schön*' he said. He had evidently expected worse treatment than he had received. The gallant officer from New France smiled, returned his salute and wished him luck. The German prisoners looked apprehensive but not ill-disposed and it was hard to understand why their three comrades had swum away to certain death.

The three other captains congratulated Edmund on his success.

'We were lucky,' Edmund replied. 'The U-boat captain made no last-minute alteration of course. He kept straight on. It can't have been any fun inside that U-boat.'

The four officers spent an hour with the admiral's chief of staff and other specialist officers. The escort commander did much of the talking and mentioned that from New York to Halifax the route had been ill-chosen and the U-boats were waiting for them. His intuition told him they should have been further to the east where asdic operating conditions would have been better and the convoy could more easily escape detection. They discussed the U-boat attacks and Edmund was surprised to learn that the admiral's staff knew specifically which U-boats had been engaged and even the names and histories of their commanding officers. The admiral himself came in towards the end and congratulated them on what was, for him, a successful convoy with few losses. *Few losses*, Edmund thought. As the meeting ended he asked if any of them had any suggestions, and Edmund raised his hand.

'If we had carried some sort of recording device,' he said, 'it could have been switched on when we first gained contact with our U-boat. The recording itself could have been used to teach asdic operators. If we hadn't sunk it the experts could have listened and perhaps told us where we went wrong.'

'That's an idea,' the admiral said. 'I wonder why it hasn't been suggested before. Will you make a note of it?' He turned to his chief of staff.

'Yessir. An organization could be set up to select the recordings, and I agree that they'd be useful for training purposes. I can imagine how someone with a very good ear, a musical person perhaps, would hear subtleties which the operators on board the ships were not aware of. It's one of those things that might produce interesting results.'

'When you think of it,' the admiral added, 'the Air Force is ahead of us. They mount cameras in the wings of their aircraft which are set in motion when the guns fire, so they get a visual record of the battle. Ours, on the other hand, is an undersea battle which depends not on sight but on sound. It makes good sense to record it. I wouldn't expect a recording machine to be very complicated or cost a lot of money. It certainly needn't cost more than a good camera.'

In a few minutes the discussion ended and the other captains were excused. Edmund guessed that the Braithwaite – Pemberton tragedy would be next on the agenda.

'Call Alastair, will you?' the Admiral said, and a few moments later a surgeon captain entered and was motioned to a chair. He had Marko's report in hand and placed it on the table in front of him. He began by expressing perplexity at the report and said that in his many years of medical practice he had never heard of a similar case. The suddenness of Braithwaite's affliction and the bizarre forms it took; the fact that he was not altogether divorced from reality yet deliberately shot Pemberton, all contributed to a unique medical case. He agreed that if there had been a surgeon lieutenant on complement, as there was aboard the destroyers, it would have been easier for the first lieutenant to make the decision to restrain his own captain.

The admiral seemed to be asking himself another question. Had there been clues to Braithwaite's mental condition which should have been picked up? By whom had he been interviewed before he was appointed to command? Were there faults in the system? 'In retrospect,' the admiral said, 'it's easy to say that it was a bad decision to have appointed him in command of his own ship. He would have been better off in say, a troopship, with a full captain in command, a doctor and proper facilities.'

He turned to Edmund.

'These papers will go to the Admiralty and I intend to add

some comments of my own. You can be assured that no blame falls on you or any of your officers.'

My officers, Edmund thought; *mine*.

The admiral paused and leaned back in his chair.

'In wartime we learn to put this kind of tragedy behind us. We have a battle to fight, the battle of the Atlantic Ocean. We are suffering losses and if we don't win, the war as a whole will be lost. I propose that Braithwaite and Pemberton be reported "killed whilst on active service". I don't see any point in saying more than that.'

'What do I tell their wives, sir? I know both of them. Well, I mean, I've met them.'

'The truth, Casswell. They are sure to find out sooner or later. It might as well come from you.'

There was silence in the room for several seconds.

'Nothing will bring them back,' the admiral said. 'You've done your best and it was a very good best. You sank a U-boat and acted as captain, asdic officer and communications officer. You deserve leave and you'll get a full month; then the Admiralty will give you a completely new appointment. How does it sound?'

Edmund could think of nothing to say so he thanked the admiral and stood to attention facing him before he left. This is wartime, he said to himself; an admiral has spoken.

In the chief of staff's ante-room he put on his coat and cap then went in search of 'Soapy' Hudson, the paymaster lieutenant.

'I don't know the procedure for paying off a ship,' he told him. 'We have to start in the morning. I'm alongside *Harp* and Dalzell-Paul may have some ideas, but I was wondering whether you could come aboard and show me. It's the paperwork.'

'Soapy' glanced at his calendar and looked up with a smile.

'Sure,' he said. 'First thing.'

'One other matter,' Edmund said. 'Is there a phone I can use? I want to make a private call.'

'In the circumstances I think that our grateful country can afford to foot the bill. I shall go down the corridor and speak to a petty officer who will assemble the papers needed for paying off a ship. Back in three or four minutes; there's the phone.'

What an excellent fellow he is, Edmund thought. He sat down

and pulled the telephone toward him. A moment later he was talking to Marguerite.

'It's me, Edmund,' he said. 'I'm in England and in a few days I'll be on leave.'

In moments of emotion Marguerite spoke in French and now it was as though the floodgates of her heart and mind had opened. The telephone connection was imperfect and her thoughts seemed less than orderly, but he sat and listened in utter joy. There had been a letter from her mother via Switzerland and her family was well. The organization to which she belonged was now being called Free French; an officer who had known her father would give her away in marriage. She had found a church with a hall where the reception could be held.

Edmund broke in.

'Please, darling, get in touch with my father and persuade him to play a part in it. He may not want to marry us himself, but he must be present and pronounce the blessing. I hope he'll agree to that. And talk to my mother. Tell her not to worry.'

They spoke for only moments but those moments were like shafts of sunlight. He reminded her that the gallant officer from New France would be his best man and that *sous-officier* Clancey who passed his youth helping to release slaves would be invited. They spoke of their love for each other and the joy they felt.

'I must go now,' Edmund said. 'The owner of the telephone is on his way.'

Chapter 24

WHEN EDMUND'S MOTHER admitted him to her apartment near Lambeth he was disturbed by what he saw. The hall and living room contained unopened boxes, the kitchen was antiquated and had only one cluttered cupboard and little counter space, the spare bedroom where he would sleep had the parts for a bed but they were ill-assorted and didn't fit each other. Heavy black curtains hung over the windows to conform with blackout regulations, but could not be drawn back by day which produced perpetual twilight.

'None of the servants came with us,' Mrs Casswell explained when greetings were over. 'We've been getting someone to come and do the cooking, but she's terribly unreliable.'

Edmund stood and contemplated the scene, then brought his luggage in and put it in the spare room.

'You haven't really got settled, have you? You and Dad have been here for how many months? Is there something wrong? I didn't expect to find you in a mess like this. I won't want to bring my wife here.'

'Wife?' she said. 'Oh please, Edmund, your father is so against your marriage. Will you talk to him? He hates to be disturbed, but this is rather an exception, isn't it?'

Well, Edmund thought, we didn't take long to get to the point. Is this how I am to be welcomed after months of war service?

She went across the living room and knocked on a door.

'Edmund is here,' she said. 'Edmund.'

'Oh yes, what a surprise, I wanted to speak to him,' came his father's voice.

His father emerged and closed the door behind him. He held

out his hand with hesitation and seemed about to withdraw it before Edmund could take it.

'I really cannot agree with any of your fiancée's proposals,' his father began. 'They are not acceptable to your mother or myself. Such a wedding would be a travesty.'

'I'm sorry to hear it, of course.' Edmund spoke rather slowly. 'Does it mean you and mother will not attend?'

'I don't think I quite understand. Are you saying you will proceed in disregard of my objections?'

'Father, I had hoped that you would want to participate in the ceremony but if not, that's unfortunate. I don't know what my friends will think if you're not there. The answer to your question, of course, is *yes*; we are going ahead with the wedding as arranged.'

His mother sat down on the edge of a crate and his father on a kitchen chair. Edmund remained standing.

'I am beginning to wonder if I have not been mistaken in thinking that you were called for the Church,' his father began. 'Your entire course of behaviour seems to contradict everything you have been taught.'

Edmund drew a deep breath. Now, he said to himself, is as good a time as any.

'I now have no intention of entering the Church. That part of my life is over. I am amazed you can't see it for yourself.'

His father's head sunk on his chest and his mother dabbed at her nose with a handkerchief.

'You are a great disappointment to me,' his father said at last.

'And as I stand and look about me I also feel disappointed. Just look at this place. Is it the best you can do? I'm asking myself how you propose to administer the lands and properties of the Church when you don't even know how to organise a few little rooms of your own.'

'But we can't get any servants. It's no use blaming us. All the people who would be in service are going into war factories. What can we do?'

Edmund turned to his mother and shook his head.

'Oh, come,' he said. 'Who did the packing?'

'Carter Patterson's, of course,' his mother replied. 'They're supposed to be the best.'

'Following your instructions, I hope. You set out the things you needed for here and told them to pack them separately. The rest would go into storage, is that it?'

'Not exactly. All the flower vases were brought here, which wasn't very clever of them. Tom was supposed to keep an eye on the work, but you know . . . And we have so many possessions. One never realises, does one?'

'Now, listen, mother; until a minute ago I had some doubt in my mind as to how I was going to spend my leave. We're not travelling anywhere for our honeymoon; we prefer to stay in London where Marguerite can carry on with her job; we feel that in wartime it would be the proper thing. Well, I've now decided that I'll be working here, getting you organized.

'It's quite simple,' he went on. 'I'll unpack everything, keep some necessities and repack the remainder, including the flower vases, to be put in storage. I'll probably do some painting and redecorating, not to mention putting in more shelves and cupboards. And it'll be an opportunity to give away a lot of old stuff that isn't needed. Plenty of people have lost everything in the bombing. Father is supposed to know that.'

The bishop raised his head. 'So you're going ahead regardless?'

'Yes, father. And if you are going to be present, I suggest you discard those old-fashioned clothes. You have worn them too long; look at you. Knee breeches, gaiters, morning coat; for heaven's sake go and find yourself a plain dark suit and send those absurdities to a theatre company.'

Edmund scarcely paused for breath.

'Now, have you got a spare key so I can get in and out without disturbing you?'

'I'm afraid not,' his mother replied. 'We were only given one key, weren't we, Jonathan?'

'Very well then, you must let me have it and I'll get two more made so we can each have one.'

'Is that possible?' his mother asked.

'And I suppose you're going to tell me that my bicycle is in storage.'

'Yes, I think so,' she nodded vaguely.

'Well, I'm going to need it. With petrol rationing and practically no cars on the roads it'll be ideal.'

He went to the door and changed the subject.

'I'm going to see Marguerite now and we'll be having supper together. You'll probably be asleep by the time I get back.'

He left his parents sitting abjectly among their crated belongings.

'The saints preserve us,' he said as he went down the stairs.

That evening Marguerite and Edmund sat at a small table at their favourite Soho restaurant. Their love hung round them like a cloud; they could scarcely eat and their conversation came disjointedly. It was enough merely to be together, to rejoice in each other's presence after being so long apart.

'I have lots to tell you,' he said. '*Troubadour* is in dock having a refit. The crew have been sent on leave. On Wednesday I have to be at the Admiralty and find out about my future.'

'Edmund,' she said. 'I failed where your parents were concerned. I tried my best. Your mother's ideas were quite impractical and your father kept saying that we should wait. We've made our plans and my heart is set. I couldn't bear to be treated like a child and spoken to as though I was a foreigner. Your mother's family was from France; she speaks French; I don't know what I did wrong.'

'You did nothing wrong, but a great gulf now separates parents and children; old and young. They caused the war by their carelessness and we fight it. The time has come to take charge of our own lives.'

Edmund had never before ventured inside the Admiralty. He walked up the steps, was saluted by a guard and stated his business at an information desk. He was led down a long corridor and instructed to wait in the ante-room of a staffing officer and when called in was confronted by a captain. There were no chairs on which visitors might be seated, which suggested that he was not expected to stay for any length of time.

'Lieutenant Edmund Casswell,' the captain began. 'Dalzell-

Paul has asked for you. He'll be getting command of a fleet destroyer. How does that sound?'

'I would have expected him to ask for Campbell, sir. They've been together since *Harp* was commissioned.'

'Campbell's going into special duties; he's not available.'

'Well, thank you, sir. I look forward to it.'

'However,' the captain went on. 'His ship won't be ready for a few months. It doesn't even have a name. We're moving toward launching a destroyer a week from British shipyards.'

'A destroyer a week,' Edmund repeated in surprise.

'In the meantime, when you've had some leave you'll be put on the staff of the Asdic Training School. The commanding officer is new and wants to make changes. I told him you had experience in U-boat warfare and your last report from . . . what was his name, Braithwaite, said you were a good teacher. I think you could help him.'

'I do have some ideas about teaching asdic, sir, using live sound recordings.'

'That's fine. Any questions?'

'No, sir. Thank you, sir.'

'We'll be in touch with you toward the end of your leave. Oh, and by the way, you'll be able to get to London on weekend passes while you're at Portland.'

A smile appeared on Edmund's face.

'Excellent. Er, sir, one thing. Lieutenant Marko Cyr.'

The captain pointed to a sign on his desk which Edmund hadn't noticed. *You are here to discuss your posting, not someone else's.*

'Aye aye, sir.'

So far so good, he thought as he left the office. A brand-new fleet destroyer with a complement of over two hundred men to serve the armament of guns, torpedoes and depth charges. Dalzell-Paul as captain; he could have asked for none better.

The next office to which he had been summoned was that of 'Honours and Awards.' His own recommendations for Harding, Hounsom and Williams had been passed to Dalzell-Paul who had become flotilla leader after Braithwaite's death. It was Dalzell-Paul, therefore, who recommended Edmund himself for the Distinguished Service Order, which was standard for an officer who single-handedly sank a U-boat. Dalzell-Paul, however, felt that Edmund had been too cautious where Marko was concerned. He knew they were friends and that Edmund had not recommended him because at the time of the battle he was struggling with a mad captain and was not at his gun position.

Dalzell-Paul, however, had taken a different view. Marko had trained the gun's crew, fought successfully against E-boats and aircraft in previous battles and if he was somewhere else while leading seaman Harding was shooting at the U-boat, he had been responsible and deserved a full measure of credit. Not only that but he had also led the team which had jettisoned the depth charges from *Northern Harvest* while fires raged. Accordingly, they prepared the papers which recommended Marko for the Distinguished Service Cross.

There was yet another surprise in store. Dalzell-Paul himself had claimed a 'possible' U-boat sinking and the Admiralty experts had identified the U-boat, knew the name of the captain and other details. There were no reports of its being engaged subsequently against our ships and the fact that the boat, its captain and crew had never again been referred to by the *Kriegsmarine* was evidence that it had not returned from patrol. This had been confirmed by a survivor who told the interrogating officer that his best friend had been killed when that particular U-boat had been sunk. Dalzell-Paul had accordingly been credited with its destruction. His report of the action was re-examined and it was concluded that he should have claimed a 'probable' kill in preference to a 'possible'. It was typical of Dalzell-Paul that he had underrated his own achievement.

The investiture, Edmund was told, would be held at Buckingham Palace. Now that he had been officially informed and his award gazetted he should go to his tailor and have the ribbon stitched on his uniform. His Majesty the King would pin the medal on top of the ribbon.

Appointment to a destroyer under Dalzell-Paul's command; three or four months in the meantime teaching asdic; Buckingham Palace; it was rather overwhelming for a single morning. He found a telephone and told Marguerite.

The wedding of Marguerite de Tilly and Edmund Casswell perfectly captured the spirit of those dark times. At eleven o'clock on a cool autumn day Marguerite rose from her desk and taking her gloves and uniform hat she and her office friends walked to the bombed church where she had chosen to be married. It stood roofless and invaded by the weather, but a side chapel had escaped the worst of the destruction and was still in use. The pews had been piled at one side and the shattered stained glass swept into a corner.

Edmund and Marko stood together below the altar step while guests and many others crowded the chapel and flowed out into the rubble-filled church. There was neither music nor flowers, and when the French military officer who had been a friend of her father approached with Marguerite, the crowd seemed to emit a kind of collective sigh, shifted its feet on the gritty floor and made way for them. He did not take Marguerite's arm, because she was in the uniform of an army nurse, he merely walked at her side, his black and gold *kepi* under his arm. As they advanced toward the altar the crowd closed in behind as though to bar their exit. Edmund took Marguerite's hand and bowed his head very slightly toward her escort whose attention seemed momentarily distracted by the blue and pink ribbon above Edmund's pocket.

'We are gathered together in the sight of God,' the clergyman began, and the murmuring of the crowd subsided. He was a kindly man, Edmund thought, white-haired and older than his father. He had blue eyes, like a sailor, and a slightly broken voice which had doubtless pronounced these very words a thousand times. A breeze from the open sky ruffled his vestments.

'Do you, Edmund Casswell, take Margaret de Tilly . . .' They planned to join their names after the war and go to work for uncle Philippe in his wine business. Edmund would inherit the firm, he had his uncle's word on it, and they would change the firm's name to *Casswell de Tilly,* confident names that combined French and English. The present name *Continental Wines* didn't sound right at all.

'Until death do us part.'

Yes, Edmund had thought about death and he wanted a marriage that would be shattered by nothing less. Visions floated before his eyes of commander Sykes, ordinary seaman Crouch, the French deputy minister, the captain and crew of *Northern Harvest* and all the other ships that he had seen sunk or damaged. Lastly there was Braithwaite and Pemberton. Death, where is your sting, and grave, your victory? This woman who was at his side; he wanted to live with her for a lifetime, for her to become the mother of his children, to go to his grave only when he had experienced the world's best, read its great books and loved with all his heart. That would be victory enough.

'With all my worldly goods I thee endow.' Oh dear, he thought, worldly goods; we haven't spent much time on that. Well, there's my bicycle and in many years I shall probably inherit a lot of theological books and flower vases.

'With this ring . . .' They had bought it at Dibdin's on Sloane Street, a plain ring with both their names engraved on the inside. Marguerite had insisted on having no other jewellery. 'Please, not,' she had said. 'Not in wartime.'

Little Brother Reece was reading the lesson slowly and carefully as though he were plotting something on the chart where a mistake could be fatal.

'Then shall a man leave his father and his mother and shall cleave unto his wife, and they shall become one flesh.' This was the youth who, at fifteen, had joined the world of men and made an allotment to his mother from his meagre pay. What a gesture, what a triumph; a few shillings a month to a mother who had spent a hundred and fifty pounds on curtains; the price of a minesweeper.

'You may kiss the bride,' the clergyman whispered, and Edmund took both of Marguerite's hands in his and looked for long seconds into her eyes. He didn't kiss her and the clergyman finally cleared his throat and climbed the altar steps.

'I make no apology for the condition of my church,' he began. 'The Germans have been here and this is what they have done to our place of worship.' The onlookers shifted their feet.

'We have not merely joined two young people in marriage,' he went on. 'We have done more than that. We have all been joined and compelled to consider our own lives, drawn into the love which they have for each other.'

He looked over their heads at the crowd that pressed into the small chapel and extended back almost to the street. There were sailors from *Troubadour*, soldiers, civilians, passersby, people who had finished their work at midday who at first hesitated then lingered to witness a drama that was not theirs but was one in which they were capable of sharing. It was a wedding of few words, the verbose and garrulous seeming to have missed their cues. For once the unspoken word had the greater power.

England, even as they stood there, was fighting to survive as that catastrophic year declined. The bombing continued, but the real battle was now being fought in the wastes of the North Atlantic where Edmund, Marko and Reece had served, where Braithwaite and Pemberton had somehow killed each other, where *Troubadour* had sailed and would doubtless sail again. The allied losses at sea were beyond contemplation, too frightful for all but the bravest to consider, far beyond the point of eloquence or fine language. If the German U-boats could not be stopped there was a danger that England would starve and then all of Europe would die the Nazi death.

It was against this solemn page of history that Marguerite had planned a wedding that was devoid of all elaboration. Her mother, madame de Tilly, was not present to deck her in the family lace, so she would wear her uniform in defiance of those German beasts who had brought this about. The bombed church would remind her of her torn and shattered country and the military officer who walked with her to her husband's side would speak silently for her father, his wounds and early death.

As Marguerite and Edmund left the chapel they were first surrounded, then followed by the crowd. They went into the church hall and it was there, some minutes later, that Edmund noticed his father and mother. He advanced toward them and presented Marguerite as his wife.

Edmund had not realised until he entered their cluttered apartment less than a week earlier how helpless his parents had become since being cut off from the elegant paraphernalia of their pre-war lives. His mother without servants was ineffectual, and without her flowers she withered into the kind of floral remnant found in Victorian scrap-books. Her life had been set in motion in ways that made no sense in the world of 1940; elegant, unhurried and gracefully served. She could not perform even the smallest task for herself, nor could she think for herself, her servants having placed her at a remove from reality, a step apart from the arena where life is truly lived.

Edmund pitied her because she had never enjoyed the pleasures of normal womanly existence; cooking a meal for her husband, going out to the garden for some vegetables or herbs that she could prepare with her own hands. His father's sonorous blessings on their food would have had a richer significance if his mother had done more than merely appear at the proper time to eat it. By the light of those years she was not a bad mother; far from it, but her accomplishments, languages and social graces mocked her in these devastating times.

The bishop, a man of great but narrow brilliance, was as much at a loss as his wife. Who needed the subtleties of theological discourse when bombs were falling and torpedoes raced through the sea like arrows of destruction? Without the tall shadows of his cathedral, the ancient ritual, the pageantry, the acolytes waiting on his every word, the choir to punctuate each invocation with glorious music; without a vast panoply of support, he seemed bereft and stranded. He knew in his heart that no one was listening to him any more as he sat in his dusty office down the corridor from the archbishop. He had a typist, but could not dictate letters, having hitherto drafted them slowly by hand. He shared the services of the archdiocesan secretariat who had been selected on the basis of church attendance and family circumstances in preference to their clerical abilities.

Lining the walls of his office were leather-bound ledgers which were said to contain information about the Church's lands and properties within the London diocese. To Edmund's practical mind there should have been a map on the wall to indicate the whereabouts of each property, a filing system in support of the ledger entries, perhaps a simple numerical system that could have shown number 25, for instance, as a church and rectory at such-and-such an address.

When Edmund had visited him in his office the bishop had sat behind his cluttered desk and looked about him in despair. His telephone was on a small table in the corner.

'Had you thought,' he asked his father, 'of hiring expert advice to get you started? There are people who specialise in this kind of work. Even a retired chief clerk would be a help, and don't tell me that an outside consultant would be beyond your means. An inefficient organization,' he looked around him, 'is a sure way to waste money.'

Although Edmund didn't know it at the time, the police had laid charges against a number of volunteer workers in one of the furniture and clothing depots. These had been set up in bombed areas to help those who had lost their possessions by giving them a modest beginning in new accommodation. It had been discovered that the more valuable articles were being stolen and sold on the black market, which, when it became known, was scarcely an incentive to those who were being pressed to give more generously.

Worse from bishop Casswell's standpoint was the discovery that the Church had owned a house of ill repute. The place had been partly demolished by a bomb and a newspaper reporter asked the standard questions about its ownership and operation. The trail led him to Lambeth where a suffragen bishop said he hadn't known it was Church property, while bishop Casswell knew it to belong to the Church but was not aware of the degrading use for which it had been employed. The newspaper ran the story with evident relish under the headline 'Bishops in Brothel Bog.'

Both the bishop and his wife, in short, found themselves in confusing and unfamiliar circumstances, and Edmund's proposal to abandon his theological studies served only to emphasise their sense of loss. Secretly the bishop admitted that Philippe, his brother-in-law, had won the contest, had attracted Edmund's loyalty where he had failed. He was glad that Philippe was away buying wines somewhere in Spain and was not present at the wedding. Edmund was also thinking of his uncle Philippe, because he had contributed half a dozen cases of wine for the occasion. His cellars near Portsmouth were said to hold five million bottles and with the fall of France his magnificent collection from Bordeaux was gaining in value almost by the day. Uncle Philippe would have wanted to make a speech, his speeches being celebrated for their risqué humour, the outrageous compliments which he sloshed out like wet cement to the ladies present, and his clichés whose meanings had long since become vacuous from overuse. He had a long-standing affair with the sound of his own voice and cherished the belief that he was holding the audience spellbound. It was just as well he was far away.

Marguerite and Edmund stood for an hour in the church basement and talked with their guests. It had been decided to put sailors in charge of the refreshments and at some point petty officer Clancey appeared with a mug of champagne which he offered to Marguerite and which she and Edmund shared. There were no speeches, no dancing, the food and drink was demolished by those who were meant to be guarding it, the cake didn't arrive from Gunter's and yet none of these misadventures seemed in the least important.

The French officer summed it up with the words *'l'esprit, c'est magnifique'*.

After an hour Marguerite and Edmund stood momentarily at attention in front of him, thanked him and took their leave. He had done what only a French officer can do to perfection, he bent over Marguerite's hand, then stiffened and gave Edmund a small, almost unnoticed nod of approval. The bishop and Mrs Casswell had already departed and with the Wreford Hays a short distance behind them they walked to the Underground station. It was only a couple of stops to Sloane Square and a short walk home.

'Hungry?' he asked. 'We haven't had lunch.'

'Not really. I just want to go home and help you unpack. Mrs Hay will cook something this evening. She's very kind. What I most want is a bath,' she hesitated, 'with you in it as well as me.'

'With my body I will gladly and lovingly thee honour; I wonder what it's really going to be like.'

'You came close to honouring me on the way back from Bordeaux. I didn't resist either.'

'It was close, very close, and would have been something new for *Troubadour*. So many acts of war were performed on her decks that an act of love below decks would have been an interesting departure. I'm glad that we go to our bath and our bed . . . as we do. I remember one of our professors who said there was virginity of the body, and of the mind, and of the soul. I don't think I fully understood; I don't see how a modern, healthy person can be pure in mind. But I think our love toward each other can be pure.'

It was an hour later as Edmund and Marguerite were settling in to their basement rooms that the telephone rang. It was bishop Casswell and his voice sounded tired as he apologised for disturbing them at such a moment.

'That's all right,' Edmund said. 'What can I do?'

'His Grace has left a message to ask if he can meet with you. He wants to discuss your suggestion about getting an office consultant. He's much disturbed by the recent disclosures.'

'Meet where and when?'

'Lambeth Palace, at ten.'

'Sorry, father. My duty is to be at another palace.'

'I don't follow you, Edmund. You're speaking in riddles.'

'I am commanded to present myself at Buckingham Palace and stand before my King. My wife will be with me.'

'I see, I see. What a shame you could not have taken your mother, she deserves . . .'

'Yes, father, but it can't be done.'

'Not even if you were to . . .'

'No, father, there will doubtless be others who want to bring wives, girl friends, parents. I expect to see many of our brave pilots receiving their decorations; like me, they will only have one guest.'

'Well then, I can do no more than caution you . . .'

'Father, the moment for such caution is poorly chosen and if you are about to pronounce your usual strictures I suggest you keep them to yourself. I don't know why you must spoil such a happy day. Good heavens, you elected to take no part in our wedding and the truth is I have no wish to hear from you now. However, I shall be at your apartment to start cleaning next Monday morning. Give my love to my mother.'

As he put down the telephone receiver Edmund was conscious that the past was finally set to rest. The war had changed everything in his life and in many ways he was grateful that he had gained the experience he could hardly have gained otherwise. It had give him new and unlimited horizons, a beautiful wife, self-confidence and a hope for the future. The urgency of war had been like wine added to the plain diet of his former studious existence. The hardship and discipline of the sea was something that he had learned to accept. Deep inside himself he believed that he and his companions in *Troubadour*, indeed, all the young men who were uniform, were paying the debts owed by their parents who had voted for lower taxes, disarmament and a life of ease. *The dancing years* those times had been called.

For Edmund's parents on the other hand, the war had ravaged the way of life they had come to accept as their due. They had turned into an ordinary complaining couple whose problems seemed trivial when compared against the suffering on the battlefields and in the bomb-cratered cities. Their loss was that of status and condition; they bewailed the passing of a social structure which maintained them in delicate comfort. 'What have we done to deserve this?' they asked, and did not know, even as they spoke, that it was not a rhetorical question but one which deserved a thoughtful answer.

Uncle Philippe, who was single-minded and harsh on occasion, might have done better than the bishop when it came to organising Church property. He would have marched into the office, changed everything to suit himself and upset every time-honoured tradition. Inefficiency would have been rewarded by dismissal and the end result would have been a solid organization with high morale and loyal employees. Yes, uncle Philippe, despite his faults, could have done it, because he was demanding and expected nothing but the best from everyone.

Uncle Philippe had a reputation that was known throughout the closed and sophisticated world of wine importers. His palate was so finely tuned and his knowledge of wine so vast that he could identify blindfold a hundred of the great growths and often put a year on them as well. He was a familiar figure at every wine tasting and elegant dinner at which importers would gather. How different from his brother-in-law, the bishop, who had cultivated detachment almost as an art.

Edmund would get to know his uncle in the months ahead.

Portland, where the Asdic Training School was located, was no distance from the cellars of *Continental Wines*. He'd spend whatever time he could with him and plan to join the firm at war's end. He'd ask him what reading he should undertake in the meantime; what study he should pursue.

He thought back to the summers when he had accompanied uncle Philippe on tours of the great vineyards; the tastings, the hearty dinners, the flirting. Edmund hadn't done much besides look and listen, but he had not given his uncle credit for his patience in teaching him the rudiments of the trade. Philippe knew that Edmund was too intelligent to be a lifelong prisoner in the narrow corridors of theology.

For uncle Philippe the war had merely hastened the process of providing him with the heir he wanted. It was a strange perversity that Philippe, who had cast his seed so mischievously after his wife's death, had never fathered a child. The bishop on the other hand, sickeningly reticent where the body was concerned, about whom it was said that if he had sex at all he had it in Latin, had succeeded in this one respect where uncle Philippe had failed.

He wondered what would become of his father now that his career had foundered. Back at university there had been talk of a bishop who had made himself ridiculous by attempting publicly to perform a miracle. He had promptly been raised to archbishop and despatched to some distant archiepiscopal see whose name was so unfamiliar that an atlas had to be used to establish its whereabouts. If his father was sent to Africa or the East his mother could at least surround herself with native servants.

Edmund sat for a moment in front of the telephone and wondered how he would say goodbye to his friends and shipmates. Reece had already telephoned to say that his promotion to sub-lieutenant was assured and that Dalzell-Paul had asked for him. He had been promised a number of training courses to fill in the time until the ship was ready.

Marko, however, was destined for the Canadian navy. Their offer included passage to Canada for himself and his intended wife, a long leave and appointment as first lieutenant in one of the new corvettes that were being constructed in Canadian shipyards. It was a generous offer which Marko's loyalty to Canada would not let him refuse.

Marko, the gallant officer from New France; Edmund would miss him deeply. He had learned so much from Marko, so staunch had been their friendship during those fifteen months of sea service. He was the lawyer who, uncharacteristically, could make sense of legalities, had worked tirelessly for able seaman Knatchbull, had almost, but not quite, saved Pemberton's life. One day Edmund and Marguerite would visit him in New France.

Edmund pushed away the telephone and stood up. He could hear water running in the bathtub.